devils+heartbreak

Aud Pitch

Book Cover by Inez Joakim

ISBN: 978-1-7637103-0-6 (Paperback)

Independently published v.1

1st edition December, 2024

For Scott.

Contrasting.
Complementary.
Exactly the same.

All things are true with you.

x

content warning

For those who think content warnings spoil the plot:
Skip the next paragraph and jump straight into the book.

⟂

For those who do appreciate content warnings:
This book has scenes containing panic attacks, anxiety, depression, alcohol and drug use, sex while under the influence of drugs and alcohol, smoking, office bullying, fat shaming, and intense sex scenes.

listen

Music played a huge part in the making of D+H.
Snap the QR codes below to access the playlist and listen while you
read.

SPOTIFY

APPLE MUSIC

A track list is available at the back of the book.

intro

How could Owen have thought showing up to an art show after-party alone was a good idea? What in his right mind had compelled him to enter Chidori, expecting it to be as it always was?

That was the crux of it, he supposed. He wasn't in his right mind.

As soon as he opened the glass doors of his favourite restaurant, tucked away down a graffiti-covered laneway in Melbourne's CBD, turbulence whirled to life in his sternum. Chidori *wasn't* as it always was; the sleek wooden dining tables and chairs were gone, replaced by industrial high tables around a dancefloor and DJ booth.

O patted his pockets yet again, wishing his hands could conjure up his missing pill case. When the hell did he lose it?

He hesitated for four breaths at the threshold of the space, the air already stuffy with so many guests, and then stepped through. *Tonight,* his brain claimed, *home alone equals bad. Out alone equals... marginally better.*

O weaved through the sea of partygoers to the bar, forgoing the free champagne. He needed something stronger to replace his missing Valium. He downed a single shot of whisky before ordering a double to lubricate his grating nerves and then retreated to a dark corner to people-watch, avoiding any lingering eye contact that could unwittingly encourage anyone to approach. He needed to silently, peacefully, soak up the energy of the space—the frenetic current that sparked through each person present.

O surveyed the guests; everyone was beautiful—boringly so. They were all *beige*. Not in skin colour or clothing (although there *were* a lot of beige outfits) but in how they carried themselves. They were all appropriately dressed and decorated. Typical creative-adjacents—the type that dissected and bought art and thought themselves better than the artists who did the work. They patted themselves on the back for being so clever and rich and laughed the way people laughed in ads—like life was perfect and nothing in the whole world could make it any less so.

Hell—*he* fitted snugly into the beige category too.

Owen Jameson: utterly boring, rich, and creative-adjacent. Beige-skinned. He didn't think he was particularly clever though, and Mario always chided him about not laughing as often as he should, so at least he had that.

He let out a weary sigh. He loved Melbourne—the secret laneways, the unpredictability of the weather... even the obnoxious beeps and slams of trucks and vans delivering goods to the hospo venues on Brunswick St early in the mornings. But some of the people he engaged with on a day-to-day basis?

Christ—it was all so stifling.

His whole body itched to flee. He *could* do it again—grab his passport and fuck right off, just like a few years earlier when he journeyed from Southeast Asia all the way to Europe, moving onto a different city when it got tiring or lonely, or when he'd met so many people he craved solitude. But he'd returned to Melbourne after that year abroad to be responsible, to show his face at work through doorways instead of computer screens, to uphold the family business. The family name.

Where would he go this time? Perhaps it was time to head home, to stop avoiding the people who missed him the most. Maybe it was time to start making new memories there...

Ecstatic squeals from the opposite side of the dancefloor interrupted his fantasy.

Heads turned toward a trio of femmes, arms flailing wildly as they rushed to greet a late arrival. They went in for a group hug, exchanging *I missed yous*, and *you look so beautifuls*, and *it's been too longs*. Then they stepped back, and O inhaled sharply at the sight of the newcomer who had evoked such a joyful reaction.

He choked on his sip of whisky. Coughing and sputtering like a fucking idiot, he pounded his chest as someone next to him handed him their napkin. He nodded sheepishly in thanks and shrunk further back into the corner, swallowing the burn in his throat.

The new arrival's golden-brown skin wrapped snugly around wide curves, her dark hair cascading over rounded shoulders like a curtain of silk that swayed as she moved. Her red tshirt had a peculiar bleach stain on one side and when she cupped her friend's cheeks affectionately, the red fabric rode up to reveal her round belly. Her arms, clinging tightly to her friends, were heavily tattooed. How much of her skin was adorned with ink?

The three other femmes were dressed to impress, their clothes and accessories carefully considered for an event that was sure to make headlines in the arts and culture sections of news sites and social media accounts. But the new arrival wore the opposite of red carpet attire; her jeans were ripped, and not in a way that said they were fastidiously picked apart by some artisan from a fashion house. Her denim was well-worn and loose; a creative's uniform.

O watched on as she brushed her long, just-got-out-of-bed hair off her shoulders with a mesmerising flick of her wrists, tucking the wavy strands behind her ears. He rubbed the spot right above his heart when the light above cast her in a soft pink glow.

He forced himself to look at the other guests, how they gazed at her also. She didn't notice—far too busy giving her loved ones all her attention. And then she tipped her head back to laugh, neck lengthening, plump cheeks rising into high rosy mounds, and… God—O was utterly beguiled. Her smile—both generous and sensual—sucked the air from his lungs, all the way from the opposite side of Chidori.

This is ridiculous, he thought. *I'm being ridiculous.*

The muted atmospheric tracks drifting out of the speakers transitioned to louder, heavier hip-house beats and the overhead lights dimmed. LEDs flashed and pulsed in sync with the music; the friends' reunion heralded the beginning of a riotous night ahead.

They drank. A lot. And O spied them discreetly passing around pills —molly, perhaps.

Fuck—he felt left out as he watched from the sidelines. He wished he had the nerve to sidle up to them and ask for one.

The lofty art-speak of the partygoers turned into slurred chats and drunken dancing, and the mysterious femme's eyelids became heavy— her movements slow and dreamy as she danced as well. She swayed with the tempo, arms high above her head as she submitted to the music, and O tried so hard to get his stupid, stubborn feet to move in her direction—to say hello and ask if he could dance with her.

She floated to the bar, and one of the bartenders swaggered her way, leaning over the counter with clear interest. She gave him a coy smile. She haphazardly twisted her midnight waves atop her crown and tied the bun with a lock of her own hair, took her drink from the bartender's hands with a wink, and let herself be swallowed up by the dancers again.

O dashed away to use the bathroom. He stared at himself in the mirror as he washed his hands and nodded at his reflection.

Okay. He was going to introduce himself. He was ready—had the right amount of alcohol in his system to feel brave. *Hey, I'm Owen. What's your name?* Simple. Hard to fuck up. And then he could follow up with, *Are you a fan of DEWI's work too?* He squared his shoulders, unlocked the door and marched to the dancefloor.

She wasn't there. Fuck—she wasn't anywhere.

The mysterious newcomer vanished while he was giving himself a fucking pep talk in the toilet. He spun on his heels, searching the crowd for that messy bun and red tshirt.

Nothing.

He clutched his chest again and this time, he didn't understand the feeling that had manifested there. Dread? Panic?

Her arrival, and the joyful exuberance of her friends, had flipped some kind of energetic switch; the atmosphere of Chidori brightened and relaxed all at once as if everyone inhaled and released a collective breath. Or maybe it was all in O's head because the night had definitely become significant to him. There was this terrifying feeling of instability, like he was standing on the precipice... of what—he had no idea. Something wonderful? A lesson he'd never forget, maybe? All he knew was that one minute, he was getting tipsy, wondering the *why* of it all and the next, he was given an answer in the form of some mysterious human with big beautiful feline eyes, mermaid hair, and thick thighs.

Christ, those thighs.

His fingers flexed at the thought.

But now she was gone and his anxiety spiked, and then he realised how stupid it was for his heartbeat to race all because of a stranger he hadn't even spoken with, and he was standing alone in a crowded space, being shoved around by hot bodies that were laughing and having fun when none of it was fun anymore and—*shit.*

He counted five things he could see, and four things he could hear. Counted his breath.

He cut across the dancefloor to reach the bar, the sweet-salty mixture of sticky air wafting up to his face. His heart pounded in his ears, almost as loud as the bass line throbbing from the speakers. Too many people. Too many slippery, undulating bodies around him, pressing and sliding, and shoving.

He fought his way out the other side, flinging his clammy palms onto the cold counter-top of the bar and breathing in deep to stave off the beginnings of panic. He gestured for three shots of whatever the person next to him was having—anything to get him out of perfectly tipsy and deep into the vicinity of officially drunk.

He inhaled the shots in quick succession and exhaled the burn with a grimace.

Okay. Three rapid-fire shots of tequila—*disgusting*—meant fifteen more minutes and he'd be perfectly drunk.

Which meant the panic would soon dissipate.

Which meant he should leave right away since his reason for staying had vanished.

If he left right now he'd arrive home too fucked to spiral or send pathetic, needy texts to any exes. Although... sending pathetic, needy texts to his best mate was firmly on the table.

He checked his watch. 7PM in Jakarta; Mario would totally pick up his—

"Owen?!"

O whipped around and exhaled the breath he hadn't realised was still trapped in his lungs.

Alexis Charles—fashion influencer and self-professed *it-bitch*—slunk through the crowd with the effortless grace of a cat, looking pristine as ever. The handsome human pushed through with a, *'scuse me, 'scuse me, 'scuse me*, and then tucked themselves into O's open arms.

"Al. Thank god. Hey." O kissed their cheeks and stifled a snicker when he eyed Al's clothes. "Are you wearing beige?"

They leaned away to look down at their outfit, pulling at the suit lapels with brightly painted nails. "Yeah. Why?"

"No reason. How are you?"

"Yeah, yeah, fine," Al said, head bobbing up and down as they took O in. They took a sip of their dark cocktail before staring up and commenting, "Have you gotten taller or am I shrinking? And your beard! Owen Jameson: ripped white Jesus. The power of Christ compels me. *Mmm.*"

A startled laugh flew out of him.

"What the fuck are you doing here, Owen?"

"Drinking."

"But you're doing it in public."

"Yeah, it's an afterparty."

"I *know* it's an afterparty. I'm the afterparty queen. This is my third one this week." Al adjusted their wide brim hat with its bright yellow satin band and O dodged the long pheasant feather sticking out the side.

O jerked his chin at Al's head. "That's a lot of hat. Very *Pharrell* of you."

Al grinned. "Good isn't it? I'm banging the designer. He showers me with hats instead of flowers." Al offered him a sip of their cocktail, and O obliged, taking the straw between his lips and sucking down a big gulp. "Oi, greedy!" They snatched the drink away and glared at him. "Anyway, did you go to the show at Norton?"

"Yeah, I got there early, and—"

"Oh. My. God," they cut in. "*Do not* tell me you got one. You did, didn't you? You fucking arsehole. I arrived fifteen minutes after the doors opened and missed *out!*" they whined. "But I bet you got your hands on one. No. I don't want to know. Don't tell me."

O shrugged. "Okay."

"But you did, didn't you? You got a DEWI piece. You fucking arsehole." O just grinned. Al groaned and dragged their slender fingers over their face. "You utter shit. Which one?"

"*'Abundance.'*"

Al's manicured brows shot up, glittery eyeshadow sparkling under the flashing lights. "You utter *shit*," they said with a smile. "Now I have to wait god knows how long for DEWI to get their head out their arse and sell more work. Honestly, it's rude of them to make me wait."

O laughed. "Well, until then, head over to Drewery Alley and stare at the mural for free."

Al's bright blue eyes gleamed. "Maybe I should buy the building. But seriously, O, I'm surprised to see you. *Here*." They gestured around. "You rarely came out to parties back in the day. Especially stag. Hoping DEWI would show up?"

He chuckled. "Yeah, actually, at first…"

His smile disappeared.

The reminder brought him back to himself—to the fast-beating heart, and the far-too-loud music that assaulted his senses. He cringed, eyes scanning the throng of bodies again. "There… was someone here before. Beautiful. Part-Asian, I think. Or maybe Polynesian. Long dark hair. Plus-sized, red tshirt with a bleach stain on it, ripped jeans covered in paint? She looked like she came straight from work or something. She was with three other femmes; they were dressed up. One was wearing hot pink. Sound familiar?"

"A bleach stain? Bit basic," Al commented with a sneer, and O couldn't help getting defensive.

"Don't be a snob," he growled.

Al raised their hands placatingly. "Alright. What—you chatted her up but didn't get her name?"

O's cheeks went very hot. "I was about to talk to her," he mumbled.

Al cocked their head to the side ruefully, the straw of their drink tucked into the corner of their mouth as they took another sip. "Oh Owen, your shyness is adorable. And fucking stupid."

O rolled his eyes. "Shut up."

"But considering you look—" They waved their hand at O's face— "I'm glad for the rest of us. Evens the playing field."

"Oh, *shut up.*"

Al smacked O's chest playfully. "I'll go ask my friends."

"No. Don't worry. It's getting—" A heaviness behind his eyes made itself known; the tequila shots were taking over. He pulled at his shirt collar—"too much."

The handsome human shoved their dark cocktail back in O's face. "Here, have some more. It's got some extra kick," Al offered, holding the straw to O's mouth.

He took the glass, plucked out the straw and gulped down the entire drink. Al squawked, trying to grab at it. "Whoa, whoa, whoa! Not all of it!"

O batted Al's hands away and finished the cocktail with an, *Aaaah.*

"My drink..." Al said, horrified.

"Oh my God—I'll get you a fresh one."

Al cringed. "But—oh, nevermind." They patted O's shoulder almost regretfully. "Just... go home. *Now.* Maybe eat before you try to sleep? A steak or something. I'll call you." They raised onto the tips of their toes to kiss O's cheek. "Enjoy," they said, flashing something between a wince and a grin.

And then they spun around and slithered away.

O zig-zagged through the sea of people in the opposite direction with far less grace than Al, and by the time he squeezed past the last partygoer, he was dragging himself through mud.

What a waste of—

No, he stopped himself. It wasn't a waste of an evening. Going stag to an afterparty had been, in many ways, exactly what he'd needed.

Something impulsive; a deviation from the usual wake up/work/wind down routine that had been his life for the past year or so.

And although it had come with a heavy dose of anxiety, he'd gotten through it unscathed. Drunk as fuck, but unscathed. He'd even bumped into an old friend he realised he actually missed.

O hesitated in the foyer. Why hadn't he left yet?

Earlier, when he mustered the courage to talk to the newcomer, only to find her gone, he'd asked himself if this night was a lesson.

Yes, he decided, a lesson to be brave, always—to follow his gut, even if it was terrifying. To remember that trying was never failing.

His dad's voice echoed, *Failing isn't not succeeding, Owen. Failing is not trying at all.*

His eyes blurred, a little bit from the prickle of tears that always formed when he remembered his father, and a lot from his brain spinning inside his skull, slowly increasing speed like a carnival ride.

O shut his eyes and pitched sideways. *Nope—don't close your eyes; makes it worse.* He rubbed his temples with his thumb and forefinger instead, and shook his head ever-so-slightly.

Something was off. His limbs were weighed down, each wrist and ankle strapped to some invisible ball and chain. He looked up; the ceiling lights all pulsated with halos. It took everything he had to keep his spine straight, to not just allow his body to crumple into a comfortable pile of meat and bones in the entranceway of—where was he again?

He leaned against the cold concrete wall by the door, needing to feel something hard and unyielding against his spine. He rubbed his eyes and scratched his beard, groaning. *"Fuuuuck."*

"Hey. You okay?" slurred a breathy voice.

O turned towards the pretty sound, and... *holy shit*—it was her. The red tshirt person. Standing close enough to touch. Without thinking, he reached for her and then froze. He still had enough sober brain cells to remember poking strangers was frowned upon, but now he was just randomly pointing.

Fuck—he was getting this all wrong.

He prepared an opening line earlier didn't he? What was it again?

"DEWI."

Her brows drew together. "Pardon?" she asked, her eyes opening wider, accusingly.

"I'm a fan."

She made a *you're-not-making-sense* face. "Of DEWI?"

O held up two fingers. "Of both of you."

"What?"

"I dunno. Fuck—I'm *high*."

She gave a sparkly laugh at that. "Me too," she proclaimed, and came forward for a high five.

He missed her raised palm, hitting her on the shoulder with his floppy hand instead. "Shit—sorry. No, no, but," he rushed out, shaking his head quickly, and thank god he was still leaning against the jarringly cold wall because he definitely would've fallen if he tried to do that without the solid building against his back, "I didn't take anything. My mate spiked my drink. Their drink. I drank their drink. Oh. *Oh!*" And then he gasped loudly. "Shit—I drank their drugged drink."

Oh no, the anxiety was back. But that was good because it meant he was sober enough to feel something other than the floaty euphoria that came just before oblivion.

"You should sit down," the pretty red tshirt person said, and wrapped her tiny hand around his wrist. She shuffled drunkenly down a cordoned-off corridor with him stumbling after her.

They turned into a dimly lit room with a long leather couch, a coffee table and a floor lamp turned down low. She flopped on one end of the couch with an indulgent sigh and O let his body go slack as he collapsed next to her.

The cool, butter-soft leather against the back of his neck made him shiver. He closed his eyes for a moment before turning to her. She was studying him carefully, her own eyes heavy-lidded.

"Hello," she mumbled.

"Hello."

She snuggled down a little and leaned her head on his shoulder, and O could not fucking believe this was happening.

"So are you a fan of DEWI?" he asked, finally able to say more coherent things now that his brain didn't have to worry about keeping his body upright.

"Of course," she murmured. "Who isn't?"

O gave a little snort. "I dunno—people they take the piss out of? I'm sure there's some religious organisation that hates the latest mural in Drewery Alley."

She lifted her face to stare up at him and the look she gave him was decidedly impish. "I like that mural a lot."

"Or what about that revenge porn guy in Indonesia? Bet he hates DEWI too."

She sneered. "Fuck that guy," she said through gritted teeth.

O nodded solemnly. "Agreed." Jesus, his brain felt as heavy as a bowling ball.

Raking her dark polished fingernails through her wavy tresses, her eyes fluttered lazily as if the caress on her scalp delighted every nerve ending in her body. A rebellious lock of hair slid over her eyes and before he could second-guess himself, he combed it over her shoulder with his fingers. The femme leaned into his touch and looked at him. Her eyes went wide like she was seeing him for the first time. She sat up straight. "Oh," she breathed, "aren't you pretty."

"Me? Look at *you*."

She tilted her head as her eyes scanned down his body and then back up again. O fidgeted nervously. "You're very big," she said approvingly, "like that tree in Denmark."

"Oh?"

"Denmark, Western Australia. Not Denmark, Denmark. The Great Tingle Tree." She lifted his arm and inspected it, giving his bicep a squeeze. "I could tie a swing to you."

He barked out a laugh. "I'd be down for that."

All of a sudden he had a lapful of newcomer, the weight of her a solid, tangible thing that made him gasp. O froze—delight and trepidation coursing through him. Blood surged down to his pelvis.

Fuck.

She straddled his thighs, her little hands resting against his stomach. "Jesus—you're handsome," she said curiously, and then pressed her cheek to his. "Mmm. You smell like summer. God—if that's how you smell, I wonder how you'd taste..." She leaned back again, tilting her head to the side.

O sat up straighter, his whole body igniting under her careful gaze. He could feel, like some phantom caress, everywhere her eyes landed on him.

"Your hair is golden at the ends! And your freckles... You know, my friend Meredith would be climbing all over you if she was still here."

"I'm enjoying *you* climbing all over me."

The red tshirt person ignored him and shook her head ruefully. "She's getting a divorce. She's so heartbroken. Heartbreak does stupid things to people..." Her voice trailed off. O watched on—mesmerised. And then she perked up again when their eyes met. "But you—" She poked his chest—"you, with your gorgeous face, and Great Tingle Tree body, Denmark. You'd *totally* cheer her up."

"I'm sorry your friend's sad. Still not interested in her though."

She waggled her brows. "You sure? She's pretty bendy. She's a yoga instructor."

"Oi—stop trying to pimp me out to your friend," he gruffed.

She giggled, and darted forward to plant a quick peck on his cheek and O's chest warmed with tenderness. He brushed his knuckles along her jaw and again, she leaned into his hand like she was touch-starved. "You are definitely the cherry on top of a very good evening," she sighed contentedly.

"Yeah?"

"*Mm hmm.* Good art, good friends. Good music, *great* drugs. Great looking guy between my legs," she said with a lascivious lick of her lips, and then ran her palms down his chest. He stared down at her hands, but she tipped his chin up, stroking the sides of his beard. "Want to come back to mine?"

O, who'd been sitting still and tense since she first began using him as her personal throne, swallowed hard. "Fuck yes."

She leaned in for a kiss. God—she was fucking hot... and so

wonderfully assertive. Exactly what O needed, because he wasn't drunk enough to make the first—

"Wait—" He put two fingers on her pretty mouth to stop her and, fuck… her lips were so soft—"how high are you?"

She grinned. "Very."

"Yeah, but if you had to rate how out of it you are out of ten?"

She pursed her lips, concentrating on his question, waiting for a voice to answer from somewhere inside her. "Maybe eleven?"

Fuck. "Really?"

"Good chance I won't remember you tomorrow. That a problem, Denmark?"

She pressed her tits against his chest, and her nickname for him came out in a sigh.

What a charming, playful little devil. She felt, and smelt, and looked so good. So fucking *good*. He wanted to demand a kiss from her… run his tongue along her neck… grab her arse and pull her closer; let her rub herself against his cock, which was very hard and very interested in the night's turn of events. But how could he? How could he let it happen when she was so far gone, while he had enough self-awareness still to wonder if this would be okay in the morning?

O realised his hand had been gripping her at the crease of her thigh, his thumb so very close to that seam in her crotch—that crosshair in the denim that he couldn't unsee now.

Jesus Christ.

He snatched his hand away. "I… shouldn't take advantage."

And then he peaked—the crown of his head tingling like he'd downed a fizzy drink too fast. That heavy pressure behind his eyes that always made itself known when he was thoroughly fucked up decided to appear with a vengeance. He scrunched his face and pressed the heel of his palm into his eye socket. He was going to kill Al. "I think.. I'm about to hit a thirteen," he groaned.

"So we both won't remember tomorrow. I'm okay with that."

"I don't know if that's a good—"

And then the evil little devil tilted her hips forward, shuffling closer, and O gasped when she rocked against his erection, and she had the audacity to fucking *laugh*.

He made a garbled sound, and the self-satisfaction written on her face made him want to punish her for her cruelty.

He moved without thinking—surrendered to his need and her pleasure. His fingers slithered up between her shoulder blades and he wrapped his hand around the back of her neck and squeezed.

She made a breathy little, *Aah*.

His other hand found its way under the front of her tshirt, over the soft folds of her belly and up between her tits. He stretched his digits wide over her chest, right at the base of her throat. O's unforgiving hold on her didn't subdue her at all; her arms wrapped around his shoulders and her spine bowed seductively, hips curling back before pushing forward to rub her wide arse against his erection again.

"I want to peel all your clothing off. Unwrap you like a present."

Fuck—she was egging him on.

"You're a menace," he answered, baring his teeth at her and pushing her down against his cock at the same time his pelvis bucked upwards.

He flexed his fingers. Soft, silky hair in one hand; fiery, slippery skin under the other. Which hand should let go to continue exploring? He hated so fucking much that he wasn't some almighty deity with multiple arms to stroke every part of her, all at the same time—to devastate her.

"Oh, Denmark," she said, her voice a low, teasing growl. She stared down at him, eyes ablaze, pushing against his grip on her until her mouth was only inches away from his. His drunken vision tunnelled until her lips—plump, and bright pink—were all he could see.

She ran her tongue across her teeth. "I'm at eleven. You're at thirteen. Who's got the power here?"

Shit—he was fighting a losing battle, wasn't he?

"Let me take advantage, Denmark."

Srinaya awoke to a swarm of bees buzzing around her head. With her eyes squeezed shut, she swiped the air to shoo them away. She whimpered; the incessant drone wouldn't stop, and her brain finally recognised the staccato rhythm of her phone vibrating rudely on the bedside table as the actual culprit.

She cracked open her lids to darkness, save for the flashing light of her phone screen, and some weird alarm clock on the strange table, its dim green digits blinking back at her.

Oh. My hotel room.

3:30AM.

The phone stopped its buzz for a few seconds before it started up again. She snatched it off the table and pressed it to her ear as she buried her head under the covers.

"Oh my god, what?" she mumbled sulkily.

"Good. You're not dead."

"Trying to sleep, Ru."

"Yeah, I know. But I know what you're like so this is a safety check."

"Can I go back to sleep now?"

"Yeah, yeah. Just don't forget you have a flight to catch today, babe."

She groaned. "Fuck. I haven't finished packing."

"Yeah, I know. This is your reminder."

"Can you remind me again in, like, two hours?"

"Fuck off. I'm about to sleep."

"I'll pay you overtime."

"Not a chance. Byeeeee."

She swore at him and hung up, set an alarm on her watch, and snuggled further under the cloud-like duvet that smelt of sweet citrus for some reason—like tropical cocktails and the summer sun. She stretched her legs, her toes spreading wide, revelling in the softness of the thousand thread-count sheets when her toes came in contact with a hairy shin that did not belong to her.

She squeaked in shock.

The mattress dipped ever so slightly behind her, and a low rumble came out from under the sheets.

In the dim light, all she could make out was long hair and a beard that both looked black in the dark blue of the night, and the size of the man's form.

His big body moved as he roused slightly, and he let out a breathy sigh. He clumsily rubbed his face and scratched his thick beard.

Well. This was awkward.

She felt the soft fabric of her well-loved tshirt twisted around her torso.

Yes. Still clothed. Okay.

Her hands travelled downwards.

Right. No underwear. Definitely awkward.

Naya's eyes wouldn't allow her to take in any more details to jog her memory; the darkness shrouded him safely as if he belonged to it.

She should get up and search for her underwear and jeans. She should quietly leave her sleeping bedmate in peace; all she had to do was find her things and slip out the door.

Naya sat up, slightly wobbly as she swung her legs off the high bed. Her stomach gave a little spasm. She rubbed her temples, brain throbbing in her skull. The buzzing returned, although this time it was just the drugs and alcohol bickering loudly at each other.

"Hey," purred the man behind her, and she started. She turned to see his shadowed hand sliding over the white sheets, reaching for her. His long fingers brushed her knuckles. "Stay."

He said it so softly—almost a whisper—but something in his cadence gave her pause. It wasn't a request… It was a plea. And even though she had no recollection of how he came to share her hotel bed, or any details of how they met, his gentle invitation was too sweet to deny.

His fingers intertwined with hers and he carefully pulled, coaxing her back to him, and how the hell could she resist the way he held open the duvet for her like the mouth of a safe little cave?

Naya lay back down and shuffled backwards and he hummed with lazy satisfaction. And then the sleepy giant curved his muscular body, his knees coming up to fit behind hers, and two tree-branch arms enveloped her and gently dragged her against his warm, hard chest. He sleepily nuzzled her ear; his scratchy beard tickled her cheek.

"Mmm. Sleep, love," he whispered languidly, kissing her shoulder and the crook of her neck. Naya couldn't help the sigh that came out of her mouth at the feel of his hot breath skirting across her skin.

And then the mysterious man drifted out of consciousness again, clutching her with care, his arm a comforting weight on her waist.

In the almost pitch-black of the witching hour, something about him made Naya's heart slow its beating, and the painful buzz in her ears faded to a soft hum.

Twelve hours before her flight departed. She could spare a few more in the loving arms of a stranger she wouldn't ever get to know—a perfect, bittersweet memory of her last night in Melbourne.

one

6 MONTHS LATER

Srinaya sat impatiently in a planning meeting at MERAHPUTIH—Indonesia's oldest private venue for arts and culture nestled among the high-rise buildings of Kuningan.

She was the first Indonesian-Australian senior curator hired at MP, a choice that baffled the department heads overseeing the meeting. Naya secretly called them *The Elders*, mainly because they were so fucking old, which was fine, if they weren't also so old-fashioned.

The Elders didn't see her as Indonesian; too much about her betrayed their conservative sensibilities—her fatness, her tattoos and piercings, her *bule* last name, her less than one hundred percent fluency in Bahasa Indonesia.

And yet, she'd still been hired. Her CV made a good enough impression to the hiring panel in spite of The Elders' personal opinions, which a few of them felt the need to share again and again. *Brazen. Western. Unrefined, untraditional, explicit.* Naya couldn't tell if those words were about her work or *her*.

They questioned the exhibition proposals and workshop ideas she brought with her to every single planning catch-up; in the six months she'd been working there, none of her ideas had been shortlisted.

Her suggestion to hold a special event to teach children the art of *batik* was denied, as was her idea to hold workshops to teach them the old tradition of *wayang kulit*. Apparently, the proposal to hold an exhibition to showcase works created by folks with disabilities was outrageous.

God forbid the gallery discuss themes more meaningful and relevant than fucking patriotism, or showcase local artists under the age of fucking sixty.

The current exhibition in Hamdan—the smaller exhibition space being used while the Purnama was being renovated—featured a nineteenth-century Dutch-Indonesian artist. The work was beautiful but, god—*enough* with old dead guys painting bare-breasted maidens bathing in rivers already.

Suryadharma Ali—board member and relative to the last living co-founder of the foundation—only allowed The Elders to approve proposals with safe themes and palatable pieces.

Because he was a basic asshole.

Other board members had no interest in the minutiae of the institution, only coming in for major voting decisions or emergency meetings. But Surya was always there, just to make his presence known… like a fun vampire, sucking everyone's happiness dry. And the shittest thing? His seat on the board meant his bullish behaviour went unchecked.

Naya should've kept her mouth shut in that very first meeting with him. But how could she not stand up for herself when Surya tried to shame her in front of a room full of colleagues? He'd glared at her tattooed arms in her white tshirt and told her to cover up. She refused, advising him not to look at her if he was so offended since there was nothing in her contract that required her to hide her ink.

Surya sputtered some bullshit about disrespect, and fatness, and unprofessionalism, and Naya just glowered at him.

If she were still in Australia, she would've made a complaint but in Indonesia, those kinds of HR woes weren't taken seriously.

In Indonesia, looks mattered. *Thinness* mattered. Acting and dressing appropriately mattered but she wasn't going to start hiding even more of herself.

It had been six months since then, and Surya had only gotten worse.

He rolled his eyes at the printed proposal he carelessly flicked through as Naya explained her latest ideas to introduce a new generation of artists—ones that weren't confined by the constraints older members of the community couldn't seem to break free from.

"It's 2024, *Pak* Surya," Naya insisted. "We have to allow for new traditions. Aren't you excited to see what the younger generation has to say?"

Surya tensed, his narrow face pinched into a sneer to look down his nose at her. "Don't lecture me about traditions, Miss Matthews. I know far more about Indonesian traditions than you do. We broke tradition the day you were hired here. You aren't even Indonesian, and your own *scandalous* work—" He clicked his tongue—"is immature and vulgar at best."

Naya's face burned crimson but she bit her tongue. She didn't want to give him the satisfaction of unleashing her *bule* side—the foreigner part of her that wanted to tell him to fuck off.

A firm, feminine voice from the doorway said, "Is this how the staff are treated when the directors aren't present, *Pak* Surya?"

Endah Ngurawan, lovingly nicknamed *Indonesia's mother of ballet and contemporary dance*, walked in. She was one of four legacy directors—descendants of the co-founders of MERAHPUTIH—and if anyone had more clout at the company than Surya, it was her.

Surya paled at being chastised in front of the lower department heads. Rich, considering he was bullying Naya in front of them.

Endah added, "I'm shocked to hear you talk to one of our senior curators in such a manner."

Surya stammered, "Excuse me, *Ibu* Endah, but do you not agree her work is—"

Endah gracefully floated further into the room and stood right behind Surya, forcing him to twist his neck to look up at her. "No, I don't agree," she said over him. "You don't speak for all the board members when you share your opinions here. You certainly don't speak for the legacy directors. And either way, *Mbak* Srinaya's resume is testament enough. You don't have to like her work for her to be an integral member of this foundation. There are plenty of people here I don't care for— "She arched her manicured brow at him—"and yet I'm able to treat them with respect."

Surya closed his mouth.

Endah turned towards Naya. "*Mbak* Srinaya. I'm sorry about how you've been spoken to today." Endah paused for effect. The room stayed silent. "From now on, please send *me* your proposals so that *I* can pass them on to the relevant parties. In fact," she added, "I'd love to see *all* of your past proposals."

The meeting ended; Naya stayed seated with her nails still digging into her legs, breathing deeply and evenly as the staff filed out.

Surya cast her a disdainful sneer as he closed the door behind him.

Naya let out a scornful sound.

Endah moved around the table to sit next to Naya. "You're right, Naya. MP tends to play it safe. People are scared of disturbing the status quo."

Naya huffed out a breath, afraid that looking into Endah's kind face would make her cry. "I think you'll find," Naya countered, "that people are more scared of Pak Surya."

"I didn't realise. I *should* have realised..." Endah said regretfully, shaking her head. "I have to make a few calls—" She pulled a business card from a shiny gold case, and handed it to Naya—"but please email me. Let's see if your exhibition proposals are as *scandalous* as your own work." Her eyes gleamed with cattiness and Naya grinned.

$$\downarrow$$

A month later, on a Saturday night, Naya received a video call from Endah.

"I have some news, dear," the beautiful ballerina said. "I submitted one of your exhibition proposals and it has been approved. Your show —the one you titled *Heartbreak*? It will reopen the Purnama."

Naya choked on the green tea she was sipping. "B-But what happened to Alex Visser's show?" she asked in between coughs.

"Cancelled. Alex Visser turned out to be unsuitable." Naya blinked, confused. "Someone posted a video of him drunkenly spouting anti-Islamic sentiment on social media yesterday." Endah made a disdainful face. "He won't work in this country again."

Naya knew Visser's reputation—knew people who'd worked with him when he wasn't quite as well-known. He was an asshole then too.

She couldn't help but feel a little bit of glee that he'd made an enemy out of Endah.

Endah's resolve knew no bounds, as did her influence. Naya didn't doubt for one second that Endah's phone had the names of some serious political heavyweights saved within it. All it would take was one phone call in that charming lilt of a voice to someone who worked in the immigration department and Visser's travel visa would never be approved.

Endah sighed. "Unfortunately, he has quite the following here, which means our patrons will be disappointed about the cancellation. Ticket sales were projected to be astronomical."

Okay. So this show had to be exceptional.

"We don't expect your exhibition to bring in the same kind of numbers but it must impress. I don't doubt that it will—that you will. Your own art shows have been very well received in New York and Toronto, no? You obviously have an eye for beautiful work that engages the viewer, and a finger on the pulse of who and what is popular. And I hear you've also worked with DEWI. That's quite an achievement."

Naya shouldn't be surprised that Endah knew. Endah seemed to know everything about everyone.

"Anyway," Endah said, "I'm sorry to bother you on a Saturday night but I didn't want you to be blindsided first thing on Monday morning when you receive the official memo, and I won't be at MERAHPUTIH to congratulate you."

Naya nodded. "Thank you, *Ibu* Endah."

Endah waved off her thanks. "I collect good people, Naya. And I can tell you're a good and capable person." Naya smiled at Endah's beautiful face. "One more bit of advice, dear? Among the lesser-known artists you invite to be a part of your exhibition, whose work will no doubt be wonderful, make sure you have some big names, yes? Perhaps you should see if you can get in touch with DEWI's people."

Endah hung up and Naya jumped to her feet and squealed. She hit play on her *FUCK YEAH!* Spotify playlist, and she danced around her living room and kitchen to a remix of 'Sex With Me' by Rihanna.

Finally. Fucking finally.

A show of her own to plan at MERAHPUTIH.

Her mind kicked into planning mode—marketing and publicity, how to reach out to artists, which of the juniors she wanted on her team…

She stopped herself.

No, Naya. Tonight, we celebrate. Tomorrow, we plan.

She searched for Arum's number in her contacts—knew her best friend would jump for joy at her news.

But another face forced its way to the fore and the joyful feeling from a moment ago turned a little…

No—not sour. Bittersweet.

Should she text Sal? It had been so long but Sal would want to know. He'd be so pleased for her. And… in some way, Naya *needed* him to know that she had reached another goal after all that had happened.

She searched for his name in her messages.

NAYA:

Hey you. I know it's been a while but I got some big news and you were the first person I wanted to tell.

SAL JONES:

Hello! Tell me!

NAYA:

I'M CURATING A SHOW AT MP!

SAL JONES:

HOLY SHIT SRI THAT IS HUGE! Kicking arse and taking names! Never doubted you for a second.

NAYA:

That means a lot coming from you.

SAL JONES:

I'm so proud of you.

NAYA:

🙁 I hope you're happy and well, Sal. Please don't be a stranger?

SAL JONES:

Never. I'm always around, love. Although I gotta go for now... need to get Chlo to sleep. Little shit is trying to negotiate.

NAYA:

LOL. Ok. I'm always around too. Talk soon xoxox

First thing on Monday, the admin department received an email announcing the cancellation of Alex Visser's show due to his disappointing anti-Islamic rhetoric, and the exhibition that would take its place: *Heartbreak*, a group show featuring local and international artists curated by none other than Srinaya Matthews, the newest senior curator.

The CuRaShUn NaSHuN 💩 group chat blew up.

CHRIS:

YEEEEEEEEEEAAAAAAAH NAYA. GOOD JOB

TINIIIII:

Dude fuck Alex Visser. What a dickwad

LASTRI:

👣👣👣👣👣👣👣👣go go go

JON F:

So happy for you Mbak Naya! Cannot believe what Visser said.

NUR:

100% I don't know his work but after he spouted that crap I HATE HIS FACE

TINIIIII:

You're not missing much Nur. His work is banal AF

GUNAWAN S:

Can't wait to see what you come up with Mbak Naya. If you need any help at all, please let us know 😊

EDHIBOBEDHI:

I'm on your team right? I'll cut you if I'm not on your team.

RAVI C:

Edhi chill she prob just found out and needs time to process.

But I better be on the dream team too, yo. 😈

†

Later that evening, after a day of selecting teammates and preliminary meetings, Naya went to the Purnama Gallery. The tradesmen fixing the water and termite damage in the east and north wings had left for the night.

The hairs on Naya's arms stood at attention as the sliding doors opened, as if she was entering some ancient house of worship. She made her way up and down the three wings, the sound of her footsteps echoing.

She returned to the heart of Purnama, the vast foyer in the very centre with its high cloister vault ceiling.

The only illumination came from one set of spotlights pointed at a bare wall.

She leaned back against the cold white concrete and stared at nothing; with the lights shining down into her eyes, blackness engulfed the rest of the room.

She was like a performer on stage—all eyes on her.

Her breath hitched.

So much responsibility.

She felt… she couldn't quite grasp onto just one emotion. Pride? Awe? Insecurity? So many things.

The smell of the fresh plaster mingling with the old wood brought back sweet memories of past visits to MP. Incredible works had graced the walls—Keith Haring, Ai WeiWei, Yasumasa Morimura, Slamet Gundono, Jean-Michel Basquiat, Pipilotti Rist, Heri Dono—artists she admired and who inspired her own work.

To Naya, the Purnama was hallowed ground.

She squared her shoulders.

Right. Ok.

She inhaled through her nose, held for four beats, exhaled, and held for four beats.

It's just like the Danks Gallery, she thought, comparing Purnama to the largest exhibiting space she'd worked with before this proposed exhibition.

She looked around the space again.

Multiplied by three. Fuck. This place is massive.

She shook the doubt away and before another barrage of insecurity could crash over her, she marched out of the gallery and out the front gates, praying to the universe for support.

She reread Sal's texts as she waited for her taxi, and looked up at the sound of a car pulling up in front of her. Surya exited through the wrought iron gates and before she could pretend she hadn't noticed him, they locked eyes.

Fuck.

"Goodnight *Pak* Surya," she said, smiling politely.

The streetlamps outside the gates cast ominous shadows onto his wiry frame, and the reflection of the rear car lights on his glasses lit his eyes in a way that made him look like some caricature of a demon—if demons were rangy, middle-aged men who wore mock turtlenecks in tropical weather.

"You must be pleased with yourself—getting *Ibu* Endah to champion one of your proposals. You were incessant with them. *Community-based projects,*" he scoffed.

He shook his head and turned away but Naya couldn't help herself. "At least I've consistently brought ideas forward in those meetings *Pak* Surya. I work hard. I *try*. It's harder to come up with ideas than it is to judge them."

Surya—ever the fan of dramatics—turned back slowly, silently. His nose wrinkled as his gaze swept from her head to her feet and back up again.

And then he opened his mouth. "You don't belong here, Miss *Matthews*." He spat out her last name as if it tasted bitter in his mouth. "My aunt co-founded this place to celebrate our history, preserve Indonesian culture. Even the name—*MERAHPUTIH*—is a nod to the Indonesian flag. And you want to plan some exhibition about *heartbreak?* How overly dramatic and self-indulgent, and so typically *western*."

Naya felt like she'd been slapped—too shocked by his meanness to say anything. The tone he used when he called out her whiteness was a brand on her forehead that said, *Other*.

Surya climbed into the back seat of his car but before he closed the door, he added, "Expect to only have the main foyer and south wing to use. I doubt the north and east will be ready in time. Probably a good thing; I can't imagine your show lasting the full season."

He slammed the door, and Naya tried and failed to hold back her tears.

two

After three days of constant rain and temperatures dipping below five degrees, it was official: winter had finally arrived.

O relished cold Melbourne days. To be fair, they weren't unlike other cold cities. Vancouver, San Francisco, and even London—they all had a similar energy but the nostalgia made all the difference.

Melbourne played a major role in his own story—reminded him of finding himself again after all the loss. It was the place in which he'd put himself back together as best he could.

Many pieces had been missing at the beginning, but over the years he'd found ways to cope. Friends and loved ones filled those spaces, and the cracks were held together by sheer determination.

And therapy. Lots and lots of therapy.

He walked down Swanston St—coffee in hand—and tucked the ends of his scarf into his coat. The rain finally stopped but the clouds hadn't parted to give way to blue skies and sun. The tall buildings in the central business district created wind tunnels which always made the city feel colder.

O flicked his collar up and hunched his shoulders.

It was bitterly cold. His cheeks and nose reddened to warm his face, his hot breath visible in front of him like a plume of smoke.

He checked his watch. Two meetings done. One more to go.

As he waited at a pedestrian crossing on Bourke St, O scanned his emails, spotting one from Endah—mother figure and fellow legacy board member of MERAHPUTIH.

His heart warmed.

Endah was an integral part of his healing. She moved to Australia for the better part of a year to be close to him, making herself available should he ever need someone.

O's uncle, Nicholas, who'd unexpectedly inherited him at the passing of his parents, was kind and loving, but ill-equipped to look after a broken-hearted Owen.

Also, Nicholas' work in the military meant he was deployed to many different—oftentimes dangerous—places so boarding school in Melbourne was where O ended up.

Endah had been there through the worst of it, a constant figure of love and patience, never smothering him but always in his periphery. Holding space for his bouts of anger and sorrow.

Endah had been a tower of strength for him while also mourning the loss of his mother, Molly—her best friend. He couldn't even imagine the pain she went through.

O was ashamed to admit he'd been avoiding Endah; in the past three years, they'd only seen each other a handful of times.

The crosswalk light turned green, and the throng of people crossed the street. O stepped onto the road as he read the subject line: *Come home. Need your help.*

He tapped on Endah's email, saw the attached photo and dropped his phone. He scrambled to pick it up off the asphalt, jogged to the other side of the street, and gaped at the message, his heart pounding in his ears.

The image embedded at the top was of the *newcomer*—the wonderful, impish woman from almost eight months ago who'd left him alone in a hotel room with nothing but a handwritten note on hotel stationery:

Thanks for a night I wish I remembered. ;)
xox N

And now he was staring at a photo of her standing in front of a large abstract painting of an Indonesian goddess. The caption read: *Our newest senior curator, Srinaya Matthews.*

The photo had been taken mid-conversation; one hand buried in the pocket of her ripped jeans, while the other blurred as she waved it about. Her eyes were bright and animated as if she was getting to the juicy part of a story. She wore an oversized black tshirt with *CECI N'EST PAS UN TEE SHIRT* on the chest, knotted at the waist. Sleeves rolled up with black Birkenstocks on, she looked so ridiculously cool.

She looked even more beautiful than he remembered.

O hadn't realised he was holding his breath and exhaled sharply as he read the email:

SUBJECT: Come home. Need your help.

Dear Owen,

It's been such a long time since we wrote to each other. How are you? I hope you're doing well in Melbourne.

We have a new curator who has joined our team. She is a wonderful addition. Srinaya's work is gritty and daring… maybe even a little too much for this country's sensibilities, but she truly has impeccable taste when it comes to curation and planning inclusive events that are not only for Indonesia's elite.

Because of Alex Visser's snafu, we approved one of Naya's exhibition proposals to replace his show. It will be called "Heartbreak". She will be inviting artists from all disciplines to apply. She plans to use the entirety of Purnama to include multimedia installations and large-scale pieces. The show will be bold, and unique, and I am very excited to see what she comes up with.

Unfortunately, some people are pushing back on these plans, labelling her a risk due to her personal artwork. But there's more to it… I think her half-white heritage is being used against her.

Aud Pitch

Yes—we're not supposed to interfere with the smaller details of MP, but I think you need to come to Jakarta and show your face. I think people have forgotten that you are proof that being not Indonesian enough is a ridiculous reason to penalise someone who wants to do wonderful work for MP. Come home, *nak*. Meet Naya. Help me support her. You will love her. Your parents would have approved of her ideas—especially your Mom. Google her. She is a coat of fresh paint on the walls of this old place.
Love,
Endah

xox N.

    N for Naya.

A startled giggle came out of him which grew into a full laugh. He laughed so hard he doubled over, hands propped on his knees, on Little Collins St. A passerby asked him if he was alright and he nodded, waving them away.

All this time.

All this fucking time the red tshirt person was in Jakarta. In his mother's hometown. Getting hired at the institution his grandmother co-founded.

For months, he thought of her every day. He'd woken up that morning, head pounding, to darkness and a cold, empty bed—a punch to the gut, his abandonment issues flaring big, and hot, and bright.

He couldn't latch onto any clear memories from after she'd asked him to come home with him. Something about *elevens*, and *thirteens*, and taking advantage?

But he did have blurry images embedded behind his lids—the arch of her back, her strong thighs straddling him on the bed, jeans off… panties on, *maybe*? Her sucking on his fingers, staring up at him with those big, black eyes. Fuck—was it his fingers that she had sucked?

His cock hardened. Thank god for his coat.

O wasn't sure how far they'd physically gone that night, but she'd managed to burrow her way into his brain, and deeper still, into some strange place that felt a lot like where a soul would be if he believed in that sort of thing.

He thought back on how close he'd come to turning into an absolute creep by calling Derek, his friend in the police force to do some dodgy detective work... maybe look at the security footage from Chidori to identify her.

It was Mario who reminded him that doing that kind of shit was definitely verging on stalker-like behaviour.

"Sometimes, O," Mar had said sagely, "when almost everything is available to you, you forget that some things? Some things just aren't *for* you."

O didn't believe in divine timing or even fate, but this revelation... Naya, working at MERAHPUTIH? An institution so grand, and special, and so connected to his family? In a completely different country to where they'd first had that intimate exchange?

O dared to say it felt a little bit like his parents had a hand in the strange coincidence.

He called his EA to divert all meetings to relevant department heads, change any and all in-person meetings to zoom calls and book his flights to Jakarta for two days' time.

three

Naya squeezed her hands into fists and stomped around Purnama, muttering angry curses and not giving a fuck who heard.

She wished the tradesmen in the gallery had a wall they needed to demolish because she really wanted to break something.

Her watch beeped at her politely, offering to lead her through a meditation to lower her heart rate. She furiously unfastened the strap to throw the stupid thing across the gallery and then stopped—told herself not to be so rash—refastened it, and followed along with the mindfulness session.

Earlier that morning, Naya was called in to discuss the use of every available room in Purnama.

Artwork profiles for *Heartbreak* had begun trickling in, and the pieces were perfect. So many artists were bravely pushing the boundaries, talking more openly about topics still considered taboo in a country trying to break out of conservatism.

The main gallery and one wing were nowhere near enough. She had to get The Elders to understand.

She sat alone on one side of the conference table while the seven department heads sat opposite her.

Ibu Lina—a fine arts docent at Universitas Indonesia—spoke bluntly. "*Mbak* Naya, this is your first curated show here. And it is being planned, with very little time, after a devastating cancellation. Alex Visser's show was going to be a huge event to reopen Purnama, but your show is filled mainly with *emerging* artists. Not only that, we're familiar with the work you're drawn to, and although we understand the need to be more progressive, we worry that some of the works you'll choose will be—" A pause for the right word. A pointed gaze—"distasteful to many."

The rest of The Elders quietly nodded.

Naya wanted to yell at them, at their small-mindedness; their cowardice. She wanted to scream at *Ibu* Lina for having so little faith in these up-and-coming artists—some of whom were *her* past students.

Naya nodded crisply. "I appreciate your thoughts. I'll remember your feedback as I choose the final pieces. My goal isn't to offend. It's to show raw emotion surrounding a theme every single one of us has experienced."

What the fuck was she doing at MERAHPUTIH? Why the fuck had she crawled back to Jakarta after over twenty years of living abroad? It wasn't like she had family connections, or at least, no one she wanted to reconnect with. There was a reason why she moved away at fourteen, begging her dad to take her so she could go to highschool in Melbourne.

She'd visited Jakarta for regular month-long stints here and there but always found herself straddling the line between feeling out of place and feeling at home. Even her intimate group of friends in Jakarta—her *bestest* friends—who always welcomed her with loving arms and made her feel less lonesome, couldn't stop the ache of not fully belonging.

She thought it would be different this time since she was moving to Indonesia for a highly-coveted job, but it wasn't, not at all. Surya and The Elders wouldn't let it be different, and she hated them for it.

And she hated herself for being so fucking desperate to make a name for herself in her birth town that she had left the city that had embraced her without question.

Naya sat on the floor in the centre of Purnama and opened an email with an attached image sent in for consideration. It was an oil portrait of an elderly Indonesian man smoking a cigarette, the paint textured and heavily applied by an angry hand.

She stared at the hollows of the old man's cheeks, his face frozen in an everlasting drag of nicotine.

Shit.

She bit her lip, her craving rising, and she gave in. It was not the day to deny herself. She fished money from her bag and went outside.

She walked out the gates of the art complex to the roadside *warung* selling ice cold drinks, sweets, snacks, and—most importantly—cigarettes.

The *warung* owner's two little children sat beside the stall and gaped at Naya. She was used to the stares; a fat half-white, half-Indonesian woman covered in tattoos must've been quite a sight. She smiled at the children as she paid for a pack of Sampoerna Menthols but they hid behind their mother.

The sprawling art complex was quieter than usual. A handful of people loitered on the steps to the Purnama while others sat on park benches under the copse of trees in the garden.

Visitors of the Hamdan gallery walked past in dribs and drabs.

Teens on a school tour blatantly gawked at Naya and talked about her in not-very-hushed tones, thinking she couldn't speak Indonesian, and she ignored them.

Fuck, she missed Melbourne. She missed her little flat in Footscray, with its wonky floorboards, the dozens of rosellas and white cockatoos that attacked the cumquat tree in her front lawn, and the sounds of her elderly next-door neighbours playing rock 'n' roll records on warm evenings. She missed getting drunk and high with friends and making her way home on the tram.

She didn't have the same kind of memories of Jakarta. Jakarta memories were *feelings* and she was starting to realise she couldn't trust them.

Maybe what she recalled were child-like feelings of *wishing* she belonged. What was that Portuguese word?

Saudade. Maybe Naya was missing something that never was.

It was an unusually clear day in Jakarta. Most days, the sky was grey or even white. The smog kept the city humid and sticky, but the sun shone brightly down at Naya and her cheeks warmed.

She lounged on the steps leading up to the administration building like some intractable stray cat and lit her cigarette.

She looked very unprofessional and she didn't fucking care. What else would The Elders do—take the *last* wing from her?

She swore under her breath and took a slow drag, letting the burn of smoke and tar tickle her throat.

Resting her head on a step with her eyes closed, she stretched, arching her back and raising her arms above her, exposing a strip of her belly to the sun. She purred deep and low when her limbs trembled, loosening the tension coiled tight in her body.

With her eyes still closed, she flicked her cigarette and took another drag, exhaling with a sigh.

And then, the Indonesian national anthem popped into her head like some weirdly cruel joke, and she hummed along.

"Permisi, boleh minta satu?"

Naya's eyes snapped open at the deep voice that came with a foreign accent. She squinted in the sunlight to focus her eyes on who had asked to bum one of her cigarettes.

Standing a few steps below where she rested was a *bule.*

An outrageously handsome one.

Naya shot up.

The symmetry of the man's striking features reminded her of the Divine Proportion—of *perfection...* but the kind of perfection that would never fade to ordinary.

His white shirt sleeves were rolled up to his elbows, revealing muscular forearms lightly covered in fine brown hair that glinted gold in the sun.

The man gestured to the steps for permission to sit, and Naya nodded. He sat with a little grateful huff but kept a respectful distance. His mouth curved into a questioning smile—almost a smirk—as if he knew a secret.

"Sure," Naya finally answered his earlier question and realised she'd spoken in English. "Oh—*silahkan*," she corrected, handing him the pack of cigarettes.

His mouth widened into a dazzling show of pearly white teeth. "Thanks," he said as his large hand reached for the pack. Naya spotted a little star tattoo in the webbing between his thumb and forefinger.

He pulled out a cigarette and slipped the filter between his lips and she leaned towards him, offering to light it. He came closer too, moving up a step and curling his slender fingers over her hands to pull the flame closer to his face.

The innocent touch sent a shiver up her spine.

His hazel irises—bright amber ringed with stormy grey—stayed locked onto her face as the cigarette burned and crackled, and then he reclined against the steps, propped up on his elbows, taking a long deep drag.

"Clove," the foreigner sighed in a plume of smoke, patrician features turned up to the sky in pleasure. "They smell like the beach and of late-night chats with friends, don't you think?"

His voice was deep and gravelly, with a mild Australian accent. He smiled at her again and ran a hand through the waves of his shoulder-length hair.

Now that she sat closer, Naya discovered freckles dusting the bridge of his nose and cheeks, and her heart thrummed. That smattering of freckles gave the seemingly unapproachable, powerful man an air of boyish charm.

His freckles and those big hands were by far her favourite things about the foreigner, followed closely behind by every other part of him: the way his hair was too messy for someone in expensive busi-ness-casual attire but no one would ever fault him for it because it just *worked* with that face, or how when he leaned forward to rest his elbows on his knees, his shirt was so tight against his broad back and muscular upper arms that it looked like skin.

Naya finished first. "Another?" he asked as he pulled a cigarette from the pack he still held.

She shouldn't, but she took it anyway, enjoying the shock of elec-tricity that fizzed through her when their skin touched.

"Here—let me," he said softly and gestured for the lighter.

She brushed her fingertips against his skin as she placed the cheap Bic in his wide calloused palm.

She couldn't help thinking about how nice those rough hands would feel gripping her hips.

His eyes never left her mouth as he lit her smoke and she licked her lips extra slowly—making a subtle show of it—and his pupils dilated.

God—if they were anywhere else Naya would've made a move, let her gaze linger on his, touch his arm a little, lean in a bit closer.

Hell—she was brazen enough to come right out and ask it: *Let's go back to mine. I'll wrap my legs around that big, hard body of yours.*

But fuck—she was at work, and it wasn't even midday yet, and he looked like he had business with MP. Totally off-limits.

She could smell him now; sweet citrus—like a tropical cocktail, and the warm salty hint of *him*. The scents mixed playfully on her tongue; he smelt like—

No. It couldn't be him. That guy from her last night in Melbourne was European—Danish, if her drug-addled brain remembered correctly.

She narrowed her eyes at him. "Have… we met before?"

His brow wrinkled but a smile tugged at his lips. "*Have* we?"

She refused to answer his question by telling him he *smelt* familiar. "Are you here for an appointment?" she asked instead, hoping her question would snap her back into focus, but her body insisted on moving closer to him.

"Yeah, I am." He casually looked at his watch. He was either eleven minutes late, or nineteen minutes early.

"Do you need help finding your way to the right office? The admin building can be a bit of a maze if you're not familiar with it. I don't want to keep you if you're running late."

The foreigner rolled his wide shoulders in a lazy shrug and flashed her another smile. "They'll wait," he rumbled.

The spun gold highlights in his hair gleamed under the sun, so bright it reminded her of Gustav Klimt's '*The Kiss*'.

God—those lips…

The foreigner glanced her way as he extinguished his cigarette on the sole of his fancy shoe. "Aside from the kooky display of patriotism before, what are *you* doing here?" he asked with a teasing grin. She must have looked confused because he sang, *Indonesia Raya, Merdeka, Merdeka.* "Interesting song choice."

Naya let out an embarrassed laugh and heat rushed to her cheeks at having been caught singing. Out of tune, no doubt. "I *was* having an existential crisis but you interrupted me. Rude."

His pretty eyes widened. "Shit—sorry. Should I leave you to continue your crisis in peace?"

"God, no. Please don't. It was stupid of me to try and resolve it in my head."

He rested his chin on his fist. "So speak it out. Come on—I'll be your sounding board. Go," he beckoned.

Naya looked at him dubiously. Airing out grievances to a stranger? He looked so eager to help though, with those intense eyes focused on her. He gestured for her to speak so she took a breath. "I think… Maybe *home* isn't a place but a state of mind. Maybe my body should be *home* so I never feel displaced."

"Shit—you're talking about a *proper* crisis."

She put her hand to her heart and declared, "I never do things half-assed."

The foreigner smiled ruefully and crossed his arms over his knees. "If it's any consolation, I know exactly how you feel." Naya must've given him another suspicious look because he pointed to himself and said, "Quarter-Indonesian. Born here. Spent almost half my life here. Speak Bahasa well, but I'll always be an outsider."

A warmth heated her chest—a knowing that appeared whenever something significant blossomed between her and someone new. The words came out of her mouth before she had time to think: "Maybe we can not fit in here together."

The man looked genuinely touched and before she could make a quippy remark to save herself from embarrassment, he answered, "We could start a club." And then they both barked, "I'm President!" at the same time and burst out laughing.

His chuckle was full, and gravelly, and beautiful.

They both went quiet, giving the spark between them permission to grow.

He studied her carefully, the honey in his eyes glowing. The man's generous smile disappeared when he said, "Sorry today's been shit. I hope tomorrow will be better for you."

She nodded. Their conversation had gotten far too melancholic.

"My name's Naya," she offered.

His gaze turned hot and she couldn't help but fidget, squeezing her knees together. He placed his fingertips on his chest and said, "Owen."

Owen. What a beautiful name. Both strong and soft. She imagined the shapes her mouth would make—loved how her lips would part at the start of it and then slowly draw closer together, and then her tongue would join in at the end, not wanting to be left out. It would be a wonderful name to moan.

Shit—her cheeks went beetroot-red, she was sure of it.

She changed the subject again. "You're a great sounding board. Thank you for helping me troubleshoot my crisis, and for joining me in my pursuit of quitting not smoking." She crossed her legs coquettishly to punctuate her sentence.

Owen squinted in confusion for a moment as he repeated her words. "Quitting… not smoking…" His eyes flicked down to the pack of cigarettes Naya held in one hand and the lit cigarette in the other. He gasped—mouth agape. "Did I help you restart your dirty habit?"

Naya gave him a scandalous grin as she nodded at him slowly.

He gasped again and snatched away her cigarette before she could take one last drag. "Uh-uh," he said, shaking his head in mock disapproval and *tsking* at her dramatically. He took it between those full parted lips before she could respond saying, "Cigarettes are bad for you." He took the last drag of it and winked at her.

Naya probably should've been annoyed at Owen's casual intimacy, how he acted so familiar… maybe even entitled. But there was some other feeling that overtook her, and it wasn't just her body reacting to his looks. It was something deeper, like recognition.

From the entrance of the admin department at the top of the steps came an unwelcome voice. "Miss Matthews, are you disturbing our most esteemed benefactor and legacy director?"

They both turned to see Surya smiling down at Owen, Surya's eyes strangely soft and expectant as if waiting for Owen to praise him for chastising her.

She whipped her head back to the *bule* next to her and looked him up and down.

Benefactor. Most esteemed?

She'd met three of the legacy directors. Surely he couldn't be the fourth. He was too young; he couldn't have been older than forty.

She scrambled to her feet, hating how Surya was so good at making her feel guilty. "No, *Pak* Surya. I— we—"

Surya waved a dismissive hand at Naya as he spoke over her, "I apologise, Mr Jameson. She's only the newest addition to our curatorial staff. She's planning a small exhibition in the coming months. Nothing worth your—"

The esteemed benefactor interrupted Surya as he stood. "I'm familiar with Srinaya's plans to reopen Purnama." His eyes met hers. "*Heartbreak*. Powerful theme. I'm pleased with the board's decision to bring in some new blood and, with her, some progressive suggestions."

Naya blinked. He knew her full first name. He knew about her exhibition. Fuck—she'd gotten weirdly personal with a legacy director. She blinked again when she noticed how tall he was, her eyes going up and up and up.

Surya's eyes flashed menacingly at her before he gave Mr Jameson a sickly-sweet smile.

Standing next to Mr Jameson, Naya couldn't see the sprinkling of freckles on his nose and upper cheeks anymore; his boyish charm and playful grin were replaced by a tight-lipped smile. He rolled down his sleeves, buttoned his cuffs and reached behind himself to shrug his linen blazer on. Her cheeks heated at the sight of his broad chest that tapered to a narrow waist.

He gestured for her to lead the way up, his eyes crinkling warmly, and Naya giggled awkwardly as she climbed, feeling his overwhelming presence close behind.

Endah appeared beside Surya and let out an elated squeak, her arms stretched out wide. "Owen! *Sayang*! Oh, I'm so happy to see you."

Owen Jameson. Stealer of cigarettes. Enabler of dirty habits.

Benefactor. Legacy director.

Holy shit—thank god Naya hadn't made a move.

Mr Jameson quickened his pace up the steps, overtaking Naya to greet Endah with a kiss to each cheek and a tight hug. Endah's brows furrowed; she was holding back tears. There was history there—a shared story.

"*Tante*, look at you," he said. "You're more beautiful now than when you were a prima ballerina. I may have to steal you away from *Oom* Agung."

Endah smacked his arm and fiddled with her hair, waving off his flattery. Mr Jameson turned to Surya, smile disappearing in an instant, and shook the man's hand curtly. "*Pak* Surya."

"Nice to see you, Mr Jameson. My aunt didn't tell us you'd be visiting."

And then Surya turned to Naya. He opened his mouth to say something, and by the sneer on his face, it was going to be patronising and derisive, but the benefactor casually stepped in front of her—tall and domineering—protecting her from Surya like a stubborn sea wall defending a little coastal town from destructive ocean waves.

Mr Jameson's back was to her, and although she couldn't see his face, it was perfectly clear from his icy tone that he expected immediate obedience: "Start without me. I'll be in shortly."

Endah smirked and ushered a blank-faced Surya inside. She turned to catch Naya's eye and winked.

The sliding doors closed behind them and Mr Jameson turned back to her. She looked at the ground, embarrassed by Surya's rebuke.

She was wrong before. This wasn't a significant connection. She could never be friends with a legacy director. There would be no silly club, and even if there was, of course he'd be president and she'd be... Naya.

"Well," she mumbled, "it was nice meeting you, Mr Jameson."

She turned and walked towards Purnama.

"Please wait," he called after her—voice expectant.

He closed the distance between them—came so impossibly close that she stepped back defensively. The esteemed benefactor reached out and enveloped her right hand in both of his.

"Srinaya Matthews," he murmured. Something akin to relief washed over his face. His eyes scanned over her as if he was learning her, memorising her features. "At *MERAHPUTIH*," he added, bewildered. She had to lean her head back to look up into his bright eyes framed by dark lashes. "I am very, very happy to meet you."

He smiled the most devastating smile, let go of her hand and headed inside the doors of the administration department of MP, leaving her in a daze.

four

Ibrahim turned the car into the entrance of MERAHPUTIH and O lost his breath when he saw the stylised form of *'Penari'* through the tinted glass of the sunroof. The towering bronze sculpture welcomed visitors to the gallery complex, its elongated body an eerie mix of Duchamp's *'Nude Descending the Staircase'* and Dali's *'Woman with Head of Roses'*: spindly arms flung high into the air, a choppy, minimalistic torso with sharp angles, all balanced on a pointed foot that looked far too narrow to hold up such a precarious-looking piece.

It was the last artwork O's grandmother had purchased for MP before she died. He always felt closest to her when he passed underneath The Dancer, imagining the great Rina Candrawatih—formidable poet and philanthropist—watching over him with a stern look on her face.

They drove past the public drop-off point to the security booth and O rolled down his window to give a friendly nod to one of the security staff who approached. The guard's eyes went round with recognition and he rushed to lift the boom gate, waving the car through.

"It hasn't changed much," Ibrahim commented.

O hummed in agreement.

He gazed up at the main trio of buildings that were his legacy—the harsh straight lines of concrete covered in creeping vines, palms and colourful tropical flowers.

He sighed.

And then he jerked forward to shove his face between the two front seats when he spotted a familiar femme sitting on the steps of the admin building.

"Stop the car, stop-stop-stop—"

Holy shit—that's xox N.

Naya.

He clambered out and strode up to her, opening his mouth to launch into his practised greeting: *Hello, we met last year in Melbourne. Did you forget me like you said you would?* But when he heard her humming the Indonesian anthem, of all things, as she ungraciously (but so sultrily) laid back against the steps with her eyes shut, his mind went totally blank.

And then Naya looked up at him—actually *saw* him with sharp eyes and a clear head—and… he panicked. Anxiety stabbed at his sternum when her brows drew together almost accusingly as she tried to place him. She outright asked him, and he'd stupidly answered with… a question?

He cringed inwardly. At least his reply had been non-committal— neither a yes or a no—which gave him more time to figure out how to tell her about their first encounter.

O wanted to wrap his arms around her when she spoke so openly about wishing she belonged. And when she offered him her name like a gift, he wanted to fucking die.

But then that spell was broken by Surya, and now he was stuck in a meeting and he wanted to fucking die again… *and* take Surya down with him.

O couldn't give a flying fuck about donations, or revenue, or approving annual budgets; not right now—not when the person who'd turned his world askew was in the Purnama. So close, yet so painfully far.

It would probably take less than thirty steps from the admin build-ing's entrance to the gallery's main doors. Seven seconds. *Four if I bolted.* He certainly didn't want to spend any more time in the same room as Surya—the little weasel of a man.

O twirled his pen restlessly between his fingers. Every time he thought of how Srinaya wrinkled her nose playfully like that night in Melbourne, his lungs spasmed. And in his lucid state, he was delighted to discover she had three little beauty spots under her right eye that his thumb itched to caress.

The conference room was stifling; he felt as if he'd swallowed fireworks and they were going to go off inside his chest cavity if he didn't get out soon.

"I think we can end there," O announced. He scribbled notes on one of the many pages of spreadsheets and graphs presented to him. "From what I can tell, everyone's working hard to ensure the donations are spent in the best possible way. And it's good to see the main focus is on the community, with a concerted effort to include those who would otherwise be left out of the arts and culture programs: underprivileged children, those with disabilities... It's progressive—I like it. It's what's been missing at MP."

Endah spoke up. "Yes. The brightest ideas have come from our newest curator, Srinaya, or have been inspired by her, I believe. The others are now coming up with plans to bring younger audiences in and community projects seem to be the best tactic."

Pride bloomed in O's belly. He'd done his research since he found out Naya's name; her main discipline was mixed media on large canvases and recycled wood, and her themes were consistently bold—angry and seductive; lots of abstracts that hinted at bodies tangled together, splashes of colour depicting hands and tongues and teeth.

But even with all that artistic talent, the best thing about her was her passion for inclusivity, for ensuring that art was accessible for everyone.

"Well, aren't we lucky that she accepted our offer to work here, then," he commented, flicking his gaze to Surya.

The man didn't respond.

The meeting ended and everyone filed out, leaving Endah and O alone.

Endah squeezed his forearm. "It's been far too long," she said. Her eyes brightened with tears. O covered her hand with his. He sat on the table; Endah smiled sadly. "I can't help but see the rowdy little O who climbed on all the furniture when you sit on the table like that."

"I've missed you too," he said. "I'm sorry I haven't been in touch. Life just—"

Endah raised her hand to stop him. "We've never been the kind of people to regularly contact each other. Sometimes I wonder if the loss made silences more comfortable."

He nodded in agreement. "But I'm always available when you need me. You can count on me to come running as soon as you ask me to."

Endah's arms stretched wide. "And here you are. I feel very powerful to have the great Owen Jameson at my beck and call."

O sighed melodramatically. "Yeah, yeah. You have me wrapped around your little finger, *Tante*." He stood again and buttoned his blazer, and Endah's face softened even more.

He knew she saw his father in him—the husband of her lost best friend. He sorted through some documents from the meeting, refusing to dwell on it.

As he straightened out the ridiculous amount of paper printed out for him, muttering under his breath about recycling and trees, Endah spoke up. "Be careful with Srinaya, Owen."

Her voice was just above a whisper as if she was worried someone would hear.

O stopped packing up his documents and blinked. "Huh?"

Endah lifted her chin and clasped her hands together in front of her. Her feet did that thing ballet dancers do, where their toes point outward. He had no idea what the position was called—First? Second? —but that stance, as well as her hair swept up in a chignon made her look every bit the prima ballerina she once was. This was *Power* Endah —not *Sweet Mother* Endah.

"Srinaya is valuable to MP," she said. This protective, almost angry spark exuding from the usually calm dancer was… interesting. "She's caught your attention."

O laughed and gave her a playful nudge on the shoulder. "Hey—

you're the one who told me to fly here to meet her. You said you needed my help. To show my *not Indonesian enough* face. Not sure if I should be offended by that, by the way, Endah." He pouted. "Anyway, you were the one who said I'd love her."

Endah smacked his arm. "You know I meant her work! I didn't expect—" She lowered her voice— "to catch you *flirting* with her."

O's mouth dropped open. "Oh my god, we were just talking! You make it sound like you caught us performing some sex act on the steps." He laughed loudly before plastering on a serious face and bringing his wrists together. "Take me away, officer," he said mock-contritely. Endah *tsked* and smacked his hands away. He bent slightly, rubbing his lower back. "Ooh. My back really hurts now though. And my hamstrings, Endah. Ouch. Those stairs are not at all comfortable. Maybe I can raise more funds to get them just right. We'll make it a permanent art installation—sell tickets. By the hour."

An adorably unattractive sound escaped her. "Oh, Owen. You're ridiculous," she said, covering her mouth.

He grinned at her and shrugged, just like he used to as a teen when he'd been caught doing something he wasn't supposed to be doing and charmed his way out of punishment.

A silent moment was shared in which they both knew the other was thinking about Molly and Teddy—O's late parents and Endah's best friends. They reached for each other's hand.

Endah looked up at him. "Srinaya is beautiful."

"Yes, she is. Unique."

The little dancer placed her other hand on his other arm and looked up at him sternly. "Be careful." O took in her words and nodded. "She's worked very hard to get where she is. On her own, with no help from anyone, Little Owen." Her nickname for him was used to remind him not to forget his place, to listen carefully.

He arched both brows, waiting. Endah sighed, her eyes flat with derision as she met his gaze. "Some of the more engaged board members don't trust her, even though she was the most impressive out of all the applicants. And she's taken their treatment of her with grace. Such a stubborn person. Like someone else I know." She poked O's stomach. "Don't play with her if you're not serious about her. You know what Jakarta's like, *nak*. You are *somebody*. People will talk if something happens between the two of you. Good *or* bad. So be sure."

He nodded slowly to acknowledge her words, zipped his compendium shut, and looked down into her face. "You know I wouldn't do that," he said. "You're right. Srinaya caught my attention. Eight months before I officially met her today. Before you even sent me that email." Endah pouted in confusion and O smiled, almost sheepishly. "She doesn't remember me, and to be honest—" He winced, embarrassed—"I don't remember much either, but we kind of… spent a night together… in Melbourne."

Endah gave him a disapproving glower, and he waved his hand at her dismissively. "Oh, don't look at me like that. I'm not a teenager anymore. Look—let me buy you lunch before the next meeting and I'll tell you the PG version."

Endah tsked but tucked her fingers into the crook of O's elbow.

As they waited out the front for Ibrahim to bring the car around, O broke their comfortable silence. "So, if the steps are a no-go, are sex acts in the south wing acceptable?"

Endah threw her head back and cackled.

five

Naya arrived at MP just before lunchtime.

She strolled up the long driveway to the trio of brutalist buildings that made up the main section of the sprawling campus.

Pak Yanto stood at the very end of the pond, leaning over the edge, clutching a bucket of fish pellets. The senior groundskeeper had to be nearing seventy—cropped hair silver and laugh lines set deep in his face. He tossed a handful of fish food in, and as the multicoloured Koi writhed and splashed greedily for their meal, Naya heard him talking to them, his voice soft and affectionate as if he was speaking to his grandchildren.

Yanto straightened as Naya approached. She dipped her chin respectfully. *"Selamat siang, Pak Yanto."*

"Siang, Mbak Naya. Nih... mau kasih makan?" *Pak* Yanto asked, handing her a cup of fish pellets.

Naya smiled at the kind old man and tossed the food into the middle of the pond. The water churned, and flapping tails and fins broke the surface. She cooed in awe at the size of them, jokingly warning Yanto they'd grow so big they'd start eating children if he kept overfeeding them. "Who will come to our children's art classes then, *Pak?"*

He laughed, friendly eyes wrinkling into little crescent moons.

Yanto's focus shifted past Naya's shoulder, his grin growing wider. "Hello *Pak* Owen. It's been a while since you visited."

Naya whipped herself around and came face to chest with Owen Jameson. His closeness made her jump and she yelped, "Jesus fuck!" and her satchel slid off her shoulder, dropping onto the pavement with a thud.

Owen stumbled back, hands up. "Shit—sorry." His laugh was low and breathy, a satisfied look of surprise on his handsome face.

He bent down to retrieve her bag, holding the long leather strap in both fists. Naya stared blankly at his hands as he gently placed the strap on her shoulder, at the way his knuckles brushed the fabric of her clothing. She cursed herself for wearing a top with sleeves and a high neckline. If she were wearing a singlet, his fingers would've caressed her skin…

His voice broke through her daydream."You okay?"

Naya still clutched her chest. "Yes. Jesus," she huffed.

Yanto chuckled behind her, and Naya flinched again, like an idiot—forgetting Yanto was there.

Her cheeks burned.

Owen stepped around her to shake Yanto's hand. *"Halo Pak, udah lama nggak ketemu. Gimana Pak—keluarga sehat semua?"*

Yanto nodded his head, thanking Owen for asking after his family and offered him a cup. Owen tossed the fish pellets close to the edge and sprang backwards, narrowly avoiding the splash made by the wrestle of scaly bodies. His eyes were alight when he teased Yanto, *"Mbak* Naya is right, *Pak.* Those fish will swallow the stray cats whole."

Yanto excused himself and continued his duties, and Naya was left standing by the edge of the water with the stunning legacy director who knocked her off kilter the day before.

"I'm sorry," Owen repeated. "I didn't mean to scare you."

Naya waved off his apology. "It's fine. Although maybe you should think about wearing a bell. *Pak* Yanto probably has a collection of them from all those cats he feeds to the fish." She lowered her voice and cupped a hand around her mouth. "Don't tell him I said that."

He chuckled, raking his fingers through his hair. He looked so put together again; Naya was a bum in comparison, in a basic black top, jeans and huaraches.

They walked towards the admin building, shuffling their feet, and paused at the bottom of the steps. Neither moved or spoke for an uncomfortably long moment.

"Um, want to sit for a bit?" Owen asked.

She knew, and accepted, that their connection wouldn't extend past the gates of MP. Whatever this was—this innocent friendship between two people that didn't quite belong—it was enough. It had to be. So she nodded, and sat on the steps where they'd met for the first time exactly twenty-four hours earlier.

"So, I googled you."

Dread slammed into her like a freight train. She hoped to the gods he hadn't gone too far down the rabbit hole. She hadn't searched her own name in ages, and last she checked, the controversy of Sal and Reginald Muse had been overtaken by flattering articles and thoughtful interviews.

She feigned nonchalance as she answered, "Oh? And what did you find out?"

"That you're very talented. Your art is incredible. And that show you curated at Danks Gallery? Wow."

Her heartbeat slowed. "Thank you." She narrowed her eyes. "Checking my credentials, huh? Making sure I'm a good fit for MERAHPUTIH?"

Owen nodded his head fervently with mock-solemnity. "Absolutely. Just doing my due diligence."

She smirked. "Wouldn't expect anything less from the *esteemed benefactor.*"

He grimaced, like the title made him uncomfortable.

"This place," Naya said, changing the subject, "you must be so proud."

Owen turned to the Purnama. "Yeah, I am. The whole complex was a total mess in the beginning. The first two floors were underwater for over a month because of a flood. The founders bought the place for next to nothing."

Naya had seen old photos of the brutalist structures before they became MERAHPUTIH, the abandoned government buildings yellowy-brown from disuse and the surrounding land covered with weeds, vines and tall grass. And rubbish. Since the property had been left to rot for years, it became a place for people to dump their unwanted *everything*.

Naya had been a regular visitor of MP since she was a child—first on the weekends with her parents. When they finally—*thankfully*—split, her mother had neither the time nor the wish to take her so she tagged along with friends or waited for school excursions.

She witnessed MP's evolution; with every visit, the place held more warmth, more soul. And now, the grounds surrounding the boxy concrete architecture were lush with trees that gave shade to resting areas and park benches, and gardens filled with native tropical plants and flowers. "And look at it now," she commented, taking it all in.

Outdoor sculptures were installed throughout the walkways and courtyards. Naya loved watching children interact with the pieces—how they touched them and climbed over them. The kids always reminded her that art was for everyone, that although facilities like MP were there to preserve historical pieces, no one had a monopoly on art, or had the right to control who was allowed to experience it.

She hugged her knees as she added, "It has to feel pretty amazing to be connected to a place that looks after so many beautiful things. It must make you feel good. Important."

The sad little smile that had plagued his face as he spoke expanded into something happy. He jerked his chin in her direction. "You're connected to MP too. You play a part here."

"Just a small part," she protested.

He scrunched his face at her, and it should've been unattractive but was—annoyingly—still *Divine-Proportion-hot*. "Rubbish," he said. "You're reopening the Purnama. Do *you* feel good? Important?"

His brows were raised, waiting for a response. Naya wasn't going to get away with dismissing his compliment. "Yeah," she answered, and she meant it. "Really good."

"Good. Would you like to go for lunch?"

She blinked. "With you?"

Owen sniffed a little laugh, rubbing the back of his neck awkwardly. "Yes, with me. We could go to Setiabudi Two maybe? Do you like sushi?"

He shrugged casually, but his eyes darted nervously from her face to the ground and then back up again.

A lunch date with Mr Jameson outside of MP... Fuck—she wanted to say yes but how would that look? Setiabudi Two was a regular lunch haunt for the MP staff. She could only imagine the quiet comments thrown their way if they were spotted.

"I... can't. I've just come in to take my team out for lunch. Oh, b-but I *have* been doing work," she rushed out. "Whenever possible, I work from home. Sometimes, I find it hard to focus in my cubicle."

Owen raised his finger. "Wait. Sorry—you're in a cubicle? All the senior curators have offices."

"No, we're working in cubicles except for Gunawan, who shares with Budi from accounts. He's been here the longest though, so it makes sense for him to get an office. He's like the *senior* senior curator," she joked.

His brow furrowed. "Gunawan's been here for, like, a decade. He's *sharing* an office?" His tone had gone lofty—remote.

Naya looked up at him, growing increasingly uncomfortable at the thought of coming across as ungrateful. "We get by," she answered, reassuringly. "It's made us good friends. And I don't mind doing most of my work somewhere else."

Owen shook his head—frown deepening. "That's all well and good but you still have the right to a proper office. With a door. That locks. It's one of the major perks of the position."

Naya didn't really know what else to say. Of course it would be nice to have a space to do her work *at work*. She enjoyed the banter between the curatorial team and was touched by how quickly they welcomed her into the gang, but working in her cubicle was difficult when her colleagues' hilarious office antics were a wonderful distraction. She wasn't going to complain or request something better though. If the rest of the team could deal, then she would too.

"Honestly, it's fine. None of us mind. *Really*," she insisted, but Owen wasn't listening anymore.

He'd taken out his phone, fingers moving at lightning speed as he typed a message that was sure to mean trouble, and Naya just sat there, unsure if she was supposed to wait or if his silence meant she'd been dismissed.

"Okay," he said, voice clipped. "I'll get this sorted for you over the weekend. You'll have an office by Monday. Promise."

The esteemed benefactor pulling strings on her behalf…

Shit.

She mumbled a thank you and excused herself to meet her team.

six

LASTRI:

OOOOOH SOMEBODY DONE FUCKED UP

SRINAYA:

What's happened???

LASTRI:

Check your emails! Meeting at 8AM tomorrow on the 5th floor!

NUR:

Uh oh

TINIIIIII:

Fess uuupppppp who was it?!

CHRIS:

Bet it was Gunawan

GUNAWAN S:

What!

CHRIS:

Did you eat Surya's Pringles Gunawan??

RAVI C:

OMG Chris, let it go. It's been almost a year.

CHRIS:

I SHALL NEVER FORGET CHIPGATE 2023

RAVI C:

You drama queen.

CHRIS:

SUCH TREACHERYYYYYYY

They were limited edition pecan pie-flavoured Pringles from the US.

GUNAWAN S:

They were terrible.

I thought they had gone off. That's why I threw them out.

CHRIS:

DTM, Gunawan.

SRINAYA:

What does DTM mean?

CHRIS:

DEAD TO ME. HE'S DEAD. TO. ME.

EDHIBOBEDHI:

Puhlease. If anyone's getting in trouble it's Tini. She got Surya's coffee order wrong the other week.

TINIIIII:

Oh ffs

NUR:

😂 😂 😂

EDHIBOBEDHI:

A latte, Tini? Really? You know he only drinks a weak flat white.

TINIIIII:

THEY'RE THE SAME GODDAMN MOTHERFUCKING THING OK

LASTRI:

Lololol

TINIIIIII:

He literally wouldn't've realised if they hadn't written it on the receipt he demands so he can expense it to the company.

RAVI C:

If it is a Surya thing and someone's in trouble, we'll deal with it. We'll support whoever it is.

CHRIS:

Unless it's a potato chip-related crime. Then you can hang.

LASTRI:

See you at 8AM tomorrow! 🤍

Dread pooled heavily in Naya's belly as she dragged her feet out of the elevator.

No one's getting fired.

The team congregated in the giant top-floor boardroom used for director-only business. They sat quietly along one side of the expansive boardroom table, chirruping away like small, restless schoolkids waiting to see the principal.

She stared at the glossy table in silence as the others continued to speculate. Her knee bounced restlessly, her jeans squeaking against the leather chair. "Sorry," she mumbled and Tini gave her a questioning look.

Surya burst through the door and the curators snapped their mouths shut, sitting up straight. Naya's heart sank. She did not have the spoons to deal with him today.

Surya leaned over the table to look down his nose at them. He punctuated his whispering words. "Why have the directors called you in for a meeting? Who screwed up?"

He glared at Naya and she glowered right back.

From down the hall, Endah's lilting laugh faded in, followed by a familiar deep Australian accented voice rumbling in response.

Naya cringed inwardly.

No one. Is getting. Fired.

Endah floated into the room looking as elegant as ever—black hair swept up in her sleek signature chignon and ruby drop earrings a perfect match to the roses printed on her flowy skirt. A bright-eyed Owen Jameson swaggered in a step behind looking gorgeous and fresh in slouchy jeans rolled up to the ankles, a light blue shirt with the top two buttons undone, and a cream linen blazer. He looked like he'd walked straight out of some Japanese fashion brand's social media campaign.

For fuck's sake. Who the fuck did he think he was, waltzing into MP looking like that, making her feel all the things she shouldn't feel?

Surya frantically gestured at the curators to stand, and they all awkwardly rose to their feet.

Owen looked horrified. "Oh god. No. Please don't do that. Don't stand up."

They all sat down again.

Naya watched the juniors gape at him. She didn't blame them. He looked as sparkly as ever; the natural blond highlights in his hair stood out against the cream blazer and his skin was a deep honey in contrast to the cool tone of his shirt. The man looked gilded. Owen Jameson was the sun and, from the looks on the juniors' faces, they would've happily whizzed around him like planets. Naya couldn't remember which planet was closest to the sun, but she'd totally volunteer to be that one.

Naya looked over at Tini, whose eyes widened and a little smirk appeared on her face as if to say, *Holy fuck who is this man and what do I have to do to see him naked?*

Naya pursed her lips to stop the corners of her mouth from curving upwards.

Lastri leaned towards Naya to whisper, "*The Golden God*'s back," and then darted her eyes in Owen's direction.

"*Selamat pagi,*" he greeted them, his voice quiet—almost a little shy—

with that beautiful show of teeth, "I'm Owen, one of the legacy directors. I'm the grandson of Rina Candrawatih." He said his grandmother's name fondly, sadly. "*Ibu* Endah keeps me up to date with your projects and it sounds like you've done some exciting stuff."

Owen's right hand slipped into his trouser pocket while the fingers of his left tapped the table. Naya stared down at it, watching those long fingers, remembering their warmth as they reached out to grab the cigarette from her hand.

Tsk tsk tsk. Cigarettes are bad for you.

Owen spotted Gunawan at the other end of the table. "*Pak* Gunawan. Good—you're here." Gunawan gave him a jerky nod, eyes wide. "I bumped into *Mbak* Srinaya on Friday and she said you're sharing an office while the other senior curators are stuck in cubicles."

Everyone blinked.

"That's unacceptable," the esteemed benefactor gruffed.

Confused faces turned Naya's way. Even Gunawan's smile disappeared as his eyes darted to her. Worst of all, Surya looked pleased as fucking punch to see her being singled out as a troublemaker.

That's not what happened, she wanted to argue, but the words got stuck in her throat.

The curators had been so kind to her, and now they were looking at her like she'd, what—complained to the hot boss about how unfair it was that Gunawan got an office when *she* was stuck in a cubicle?

Owen pulled out the seat opposite Naya and sat, the sheer *Golden Godness* of him palpable from across the wide boardroom table. She fantasised about sliding off the leather chair and crawling under the desk to slink out of the room.

Owen's eyes swept over them all, his disapproving scowl turning into something like… contrition?

"Curators," he explained, "are supposed to get personal spaces. The seniors are assigned offices, and the juniors are assigned cubicles." The team didn't move a muscle—holding their breath. "And you, Gunawan. You *definitely* deserve your very own office. You've been a loyal employee for thirteen years this coming September."

Now they were looking at Naya with… hope?

Her gut churned. This was far too much anxiety for a Monday morning.

"From the outside," Owen mused, "the directors and board members are the people who make the magic, but it's not us at all, really. *You're* the ones who come up with the ideas, the ones who do the hard work. You make us look good. And we look *very* good thanks to you." He grinned, pulling at the lapels of his perfectly tailored jacket. The juniors giggled. "Wouldn't you agree, *Ibu* Endah?" he asked, as he turned to the willowy woman standing proudly behind the chair next to him, hands resting on the top of the high leather back.

"Yes," Endah answered, reaching over to pat his shoulder. "My mother would be very proud. Yours too."

Owen squeezed Endah's hand, and then turned his gaze to Surya. All warmth disappeared in an instant as he bared his teeth at the lower board member, his smile cold and cutting. "You spend *a lot* of time here, Surya. I hear you sit in on meetings that don't concern your business with the company. Such... *dedication*. You've noticed their hard work, I'm sure. Care to congratulate them?"

Surya's brows raised high, nodding fervently. "Y-Yes, definitely," he sputtered. "Well done, all of you. I'm very pleased. Very proud."

Naya wanted to laugh bitterly at the bald-faced lie; she crossed her arms aggressively. Owen noticed.

Endah spoke up in her sing-song voice. "I think the team deserves a night out on us. Next Friday? Cocktails at Cinq-Huit?"

Tini and Nur gasped.

"What a fantastic idea, *Tante*," Owen answered. His eyes scanned the curatorial staff before settling on Naya. "Does that work for all of you?"

Naya nodded silently.

"Wonderful," he said in a clipped, professional tone. He stood up, and buttoned his blazer. He manoeuvred around the chair, tucked it under the table and proclaimed, "You're all moving to this floor."

More whispers of excitement from the staff.

New offices... and on the same floor as the directors. This was definitely not what Naya expected when Owen promised to sort out the space issue.

I am a pot-stirrer. A feather ruffler.

Owen continued, "Senior curators, you'll find your names on the doors to your new offices. Junior curators, your personal desks are in the centre of the space." Tini looked like she was about to burst at the thought of having a space of her own. "Welcome to the fifth floor. Enjoy your new offices. Turn them into spaces that'll make you happy to be here, because *we* are happy to have you here."

The last person he looked upon was Naya. She smiled weakly at him.

Endah led the way out of the boardroom with Surya scurrying out a few steps behind. Owen wished the team a good day and disappeared through the door.

The curatorial team all stood up, the fancy chairs rolling about as they huddled in small groups to celebrate.

Lastri waggled her brows at Naya and murmured, "Think you could get him to implement a four-day work week?"

Naya rolled her eyes. "Shut up," she said, cringing inwardly. Lastri's words brought back an old feeling she did not like.

"Srinaya—" The esteemed benefactor popped his head through the doorway and they all froze in place—"your request to use the entirety of the Purnama has been approved. I'd like to hear your plans for the show at your earliest convenience."

✝

O sat in his suite as the curators made their way to their new offices.

The juniors scurried around the open space in the middle, their shoes shuffling on the polished wooden floors as they searched for their names on the partitions—for now, only handwritten on a piece of masking tape and stuck onto their desks, but laser-cut name plates had been ordered and would arrive in the next few days.

They *oohed* and *aahed* at the walls of glass that kept the entire floor bright with natural light.

Naya walked with Chris along the wall of glass separating the main area from the private offices. Chris rushed inside his shiny new space, bouncing about the room to touch all his new furniture, and Naya beamed.

They *all* beamed, and O basked in it.

He spent all weekend working with Endah and his PA to choose furniture for the spaces. He'd picked the pieces with Naya in mind— *would she prefer a glass desk? Does she like painted cabinets or stained wood?*

He knew (and recalled) so little about her. He hated it. He knew she liked to dance and drink, and created beautiful paintings. She liked smoking Sampoerna Menthols and straddling his lap... What paired well with drunken kisses, ripped jeans, and fantasies—or were they blurry memories?—of her long, dark hair tangling around his fist? *Stained wood. And a complementing coffee table. And a two-seater couch in a textured taupe fabric.*

The floor turned vibrant with them there. Even their clothes were less stuffy. They injected colour and personality to a rather cold expanse of glass and concrete, just like the colourful trees and hulking sculptures brought vitality to the silver-grey exterior of the art complex's structures.

Surya sat in his own office at the far end, glowering at the new additions. He jumped to his feet to shut his door with a pointed thud when Edhi—one of the juniors—chortled. He looked so put out, and O's mood soured when Surya closed his roller blinds to isolate himself from the rest of the staff, as if the light grey fabric could protect him from their germs, and their joy.

The plan had always been to bring in the curators and creatives from other departments. O had assumed someone would sort it out— he was sure there were conversations about it the last time he'd visited —but nothing had been done, and he couldn't help feeling responsible for not being around to stay on top of it.

Even though the legacy directors had the power to overturn pretty much any decision at MP, they weren't there to rule with an iron fist; that's why they had department heads in place. But were those heads scared of one particular board member who seemed to be everywhere, all the bloody time?

He glared at Surya's closed door.

"What the hell," O asked Endah with a grumble, "is up with Surya?"

Endah sat on his deep brown leather sofa, legs crossed, drinking *teh panas*. She shook her head. "I don't know, *nak*. My mother was here when he joined the board, so don't blame me for that. It was supposed to be a kind of—" She paused, her dainty hand doing a queenly gesture —"*decorative* role. You know what I mean. He wasn't supposed to take the role so seriously." She took a sip of her tea, and then settled further back into the cushions. "I made a complaint, but the contract we have with his factory does protect him somewhat. As does his connection to *Bu* Tuti."

"Does it have to complicate things? He's just her nephew or something, isn't he? It's not like he's going to inherit her legacy title." *Thank god.*

Endah gave a delicate shrug. "I'm not sure. I never had a reason to question it before." She shook her head. "I haven't been around... I don't have an excuse besides MP being so well-run that it doesn't need our constant attention, and," she sighed, "We got complacent... and that emboldened him. To be honest, we all thought him a bit ridiculous and ignored him."

"I'll get the contract reviewed, then," O murmured.

"And visit *Tante* Tuti. Let her pinch your cheeks."

Naya strolled out of Chris' office and knocked on Ravi's door. Ravi stretched out on his new sofa and smiled lazily up at her, beckoning her inside. Her round arse and wide hips swayed as she sauntered in— her black jeans tight over her belly and thick thighs. She moved to his floor-to-ceiling window, staring out at the view.

From where O watched her, the daylight pouring in bathed her in a blue-white glow. Her thick-rimmed frames that sat atop her head during the meeting were now balanced on her adorable nose. She wore an oversized white shirt with one side tucked in at the front, her sleeves rolled up to her elbows. She looked effortlessly cool again.

O fidgeted, his trousers feeling far too restrictive as he stared at her arse.

"I'm concerned about his interest in Srinaya," Endah commented.

O blinked in Endah's direction. "Interest?"

She set her teacup on the side table. "Well, I say *interest* but I'm talking about his hostility."

O clenched his teeth. What was Surya's issue with her? Could it really be her heritage? He looked over at Naya, leaning against the wall in Ravi's office, and all of a sudden, she tipped her head back and laughed. The sound was as lovely as when he'd heard it in Chidori all those months ago.

Endah spoke in a discreet tone. "You know, maybe her size..."

O couldn't control his scowl. "What about her size, Endah?" he challenged her.

"Oh, Owen—" She rolled her eyes—"you're being ridiculous again. I think she's absolutely beautiful. Don't you dare think I would judge her for being plus-sized." She shook her head at him, unimpressed by his presumption. "People can be unkind though. Anyone on the board, and —let's be realistic here—in this country would think she is..." Endah pursed her lips as she tried to think of the word she was looking for. "Unacceptable."

Unacceptable. How fucking absurd.

He looked over at Naya again. She walked into her office situated exactly opposite his own and his head snapped Endah's way. Endah gave him a knowing wink; she had assigned everyone's workspaces.

Endah stood, taking her teacup with her. "I'm going back to my suite. Now that I'll be spending more time here, I think I'll redecorate. Enjoy the view," she teased, and left the room.

O discreetly watched Naya as she dropped her bag on her sofa. She slowly turned to take in the space, her head tilted in thought like she was imagining how to decorate and make it her own. She sat down on the couch, tucking her legs under herself, and nestled her shoulders into the cushions. A satisfied smile appeared on her face.

She was pleased. *Good.* He'd pleased her.

And then she rifled through her bag for her cigarettes, lighter, and phone, and walked to the elevators. O felt a familiar panic—that same panic he experienced when he lost her at Chidori—and found himself standing next to her as she waited for the lift to arrive.

She stood with her ankles crossed, hands behind her back, staring up at the digital numbers above the elevator doors. O glanced down at her ample chest, and then she looked up at him, a pink flush sweeping across her face. "Hello," she said.

"Hey." His palms were clammy and his cheeks heated—was he blushing too?

Time to tell her, his brain commanded. *Tell her she knows you.* "So," he rushed out, "the thing is—" The elevator dinged and the doors slid open.

O gestured for Naya to go in first. "Thank you," she said, leaning back into the far corner of the lift. "And thank you for the offices. I didn't mean to trouble you. I hope you know I wasn't complaining the other day, or trying to blame anyone."

O leaned back on the opposite wall. "You didn't trouble me. *I'm* sorry it took so long for us to realise the oversight."

She nodded in acceptance, and gave him a shy smile. O needed more—was desperate for her validation. "*Do* you like your office?"

Her reserve disappeared instantly. "Oh my god, yes! I would have been happy with something the size of this elevator. I wasn't expecting an office the size of... *eight* elevators. So fancy." She lifted her chin loftily. "*I* have a window. Bet you don't have a window."

He shrugged. "Sorry. Windows—*plural.* Big windows."

Naya pouted. "*Mine* has a couch though. I bet *yours* doesn't have a couch." He held up two fingers. Her mouth dropped open. "You have *two* couches? That's a bit excessive..."

The lift *dinged* again.

As they walked out the doors and down the steps of the admin building, Naya was incandescent, teasing him with attempts at one-upping him and his *Presidential Suite.*

O said haughtily, "I have a six-seater meeting-slash-dining table."

"Oh, come on!" Naya crowed. "Now you're just showing off. Whose dick do *I* have to suck to—" She gasped and slapped her hand over her mouth. O gasped as well and burst out laughing, but Naya's smile had completely disappeared; her face went white, and eyes big with fear. "Oh my god, I'm sorry, Mr Jameson. I'm so, so sorry."

O frowned when he realised she was serious, that she really thought she was in trouble. "Hey—it's fine…"

She rubbed the space between her brows with the heel of her palm. "I shouldn't have said that. To a *director*. Jesus. I forget my place sometimes. I forget…" Naya's arms swept up as she gestured around. MERAHPUTIH. Jakarta. Indonesia. This was about the other day on the steps, about feeling *out* of place.

She hurried to the cluster of trees at the top of the driveway. O followed, his hands back in his pockets and keeping a respectful distance. She took a cigarette out of the pack and lit it, taking a deep drag, her head shaking in embarrassment, or maybe annoyance, at herself.

The crackle of the cloves slowly calmed her, the wrinkle in her brow fading. O motioned for one, and Naya handed over the pack. The sugary taste of the paper was a welcome distraction to the weirdness that had forced its way between them. "Please don't be sorry. I like this banter."

Naya sat down on one of the park benches while he stayed on his feet. She didn't speak now, all signs of the pleased woman gone. She didn't look at him, which gave him the perfect opportunity to study her up close once more. *Ah. There they are*, he thought, as he found those little beauty spots on her cheek, obscured by her frames.

She held her cigarette between her index and middle fingers, and ran her fourth finger along her lips absentmindedly, staring at the long rectangular pond not far from where she sat.

Naya looked up at him and blinked. "Sorry—was there a reason you came out here? Did you want to have a chat about the exhibition right now?"

O shook his head. "I came out for a smoke."

"You didn't bring any."

He held up her pack, which he hadn't yet returned to her, and grinned. Naya stared at his face, eyes narrowing slightly, taking measure.

O wished he could read her mind.

They smoked under the shade of the trees, giving them a reprieve from the bright hot sun. A little sheen of sweat covered Naya's nose, causing those adorable glasses to slip down a little. She pulled them off her face and set them beside her, and wiped her nose with the back of her hand. The heat was getting to her—or maybe it was the rush of nerves—because she pulled at the front of her shirt, and O spied the tattoo peeking out.

An image appeared in his brain: Naya laying on her front, white sheets twisted around her naked hips as O slid her bleach-stained red tshirt up to expose more of her soft skin, unveiling a tattoo—something intricate in black and white. Flowers, maybe?

Shit. He really needed to tell her, and soon; this definitely wasn't the time.

Naya huffed and balanced her cigarette between her sinuous lips as she undid her half up-do. O's mouth went dry when her hair came tumbling down, and almost choked on his tongue when she raked her fingers through her hair, chin up, eyes shut. In an effortless move, she grabbed all of her hair in both hands, flicked it up and re-tied it atop her crown, her nape exposed. His eyes zeroed in on the little curls along her hairline that stuck to her brown skin.

He almost burned himself with his cigarette.

O wanted to see her do that wearing nothing—wanted to see her head fall back and neck lengthen and belly stretch as her hands raised up above her head. He wanted to commission a painting of it.

"I hope you'll ignore what I said," Naya said.

O smiled impishly. "Absolutely not."

Naya tugged at her earlobe and her mouth set in a harsh line.

Okay. Not the best time to tease her. He sat down next to her instead. "Really," he said in earnest. "Please... forget your place. It means you forget *my* place. I'm not going to hold it against you for saying something funny, even if it probably is *inappropriate language for the workplace*"— He made his voice all low and monotone as he made air quotes with his fingers—"I don't care. I'm not a fucking priest. I'm certainly not Surya, Archbishop of the fifth floor."

Naya squawked out a *Ha!* before clamping her hand over her mouth.

There she is. There's that lovely lighthearted Naya.

O made his face as deadpan as he could muster. "But in answer to your earlier question, it is, in fact, Archbishop Surya's dick that you would have to suck to get a six-seater meeting-slash-dining table."

Naya squealed through the hand still covering her mouth, her eyes wide. Her shoulders shook as she laughed, trying to keep her voice down as three staff members from the accounts department walked passed.

"Oh, to be so lucky," O blurted out, grinning like a Cheshire cat.

Naya groaned and covered her face. "Oh, for fuck's sake," she said, snatching her pack of cigarettes from his hands and taking two out. She passed one back to him, without even thinking, as if this was expected—as if they'd always sat down under the shade of the trees to talk and laugh together.

She leaned back against the thick trunk, legs now straight out in front of her, ankles crossed. She sighed and shook her head. "Me and my big fat mouth. I've started something with that comment, haven't I?" She tsked.

"Please," O drawled, lighting his cigarette. He pointed to the steps of the admin building. "You started something when I found you stretched over those steps, purring like a cat."

seven

O dropped in at MP after a day of Jameson Publishing meetings to pick up some paperwork—literal work printed on paper; *was MP run by Luddites?*—left on his desk.

He'd been busy over the past week catching up on the goings on at the gallery, but JP also needed his attention. It was a precarious balancing act; everywhere he turned, there were problems to solve, questions to answer, people to praise and encourage... A beautiful femme to charm and befriend.

He walked through the deserted complex, the staff of MP already celebrating the Idul Adha long weekend.

Laughter and music greeted him as the elevator doors opened onto the fifth floor. His feet followed the sound to Naya's office; Gunawan and Tini lounged on the couch, and Ravi and Edhi sat on the floor, their backs against the wall of glass. Naya perched on her desk wearing a batik knee-length skirt, her tattooed legs dangling as she grinned at something Edhi was saying.

All of a sudden, they erupted into laughter, Naya covering her mouth as her shoulders shook.

Naya spotted him before the others did, and she bit her lip as she waved.

O's heartbeat skipped.

The others turned their heads to the glass, and as O poked his head through the doorway, they greeted him warmly.

"Mr Jameson," Naya said.

"Ms Matthews," he answered coolly. He leaned against the door frame and crossed his ankles. "Hello, *Heartbreak* team."

Naya scrunched her face just as Edhi shot forward and exclaimed, "See? *Heartbreak team?* It sounds terrible. We need a better name."

The rest of them groaned. Naya rubbed her temples.

O raised his palms. "Uh oh—did I just start something?" he asked.

"You *re*started something *Pak* Owen," Tini said with glee.

Gunawan asked, in that nerdy-dad way of his, "What's so wrong with the Heartbreakers?"

"It's boring! We are not boring. I refuse to be boring. Do I *look* boring to you, *Pak* Gunawan?" Edhi said in one breath.

O studied Edhi's oversized white tshirt covered in huge colourful flaming hearts. He wore white skinny jeans, and a gaudy gold chain necklace. Edhi definitely didn't look boring.

Naya winced.

"So, why are you all still here?" O rushed out, changing the subject. "The long weekend started at lunchtime didn't it?"

"We're celebrating our new workspaces," Naya answered, "and the use of the extra wings, and discussing some other *Heartbreak*-related stuff before we go away for the weekend. Would you like to sit in? We ordered food."

O looked around the room. "That'd be great," he said, "but do you want to do this in my office? It's a little bigger."

"Oh, yes, bigger. That's right."

"Two couches and a six-seater meeting-slash-dining table."

Her deep chocolate eyes sparkled brighter at the memory of her little faux-pas from earlier in the week. She parted her lips, and he wondered if she imagined what *he* imagined at that moment.

Everyone moved into his *Presidential Suite*, as Naya called it, to continue the celebration. The team walked in with a strange kind of reverence, as if they were entering a library.

"*Silahkan.* Make yourselves comfortable," he encouraged, grabbing bottles of water from his mini fridge.

Tini and Edhi cooed as they sat at the table.

Once the food arrived—four pizzas, fried mozzarella sticks, and garlic dough balls with ranch dressing—*the food of champions and curators alike,* Naya declared—O asked them to share their plans for *Heartbreak.*

Naya started, "It's going well. We get to show more works now, so thank you for that."

They nodded and murmured their agreement.

Ravi added, "There are some amazing video and 3D installations that we'll be able to exhibit now. Ones that require their own room."

"We've sent emails to some well-known artists that have been supportive of MP, as well as a few of *Mbak* Naya's contacts," said Gunawan before biting into a mozzarella stick.

"That's exciting. Anyone I'd be familiar with?" O asked, looking at Naya. She was licking her thumb clean absentmindedly. O swallowed.

"Yes," she answered, but didn't elaborate.

O raised his brows and waited. No one said anything although everyone was either smirking or holding in a laugh, so he responded, "Not going to share?"

"She's not allowed to," Tini blurted in a warning tone.

Ravi rolled his eyes. "Tini's superstitious."

Tini looked affronted and a little embarrassed. "Shut up—I am not."

"You are!" the rest of the team retorted.

Edhi made his voice go all high. *"Just in case we jinx it by telling every-one.* Literally what she said." He made a ghostly *Oooooooh* sound, with a twinkle of his fingers for good measure, and Tini covered her face.

"I like that you care enough to be nervous, Tin," Naya encouraged. "Some of the established folks are bound to say no, and that's fine. We don't want too many well-known people anyway. The big names would overshadow the emerging artists, and I'm more interested in giving them a leg up."

"Imagine DEWI at this exhibition though," Edhi exclaimed dreamily.

O almost fell off his chair. *"DEWI's* showing at *Heartbreak?"*

Gunawan answered, "Not yet, but Naya is hopeful," and then his eyes went big as he pointed his thumb at Naya and added, "She's worked with them."

O's jaw dropped. "You *know* who DEWI is?"

Naya shook her head. "A bunch of us receive DMs whenever they're planning large scale pieces and need volunteers. I helped put up that Drewery Alley piece and happened to be in Perth when they needed people for the giant paste up on Grand Lane. Both times, there was a guy there—Ruben—putting us into teams and giving us directions. *I* think *he's* DEWI. He went to one of the international schools here. It's a good diversion, right? A white cis-dude using the Indonesian word for *goddess?"*

The team grinned at O, but their smiles were all for Naya as if they were all silently saying, *How cool is she?*

O recalled their conversation in Chidori—how Naya had grinned at him and told him how much she liked the Drewery Alley piece. But it wasn't just appreciation. There was pride in her voice that night.

Volunteering to help an anonymous artist, known for their incendiary murals, install their work... Whoa.

DEWI caused an uproar in Yogjakarta a few years earlier when they created a portrait of a university student who circulated sexually explicit videos of himself with his ex-girlfriend after she broke up with him. The videos spread like wildfire throughout the campus and ended up on all the porn sites. The police were called in, since pornography laws are *very* strict in Indonesia, and both students were arrested. Unfortunately, the young woman didn't come from a well-to-do family like the abuser. He was never convicted of any crime while she—the *victim*—was. She ended her life the day before her sentencing.

DEWI mounted a portrait of the young man on two gigantic billboards—the first faced his parents' apartment, who were rumoured to have bribed the police or maybe even the judge, and the second stood opposite the entrance of the university. Underneath the portrait of the man were the words: *CAN'T FACE REJECTION.*

DEWI paid for advertising on the billboards for an entire year but the abuser's parents used their connections to get them taken down within a week. DEWI printed posters and pasted them everywhere instead. The city was divided; some applauded DEWI, and the rest victim-blamed or found the whole case distasteful.

"Wow, Srinaya," O breathed. Naya blinked at him but no one else seemed to notice. He cleared his throat. "I was at their last exhibition in Melbourne."

Naya pouted. "You and everyone else," she sighed. "Their one-night-only show was the closing day of my own exhibition at Underwood Gallery. I was packing up."

Naya's arms were crossed on the table, her tits pushed together. His focus flicked down to her cleavage. "It was a very memorable night," he said, crossing his own arms and leaning back on the chair.

So *that's* why she'd been late to meet her friends at Chidori—she was packing up her own show. "I hope your exhibition went well. I wish I'd known about it."

She smiled. "It did go well, thank you. I'll send you an invitation to my next one."

Their gaze lingered on each other as the group kept chatting, and O noticed her mouth part slightly, her little pink tongue sweeping across her bottom lip. She broke eye contact to reach for another garlic dough ball, dipping it in ranch dressing, and taking a bite. The way her eyes crinkled in pleasure made his mouth go instantly dry.

They continued discussing the show, Naya sitting back to allow the other members—even the juniors—a chance to speak. She listened to their opinions, and happily changed her mind when she believed their ideas were better than her own.

Naya's determination was infectious; each member talked about their own role with solemn focus and a passion he hadn't seen or felt at MP in ages. Even Gunawan, who'd been there the longest, talked about the exhibition with youthful excitement.

After the rest of the team left, O and Naya stayed back to clear up. Naya babbled excitedly about all the ideas she had for *Heartbreak*, her hands gesturing wildly as she talked about products to sell in the gallery's design store and website. O put his hands in his pockets to stop himself from biting his nails.

"The team really likes working with you," he said.

Her lips curved up. "And I love working with them. They're really dedicated."

"I think they're dedicated *because of you*. You've made them passionate. It's not an easy task—putting together an exhibition like this in less than four months." He smiled. "You're fantastic."

Naya flushed deep pink at his praise; he loved seeing that shade on her skin. He'd remember to compliment her more often.

She cleared her throat. "It's the theme," she said, dodging the compliment. Her lashes fluttered as if she was too shy to look at him. "Heartbreak's universal. Everyone understands it, has experienced it. And as humans, we're built for communion. We're built to—" She clutched her chest—"*care* too much. Sympathise. Do you know what I mean?" She wasn't looking at him as she asked. She was just speaking openly—her voice soft and serious, and her earnestness was a beautiful thing. "I love evoking that kind of emotion. I want people to hurt as they see the work. That probably sounds silly, but I want them moved to tears. I want them feeling a bit maudlin."

O was rendered speechless on the opposite side of the table, enthralled by the pleasure on her face. Naya looked up at him then, a self-conscious smile appearing in the wake of her excitement.

Jesus—he wanted to kiss her.

She giggled in embarrassment and touched her blushing cheeks with her hands. "I got swept up."

O stepped forward and her smile faltered. "You're lovely when you get swept up," he rasped. "You're lovely all the time."

Her eyes widened as she took a little ragged breath in, wringing her hands nervously.

His office instantly turned into a sauna at the sight of her nipples stiff and daring to be touched underneath her singlet.

Her hand was on her chest again, rubbing her little fingers over the hollow of her neck, and another drug-fuelled memory appeared... of him dragging his tongue right in that little dip.

Fuck—he wanted to caress those little beauty spots on her cheek. He wanted to touch her again… so badly. So much of her skin was uncovered. Her tattoos—bold and bright in contrast to her black singlet—were as beautiful as he remembered. Her left shoulder and her whole left arm completely covered, the tattoo spreading down over the left side of her chest. How far down did it go? He had no recollection of that. He wanted to relearn it—relearn *her*. Wanted to spend an entire night tracing every line with his fingers—run his tongue over the snake inked on her forearm.

Srinaya Matthews looked so fucking pretty and soft and bold and it made him ache all over.

His erection strained in his trousers.

He took another small step towards her. Her feet didn't move but she clearly swayed closer. Her eyes were hooded with arousal—he was sure of it—as she looked up into his face.

He leaned in, his voice just above a whisper, and asked, "May I touch you, Naya?" He licked his lips and Naya focused on his mouth as she let out a little sigh.

Her lids shut as she murmured, "I *really* want you to, but no."

O flinched at her words and stepped back.

Naya swallowed and then looked up at him again, pupils dilated. Her voice was low and husky as she said, "God. You're lovely too, and that's why I have to go now."

And then she finally moved past him and exited.

O—dumbstruck—turned and watched her return to her office to grab her things and then rush to the lifts.

Before she stepped into the elevator, Naya glanced back at him. He couldn't decipher what was written on her face.

It took every ounce of willpower for Naya to say no to Owen—to leave him. She'd wanted so badly for him to bend down and kiss her, to feel that big, solid body against hers.

She smelt his lovely summery cologne when he got close. She still tasted it as she waited for the elevator. Why did that scent make her feel so much?

When Naya glanced back at him before she stepped into the lift, Owen looked shocked—wounded. She felt hurt too, for being the cause of such a look—his stormy eyes wide, brows drawn together.

As soon as Naya got into the rideshare—which took *forever* to arrive and she prayed Owen wouldn't follow her out to talk—she took out her phone, hands trembling, and sent a message:

> Are you free? Come to my place right now? Please?

She received a reply:

> omw xox

She arrived home—her whole body tense and needy—and swore and ranted in shame as she stomped around her house. She couldn't believe she'd turned Owen down.

Lastri had called him the *Golden God of MP* and Jesus—that name was appropriate. That lovely golden skin. The warm honey in his eyes. That burnished copper hair with the light golden ends.

Fuck.

She'd said no to Owen Jameson.

Damn her fucking rules.

Think of Sal, she reasoned with herself. *Think of Reginald Muse. They called you a slut, Naya. You were a pariah. Don't let it happen again. No one is worth it. Not even him.*

Her skin was on fire and her pussy throbbed.

Naya hadn't missed Owen's erection in those trousers. She'd wanted to reach out and brush the back of her hand over it. She wanted to be taken over his table, and desk, and couch.

No. No man is worth your reputation.

She sat on the bottom two steps in her foyer waiting, feet tapping restlessly on the tiled floor.

And then she heard Stefan's footsteps approaching her front door and she hurriedly opened it, and there he was, running his fingers through his silky black hair, roguish eyes on her.

His smile brightened as he opened his mouth to say hello but Naya didn't have any time for pleasantries. She pulled him in, and Stef's eyes went wide with surprise at her roughness.

"Shit, Sri," he exclaimed, but she closed the door behind him and pressed him back against the wood.

Naya fumbled with the buttons of Stef's shirt as she tiptoed to kiss him, making a sound of frustration as her stupid fingers seemed to find buttons too difficult to master in her desperation.

Stef laughed wickedly into her mouth and took over. She moved her hands down to his jeans—only one button, thankfully—unzipped them and pulled his jeans and jocks over his hips.

"Baby, what's gotten into you?" She hushed him. "Not that I'm complain—*fuck*!" he hissed as he almost tripped over his own feet since his shoes were still on and his jeans were now off his hips and halfway down his calves.

"Sri, wait-wait-*wait*," he said, laughing. "Let me take off my shoes at least—bloody hell." And so she let him kick them off, all the while refusing to stop kissing him, whimpering into his mouth.

She slipped down to the floor and pulled his jeans off his toned legs, wrapped her hand around his dick and stroked him.

Stefan's body tensed as he swore under his breath.

Naya looked up at his handsome features—so different from Owen's face—at the way his lips parted as she took him into her mouth.

He felt silky against her tongue, his saltiness so familiar.

Stef stroked her face with care. "Baby, yes," he moaned. "You look beautiful," he said sweetly.

Naya pulled his cock out from between her lips and shook her head. "Don't be kind."

Stefan's lips twisted into a cruel smile. He squared his shoulders. He combed his fingers through her hair and then grabbed a fistful, his knuckles digging into her scalp.

She gasped at the sting.

"Up," he commanded, and Naya did as she was told.

He kissed her roughly, his tongue forceful and demanding, just like she needed.

Stefan let go, pushing her away a little. "Strip."

She obeyed without question, peeling off all her clothing, and stood in anticipation.

She was soaking. Her clit ached and her nipples screamed for attention, the dark skin pebbling painfully.

He pulled his shirt off his tattooed shoulders—broad, but in no way as broad as Owen's. Stefan was far leaner than Owen's bulky frame too, and Stef's skin was a deep bronze under all that colourful ink; hardly a hint of pink appeared on his face when he flushed with arousal.

Stef's erection was so, so beautiful.

She wondered what Owen looked like naked.

Focus, Naya.

She shook her head to free herself from the image of the *Golden God.*

Stefan touched her then, and she opened her eyes to let his face fill her vision. He was so pretty, with that curtain of jet-black hair.

"Please, Stef," Naya whispered.

"*Shhh.*"

He flicked his tongue against her lip and then shoved her up the stairs. They stopped on the landing in front of her bedroom.

"Down," he ordered.

Naya sank to the floor, her whole body taut with anticipation. She raised her chin, staring up at him, waiting silently.

Stef glared back at her with heavy-lidded eyes. "Stroke your cunt for me, Sri. You know how I like it."

She drew her bottom lip between her teeth and spread her thighs, and he made a low sigh of approval.

"Precious girl," he said, and Naya whimpered at his praise.

She slowly circled her clit, letting out a high pitched moan as she caressed the sensitive hood between her fingers.

Naya never took her eyes off Steff's rapt face, his eyes big and black and feral. She was so wet and ready—her juices covering her fingers as she stroked up over the cleft above her clit and down to the opening of her pussy.

She reclined on her elbow and slid her fingers inside. Her back arched as she sobbed Stef's name. "Please, please, please," she begged him, "fuck me, touch me. Anything. I need... I *need—*"

She couldn't get the words out, how she needed Stef to erase Owen from her mind—*please, take him away, get him out, distract me*—but she didn't want to say his name aloud, didn't want him to taint this moment with Stef, her beautiful friend who made her feel so many marvellous things.

She closed her eyes to focus on the overwhelming pleasure—how her clitoris was so hard and her body burned so hot, like the crackling clove when Owen inhaled—

Fuck.

She snapped her eyes open. That was the key—not closing her eyes.

Keep looking at Stefan. Don't take your eyes off Stefan. How beautiful is Stefan? Stefan, with his smooth brown skin, and pierced nipples, and brightly tattooed arms and legs.

He was stroking his cock, his slender fingers wrapped tightly around his shaft while his other hand raked through his midnight hair, witnessing her come undone.

Naya mewled in frustration. "I said touch me," she said sulkily, and he let out a low, mean chuckle.

He lowered himself to crouch before her, holding her chin and kissing her sweetly on her lips. "So petulant," he cooed, and then he slapped her—hard enough that it stung her cheek and made her yelp in surprise, but gentle enough that the redness wouldn't last longer than the evening.

She sighed as the sting faded to a dull ache. She pressed her cheek with the back of her hand; her blood had rushed to the surface—her skin hot.

Stef shoved her, and she fell back on the cold tiles, quivering. He held her legs open and very slowly lowered his mouth onto her pussy, his soft lips sealing around her clit. "Oh god, yes. *Yes,*" she grunted, and her pelvis bucked against his mouth.

He flattened his tongue and dragged it upwards, sucking hard one minute and licking softly the next, and Naya's hips shook.

Stef pushed two fingers into her roughly, and she tilted her hips upwards as he fucked her. She couldn't wait to feel that bruisey ache from where his knuckles met her pussy lips over and over again as he pounded her with his fingers.

"So good," she growled, and swept his dead-straight hair off his face so she could watch the hollows of his cheeks appear as he sucked on her.

Her whole body was wrecked with pleasure, and pain, and even a little bit of fear. Tears formed and she closed her eyes to let them spill down her face, but Owen reappeared behind her lids and she swore.

It wasn't enough. None of this was enough to chase the esteemed benefactor away.

"Stef... I need more," she said, and Stefan glowed with satisfaction.

He lifted his mouth from her slippery skin and tilted his head, assessing her, and the anticipation of what he might have in store for her terrified her and got her even wetter.

He stood and pulled her up with him, tugging on her upper arms with a vise-like grip, and then dragged her into the bedroom, commanding her to kneel on the hard floor, her knees and thighs protesting as he fucked her mouth hard enough that she gagged, spit and tears dripping down her chin onto her tits while he grunted filthy things at her—*take it, Sri, my little slut. You're prettiest when my cock is in your mouth. Quiet. Did I say you could speak?*—until she was delirious and desperate, her whole body trembling with need.

Only then did Stef allow her on the bed—face down, ass up. He fucked her from behind, Owen still present in the back of her mind like a ghost, and she cried hard and loud because it felt so fucking good having Stef's hands digging into her skin and pulling her hair.

But when she finally came, the last image that appeared behind her eyes, even with Stefan's gorgeous voice praising her for being such a good girl, was Owen bending down to almost kiss her, telling her she was *lovely all the time,* and she cursed.

eight

Monday was the last day of MP's long weekend, and Naya spent the day enjoying the empty fifth floor as she set up her office.

The sun was out again—uncharacteristically sunny days in Jakarta seemed to be becoming a regular thing—and light streamed into the window.

She'd spent the last couple of hours decorating, moving plants around and looking through piles of artwork to stick up—a poster of her favourite Basquiat painting, a large screen print that Sal had given her, and a handful of smaller prints from her collection.

A Venus of Willendorf figurine now sat on her desk next to a philodendron in a gold ceramic pot. A one-metre-tall *Dewi Sri* sculpture stood proudly by the window next to a massive bird of paradise. A devil's ivy and a monstera adonsonii hung from the ceiling. By the end of the year, her office would look more like a greenhouse.

She heard the *ding* of the elevator and turned to see Owen heading to his office, humming something—earpods in—and then he glanced her way and flinched in surprise as he came to a halt.

She waved at him and he smiled, but it was small, and then he slowly—maybe even reluctantly—made his way to her, eyes down, looking at his hands.

"Hello," he mumbled.

"Hey," she said, a little too eagerly. She felt the warmth on her cheeks, knew the flush of colour would spread downward and didn't care.

Owen blinked in surprise, disarmed by her welcome.

His smile was tentative—his voice unsure. "So, did I make this more awkward than when you made that dick-sucking comment?"

Naya laughed, waving her hand dismissively. "Not you—*we. We* made it more awkward. I played a part. It's really nice to see you."

She had the sudden urge to hug him to make it all better.

Owen's smile grew bigger, more beautiful, although his shoulders curled in like he was trying to make himself appear small. Or maybe he just felt defensive—she couldn't tell. He leaned against her door frame, one hand in his pocket, wearing dark blue joggers, a white tshirt and white sneakers.

She couldn't believe how fancy he looked in fucking joggers, for god's sake. It was ridiculous and unfair.

His chest looked massive under the soft knit; she didn't understand how a tshirt could make his shoulders look even broader than when he wore a blazer.

She bit her lip as she looked away, cleared a space on her desk for her to sit, took a quick breath to focus, and then turned back to him.

"Look," she said, clearing her throat, "how 'bout we just go back to *before* that moment? Could we do that?"

Owen cocked his head to the side in thought, definitely checking out her tits in her *CECI N'EST PAS UN TEE SHIRT* tshirt, twirling his keys around his finger as he said, "I think it depends on which moment you mean. I asked if I could touch you and you said *I want you to, but no.* Could we go back to just before the *but no?*"

His pretty eyes darted up to her face. He looked hopeful.

Naya gave him a rueful smile. "I'm tempted…"

"But no?" His voice held no cadence even though he asked a question.

She didn't think he meant to, but he visibly slumped.

Naya inhaled sharply to speak and a jolt of sensation shot down her spine as she warred with herself about what she wanted versus what she *should* do. "I'm *very* tempted," she answered with a sigh. She bit her thumbnail.

Owen stayed quiet for a moment, watching her. He gestured to her couch for permission to sit and she nodded. "Okay. Here's a question then, because I don't want you to be uncomfortable."

"Go on."

Owen sat and leaned forward, forearms resting on his knees. "Do you want the flirting to stop?"

Naya shuffled back to sit on her desk, feet dangling off the floor, toes tapping the air. "God no. But it should."

Owen groaned and gritted his teeth in exasperation. "Jesus Christ." He brought his fists up as if cursing her or the gods. Maybe both.

Naya was exasperated too. This was a complication she didn't need and yet wanted so fucking badly. She raked both hands through her hair, and then gestured to the office they were standing in, the building the office was in... the complex the *building* was in. Owen looked around to where she was gesturing but didn't understand.

Naya pointed to him. "Legacy director," she said. And then she pointed to herself and added quietly—sadly, "Curator. Lowly staff member."

He lifted his chin and his mouth opened. "*Ah.* Company policy," he said, doing a thing with his hand in the air, almost dismissively, as if he didn't really think it was a big deal, as if he was above it, which *of course* he was. He wouldn't get burnt if they started something and it went sideways.

He sat back against the couch and took a deep breath in, then out, eyes still locked onto hers. He mused with a smirk, "I guess I could fire you." Naya arched her brow. "But you're an asset here. Plus you'd hate me and then I'd *never* get to touch you." And then he gave her the biggest toothy grin as he added, "Maybe you should quit?"

Naya burst out laughing then. "Fuck off."

He shrugged and crossed his arms, biceps flexing. The golden hairs on his forearms glowed under the sunlight. And then he rolled his shoulders, his tshirt tightening across his impressive chest.

So fucking tempting.

The elevator dinged again. "That's probably Endah," Owen said. "We're having lunch."

They expected the graceful old dancer to appear, but Naya's smile vanished when she saw Surya instead.

Surya kept his hostile gaze on her—was obviously happy to glare without saying a word as he stalked towards his office until he noticed Owen sitting on her couch when he walked past her open door.

An exaggerated smile appeared on Surya's face. "Ah, Mr Jameson. Happy Idul Adha," he said reverently, with a small bow of his head.

Owen didn't smile back. "You too."

Surya turned to Naya and he kept the show of teeth plastered on his face, but his eyes went dull. "And you, *Mbak* Srinaya."

"*Selamat Idul Adha, Pak,*" Naya said with a forced smile of her own.

Owen turned back to Naya, a clear message for Surya to fuck off. Surya continued to his office; his eyes darted back and forth between her and Owen, a smarmy look on his face like he was making up stories in his head about what they were up to, all alone on the fifth floor. Naya shuffled uncomfortably and crossed her arms.

Owen went to close the door, and she blurted, "Please don't close that. I don't want him to gossip."

Owen put his hand up with authority and she stopped talking. His whole demeanour changed in the instant it took him to stand. The *esteemed benefactor* was in the room now; the casual dress did nothing to make him less commanding.

"What's that about?" he asked, his tone sharp and—frankly—thrilling.

"I don't know," she answered.

"What's going on?"

Naya shook her head quickly and shrugged. "He dislikes me."

Owen frowned. "Why?"

He sounded accusatory, but it wasn't aimed at her.

"I stood up to him in a meeting. He told me to cover up and I told him to fuck off. Not literally—" She quickly clarified when the wrinkles in Owen's forehead deepened—"like, I told him to look the other way if he found me so offensive. You know—because I'm fat, and tattooed. He said MP broke tradition when I was hired. That I'm not Indonesian enough. I push community-based projects… highlight women, non-binary and trans folk. My art is *pornographic…*"

He widened his stance like a bouncer hoping for trouble, arms crossed and pectorals flexing. His face was stony as he craned his neck to glare in Surya's direction through the glass. "I'll talk to him," he said. "I'll tell him to back off."

She slid off her desk and took a step forward. "No—don't. I can handle him. Thank you, but no."

Owen stared at her, and Naya wondered what he was thinking. He looked… forbidding.

Fuck—Naya never wanted to be the focus of Owen's rage. He sucked all the oxygen out of her office. She absentmindedly rubbed the hollow of her throat.

He dipped his chin. "Are you alright?" he gruffed.

Naya nodded.

"Really?"

She nodded more slowly—gave him a reassuring smile. "Promise. I'm fine."

The tension in his shoulders loosened a little, and he exhaled sharply. "Well, in that case, I demand to see these *pornographic* pieces. For the sake of… I don't know—science."

A squawk of laughter escaped her, and she winced at how loud the sound was.

He relaxed, chuckling along with her.

Owen Jameson: playful and vulnerable, cold and untouchable. She watched him carefully, those intense eyes that were eerily pale as they reflected the sunlight through the window, the pink sun-kissed cheeks. He was standing too far for her to see his adorable freckles, but she loved them all the same. The strong jaw, his wavy chestnut hair that almost touched his shoulders. Fuck—*those shoulders.* She almost sighed loudly as her gaze swept from left to right.

And his thighs… They belonged on a rugby player. Naya only ever watched the rugby to see the players' legs.

She'd pay good money to see Owen running around the pitch in those teeny tiny rugby shorts, getting all sweaty and dirty.

Maybe she could break her rule just once with him. There wouldn't be any harm. The only trade between them would be mutual pleasure —nothing more.

Naya was lost in her daydream as their eyes met.

His pupils had widened a touch, his mouth slightly open. He wasn't smiling, but there was humour somewhere in that face. Something about his expression made it clear.

He knew.

He fucking knew her determination was crumbling.

He took a step closer and murmured, "Nothing about you is lowly, Srinaya. Please don't ever say that." She just nodded. "Do you want me to stay here with you?" he asked.

"Because of Surya? No, I'm alright."

"*May* I stay here with you? Until Endah shows up?"

"I want you to—yes," she answered plainly, and Owen's eyes sparkled.

nine

THE STREETS SURROUNDING MP WERE MAINLY RESIDENTIAL, WITH LARGE houses that took up all the land space, save for swimming pools at the back and tiny patches of lawn at the front.

Every home had high fences and gates—typical of Indonesian houses. The suburb was a popular place for military families and government officials to live; streets in Kuningan were swept more often, and maintained better than in some other areas of Jakarta.

Butted up against the north wall of the complex stood a small row of eating houses that had been there for as long as MERAHPUTIH had.

They sat proudly out of place—a little rundown with discoloured paint and faded posters gracing the walls.

The little family-run eating houses heaved day and night. Most of the MP staff lunched there at least two or three times a week; they only had to stroll along the front gates and turn right down the quiet leafy street to eat.

Naya, Edhi, Ravi, Gunawan and Tini crowded around a table at *Warung Pak Mudi* and waited for their *mie ayam bakso pangsit*, the tiny shophouse-turned-eatery chock-full of MP staff eating delicious hearty Indonesian noodle soup with beef balls and crispy fried wontons.

They raised their voices to speak over the din, discussing a multimedia installation submitted by a local artist that featured nude images of their wife who died of cancer.

The photos were taken at different stages of her sickness, the viewer able to see the beautiful woman slowly waste away as the cancer progressed. Those photos would be projected onto a life-sized sculpture of a tree made from white cotton—the same fabric used to wrap bodies of the deceased in Muslim tradition.

The heart-wrenching piece was called, '*I Am Just Waiting To Join You*' and it was fucking perfect.

"The problem is," Gunawan said, "nudity is still a weird grey area here."

Tini groaned in frustration. "It's like, *European* nudes are okay."

Naya cut in, "—*Or*, if it's Indonesian, as long as they have a basket of offerings to the gods balanced on their head..." She rolled her eyes, chin propped up on her fist.

Edhi pointed at Naya, exclaiming, "Oh my god, yes! So true."

"But it's such a beautiful piece," Naya moaned. "I'm tempted to use the image of the tree as the main artwork for advertising." She took a bite of some *krupuk mie* as they waited for the noodles to arrive.

Gunawan nodded. "It's very poignant work." He grimaced. "Look. I support your choice to have it in the show. It's perfect for our theme. But *Pak* Surya..." Edhi made a dramatically loud sound of derision and Gunawan laughed. "I know, I know! But he's seriously got it in for you, *Mbak* Naya."

Naya felt a pang of hurt, to be the focus of someone's hostility.

"My advice? Use the piece in the show, but don't put it on the posters. *Pak* Surya will make a big deal of it if you do. I wouldn't be surprised if he tried to pull the piece altogether just to spite you and blame it on pornography."

Ravi's voice was stern. "It's not pornography. The nudity serves a purpose."

Naya nodded in agreement. "Yes. It's intimate, but not sexual."

Gunawan shrugged, pushing his bright red-framed glasses up his nose and running his fingers over his moustache. "Intent doesn't always matter here."

Ain't that the truth.

She was a perfect example of that. All she wanted to do at MP was plan exhibitions that showcased the talents of local artists as often as international ones, and to ensure the conversations they were having, and messages they were conveying, were progressive and inclusive.

Edhi waved at someone over Naya's shoulder and Tini squeaked. Naya glanced around to see Owen zigzagging through the maze of tables to reach them. Her mouth pulled itself into a smile involuntarily, instantly feeling a tingle spreading up her spine to her crown.

Oh god—her cheeks were burning. She always fucking blushed when he was around. She took a huge sip of her *es jeruk* before turning back to watch him weave through the throng.

Everyone gawked as he walked by; he looked ridiculous squeezing through the crowd. His just-got-out-of-bed hair flopped in his face as he looked down to apologise to *Ibu* Aida—head archivist—for accidentally bumping her roughly with his hip.

He gave her a lopsided grin as he flipped his hair back and kept moving, and Tini grabbed Naya to murmur, "If you don't sink your teeth into him, can I?" Naya hushed her but Tini smacked Naya's hand. "Oh please. He looks at you like you're ice cream on a hot day."

"I wish someone would look at me that way." Edhi pouted.

And then Owen was there, smiling, and perfect, and—*fuck.* He blew out a dramatic breath. "Could you have chosen a more difficult table to get to? I think I gave *Ibu* Aida whiplash."

Tini checked out Owen's ass as she muttered, "I'm sure she enjoyed it."

Naya gave her a *can you please not?* glare. Thank god Owen was too busy looking around for a stool to notice. Tini just feigned innocence, before asking, in that shit-stirrer way of hers, "*Pak* Owen, what's your opinion on pornography?"

"Versus art," Naya rushed out when he blinked.

She looked up at him, silently apologising for the twenty-six-year-old child next to her. A crooked smile slowly appeared as Owen answered, "Art is social commentary, right? Poses questions. Makes statements. It'll always offend. It *should*. I bet someone looked at

Michelangelo's *Creation of Adam* and found God's nipples too perky. You snort, Ravi, but you'll be googling them and zooming in later this afternoon—I guarantee it. His nipples would've poked Satan's eye out all the way from up there. Why am I talking about nipples? What was the question? Pornography?"

Naya barked, "Versus art!" and then covered her face.

Owen nodded with a chuckle. "For all the people that will hate a piece, an equal number of people will love it. So, as long as no one's being exploited, and anyone involved has given enthusiastic consent—" He shrugged and waved his hand to end his point.

And then he held up a finger as he spotted an empty chair a few tables down that he dashed away to grab.

Tini dipped her chin and said quietly, "He's smart. Give enthusiastic consent to that dick, *Mbak* Naya."

Gunawan, ever the voice of reason, said, "Tini, come on. Let's not treat him like that."

And then Ravi interjected again. "Oh, come on, *Pak* Gunawan. *I'd* even go there. Look at the guy. He's like the fucking love child of an Ancient Greek statue and an Avenger. It hurts my eyes to look at him."

Tini and Edhi cackled and Owen reappeared with a stool, placing it next to Naya. He sat down, angling his body to her. The length of his thigh pressed up against hers as they all huddled around the small table. "Hello there," he said, his voice the perfect mix of soft and rough.

Naya locked onto his mouth, his bottom lip glistening. "Fancy seeing you here."

"Edhi invited me." He pointed to the little shit, who was feigning innocence like Tini.

Naya made a mental note to split them up so they'd stop their schemes.

"Did I interrupt your meeting?" Owen asked.

Naya shook her head. "We've been talking about a submitted piece that we all love but it has nudity in it."

A little vertical wrinkle appeared between his brows when he frowned. "So?" he asked.

"Thank you!" Edhi and Tini exclaimed at the same time.

Naya ignored them. "We're worried about pushback."

She took out her iPad and tapped on the video of '*I Am Just Waiting To Join You*'.

Owen was silent as the first image of the naked woman appeared, projected onto the trunk of the white tree. Her body still looked strong and healthy. Her pose was relaxed, one hand straight above her head with the other crossed over her belly. Her eyes twinkled with humour. She looked like she was dancing.

One by one, as the photos progressed, Owen's brows drew closer together. Full firm flesh disappeared, bones jutted out, skin turned almost grey. But through it all, the affection for her husband was clear in her eyes.

"He watched her fade away," he murmured. "This is a beautiful piece." His voice sounded distant as if he was latching onto a memory. "What a real privilege it is to be with your loved ones on every step of their journey—to not have them snatched away suddenly. I wish I got that chance."

Naya glanced at Tini, who looked taken aback.

Gunawan broke the tension by bringing the conversation back on track. "Do you think we'd get pushback on it?"

Owen rubbed his stubbly jaw as he said, "About the nudity? You shouldn't. It's about loss. Documenting the loss of his wife frame by frame as her body admits defeat. Nothing tops that kind of heartbreak." He turned to Naya. "This should definitely be in the show."

Their food arrived, and while Owen ordered a drink, Tini said quietly in Naya's ear, "I kinda feel bad about objectifying him now because dude is *deep*. Give him enthusiastic consent to deep-dick you."

Naya pushed Tini's face away.

A giant plate of *pangsit* was plonked in the middle of the table and Owen made an absurdly erotic rumble of pleasure. "I can eat thirty of these. Have some."

Owen's freckled cheeks and lips went red from the impressive amount of *sambal* he squirted into his bowl, and in between noodle-slurps and serious chats about pornography versus art, Naya found herself softening to more than just the way he looked (Rav was right though—it always hurt to look at him, ache deep inside her) or the fact that he was flirtatious in a way that was innocent but *not* at the same time. He was clever, and funny, and respectful. He cared about art—had been to many of the same shows as her. But the thing she really liked about him was how unpretentious he was about everything. It was easy to forget his title.

"How did you come up with heartbreak as a theme?" he asked, his forehead beaded with sweat from the chilli. He reached over the table to get a paper napkin to wipe his sniffly nose.

"A conversation with a friend who decided to get divorced after a pretty shitty marriage. It was the night of that DEWI show, actually," Naya said. "After I finished packing up I went to the afterparty with her."

"And what happened?"

"She said, *It really hurts, but what's a few more shattered pieces when your heart's been broken for years?*"

Naya took the last sip of *es jeruk*, savouring the ice-cold orange juice on her tongue. She made a mental note to call Meredith later—to see how she was coping after being in a dark place for so long.

Owen didn't say anything for a while, lost in thought. And then he rested his elbow on the table and ate the second last *pangsit*. "How's your friend doing now?"

Naya half-heartedly shrugged, running her finger along the edge of her glass. "They've separated. They have another couple of months before they can finally divorce but Ben's already engaged to someone else—someone he met while he was with Meredith. Mer's staying at my place. She refuses to step foot in the house they owned together but won't give it up either."

Owen rested his chin on his hand and murmured, "Heartbreak does stupid things to people."

A disorienting deja-vu crashed over her like a tsunami and her glass slipped out of her hand.

Owen caught it before it smashed on the floor. "Whoa. You alright?" he said.

She stared at him wordlessly, goosebumps rising on her forearms.

He looked different—*felt* different.

No—not him, she realised. He hadn't changed at all. It was Naya… something had changed in *her*—a feeling that was very much the opposite of *saudade*. A missing puzzle piece had been found and finally put in its correct place; a sense of belonging.

Naya's eyes flicked to her team. Edhi and Tini were giggling like school kids as they googled *Creation of Adam* on Tini's phone and zoomed in on God's nipples while Gunawan and Rav discussed the budget. She looked back at Owen blankly, his dark lashes making the pale gold in his irises burn bright.

He tucked his hair behind his ear and breathed, "Let's go somewhere."

Naya canted her head as she focused on his ear. God—even his ears were perfect. And that beautiful neck. She wanted to nuzzle into it.

Her eyes followed the line of his shoulder, down his chest and made their way to his lap… and then she realised she was basically staring at his cock and her eyes shot back up to his face.

"Pardon?" she asked.

"Walk with me. We have some important business to discuss," he said with promise in his voice.

$$\downarrow$$

O led the way out from the throng of diners but Naya had more trouble squeezing between the seats.

She apologised to the people who shuffled their stools further in to make room for her to pass, but they were all charmed by her captivating smile. Every patron reciprocated, blank grins on their faces, as if they weren't able to control themselves.

She tiptoed through the last tight spot, her thick body sandwiched between two men. Naya's arse brushed roughly against the upper back of one guy as she leaned forward against the other, with whom she must have been friends because he patted her hand as she braced herself on his shoulders.

And then she was through, round cheeks rosy and big dark eyes full of mirth.

Seeing her pressed against all those bodies made O's cheeks turn red too.

"Far out," she said, exhaling in relief. "That was an adventure." She delighted him even more when she blurted, *"Now a question of etiquette —as I pass, do I give you the ass or the crotch?"* lowering her voice an octave and putting on a forced American accent as she quoted *Fight Club*.

She laughed at herself.

It was so fucking lovely he couldn't stop himself from rubbing the ache in his chest.

God—he desperately wanted to lick the trickle of sweat on her temple. She wiped it away, and ran her fingers gently through her hair, fixing a bobby pin that came loose.

She continued, "Squeezing my way through a restaurant used to be my worst nightmare. Now, it's the only time I ever apologise for my body."

"I'm jealous of them. They should be thanking you," he drawled.

Naya sniffed a little laugh and fiddled with an earring to brush off his flirty words. O took a few steps but Naya stopped him. "Where are you going?" she asked, pointing the other way.

O jerked his chin in the opposite direction. "Let's go the long way," he said.

They walked past the row of eateries, weaving in and out of cars and motorbikes parked haphazardly in any available space along the street.

As the chaos of the eating houses faded and fewer people walked by, Naya cleared her throat. "May I ask a very personal question?" she said quietly, hands deep in the pockets of her dark red trousers, rolled up at the bottom.

Her satchel's strap cut diagonally between her cleavage, her tight black top cut low. She turned her head to look up at him and he glanced away, kicking pebbles out of his path as they strolled down the tree-lined street.

"You can ask me anything," he answered.

"Who did you lose?"

He wasn't expecting that question.

He swallowed at the memory of getting pulled out of Biology and going to the counsellor's office to find Endah waiting there. Her eyes were red and puffy, but when she informed him that his family had been in an accident, she'd steeled herself so she wouldn't cry, breaking the news—and his heart—in a soft, even tone.

"My parents and sister. Car crash," he said, chin almost tucked to his chest as he looked at the ground.

O didn't realise Naya had stopped walking until he couldn't see her in his peripherals anymore. He turned back to find her frozen in place with her hand pressed to her chest, deeply troubled by his revelation.

And then she approached him—came right up to him and placed her little hands flat on his sternum as she looked up at him.

It was the first time she touched him deliberately and he couldn't help the rasp that escaped his throat.

Is this an invitation?

The dappled sunlight filtering through the trees reflected off her irises and revealed flecks of gold he hadn't noticed before. Her expressive brows furrowed, big eyes staring.

"I'm very sorry," she offered.

He chanced caressing her cheek, brushing stray hairs from her forehead, and he was pleased that she didn't flinch. "Thank you," he said. "It happened a long time ago though."

O said it dismissively—had even given Naya a little shrug to make *her* feel ok about it, and he hated himself immediately after. His family didn't deserve something as shallow as a shrug. His dad, mum and sister deserved full-body sobs and big fat tears even twenty-four years later.

She shook her head and continued walking and he fell into step with her. Their bodies were close, almost touching.

"I don't really know you at all—" Her rosy cheeks pulled her mouth into a smile—"but you've been really kind to me. I bet your family would love the person you've become."

He didn't know how to respond to such sweet words, so he just smiled back.

They turned onto another quiet residential street, and something about turning that corner made it easier to leave the heartache behind. He took a deep breath and then exhaled, shaking off the remnants of sadness.

He stepped in front of her, walking backwards as she continued on. "You know what I've realised?" he asked, breaking the silence between them. "You haven't offered me a cigarette today. This displeases me."

She snorted and rolled her eyes dramatically. "Apologies, oh *esteemed benefactor*," she snarked, bowing low, hands in the prayer position.

When she straightened she looked undeniably bratty, and O—who had never found the idea of spanking particularly hot—felt the strongest urge to take her over his knee.

She swaggered—hips swaying confidently. "You know, before you came along, I'd take three weeks to finish a pack." She pulled out an unopened one from her bag and gave it to him. "This is my second in just over a week."

She tried to sound scornful but her amused eyes, shaped like crescent moons, gave her away.

O wasn't sorry in the slightest. How could he be? The first time he saw her after so many months, she'd had those soft arms raised over her head, torso stretched like a mermaid sunning herself on the shore, her lovely dimpled belly peeking out of her tshirt as she took that first deep drag and fucking *purred*.

He lit her cigarette for her and she cupped her hands over his, her touch lingering, and there was something in the way she looked at him through the flame that definitely felt like an invitation.

She inhaled, her lips puckering.

He clenched his teeth and he put his hand in his pocket to distract from his semi-hard dick. "I'll happily be the one to bring the Sampoernas if you agree to keep smoking them with me. You actually seem less intense when you've got one between those pretty lips of yours," he answered.

A devilish smile appeared on Naya's face. She tapped her chin. "Hmm. For the sake of our lungs, we should probably just learn to not be so intense around each other."

"Intensity doesn't scare me."

"Really?" She didn't believe him. Or maybe she was surprised.

He nodded. "Yes. Are you scared?"

"Of you? No, not at all."

He stopped, and she did too, and then he stepped closer. She leaned her head back to look at him, and her lashes fluttered in response to his closeness.

"Not of me. Of how you feel about me."

Now she looked nervous. He probably shouldn't be happy about that, but he enjoyed challenging her.

She didn't give him an answer—just kept her blazing eyes locked on his. Was she trying to play chicken with him? *Oh, Srinaya.* Stretching out silences was his specialty.

They stood in the middle of the street, Naya staring back at him defiantly. She brought her cigarette up to her lips and took a deep drag and before she exhaled, she licked her lips to taste the sugary filter paper. He mirrored her, and he delighted in watching her eyes follow his tongue.

But then a car materialised out of nowhere and honked at them, interrupting their game. Naya startled and an awkward squeak escaped her.

O guided her onto the sidewalk, shielding her as the car drove past. His hand found its way to her waist, keeping her soft body close.

With her on the sidewalk and him still standing on the road, they were almost eye to eye. His heart pounded as her fingers reached up to touch strands of his hair that fell over his eyes. She rubbed them between her fingers.

"Jesus—you're handsome," she blurted out quietly, and O was immediately brought back to that private room when she'd said the same fucking thing, straddling him, grinding into his lap.

Present Naya looked so surprised, and that was so ridiculous to him. How the fuck could she be surprised at how much he wanted her?

She was wonderful. Kind. So smart. Funny. Insightful. She was loved by her colleagues. Shit—even Endah loved her, and *that* was impressive.

He wasn't being subtle—he was sure of it.

Right then. He moved closer and ran his thumb over those goddamn perfect beauty spots on her cheek.

Naya's eyes shot sparks, the dark gold flecks igniting against her black pupils. Her hands pressed firmly to his chest—her fingers touching the skin at the base of his throat.

She burned against him; the combination of her heat and the sticky Jakarta air made sweat well up between his shoulder blades and trickle down his back.

"May I ask you a very personal question?" he spoke quietly. Naya's brows angled together. "It's only fair since you asked *me* a personal question. I'm all about fairness."

Naya's nose wrinkled but she smiled. "*Yeeeeeees?*" she said hesitantly, her voice trailing off and upwards at the end. She grimaced.

O ran his fingers along the side of her neck and she made a breathy high-pitched sound. He pressed his cheek against hers and then angled his head to brush his lips lightly along her cheekbone.

"Let me kiss you," he purred in her ear.

Naya jerked away to gape at him, although her hand gripped his shirt tightly. "*Um,*" she managed.

Again with that surprise. She really had no idea how much he wanted her. His eyes roved over her—her almost-black hair swept up and away from her face in messy twists, her large cat-like eyes, her slightly aquiline nose. Those beauty spots on her rosy apple cheeks. That fucking mouth.

"Sorry—that wasn't a question. *May* I kiss you?"

She still didn't say a word but deep pink spread across her cheeks and down onto her chest. O wondered what Pantone would call the shade.

Her lips were parted; she panted slightly. Standing this close, he could smell her—the faint scent of vanilla, sandalwood, and something else.

Naya's mouth parted a little wider as if she was about to say something.

"Wait," O said abruptly. "That wasn't a very *personal* question, was it?"

His hand slid to the small of her back—just above the swell of her deliciously big arse—and tugged her nearer, their torsos meeting, his erection pressed against her belly.

She gasped.

"How scared are you about parting ways today without feeling my tongue sliding against yours, Srinaya?"

That sinful mouth opened as her breath hitched, the corners pulling upwards.

Good. A smile of sorts. This was definitely welcome.

Her lids hooded and her brows slanted steeply downward. She looked pained, but it wasn't pain at all…

And then she gave O the most perfect fucking answer: "Terrified," she replied, their faces so close he felt her warm breath against his mouth. She lifted her chin—an official invitation.

It was all he needed.

He gently pressed his lips against hers and sighed as the relief of finally tasting her overwhelmed him. Naya's arm wrapped around his neck. Her kiss became heavier, fervent, and he mirrored her movements, desperate to taste more.

O's tongue flicked against the inside of Naya's upper lip, and she let out a quiet sigh, opening her mouth wider for him. Her tongue stroked his in return, and they found their rhythm.

God damn all those bobby pins holding up her hair. He wanted to run his fingers through those silky waves, coil them around his fist.

Instead, O's fingers fanned out over her chest at the base of her throat—an intimately possessive gesture—and she withdrew her mouth from his, lifting her head back, inviting him to kiss her there.

He ran his swollen lips along her skin. She was so tense that she trembled, clinging tight to his shoulders.

"Fuck, you're lovely…" O growled, and Naya responded by growling back—a gorgeous rumble in her throat—and raking her sharp nails against his scalp.

One hand slid over his sternum and undid a button halfway down his shirt. She slipped her hand under the fabric and pressed her palm over his heart, igniting every nerve in his body.

And then, as if she had just woken up from a dream, she gasped and snatched her hand out. "Wait. No. Someone might see."

Naya drew her lower lip between her teeth as she pulled away from him, looking flustered, and checked the street to see if anyone was around.

For a brief moment, he thought she was ashamed. Rejection lanced through him, but then he remembered where they were: standing on the side of some street in a city that valued modesty.

This wasn't Australia.

Naya took another step away, running her fingers over her mouth as if checking if her lips were still there. He smiled and checked his own. Yep, still there, so sensitive—tingly. They already missed her terribly.

She took a deep breath through her nose and exhaled through her mouth. She was trying to catch her breath, or maybe slow down her heartbeat. Fists on her hips, she paced a few metres up the road and back to him.

He cleared his throat. It was starting to feel cold like she was closing herself off. O didn't like it.

"Everything okay?"

Naya stopped pacing and faced him. She shook her head, running her fingers over her lips again. "That felt—" She squeezed her eyes shut as if recollecting the sensations, her brows knitted.

He needed more words. He needed to understand. "That felt...?"

Naya absentmindedly tried to run her fingers through her hair but they caught in the twists and pins, loosening sections and ruining her up-do. She huffed in frustration and started pulling out the bobby pins, stuffing them in her pocket as the dark waves fell down over her shoulders.

O gawked at her—all mussed up with puffy lips, eyes glassy with arousal.

He marched right up to her and surprise crossed her face.

"*Was* that okay?" he pleaded, his hand sweeping down the sides of her arms to take her hands in his.

She wouldn't look at him as she confessed, "It was *infinitely* better than okay." Her words came out slow and almost slurred as if she was drunk.

O swelled with pride. *Thank god.*

The relief of her praise eased the tension in his chest. He lifted her chin but her eyes were closed again, and the way her lashes quivered against her cheeks made her look like she was replaying their kiss behind her eyelids.

He bent down to brush his lips between her brows. "For me too."

At his compliment, she hummed, her expression soft and wanting. His words emboldened her, giving her the courage to come up onto the tips of her toes to nip her teeth on his lower lip. "I want more," she murmured, "but... not here..."

O inhaled the coconut scent of her hair so deeply he could taste it in the back of his throat. "We'll do it again. There's plenty of time."

ten

NAYA FELT LIKE SHE'D BEEN DUNKED INTO A VAT OF MENTHOL WITH THE way her body wouldn't stop fucking tingling. Was her skin burning? Was it freezing? Her brain couldn't make up its mind. Either way, she hated being so close, yet so far, from Owen.

She kept leaning towards him. She bumped into him twice as if she was drunk. He laughed, running the back of his hand against her arm and... it hurt.

They neared the end of the street, getting closer and closer to MERAHPUTIH's entrance.

The heat and heaviness between them wore away; the lustful Owen slowly morphing back into Owen the legacy director—friendly, kind, beautiful. Untouchable. Very important. *Very very far away...*

His hands were in his pockets, eyes forward. She wasn't sure if she imagined it, but he even stood a little straighter—head held high.

The thought of it saddened her. Turning that corner was like erasing everything that happened. MP had always been a haven for Naya. Hallowed ground. But at that moment, it felt like punishment.

Like goodbye.

"Wait," Naya said, and she grabbed his hand and pulled him up onto the sidewalk to stand behind the last tree. Shielded from the main road, she pressed her back against the trunk. She cursed as she looked up at him.

His hazel eyes twinkled with amusement, those lush lips pulling into the most devastating smile.

She mindlessly opened to him, shoulders pulling back, chin up to expose her throat. Even her spine bowed backwards against the tree, her hips pushed forward a little. It was like her body was submitting to him all on its own, animal instinct kicking in.

Her nipples were so hard they ached. She saw the moment Owen noticed them through her bodysuit, the way his jaw tightened. He took a long breath in—it was almost a hiss—and he shook his head. "Naya…"

She had never loved the sound of her name more than when it came out from between those perfect lips of his. Her pussy clenched as Owen said it, and she bit her lip. "Just one more kiss," she pouted, voice high and sulky.

Owen looked utterly pleased that she was practically begging him. She didn't care. She needed it, pride be-damned.

He leaned his big, hard body against her, one giant hand wrapped firmly around the nape of her neck while the other slipped under the waistband of her trousers, gripping her ass.

She cursed herself for her choice of outfit. "Of all the days for me to wear this fucking bodysuit," she panted, and he rumbled out a laugh as he grazed her neck with his teeth.

"If I had my way you'd never wear clothes again," he murmured, his breath cold against the trail left by his tongue.

She cradled his jaw in her hands, pulling him to her mouth.

Their kiss was desperate—teeth knocking together, tongues entwining.

And then Owen's kisses slowly lost their intensity until he planted a gentle peck on her cheek and pulled away. He stepped back, combing his fingers through his messy mop of hair to tame it.

His lips were swollen and red.

Naya peeled herself off the tree and did the same, bringing her hair up and tying it into a bun, the fresh air on her neck and shoulders a welcome sensation.

She touched her mouth, felt the tingling left by his stubble rubbing her skin. "I look a mess don't I?"

His eyes flickered with satisfaction. "You look like you just made out with a boy against a tree."

She covered her face. "Oh my god."

He laughed. "You look beautiful. A little... glowy?" He tilted his head and rubbed his chest. He looked at his watch and gasped. "Shit, I have a meeting in ten minutes, and it's going to take me twenty minutes to get there, and I really need to splash cold water on my—*everything*."

Naya giggled and nodded in agreement. "Go. I'll quickly run a half-marathon to get rid of some of this pent-up energy and then I'll make my way back."

"Dinner?" Owen asked.

That weird icy-hot tingling appeared again. "Yeah, okay. I'll be done by five."

Owen hesitated, not wanting to leave. He growled, "Fuck. Okay," and then hurried off around the corner.

†

The *Heartbreak Bevy*—the name Edhi came up with for the team (*tshirts coming forthwith*, Edhi promised)—sat on the floor of Purnama.

So far, twenty-four pieces were in the bag.

Choosing the placement of the larger works gave them a better idea of how many more they could accept.

Naya used her portable projector to cast images of the chosen pieces onto the large wall in the main foyer. "So, the dimensions for Joyce's is about five by seven metres," Naya explained, "but it's also very dark. She's used Stuart Semple's *Black 3.0* on it." The group cooed in awe. "I know. It's intense."

Naya's heart thundered in response to the moody abstract piece. The rage in *'The Moment I Realised You Didn't Know Me At All'* was palpable—the splashes of matte black, deep purples, blue and grey, and the frenzied scratches of blood red with flecks of yellow reminded her of a tornado obliterating everything in its path. Malevolent. Violent.

Who was the focus of all that hatred?

"Hey Ravi, could you measure out seven metres on this wall?"

Ravi stood with the measuring tape, and Naya scooched the projector further away from the wall, enlarging the image. The Bevy also stood and stepped back.

The painting would be the first piece to greet visitors when they entered Purnama, the boldness of the image setting the tone for the show.

"Yes," Gunawan said.

"Perfect," Tini added.

Ravi nudged Naya's arm with his elbow. "That painting is made for that wall."

Naya smiled. Getting groped against a tree by a hot man may have been the highlight of her day but the people currently in the room with her came a very close second. She pouted and said, "Hey, can I be vulnerable for like, thirty seconds and tell you all how great you are? I am so glad you're doing this with me. I couldn't imagine a better team."

Edhi put his hand out in front of her.

Tini put her hand on top of his.

Gunawan and Ravi both rolled their eyes but did the same.

Naya laughed as she placed her hand on top.

Edhi put on his best deep American footballer voice as he said, "Heartbreak Bevy on three! One—"

Surya burst into the room with two *very* rich-looking people in tow.

"—have been extensive. We've installed state-of-the-art equipment: better lighting, built-in speakers, projectors and screens. Oh, *selamat siang*," he said, his bright tone at odds with the sneer on his face when he noticed the Bevy standing in their circle.

Naya plastered a calm smile on her face. "*Selamat siang, Pak* Surya. We're going through some of the artwork for the show. Would you like us to leave?"

One of the VIPs motioned with her dainty hand and answered, "Please, don't let us chase you out of here." She moved closer to study

Joyce's work projected on the wall. "What a moving piece. Is this life-size?"

Naya nodded. "Thereabouts. The artist used a very special paint called Black 3.0, a matte pigment so black it absorbs about ninety percent of visible light."

Surya subtly rolled his eyes.

The man stepped forward and tilted his head. "How fascinating. I can't even imagine seeing something so dark. It'll look like a hole in the wall."

Naya's mouth curved upwards. "I'm very excited to see it in real life too. The other colours are less matte and I think the combination will play tricks on the eyes."

The elegant middle-aged woman introduced herself and her partner, explaining their interest in becoming patrons of MERAHPUTIH. The woman took Naya's hand and said, "I have a feeling this exhibition is going to be very different from other MP shows. We'll be at the opening. We can't wait to see what other pieces you choose."

Naya thanked them, adding, "We look forward to seeing you on the night. But we should probably get on. We have a lot more pieces to select if we want to fill this entire building."

Naya caught Surya's flash of angry confusion before he smoothed back the sleazy used car salesman's smile on his face. He turned to the couple and encouraged them to walk through the wings by themselves while he consulted with the team.

When the VIPs moseyed into the north wing, Surya whirled around to the Bevy and grated, "We made it clear you only have this main section and the south wing."

Naya—who was probably three or four inches shorter than Surya, and had about thirty kilos on him—felt an all-consuming urge to body-check him like a bull being antagonised by a matador. Maybe she'd run her horns right through him and use his blood to paint a piece to add to the show.

She blinked. *Such dark thoughts.* She needed to work off that pent up energy from earlier in the day.

An image of Owen slurping *bakmie* appeared in her mind, cheeks and nose sweaty from all that spicy *sambal bakso*. She exhaled a calming breath.

Before Naya could respond, Gunawan spoke up, "Actually, *Pak* Surya, Mr Jameson and *Ibu* Endah approved the use of *every* wing."

Tini nodded. "It was at the meeting last week? When we were assigned our *proper* workspaces?"

Ravi drawled, "Yes, thank you *so* much for our new workspaces, *Pak*."

God love them.

Edhi pursed his lips to hold in a laugh.

Surya gritted his teeth.

Naya turned her back to him and chose that moment to test Gunawan's theory from lunch. She swiped through more projected images while Surya stood back, scanning them like a *cicak* clinging to a wall, waiting for a chance to snap its mouth shut on a fly buzzing too close.

'I'm Just Waiting To Join You' appeared and Surya made a sound of shock. Rav bowed his head, rubbing his thumb between his brows.

"You *cannot* display that work in the show."

And snap.

"We can't?" Naya asked innocently. "Why not?"

"It-It's inappropriate," Surya sputtered.

Naya breathed evenly through her nose, pictured puppies and rainbows and Owen sighing into her mouth. "How is it inappropriate?"

Surya gesticulated wildly at the projection. "Look at her. She's skin and bones!"

Naya swiped to the first image of the woman. "She isn't skin and bones here," she argued.

"Well—she's naked."

"And?"

"It's *inappropriate*," he insisted.

The rest of the Bevy looked back and forth between Naya and Surya like they were watching a tennis match. Naya shoved her hands in her pockets and bounced on her tiptoes. "I don't understand what you're saying," she said, swiping back to the last image where the model's skin was grey and papery. "Does this make you uncomfortable?"

"It's tasteless!" Surya retorted, almost shrill, before remembering the VIPs walking around the other wing. He lowered his voice as he said, "It's pornographic and has no place at MERAHPUTIH. This isn't Australia."

Again with that constant othering.

She tapped her chin. "Hmm. Maybe we should ask those VIPs what they think," she said, nodding in their direction.

Surya's tutted. "Why must you cause trouble? Why must you make everyone uncomfortable?"

Naya caught her snort in time. "It doesn't make *us* uncomfortable. *We* don't find the nudity inappropriate."

Tini gazed at the image thoughtfully. "I think it's moving," she commented.

Gunawan spoke up, "I've seen far more confronting pieces exhibited in this gallery."

"It's a beautiful piece about loss," added Rav.

And then Edhi quoted Owen from lunch: "The artist is documenting the loss of his wife frame by frame as her body admits defeat."

Naya's heart swelled. She quoted Owen too: "Nothing tops that kind of heartbreak."

Surya looked like he was on the verge of throwing a tantrum. Naya wouldn't've been surprised if he started stomping his feet. "It's morbid and cannot be in the show. My aunt would not approve of this."

Ugh. Surya hiding behind the skirts of the powerful *Ibu* Tuti. Naya put her hand up to get him to stop. "Then ask *your aunt* to tell me herself." She tried with all her might to hide her sneer. "I am curator and art director, and I will only change my mind when the legacy directors personally voice their concerns to me."

"So, you're filling Purnama with pornography and images of dying women—"

"It's one dying woman, *Pak*," she cut in.

"By no-name artists who won't bring in visitors and money?" Surya accused. "Ali Suleiman? Mina Wirendra? Joyce Setyaningsih? Who are these people?"

God—did this fucking clown know *anything* about art? What was he doing on the board of a prestigious art institution?

Naya swiped back to that first projection of the angry abstract painting that the wandering VIPs approved of. "Joyce won the most prestigious art award in Surabaya last year. Mina Wirendra created that public art piece in front of the new science complex at UI. Ali Suleiman's photographs have been featured in National Geographic and Time Magazine."

Gunawan added, "And Indonesia Business Review."

"Oh, that's right. Thanks, *Pak* Gunawan," she said, smiling sweetly at the person Surya probably hated the least, although the fact that Gunawan was defending her probably meant he was going to be on Surya's shitlist now too.

Naya crossed her arms as she continued, her tone deliberately patronising. "In terms of international artists, so far, we have Val Seaver, who has exhibited at the Guggenheim—that's in New York, *Pak* —" Tini choked—"Li Huan, who exhibited in a group show at the Tate, Tony Jones, whose installations are all over Western Australia, and Melissa Tran, who is currently exhibiting at the NGV."

Oooh if looks could kill, Surya definitely would've stabbed them all a million times with his beady lizard-like eyes.

Naya couldn't help herself. She'd planned to keep one bit of news between her and Gunawan, but it had been *such* a good day, and Surya really did need to be put in his place. "And if those names aren't exciting enough—Gunawan, why don't you tell them the exciting update we got today?"

The Bevy turned to look at Gunawan who announced, "DEWI is interested."

They gasped at the news and Edhi actually squealed.

Surya's chin lifted in recognition and yet he still looked down his nose at Naya.

She mirrored his glare, eyes boring into his, and shrugged. "I've worked on a couple of their projects. There's still a lot to be worked out, but we *will* have a DEWI piece."

"Well," Surya said, "It seems you have everything under control, *Mbak* Naya."

He skulked out to find the VIPs.

†

It was almost 5PM when Naya exited the admin building and sat under the trees on the park bench.

The sky darkened and a breeze came through, cool enough to make the hairs on her forearms rise.

She lit a cigarette as she waited for Owen, sighing as she recalled her day. It was certainly one of the more eventful work days since starting at MP. From connecting with her team, to making out with Owen against a fucking tree like a teenager, and then putting Surya in his place...

She exhaled sharply. Today was totally a *Dear Diary* day.

Naya bit her lip as she waited for Owen to return, her knee bouncing impatiently. She checked her phone. She didn't have his number; did he have hers? She hadn't given it to him but maybe someone else had. Anyone could have. He'd only have to ask and—of course, they'd hand her contact info over to Mr Jameson.

Naya blinked.

She took in his name again—*Mr Owen Jameson.*

Her heartbeat quickened.

What happened to no one is worth it, *Naya?*

Somewhere between eating noodles with him in a crowded eating house, and having him pressed up against the length of her, she had disregarded the gravity of the situation: Owen wasn't just *Owen.*

Owen was a legacy director. The *Golden God.* Of *MERAHPUTIH*— her workplace, where people talked. Where people were probably already talking. Four eateries full of people saw her walk out with him that very afternoon.

Naya squeezed her eyes shut.

Oh my god, and we went the long way *back. Shit.*

It was why she'd said no in the first place.

Owen, the esteemed benefactor. Even when she teased him earlier that day—*Apologies, oh esteemed benefactor,* she said—those words hadn't really hit her.

Her lust blinded her.

Fuck—

Naya rubbed her eyes with the heels of her palms and Sal's face appeared.

No, it wasn't the same as Sal and her being accused of inappropriate behaviour. It had to be so much more. A legacy director was *bigger,* right?

She could hear what they'd say. She'd heard it all before... *There goes Srinaya Matthews—fucking her way to a win.*

She recalled the comment sections of articles written about her. Cancelled interviews and exhibitions. Letters arriving at her home that called her names. Sal's face when he shook her hand on the stage at the awards ceremony, as if he didn't care about her anymore.

Naya wasn't sure she was doing anything wrong with Owen, but it took a long time, a lot of work, and a very broken heart to get to where she was now. And risking it all for the esteemed benefactor felt like a really stupid thing to do.

She put out her cigarette, and as she walked down the driveway, she saw his towering form stepping out of a car.

He hadn't spotted her; he was on the phone.

He laughed down the line—*such a beautiful, gravelly sound*—and she dashed over to the gardens, concealing herself in the shadows.

Owen hurried past, and Naya heard him say, "—can't tonight. I want to take her out. Any suggestions?" and then he leapt up the admin steps with those long legs and disappeared inside.

Naya rushed out the gates and went home.

eleven

O's HEARTBEAT PULSED LOUDLY IN HIS EARS AS HE JOGGED AROUND Senayan Stadium, replaying the previous day. He cursed over and over again in time with his feet hitting the pavement.

The weather reflected his mood; the skies were shades of silver and grey with the threat of rain that never seemed to come.

The air was thick and heavy with moisture and as O ran, his lungs burned like he was inhaling mouthfuls of water, and yet he refused to stop.

Something must have happened when he left Naya on that street. He wanted to stay—he *really* did. But his work at MP was only one of many responsibilities, and although he didn't need to keep a constant watchful eye on Jameson Publishing, it was important for O to be regarded as the kind of CEO who was present—who gave a shit.

MERAHPUTIH may have been his mother's legacy but Jameson Publishing was his father's.

Still. He shouldn't have left her.

He was practically vibrating with excitement to see her again the night before.

When she pulled him onto the sidewalk and behind that tree, the way her full lips pouted as she begged for one more kiss, her fear of them being discovered overridden by her desire to feel him against her one more time, O felt victorious.

This is eight months in the making, he thought to himself, *and it was worth the wait.*

He'd asked Ibrahim to drive him back to MP as quickly as possible after his meeting, which was a ridiculous thing to request when the traffic was at a slow crawl the entire time.

He made it back at 5:07pm but she wasn't there.

He tried to logic his way out of the deluge of irrational thoughts that washed through him. *Maybe she got sick. Maybe she got hit by a passing motorcycle. Maybe she just fucking hates my guts and regrets everything that happened.*

Even Mario, who'd been on the phone with him as he searched the entire admin building, tried to talk him off the ledge. "Or... maybe something less dramatic happened," Mar said gently. "She could've been really tired, O. That's also a perfectly reasonable excuse. Don't get sucked into the void when you don't even know. *Stop* speculating. Respect her enough to trust that she wouldn't just leave without a good reason. Besides, you both have offices on the same floor. You'll see her tomorrow and she'll explain herself."

Of course Mario was right.

He was always right.

O's fear of abandonment was rearing its ugly head and he needed to sort himself out before he got pulled under.

He called his therapist back in Australia and after their conversation, he breathed easier.

He tried to release the last bit of anxiety by working out in the gym. When that didn't work, he jerked off in the shower to the image of Naya's hips jutting forward in invitation as she pressed back against the tree trunk, her nipples—small in comparison to how large her tits were—so hard and perfect.

He went to sleep feeling better.

But then she hadn't shown up at work the following day.

Why hadn't he asked for her fucking number? How could he have forgotten?

He refused to get it from her team members without her permission and he didn't want to ask after her without causing office gossip.

His therapist was fully booked, and Endah was unavailable, so he drove to Senayan after his late afternoon meeting to release his frustration, which seemed like a much more adult thing to do than meet Mario at some bar and get wasted. Although, who knew. The day was young.

Jesus—a spiral was imminent. Naya felt so out of reach again.

I may as well be back in Melbourne, O sulked.

His body began to feel heavy. He pushed himself further than ever yet his insides were still tightly coiled as if he needed to break something to get some kind of release. Even a sixteen kilometre run couldn't ease the insecurity that burned inside.

His t-shirt soaked through with sweat, he pulled out his earbuds as he slowed his pace and was confronted with the sounds of Jakarta—the incessant car horns, the revving of thousands upon thousands of cars, buses, and motorcycles during the city's infamous peak hour traffic, and the chatter of the other walkers and joggers using the old stadium grounds as their exercise track.

He slowed his pace as he tried to calm himself, taking in the atmosphere of the chaotic city—his second home. The mayhem of Jakarta was as much a part of him as his local fish and chip shop back in Melbourne.

He passed a group of elderly women wearing matching bright red Adidas jumpsuits and visors power-walking in the opposite direction, one of them muttering in Indonesian, "You only run like that when you're angry at your woman, or if you want to screw her."

The other ladies all squealed gleefully.

O turned to smile devilishly back at the group, and one of them looked horrified as she said, "I think he understood what you said!"

O nodded and replied in Indonesian, "Yes, I did," and winked at them.

They all squealed and cackled some more, covering their mouths in embarrassment as they waved and continued walking.

O's mood lifted a little.

twelve

A nightmare jolted Naya awake.

She cried out in the dark, her heartbeat racing at the memory of thumping on her front door in the night, the phone ringing incessantly with no voice on the other end, and a mailbox full of postcards with *SLUT* and *CHEAT* written next to her name.

She stared at her ceiling, her body refusing to fall back to sleep. Her head and heart were heavy, weighed down by her past—a ball and chain from which she couldn't escape.

She gave up on sleep and padded down the stairs in the dark to her studio to distract herself, opening her laptop and writing notes. She fleshed out the ideas brewing in her mind, slowly taking form: she wanted to learn how to incorporate traditional *Batik* techniques with natural dyes made from dirt, tea, coffee, and flowers, and refreshed her original proposal to hold month-long workshops at MP to teach people how to create their own *Batik* scarfs.

She made changes to her *wayang kulit* proposal, turning it into an art project of her own, tickled by the idea of creating a soap opera miniseries using the traditional shadow puppets, written in the same tone as a trashy *sinetron*, or Australia's own *Home And Away*.

She clicked a folder she hadn't looked at in years: her research on Indonesian deities. Naya had always felt a kinship with *Dewi Sri*, the goddess of rice fields, fertility, and abundance, whose tragic circumstances were completely out of her control. Gifted to the king of the gods as a baby, *Sri* grew into a beautiful goddess but all the male deities—including her adoptive father—began to look upon her with lust, causing unrest in the heavens.

Instead of letting *Sri* make a decision for herself, the deities killed her to keep the peace. *Sri's* kind heart, innocence and beauty blessed the earth, and from her body, nourishing plants of all kinds grew in abundance.

Naya then scrolled through images of *Nyi Roro Kidul*, the queen of the Southern Ocean. The sea goddess resided off the coast of *Pelabuhan Ratu*, a fishing town in the southeast of Java. Any mortal who dared to wear green, blue, or turquoise—her signature colours—near the water's edge was taken under the waves.

Naya remembered wearing a turquoise bikini as she and Sal ran into the water at Torquay late one afternoon when they were still at uni, her legs wrapped around his waist as they kissed.

She told him the story of *Nyi Roro Kidul* then, and Sal called her his queen, and she'd scrunched up her face because it was a ridiculous thing to say, but then he said, "I'd let you drag me under, sweetheart—Sri, my goddess," as his fingers found their way under her bikini bottoms and into her pussy.

Then, she recalled the argument she and Sal'd had right after they were accused of cheating, and how she told him she could never forgive him for not being selfish—for choosing to become a martyr by doing what was *right* instead of choosing her. "What's one lost award if it means we can be together? You didn't trust me enough to tell me! You decided for me!" she sobbed.

She shut her laptop and rubbed her eyes.

Why was this coming up again? She texted Sal just weeks ago when she first got *Heartbreak* to tell him the news and it was fine. She felt the familiar pang of heartache that always came with memories of Sal, but it hadn't been attached to so much fear.

No—this new fear was because of Owen Jameson. This was so

much bigger than what happened ten years ago; Naya had more to lose now.

When all of that Reginald Muse shit happened, she was just starting out—didn't have much of a reputation to lose. But now? People knew her—recognised her work.

Instead of winning an art award, the prize was curating the biggest show Naya had ever done. Instead of Melinda, the disgruntled former classmate, there was Surya, the board member. And instead of Sal, there was Owen... beautiful and shiny. A life-sized Oscar statue.

At 4:30 AM, Naya finally climbed back into bed, still yearning for the beautiful man who appeared mysteriously out of the hot, thick air of Indonesia's capital city.

She closed her eyes and replayed him in her mind: those penetrating hazel eyes that reminded her of both warm sticky honey and a dark, stormy day. The playful freckles that dotted his nose and cheeks... that strong broad chest... his big hands with those long fingers that wrapped perfectly around her nape. The smoke that billowed out from between his full lips.

She fell asleep wishing he was curled around her in bed.

$$\downarrow$$

Her alarm went off at 7:30am, eyes puffy and emotions raw.

She messaged the Bevy:

> I know mental health struggles aren't talked about openly here in Indonesia, but I want to be honest: I'm feeling pretty blue so I'm not coming in today. Feel free to work from home if you'd like, and please know that I urge you all to take time off whenever you need to look after yourself. Xoxo

Naya would usually bury herself in work to stay busy, but as she sat up in bed with her eyes closed and her hands on her heart centre, her body asked for love.

Gentleness. Sleep.

So that's what she gave it.

She turned on some soft music, popped a couple of weed gummies in her mouth, hid under the covers and closed her eyes.

She was startled awake by her phone ringing.

Arum's pretty face appeared on the screen.

Naya grunted sleepily and Arum laughed. "Did I disturb your nana nap?"

She searched for the switch to turn her lamp on. The burst of light blinded her and she grunted again.

Naya squinted at the screen. "Didn't work today. What time is it?"

"It's 7:45. What's wrong?" Arum asked with a frown.

Naya sat up in bed, her body stiff from not moving a muscle during her sleep. "Reginald Muse flashbacks," was her bitter response.

"What the hell got you thinking about that?"

Naya massaged her temple and closed her eyes but didn't respond. The image of Owen's mouth appeared behind Naya's lids. She blinked a few times to make him disappear, to no avail.

Arum's sweet voice asked, "Is Surya still making life difficult?"

Naya's nose wrinkled at the name. "Ugh. Among other things." *People. Hot... freckled... people.*

Arum's pixie-like face turned satanic. "Want me to hex him? It's a full moon tonight. I could—I dunno... send him some epic dick-shrivel-ling vibes."

Naya scoffed as she leaned back against the pillows. "If that actually worked, Surya's dick would have fallen off the first day I met him, or any of the other fucking times I've cursed him since."

"I know, he's the *woooooorst*," Arum groaned. "Honestly don't know how Dad has tolerated the guy for the decade he's been on the board."

Weariness weighed Naya down again—even after a whole day of sleep. Curating at MERAHPUTIH was losing its lustre very quickly.

Arum tipped her head to one side. "Hey. What's going on?"

Naya shook her head as she massaged her neck. Complaining about her responsibilities for *Heartbreak* would make her sound ungrateful, especially when she was getting what she wanted—save for some board member and esteemed benefactor-shaped hurdles that slowed her down but wouldn't stop her.

Naya was nothing if not stubborn.

Arum's voice cut through Naya's self-pity as she said, "Come on. Meet me at Le Roy. Let's have a meal and a drink. I miss you."

Naya smiled weakly as she shuffled off the bed. "Give me an hour."

✝

Le Roy stood out like a sore thumb in a row of shops and restaurants in Kemang. To its left sat a high-end jewellery store and a sushi restaurant, and to the right, a very expensive day spa.

The other businesses came and went but the well-loved dive bar always remained, with its infamous mediaeval-inspired DEWI mural, featuring depictions of hell that stretched from the front of the building to the alley down the side.

Above the entrance were the words, *Abandon all hope, ye who enter here.*

The religious folks had a lot to say about the work although their call for a boycott only made the bar more popular, and Naya couldn't be more pleased, because who didn't love fucking with evangelicals?

She bought Stef a tacky 1970s Jesus clock that flashed disco lights every hour on the hour which was lovingly displayed behind the bar for all to see.

The bar was a favourite spot for expats living in the area, especially Australians and Brits who stopped in to eat Le Roy's signature fish and chips, or steak and mushroom pie—a taste of home.

It was also the only place in Indonesia that served Corn Jacks. Naya loved biting into the deep fried pastry seasoned with chicken salt; she burnt the roof of her mouth on the piping hot corn filling far too often but it was always worth it.

Arum sat at the bar, leaning over the bulky counter as she flirted with Stefan—publican, pleasure pusher, and painfully handsome bartender extraordinaire.

Arum's silver-blue pixie cut was like a beacon in the sea of natural (or at least natural-*looking*) haired customers. She wore giant snake hoop earrings, and her dark plum lipstick looked almost black under the red downlights above the bar.

Naya slid onto the barstool next to her and harrumphed. "Stef, these barstools are absolutely subpar for my fat ass," she chided.

Stefan leaned over the bar to cop a look. He bit his lip seductively. "And what a fine fat arse it is," he drawled in his fancy British accent.

He leaned over even further to kiss Naya on the cheek, so very close to her mouth, his silky jet-black hair swishing forward and tickling Naya's chest. "I'll pass your comment onto management for review," he said in his best customer service voice. "But yes, I'm planning on updating the furniture in here since business has picked up. Perhaps you could help me pick them out. Something fitting—" He reached for Naya's palm, pressing his forehead to the back of her hand in an over-the-top display of humility—"for a goddess." He winked.

Naya giggled as she shoved his face away.

Arum piped up. "I should hope so. We spend enough of our well-earned money in this shithole. And you do love our company, don't you Stefaaaaaaan?" Arum let her voice get louder as she practically shouted, "Best tips in town, right Stefaaaaaaaaan?" letting the second syllable of his name last for a good three seconds.

People turned in their direction. Stef laughed loudly as he shook his head, flicking his hair over his shoulders and tying it up into a ponytail.

Naya admired his broad shoulders in his bright green tropical print shirt, sleeves rolled up to show off the tattoos on both arms.

Stefan's eyes met Naya's and he winked again, and Naya bit her lip as her mouth curled upwards.

If only she and Steffy could make it work as a couple. They'd tried twice, but their temperaments didn't match for something serious. The sex had always been fantastic though; she'd lost count of how many times they'd ended up fucking in Stef's bathroom high on coke, or molly, or mushrooms, or all three, Naya bent over the sink with him taking her from behind, staring at each other through the mirror.

Stefan Wardhana was fun, easy, and uncomplicated. He made her feel good and didn't make her doubt herself.

God—she really needed someone to take the edge off, and Stef was always good for that. But as she planned to signal for him to play with her later, there was a twinge of... *something*. Guilt, maybe. Whatever it was, it made her stay quiet.

Stefan served rum for Naya and whisky for Arum. Then he grabbed three shot glasses and poured some tequila.

He pushed one towards Naya. "For you and that delicious fat arse," he purred, eyes full of mischief which made her clit throb and her cheeks flush, and then pushed the other to Arum and nodded to her chest. "For you and your very nice tips."

The three of them raised their glasses and downed their shots.

A few hours later, Le Roy was packed full of people, and Stefan worked his devilish magic on another group down the other side of the bar.

Arum and Naya finished their dinner.

The tension in Naya's shoulders released, although that could've been more to do with the five drinks she downed which settled warmly in her belly and behind her eyes.

She rested her cheek on her fist, lids heavy. Arum mirrored her pose. "Righto. So come on then. Out with it. I don't like sad Sri."

Naya shook her head and pointed her finger right in Arum's face. "Do you think I got the curator job because I'm best friends with the daughter of a legacy director or because they really like what I do?"

Arum's dad, Bakti, had known Naya since her Melbourne uni days, when she and Arum rented a small flat in Carlton together.

She had collaborated with *Pak* Bakti on a community event at MERAHPUTIH a few years ago, but still—Naya had been surprised to receive the call-back for her application.

Arum laughed at Naya's question, plum lipstick now faded, her head falling back. "I think... *you* think... I hold more sway with Dad than I actually do."

Naya stared at her drink silently.

Arum patted her knee. "Wow, you weren't kidding about the Reginald Muse flashbacks," Arum commented. "Bud. One—you didn't do anything wrong back then, and you handled that whole situation with way more fucking grace than I would have. Two—that was a long time ago and you have proven yourself since then time and time again. You are a fantastic artist and curator. You *know* you are."

Naya smiled sadly at her sweet friend.

She knew without a doubt that Arum would never lie to her. She always told the truth, but had this amazing way of being blunt *and* diplomatic.

That's what Naya needed. A kindly spoken truth.

Her brow furrowed and she looked away as she asked another question. "Would you judge me if I kissed a board member?"

Arum's heavily lined eyes widened. "You *what?!*" she screeched.

Every person by the bar turned to look at them. Naya grimaced at the high-pitched sound and shushed her friend. "Inside voice, Arum."

Arum drunkenly asked, "Who on earth would you have made out with?" She thought hard, eyes blinking lazily. "I mean, I guess Patrick Ho isn't so bad. And Adeline Soediarto looks a little bit like that girl you had a fling with a couple years back, although... twenty years older. But hey—nothing wrong with that if you're into her." Naya buried her head in her hands as she swore under her breath but Arum wasn't finished. "Ew, I hope it wasn't that asshole Julian because I have it on good authority that he is a terrible lay. Oh! But you know who is surprisingly good in bed?"

"Oh-my-god-Arum-it-was-Owen," Naya blurted to distract her friend before she started giving them all scores out of ten.

Arum frowned. "Owen? Who's—" and then realisation dawned on her face, and her eyes lost their glaze as if the news instantly sobered her up. "Owen *Jameson?*"

Naya grimaced again as she nodded her head.

Arum's gape turned into a terrifying open mouthed smile. She dramatically put her hand on Naya's upper back and patted. "Well done, you," Arum commented. "That boy..." Arum did a chef's kiss. "He's-it's-like-just—" She exhaled a sharp breath. "Well. Done. You," was all she could say, punctuating each word with more pats.

Naya groaned and rested her forehead on her arms.

"What's with all the negativity then? Was he a terrible kisser or something?" Arum prodded her.

Naya's head snapped up to glare at Arum in defence of Owen's skill. "It was the best fucking thing ever," she declared fiercely.

Arum brought her hands up as she shrugged. "So what's the issue?"

Naya hated that she had to spell it out. "Arum. I don't have a legacy director as a father. I can't go around banging people who work there. I'm not even sure *you're* supposed to be doing that, although I'm not judging. I'm just a curator."

Arum flashed her the biggest shit-eating grin. "I have fucked a few curators in my time..." she said, voice going distant as she got all nostalgic about her very long list of bedmates.

"Oh my god," Naya said as she shook her head in mock disapproval.

Arum giggled as she punched Naya's arm but then she went serious. "Look. Was it consensual?"

Naya nodded.

"Do you want it to happen again?"

Naya nodded and pouted.

"Does he?"

Naya nodded and shook her fists at the heavens.

"Sooooooo... what's the issue?"

Naya's fists opened into frustrated claws as she raked her nails through her hair. "You know how hard I worked after what happened. I don't know if I can start from scratch all over again, Arum. And I definitely don't want people accusing me of getting to where I am by—"

Arum finished her sentence for her. "*Fucking your way to a win.* I remember, bud."

Of course Arum remembered. Arum was the one who had picked Naya up off the floor when her gallery exhibition was cancelled. Arum was the one who had answered the phone when the prank calls started.

"Ugh. I don't feel drunk enough," Naya said, words muffled as she buried her face in her arms again.

Arum signalled to Stefan for a couple more rounds of drinks. "Look. I'm going to say this once, and then we're going to get thoroughly fucked up. Stop giving a shit what people you don't even like think about you, Srinaya. People are always going to dislike you. People are always going to gossip. And those people? They are not your people so they *don't fucking matter.*"

Naya took in her words carefully, nodding slowly. "Also," Arum added, "I met Owen at a fundraiser Dad dragged me to a couple years ago, and it's kind of disgusting how lovely he is."

Naya's eyes went wide as she pointed at Arum. "You haven't—?" she sputtered.

Arum laughed. "Fucked Owen? *God* no. Lovely, but way too intense. We'd cancel each other out."

Naya's lip quivered a little at Arum's encouragement. "Thank you. I love you," she said as she grabbed her hand and gave it a loving squeeze.

"Of course you do. I'm the best," Arum said. "But seriously. Surya. Full moon. I've got the perfect hex in my grimoire. It's there if you want it. I'm totally in."

At that moment, 'Close to Me' by The Cure started blaring over the speakers, and Naya and Arum squealed, fists pumping in the air. Stefan turned up the volume and more folks mingling by the bar danced and sang along. Stef took out his phone to record the impromptu choir.

He posted a video of Arum and Naya belting out the words with a crowd of randos on Le Roy's socials.

Then the three friends took selfies, the first with Stefan in the middle getting kissed on both cheeks by Arum and Naya, another with Naya arching her back to show off her cleavage while Arum motorboated her as Stef threw his head back, laughing, and the last with Arum pulling in some hot stranger who had appeared next to her and making out with him while Naya and Stefan watched on in surprise.

Stefan posted them with the caption:

The best tips in town.

Naya, of course, couldn't resist reposting the photos to her own account, amending Stefan's caption to say:

The best tips {and ass} in town.

thirteen

Naya awoke at 5.30 after an abysmal sleep, still faintly stinking of booze. She stared at her ceiling fan spinning slowly, the *click-click-click* of the blades pulling her into some kind of hypnosis. The fan's lazy rotations did little to cool her but it agitated the warm air around her room enough for her to feel a faint whisper along her skin. Almost like Owen's breath against her neck.

If I had my way you'd never wear clothes again.

That face. That easy, unpretentious smile. Fuck—now she was losing sleep over him. Losing sense. She rolled over onto her belly and groaned into her pillow.

She googled him after getting home from her rambunctious night with Arum and Stef, and went down the rabbit hole of articles, links, and photos from interviews and society functions.

He'd graced the covers of some niche rich people magazines. Understandable; his looks guaranteed good sales.

Owen Mansur Jameson. Thirty-nine years old. Only son to Edward "Teddy" Boswell Jameson—a British-born Australian publishing magnate—and Margaret "Molly" Candrawatih—half Indonesian, half British daughter of Indonesia's first British ambassador and the beloved feminist poet and co-founder of MERAHPUTIH.

What a legacy to be born into.

Interviewers couldn't get a read on him. They called him *serious, remote, aloof. A private man. Too careful with his words so one couldn't know if his answers are truly his.* Naya didn't know the stranger they described and it angered her to read such nonsense written about him.

Fucking hell—some of the pictures of him though. There were photos from a black-tie fundraiser last year—his hair longer and tied up. He wore a navy silk brocade jacket which would've looked over-the-top on most men, but it suited his hulking frame. Maybe the full beard he'd grown helped to smooth the edges of his beauty just a little.

That beard though. He looked so familiar with that beard... She wondered if she'd seen him at some past event.

No. I would've sidled up to him.

She kept swiping and tapping, and stumbled across a photoshoot from five years ago at a beach house in *Pulau Seribu.* The images were warm and grainy with light leaks as if they were taken on one of those plastic Lomo cameras. He looked old Hollywood beautiful—the orange tint bringing out the gold in his skin and honey in his eyes. In her favourite photo, his gaze was fixed on something over the photographer's shoulder. A breeze blew a lock of his hair over his face.

His almond eyes were the only part of him that hinted at his Indonesian heritage. Framed by long dark lashes and shaded by his furrowed brow, he looked pensive—almost sad. She wondered what he'd been thinking about when the shutter clicked.

That top lip with its pronounced Cupid's bow was... Naya looked up and acknowledged the heavens. *Well done, God. That face cannot be some random explosion of matter. That face was carefully, lovingly, meticulously created. Hallelujah.*

Then she came across Owen's net worth and choked on her own saliva. She blinked and raised up onto her elbows. It sobered her up instantly. *No.* Was this a ridiculous thing to pursue—hoping for something with MERAHPUTIH's Golden God? Surya's words kept replaying in her mind. *Most esteemed benefactor.*

She groaned. *Ugh. Surya.* That brought on the hangover.

Exhaustion hit her again. She closed her eyes for a few moments and then—*goddammit*—she recalled Owen's kindness for the entire team at lunch, how he listened, engaged, and learned. Made them all laugh—even Ravi. And how, when they walked back together he'd gently coaxed her out of her shell, challenging her, and she opened herself up to him willingly. *Desperately*, even.

She shouldn't have run off like that, leaving him wondering, and probably blaming himself. What a thoughtless, uncaring thing to do.

She awoke again when the sunlight touched her through the blinds, enveloping her, heating her skin and making her sweat. And, of course, *he* was there again like a fucking phantom. How would those rough hands feel on her belly? Gripping her inner thighs? Naya bit her lip. The thought made a familiar heat throb through her, but it started lower, below her belly and deep between her legs. Naya moaned, acutely aware of the flow of sensation settling at her clit, and brushed the soft folds of her pussy with a feather-light touch before pressing her thighs together. Her nipples hardened in an instant.

She reached into her bedside drawer for her sextoy, turned it on and pressed the soft silicone to her clitoris as two fingers delved inside her. *So wet.* She was always aroused—ever since Owen had appeared on those steps at MP.

It didn't take her long to feel the heaviness in her calves, the muscles in her hips tightening. Then, the pressure travelled to her tits, making them ache so deliciously that she panted. And then she let out a cry as the orgasm exploded through her—radiated to her fingertips and toes —wishing Owen could witness her body quake as she came to the fantasy of him sliding in and out of her.

Naya sat up quickly and rubbed her eyes, trying to shake the image of his smirk and those pretty freckles from her mind. She drowned out her thoughts with far-too-loud music under the cold stream of her shower.

Afterwards, she stood in her kitchen waiting for her coffee machine to grind and brew as she scrolled through Le Roy's posts from the night before. She giggled at the pic of her and Stefan staring slack-jawed at Arum making out with the random guy who materialised next to her.

Naya scrolled through more photos. Yep—there Arum was making out with this new friend. Oh, there she was staring intensely into his face. And there they were laughing and snuggling each other on the vinyl bench near the DJ booth. Naya sent Arum a text.

NAYA:

Yo. You still with Old Mate Trout Pout? Just checking to see if you're alive. If I don't hear back from you in 15 minutes, I'm telling your dad you touched a boy's penis.

ARUM:

LOL I just told him you called him Old Mate Trout Pout and he asked if you were Tits McGee from Le Roy.

NAYA:

UM EXCUSE ME

It's MS. Tits McGee to him until I get to know him, tyvm.

ARUM:

NAYA:

But srsly, u ok tho?

Arum sent back a video of her and Old Mate all dishevelled in bed. He sat up drinking a coffee, and Naya could make out Wordle on the phone he was holding.

A Wordle man. He won extra points for that.

He waved to the camera and said, "Hi *Ms* Tits McGee. This is Trout Pout, AKA Mario." His voice was soft and relaxed. When he grinned, dimples appeared on his kind face. He rubbed his lightly stubbled chin. "Arum is fine. I've added you to my socials so you can stalk me to make sure I'm not a freak."

Arum giggled and then the camera turned to face her. She looked tired but very, very sated—eyes twinkling with mischief. "He is *abso-lutely* a freak," she said as she waggled her eyebrows scandalously. "I'm fine. I'm going to drink some coffee, make out with this guy a bit, maybe do him a couple more times—" Old Mate laughed in the background—"and then I'll message you. Love you. Oh! Also... highly recommend you don't go to work today. Take a four-day weekend will you? Go and rest. Or do something fun. Please? If not for you then for me? You deserve it. Love you."

Naya sent a heart reaction to the video message and accepted Mario's follow request. She made the very grown-up decision to ignore Arum's suggestion and worked outside on the balcony.

By the time the sun had travelled halfway across the sky and her enclosed balcony turned into a stifling little greenhouse, eight more pieces were chosen for the show.

She went back inside for a coffee refill when her phone buzzed. She'd been tagged in a comment under the image of her smoking in front of the giant Le Roy mural.

OH.EM.JAY: @SNMxx Permisi, boleh minta satu?

Naya's chest constricted. "You're joking," she breathed, as she clicked on the username. The profile pic was of Owen laughing, lips pulled back to show his perfect straight teeth, a baseball cap obscuring the top half of his face, but Naya recognised that mouth anywhere.

The top of his profile had a bright yellow banner: *Respond to this user's follow request.*

Naya couldn't tap *Accept* fast enough. She quickly scrolled through his posts. So many travel pictures. So many ridiculously hot selfies. She sent him a DM.

fourteen

MARIO WAS LATE TO MEET O AT JAVA JAVA—THE NEW COFFEE SHOP Mar and his older brother, Hendra, recently opened.

The hole-in-the-wall cafe had the feel of an old Melbourne bungalow's sleepout-turned-sunroom. The mismatched recycled window frames and indoor plants hanging from the ceiling reminded O of life back in Australia, *Before Naya*.

BN and *SN*; Naya was a red mark on his timeline, a dropped pin that pronounced an incontrovertible plot twist in his arc, and sitting in the tiny slice-of-Melbourne coffee shop in Jakarta felt... *aligned*, very appropriate for his life *Since Naya*.

He missed her. He fucking hated it.

He ordered his third cup of coffee just as Mario texted him.

MAR

Not gonna make it to breakfast mate. Soz. valid excuse tho-promise

O gritted his teeth. That fucker. That absolute fucking fucker.

OWEN:

You shit. I'm sitting here waiting for you. Could've let me know an hour ago

MAR:

NO, I couldn't 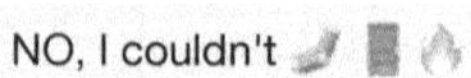

Oh. O ran his hand through his hair and let out a breath. Proverbial sock on the doorknob. Apparently, he and Mario had regressed to being twenty-two year olds living together in their old Fitzroy unit again.

Mario's quiet confidence had always been a drawcard, even back then. He was always meeting strangers—always bringing home some newly-made friend.

Oftentimes, O would arrive at the flat to find Mario at home with a few noisy guests, half of whom Mario had just met. But there was an openness about him that meant he'd know everything about them by the time the gathering ended. Mar knew how to put people at ease and O was always grateful to have him close by. O liked the energy of other people around him without having to make any effort to awkwardly engage with them if he didn't have the spoons to do so. Even when his introvert batteries were depleted and he needed to shut his bedroom door to the noise and chaotic energy in the living room, he relished knowing that life was happening on the other side, and if and when he was ready to rejoin them, he could and it would be okay.

Mario's affability also meant many folks spent the night in his bed, and O couldn't recall even one instance of him having intense arguments or uncomfortable disagreements with any of his lovers. He was respectful of everyone he met which meant when things drew to a natural close with the people he had flings with, everyone moved on without major fallout.

Basically, Mario was a lovable freak of nature.

The memories of their time in Melbourne were interrupted by Fabian, the douchey (but expert—O was loath to admit) barista of JAVA JAVA setting down O's strong flat white in front of him.

"Here's your long mac topped up," Fabian announced, a shit-eating grin plastered on his annoying face.

O rolled his eyes, disdain sweeping over his face. "Piss off with your Western Australian garbage language, Fabian."

Fabian howled with laughter. "Fuck—you Victorians act like you invented coffee," he called out as he swaggered back behind the counter.

OWEN:

Now I'm stuck at your cafe with Fabian who's calling my coffee filthy names. Fire him pls.

MAR:

Be nice to Fab. He's the best barista around. Won awards and shit

OWEN:

He started it.

MAR:

Talk later. Playing Wordle with a rad person. We already tried PENIS and VULVA and still haven't gotten a green or yellow letter! High stakes game. Shower sex if we get it in 4 tries.

OWEN:

You can't help yourself can you?

MAR:

BRO. I was ordering drinks at Le Roy when she grabbed me and stuck her tongue down my throat. How was I supposed to resist? Plus she's cute af

OWEN:

MAR:

Don't believe me? Look at Le Roy's socials!! LITERAL PROOF @leroyjakarta

He swiped over to the socials and went down the rabbit hole of images in which Mar had been tagged. What an adventure Mar'd found himself in less than twelve hours ago. So on brand.

He worked his way through the pics and found them—Mar and a familiar looking blue-haired femme pressed up against each other on the dancefloor among a throng of people. Mario's arms wrapped around her shoulders as she leaned her head back on his chest. She scrunched her nose puckishly as she grinned. Where did O know her from? He couldn't recall. Her colourful full-sleeve tattoo shone brightly from the camera flash. She really was *cute af*; definitely had a confident and seductive quality about her.

He felt left out as he scrolled through photo after photo of rowdy patrons lapping up the night. He tapped on a video taken from behind the bar. Mario and adorable Pixie-Goth were at one end of the bar, Mar running his hand along her arm as the camera panned from left to right and then, appearing in frame, leaning right over the bar as she waited her turn to order, was Naya.

He almost knocked his coffee off the table.

O scrolled back through the video. She was sweaty, long tangled hair sticking to her neck and shoulders. She pulled it absentmindedly into a messy bun, tying it up with a lock of her own hair and fanned herself with her hands. When she ordered her drink, she smiled seductively at the bartender—*another pang of envy*—and then she disappeared into the crowded dance floor.

He searched through more posts and found her in a video, dancing with the bartender by the DJ booth. Naya's hands reached above her head, hips swaying. The bartender eyed her with obvious interest and pulled her close to say something in her ear, and she tipped her head back and laughed. She replied—pressing against him—and then she pecked him lightly on the lips, and walked away.

O swallowed. He had no right to be jealous. Despite his feelings for her, he and Naya weren't anything. She was free to see anyone she wanted, but he couldn't help the little sting at the thought of her not waiting for him two nights before.

He continued swiping through to earlier in the night and discovered the photo of Pixie-Goth pulling in a very surprised Mario for a kiss—proof of Mario's claims. And there, next to Pixie-Goth making out with Mario, was Naya, staring on in amused surprise with the bartender. Pixie-Goth was friends with Naya. Of course she was.

The universe was *absolutely* fucking with him.

The last photos were taken outside in front of the DEWI hellscape mural, Naya holding a cigarette between her lips as she leaned against a dog-like demon biting a man in half, hands in her back pockets, her low-cut white tank tucked into her high-waisted ripped jeans, with white Adidas sneakers. She stood out against the deep red and black of the wall behind her—an angelic creature communing with sinners. Her round face was still pink and shiny from a hot and wild night.

The caption read:

DEWI + SRINAYA. What a combo x

O tapped the little tag button on the post for her username and there she was: SNMxx

Finally, a way to contact her.

@SNMxx Permisi, boleh minta satu?

He requested to follow her private account. Giddy with excitement, O waved at Fabian to order another coffee—a plain old double espresso to avoid any Perth-Melbourne rivalry. As he waited, he went back through the photos of Naya, saving his favourites.

And then a notification popped up—Srinaya had accepted his follow request and sent a DM.

fifteen

SNMXX:

I finished yet ANOTHER pack last night. I can't blame you this time and this displeases me...

OH.EM.JAY:

I'll make it up to you.

SNMXX:

I don't doubt that.

OH.EM.JAY:

Well, that sounds promising. 😏

Hi, by the way. Happy Friday.

SNMXX:

Hello to you too. 🙂

OH.EM.JAY:

You have an unforgettable singing voice. Loved your rendition of Close to Me. Remind me to book you for our next fundraiser

SNMXX:

🔔 I'll only agree if you're raising funds for the hearing impaired and every single person in the ballroom is deaf. Also cannot promise wine glasses and crystal chandeliers will survive the ordeal. Still game?

Aud Pitch

OH.EM.JAY:

Aaw. But I enjoyed your musical stylings so much

SNMXX:

Pfffft using the term "musical" veeeeery generously there, my dude. Just make sure you squeeze as much money out of the donors before you get me on stage.

OH.EM.JAY:

Perhaps I need an in-person encore to make up my mind? I watched that vid a couple of times but I'm out atm so the volume was low. Tbh I was mainly staring at your mouth

SNMXX:

Is esteemed benefactor and legacy director of MERAHPUTIH Mr Owen Jameson sexually harassing me? You're like my boss' boss' boss' boss' x infinity boss.

OH.EM.JAY:

...

SNMXX:

that was a joke, btw

Sorry — I forget that tone falls pretty flat over text and that you don't know me well enough to get my sense of humour

OH.EM.JAY:

you sure?

SNMXX:

Ohmygod yes. Promise

OH.EM.JAY:

Fuck, I was seriously worried

Guess I'll just have to get to know you better to understand your sense of humour then

SNMXX:

I guess so, Mr Jameson.

OH.EM.JAY:

Owen.

God—please don't call me Mr Jameson.

I can't be more than five years older than you and I doubt you call new friends by a title

SNMXX:

Untrue. Had a friend called Mistress Starla once. I got to know Mistress very well.

She even taught me a special language.

"Green", "Orange", "Red"

"Onomatopoeia"

OH.EM.JAY:

...

SNMXX:

OH.EM.JAY:

I'm gonna go out on a limb here and assume you're joking again

SNMXX:

Perhaps.

Here's a tip though: when you're strapped to a St Andrew's cross getting flogged, "Onomatopoeia" is a surprisingly difficult safeword to remember so make sure you choose an easy one.

OH.EM.JAY:

oh my god

SNMXX:

No, "oh my god" is rubbish. You'd say that too often and then the scene would be ruined. Start, stop, start, stop.

OH.EM.JAY:

Naya

SNMXX:

I'M your safeword????

OH.EM.JAY:

No, Naya, you are very much green to me.

SNMXX:

I'm sitting here trying to come up with some quippy remark to cut through the tension right now but I can't think of anything so I'll just say... that was very sweet.

OH.EM.JAY:

Feeling the tension on this end too. Maybe the best thing is to steer clear of S&M-related topics and other double entendres?

I'm sitting at a cafe right now and my jeans are feeling very restrictive.

SNMXX:

Hmm. What a nice image

OH.EM.JAY:

Don't think I didn't notice your username btw

SNMXX:

Excuse me! Those are my initials!

OH.EM.JAY:

sure

SNMXX:

Moving on...

You're out in public at a cafe wearing restrictive jeans. Where?

OH.EM.JAY:

At JAVA JAVA. You know it?

SNMXX:

Yeah I do. Great coffees

OH.EM.JAY:

Barista's a dick though

SNMXX:

You got beef with the barista???

OH.EM.JAY:

Friendly beef. He's friends with the owner, who is my best friend, although I'm seriously thinking of demoting him for blowing me off for brunch

SNMXX:

Oh no! That sucks. I'm sorry

OH.EM.JAY:

Nah don't be. If he had made it you and I wouldn't be DMing right now.

Anyway. You know him. He was at Le Roy last night as well. Mario?

Not sure if you were properly introduced to him since his mouth was suctioned to your pixie-goth friend's face the entire time.

SNMXX:

1. Her name is Arum but pixie-goth is a fair description

and 2. HOLY SHIT OLD MATE TROUT POUT IS YOUR BEST FRIEND????!!!!

OH.EM.JAY:

HA! Does he know you call him that?

SNMXX:

Oh yeah, I checked on Arum this morning to make sure she hadn't been flayed and dumped on the side of the road and they were still in bed.

He called me Tits McGee

OH.EM.JAY:

Um excuse me?

SNMXX:

and he plays Wordle, so I approve.

I don't think you'll be hearing from Mario for the rest of the weekend, I'm afraid. Arum has her tricksy pixie-goth ways...

OH.EM.JAY:

Let's circle back for a second to the whole "Tits McGee" thing

SNMXX:

Why? Jeans getting tight again, Owen?

OH.EM.JAY:

shut it.

and maybe.

I'm assuming this is some inside joke from last night?

SNMXX:

It was a very very good night

OH.EM.JAY:

Getting a severe case of the FOMOs rn 💀

You know the shittest part? I dropped Trout Pout off at Le Roy after we had dinner and then went home

SNMXX:

Really??? Why didn't you come in?

OH.EM.JAY:

Sensory overload.

I didn't have the spoons for a rowdy pub.

SNMXX:

Does that happen often?

OH.EM.JAY:

Sometimes. If I'm not careful my anxiety spikes.

SNMXX:

How are you feeling today?

OH.EM.JAY:

Better, thanks for asking.

SNMXX:

I'm glad. 😊

OH.EM.JAY:

Anyway, will follow Mario around like I'm his shadow from now on.

Should've known better than to leave him. Dude has a knack for attracting fun and interesting people.
Always has.

SNMXX:

Well, he attracted you to him so I believe it

OH.EM.JAY:

Wow.. thank you

Right.

I'm going to cut to the chase now.

We have about 9 hours before we have to be at Cinq-Huit

I'd like to see you before. Meet me somewhere?

SNMXX:

Cinq-Huit? That's tonight????

OH.EM.JAY:

LOL yes

SNMXX:

Is that... compulsory? 😊

OH.EM.JAY:

Endah would not be impressed if you didn't show.

SNMXX:

Ugh really?

OH.EM.JAY:

She'd punish you for sure.

SNMXX:

What kind of punishment?

OH.EM.JAY:

Endah has her ways

SNMXX:

I don't doubt that one bit! Would she take a hit out on me? Send some thugs my way? I can just imagine the contacts she has on her phone. Lol

OH.EM.JAY:

Maybe I'll offer my services and deal with you myself

SNMXX:

I'm not scared of you

OH.EM.JAY:

We've established that.

You *are* terrified of never feeling my hands on you again though, aren't you?

Of never finding out what it would be like to have me pressed against that lovely arse of yours

SNMXX:

Is that how you'd punish me, Owen?

By not touching me?

That seems a lot like self-torture

OH.EM.JAY:

It would 100% be torture. Is that what you want?

Because you've already succeeded if that's the case.

Seeing those images of you at Le Roy all hot and sweaty and sticky was fucking torturous.

Where were you the other night, Srinaya?

SNMXX:

Owen, I'm sorry about that.

Truly

OH.EM.JAY:

What happened?

SNMXX:

Honestly, I got scared.

I *am* scared.

OH.EM.JAY:

Of me?

SNMXX:

NO

God.

No.

OH.EM.JAY:

Then what?

SNMXX:

Look, I have some personal and professional trauma when it comes to gossip and bullying.

It got bad.

Really really bad. The police were called.

OH.EM.JAY:

Shit.

I'm sorry. That sounds horrible.

SNMXX:

It was. I don't want to talk about it.

OH.EM.JAY:

Of course. I understand

so... you're afraid of the implications of seeing me

of people spreading rumours?

SNMXX:

yes

OH.EM.JAY:

Ok

I don't want to complicate your life, Naya. If this is too much you just have to say so and I'll leave you alone.

SNMXX:

I don't want that 🙁

I made a mistake not meeting you the other night...

And I'm scared to meet you again

Both things can be true

Last night was torture for me too. You were all I
thought about.

I regret not waiting for you

OH.EM.JAY:

Let's talk about this. In person. Please.

Can we meet somewhere?

Anywhere, I don't care

As long as we can have some privacy.

SNMXX:

Ok... Come over.

sixteen

Owen DMed to say he was stuck in traffic, and he was sorry, and that he was only fifteen minutes away as the crow flies, and he wished he owned a helicopter.

Naya replied with, *Calm down, Fifty Shades,* while cursing all the other drivers on the roads.

He said he'd be there as soon as he could.

It took him a whole hour, and her insides bubbled over with impatience when she heard his car engine switch off.

She opened her door just as Owen stepped out of his absurdly beat-up four-wheel drive. A man who could afford anything driving around in what looked like a stunt car from an early '80s cop show? In Jakarta, of all places? It was utterly ridiculous. She loved it.

He sauntered up her driveway with long purposeful strides. Naya's cheeks burned like a teenager's when his gaze swept down her body.

He climbed her front steps, taking two at a time, and she suddenly stiffened as if her limbs weren't hers and she had no idea how to stand. She fussed with her clothes, fiddling with the knot on her tshirt.

God—she was as utterly ridiculous as his car.

She blinked up at Owen when he stood, all intense and sexy, before her. "It took forever," he said, pouting.

The impatient bubbles inside her spun around, sinking down, down, down into deep dark places.

Owen reached out his big hand. He moved forward with slow deliberate movements as if Naya was some flighty prey he wanted to snare. She went taut again as he neared.

"You're wearing green," he noted, kissing both her cheeks softly. The rough stubble rasped wonderfully against her skin. His breath was hot against the shell of her ear and she bit her lip to stifle a moan.

She lingered against him on the second kiss. "So I am," she sighed, her voice low and breathy.

When she looked down, she was surprised to find her hand holding a fistful of his grey shirt—so dark in contrast to the honey in his eyes that glowed like tumbled amber illuminated by light.

She laughed and let go, shaking her head absentmindedly as if to shake off her embarrassment. Owen chuckled quietly too, and the lopsided smile that appeared on his face as he shuffled back mirrored her own nervousness. Arms crossing over her chest, she rested against the door frame. "Your ride," she commented as she nodded towards his car.

Owen turned to look lovingly at the light blue Ford, with its large patch of paint missing from its hood. "Ah, yes. The trusty steed," he said proudly. "Isn't he a beaut?"

"I love it. So unexpected."

"Not *it—him*."

Naya put her hands up. "Sorry. *Him.*"

Owen looked back at the car again and paused. "He was my dad's. He's definitely on his last legs, but I just can't get rid of him."

She watched him carefully, at the way his lips thinned and forehead wrinkled, appreciating the small token of vulnerability he offered her. Hearing him share a hurt so openly made him feel not so out of reach.

He turned back to face her with an expectant look in his eyes, and Naya was struck with a heavy sense of responsibility. The direction of this relationship rested on her shoulders. She should have been grateful for Owen giving her control—should have felt safer knowing today, they would go as far as *she* wanted. Part of her softened at the thought while the other resented the burden.

Naya's faltering resolve must have become visible because Owen's smile faded and he leaned away. "Have you changed your mind?" he asked. "I'll go if you want?"

He took another half step backward, and she panicked at the thought of him turning around, leaving her. She blurted, "No, please—" before catching herself.

Okay. So perhaps she wanted it more than she resented the burden. She groaned and covered her face with her hands. "This was easier over DMs." She shook her head, face still buried—unwilling to look at him.

Owen huffed and peeled her hands away. He ran his knuckle over her temple and then unfurled his hand to press his palm on the side of her face. His thumb brushed the corner of her mouth and her lids closed. She had never known her lips to feel so sensitive but at that moment, she needed him to stroke them. She angled her head up to invite a deeper caress, and Owen obliged, running the pad of his thumb over her top lip, and then bottom. When he caressed both together, Naya kissed his thumb. He leaned down to kiss her brow and press that delicious stubbly cheek against hers again.

"Let me in?"

She took his hand.

⸸

O fought the urge to bolt up the driveway and grab her. He balled his hands into fists at the sight of Naya's tattooed shoulder poking out of her tshirt, the fabric thin enough to see her emerald-coloured bra. *You are very much green to me.* He wondered if that had been a conscious choice or another wonderful coincidence.

She smelt so sweet. Earthy. He wanted to pin her against her front door, press his face into her neck and breathe her in. Maybe if he inhaled deep enough her scent would meld with his cells and never fade. He swallowed his sigh and picked up the grocery bag he brought with him. She looked at it quizzically.

"Food," he answered. "I didn't know if you'd eaten. I ordered some *mie goreng* and *martabak* from JAVA JAVA, but wasn't sure if you wanted that so stopped at Clementine's to get chocolate croissants, bagels, camembert, honey-cured ham, cream cheese, bacon bits. And wine. Red and white. I don't know your preference."

Naya made a sound of delight and bounced on the balls of her feet. "I'm starving. Thank you."

He removed his boots and socks, placing them neatly by the door, and then looked around Naya's split-level townhouse, filled with a mix of traditional Indonesian furniture and modern pieces, creating a space that was entirely her own. Large painted canvases—many still unframed—leaned against the wall in the hallway next to her staircase.

She led the way up.

They passed her bedroom and he peeked inside. The scent of vanilla and sandalwood wafted out. He bit his lip as his eyes darted around, taking inventory—the soft furnishings in sedate tones: white, cream, gold, and silver, while the artwork splashed the space with bright colours.

Her mattress lay upon a bulky teak frame—the tall headboard intricately carved with an Indonesian floral design. Her white bed sheets softened the overpowering red-brown wood. There was something endearing about how her bed was haphazardly made... God—he wanted to wrap himself in those sheets and never leave.

"Feed me first," Naya said huskily as if she'd heard his thoughts, and O did a double-take. Was that a promise of what was to come?

Naya's mouth curved upwards as she took his hand and pulled him up to the third floor. The way she looked over her shoulder at him mischievously, long dark hair framing that adorable plump face, *killed* him. From this vantage point, three steps behind her, he watched her round arse and wide hips sway with every step she took. That band of soft brown skin between the end of her tshirt and the beginning of her linen pants made his fingers itch.

The kitchen island was cluttered with sketchbooks, papers, and notes. Naya started clearing away her things without a hint of embarrassment. She wasn't apologetic about the piles of books stacked up in corners, or how her dining table had been converted into a workbench, covered with the tools of a working artist. This was, after all, her space; she was extending to him the privilege of sharing it with her.

"Your home is wonderful. It feels like you."

Naya's brows hooded over her eyes and she wrinkled her nose at him. "How do you know what feels like me?"

O shrugged, unpacking the canvas bag. "I did my research—remember? Your last show in Melbourne, the one that juxtaposed traditional Indonesian imagery with modern mixed media? The collages were my favourite. All that white textured negative space balanced with smooth bright colours. Your home feels the same. Balanced."

Naya didn't answer and her narrowed eyes morphed into something else. Intrigue, maybe? She nodded her head slowly, absorbing his words, studying him and mentally taking notes.

"It feels a lot like DEWI's work, actually."

Naya twitched. "You think my work is like DEWI's?" she asked incredulously.

"Not in technique, but something *feels* very similar. I think… you're both a little angry."

Confusion swept across her face before she locked it away. He asked, "Did I offend you? Do you not like them? Because you should know I'm a serious fan of their stuff."

She seemed to soften before answering. "No, their work is great. I'm flattered, I guess. Thank you."

"That Drewery Alley piece that you helped with…" O did a chef's kiss, and then ripped a chunk of pastry off one of the chocolate croissants and ate it.

The five-storey tall mural featured a stylised naked femme, legs splayed open, back arched in an orgasm with the stars and planets pouring out of their vulva in a rainbow of speckled colours. Sexy. Confronting. Beautiful. "What part did you help with?"

Naya bit her lip and grinned, her cute little crooked tooth in full view. She popped some bacon bits into her mouth as she answered airily, "The cosmos."

He swallowed, the salty butter lingering on his lips and tongue. O couldn't help but picture Naya on the side of the building. He wondered if she gushed when she came. If, when she closed her eyes at the first wave of pleasure that crested, constellations flashed behind her eyelids.

He cleared his throat. He knew Srinaya was keenly aware of what he was thinking by the way the corners of her mouth pulled up ever-so-slightly. Her little pink tongue slid across her full upper lip. She leaned forward, elbows resting against the kitchen island again, tits pressed together to show off her deep cleavage. She licked her fingertips clean of the taste of bacon, her eyes never leaving his.

"Careful, Srinaya," he warned in a sing-song voice.

"Are you going to punish me?" she enquired innocently. Her eyes were full of mischief. She bit her thumbnail.

O wrapped his hand around her wrist, bending over the kitchen island towards her and pulled her hand closer. "You definitely deserve to be punished," he commented, more breath than voice. He took her thumb into his mouth and sucked, running his tongue along the length of it, tasting the saltiness. Naya's breath caught and heat coloured her cheekbones. The feel of the soft pad against his tongue made his cock pulsate. His lips smacked when he popped her thumb out of his mouth and swallowed. Naya blinked rapidly, long lashes casting feathery shadows on her cheek. "Mmm," he hummed.

She inhaled sharply, breath catching again before swallowing nervously. He let go of her wrist and cradled his chin in his hand, and gave her a placid smile. Naya still couldn't speak.

And then he forced himself to move away. "I need a fucking drink."

⊥

"Wine glasses?"

Naya's mind kicked back into gear. She huffed out a breath to focus on anything but that warm mouth wrapped around her thumb and opened the cupboard next to him. She rose onto the tips of her toes, reaching into the back of the cupboard above her, one leg bent to keep steady. Her fingers grazed a glass stem but she couldn't grasp it. She strained as she pushed herself up higher before giving up with a frustrated sigh. She lowered her heels and looked up at Owen who was barely holding in a laugh, hands in his pockets—ankles crossed. Naya pouted. "Help, please."

"That was fucking adorable," he chuckled, hand over his heart. He grabbed the wine glasses and handed them to her. "May I suggest *not* putting them so far in the back since you're so little?"

She stared at him blankly as if he'd spoken a different language. "*Little,*" she repeated—bemused. "How novel."

She placed the glasses on the island and approached him, standing upright. Naya was a couple of inches taller than the average Indonesian woman, and probably close to double in weight—*Little... how ridiculous,* she thought—but she still didn't reach Owen's chin. She looked down at her body and compared the widths of their shoulders. He was definitely broader there. Her hips were much wider than his though, and where she had a round belly, Owen was a trim muscular column.

He'd seated himself on the edge of the counter, watching as she studied him, but then he pushed off the bench and straightened his spine, towering over her. "What are you doing?"

He stood so fucking close now—the hard angles of his shoulders, neck, and jaw, the severity of his brow and the straight line of his nose reminding her of the austere brutalist buildings that were his legacy. She felt the same wonderment, staring up into those eyes as she did when she walked through the doors of Purnama. God—she couldn't help but feel important when he looked at her like that. So much care, and hunger, and maybe even a little bit of danger.

Naya let out the softest moan—breathy and low—and Owen's chest expanded. His gaze swept downward over her tits and he gulped. She wanted to summon more reactions, watch him war with himself as he tried to keep his body in check. She lifted her chin, lengthening her neck and casually combing her fingers through her hair. He loved her hair; she'd caught him staring in fascination as she tied it up.

"Srinaya," Owen gruffed, his tone caught between a reprimand and a plea.

"Yes?" she answered sweetly.

He made the smallest gasp when Naya's tshirt rode up. His hands fisted at his sides, knuckles turning white.

Naya's eyes fixed on his mouth. He tensed his jaw, and she watched, utterly mesmerised as his pupils dilated, the inky blackness and gold overpowering the grey. "We should probably talk..." His voice was rough; he was trying so hard to be sensible.

Naya reached for his shirt, fiddling with a button halfway down, and she blinked up at him. "I know, Owen," she said, her own voice almost hollow—too distracted.

"God," he rasped, eyes rolling back before he squeezed his lids shut, "hearing you say my name..."

Owen grasped her waist and led her backwards. She gave a little yip when she bumped the counter behind her. Owen loomed over. Her pulse thrummed. His hands rested on the countertop on either side of her, and she *did* feel little, caged by his broad shoulders, thick arms and solid torso. She found it harder to maintain eye contact. "Turn around, please." His tone was clear; it wasn't a request—it was a command.

"No."

Owen's eyes cooled slightly as he searched her face. "Is that a red *no*, or a green *no*?" he asked, his finger trailing the strap of her bra.

The feel of his finger—one fucking finger—on her skin felt like he was caressing an exposed nerve. Painful, wonderful, terrifying... *More* was all she could think of. "A green *no*," she exhaled as she moved her head to invite him to touch more of the sensitive skin of her shoulder.

He nodded, those bright eyes ablaze again, placing his palm flat just below her nape and slowly caressing upwards. She rested her weight against him, becoming pliant, when all of a sudden, Owen wrapped his hand around the back of her neck, placed his other hand on her hip, and firmly whirled her around. His strength and quickness made her gasp, and when he pressed his pelvis into her ass to pin her to the counter, she couldn't help the moan that came out.

"Didn't I warn you to be careful?" Owen's voice was low and

guttural as if it came from deep down in his belly instead of his throat. He caged her with his giant body again, hands curled into giant fists on either side of her.

"I'm not always good at following orders," Naya said. She put her hands right next to his on the counter and his long fingers captured hers, gripping roughly.

"Not always good," Owen repeated, blankly. "I believe that." Owen brought her wrists together, holding both with one hand, the other sweeping her hair aside so he could press his cheek to the join of her jaw and ear.

A breathy laugh escaped her and she teased, "I bet you're very good at giving orders, aren't you, Mr Jameson—*esteemed benefactor?*"

Naya felt it; the moment she said those last two words, the heat between them flickered and died out. He peeled his stubbly chin from her neck, his body stiff and distant. Naya looked back at him and her heart sank when she saw the genuine hurt in his eyes. He looked beautiful though, with his cheeks all pink, highlighting his freckles, and a shiny film of sweat on his forehead and the bridge of his nose.

"Owen, I—"

Owen raised his palms to stop her. "No, it's okay. We need to talk about this," he said, attempting to make his voice sound less gruff. He cleared his throat.

He tried to laugh and shrug off his embarrassment, and it made him look so vulnerable that she reached for him. She tugged on the bottom of his shirt and murmured up at him, "Please look at me."

Owen closed his eyes, took a deep breath, and when he opened them the stormy grey had returned. A wall separated them now, and it was all her fault.

Shit—this was getting complicated.

He shoved his hands deep into his pockets as if he was scared to touch her. Naya held onto the soft grey fabric—so close to the shade of his eyes. She came up onto the tips of her toes, arms raised to wrap around his neck.

When he melted into her touch, his arms enveloping her shoulders, she buried her face into the crook of his neck. His faint body odour mixed deliciously with his cologne. God—he smelt so right. So famil-iar. "I'm sorry. I misspoke."

"No you didn't," he answered. "We really should talk about this. This is a big deal to you." Naya opened her mouth to argue but Owen spoke first. "It *is*, Naya. It's a problem for you."

He unwrapped her arms from his neck, kissed both of her knuckles and stepped out of her embrace. "So let's talk about this, yeah? You asked me to feed you. I'll do that. And we'll talk."

Naya nodded, feeling a little raw. He cleared his throat again and grinned at her sheepishly. "Where's your bathroom? I need to douse myself with cold water to get rid of this hard-on."

seventeen

O BENT OVER THE SINK AND CUPPED COLD WATER IN HIS HANDS. HE RAN his fingers through his hair. The cool, wet strands felt amazing on the back of his neck—a sobering jolt to the system. *Fuck.* He really wanted a shower. He stared at himself in Naya's mirror.

That was close. The way she went soft in his arms, yielding. So fucking wonderful. And when he bent down to bury his face in her neck? He swore he caught the faint scent of her arousal. She *did* want this. Or, at least, her body did, but that didn't matter at all if she couldn't work through her anxiety.

Gossiping and bullying escalating to the police being called. Jesus Christ. He couldn't even imagine the terror. He frowned at the thought.

He looked at all her products on her bathroom vanity to distract himself, unscrewing jars of creams and smelling them. He picked up a pretty bottle of body oil with gold shimmer powder settled at the bottom and gave it a shake, watching the powder float through the oil, turning it into liquid gold. Unscrewing the top, he gave it a sniff, and his eyes rolled back as he sighed. Vanilla, jasmine and sandalwood. This was Naya. This, minus that spicy natural scent of hers.

He put a few drops on his hands, rubbed them together and inhaled. He memorised the label.

O's shirt collar was damp, as were the shoulders and edges of his rolled-up sleeves. He looked like a fucking disaster. But he'd been in her bathroom long enough; any longer and Naya would think he was doing something unseemly. God, he needed to take the edge off. One more splash of water on the face, and then he walked back out into her kitchen.

Naya faced away from where he entered, sitting on her kitchen island and eating what was left of O's chocolate croissant. Her feet rested on the bar stool tucked underneath the marble benchtop. She'd tied her hair high above her head and the short curls at the back of her neck were damp like his; obviously she'd needed a cold sobering jolt to the system too.

When O rounded the island to her side, she perked up and touched her lips as she swallowed. She looked truly happy to see him, face beaming, and it took all of his strength not to move the bar stool out of the way so he could nestle his hips between her thighs and hold her. Instead, he kept a little bit of distance—still close enough for her to touch him if she wanted to reach out—and gestured to the spread of food in front of him.

"So, what would you like?" he asked. "Some *martabak*? *Mie goreng*? Honey cured ham and camembert bagel? Cream cheese bagel with—" He held up the container that *was* full of bacon bits before he went to freshen up. He raised his eyebrows at her.

Naya shrugged as she reached past him for the container of ham, picking a few slices with her fingers.

"You took too long in the bathroom," she pouted, tilting her head back slightly to drop the slices in her mouth. O huffed at her, shaking his head, and she laughed mischievously. "I'm actually enjoying just picking at all the meat, but will you share a slice of cream cheese bagel with me?"

O grumbled playfully. "Cannot believe you ate all the bacon," he said, slicing a bagel in half, and then halving it again.

Naya leaned back lazily, completely unapologetic. "I'll make it up to you," she said with a soft smile, crossing her legs.

He couldn't tell if she was being coy, or if it was just a passing comment. A kind of flutter appeared in his stomach, followed by a pang of annoyance. He put down the knife and rubbed his forehead before running his fingers through his damp hair. When his eyes met hers he frowned, and Naya's smile disappeared.

"I didn't mean—" she answered, suddenly aware of how her words sounded. "Well, no—that's not true..." Her cheeks flushed slightly. "I kind of did mean it that way. Shit. I've made this really messy, haven't I?"

O didn't respond. He leaned both hands on the counter, feeling a rising anger—not at Naya, but at the root cause of her doubt. If he ever found out who'd hurt her…

His violent thoughts were interrupted when she said, "I'm not trying to be difficult," in a small voice.

He exhaled sharply as he pressed his hip to her knee. She leaned closer, and O tucked her into his side, her cheek resting against his chest. "I'm sorry. I'm frustrated. Not at you, but at this whole situation. It shouldn't have to be this difficult, but it is, and that's not your fault."

Srinaya wrapped her arms around O's torso, gripping his shirt. Fuck—this was lovely, her holding him tightly, finding comfort in him. She purred into his chest and then looked up at him, dark brown eyes focused. She took a slow, deep breath in and then hummed her breath out. "Okay. Let's lay all our cards out on the table."

He nodded and pulled out the seat next to hers to sit.

Naya still perched on her benchtop, little feet tapping on the barstool in front of her. She angled her body to face him, her knees together, hands clasped around them. She looked him square in the eye. "I want you," she said, face serious, no-nonsense.

O heard fanfare in his brain, envisioned confetti and one of those second line New Orleans bands going round the block.

"And I want you," he answered, and gave a lazy shrug as he spread the cream cheese on the bagel. "It's that simple for me. But I know it's not that simple for you."

Naya shook her head in agreement. She restlessly picked at a nail as she began, "So the thing is, working at MP hasn't been without its challenges. Don't get me wrong—I love working there. It's been a dream of mine for ages. But... some people have been difficult, and—I don't know." She rubbed the back of her neck. "It feels like it has nothing to do with my experience as a curator and more about *me*—my own artwork, my size, that I'm not full-Indonesian… I'm honestly surprised they approved my proposal for *Heartbreak*. I know they were in a bind with the whole Alex Visser thing but I'm sure there were other proposals they could have chosen." Naya paused. "I bet Endah charmed the board into letting me have it."

He nodded, silently agreeing, as he passed Naya her half of the bagel. She took a bite and let out a little *Mmmm*.

They both sat quietly as they ate and O couldn't help praying for more moments like this—sitting together in her kitchen. He wanted to do this with her every morning—fantasised about lazy weekends spent together, eating their fill of bacon bits and chocolate croissants after a morning of pleasuring each other.

"Anyway," she continued when she finished eating, "Surya said they gave me the show to shut me up." A flash of annoyance passed over her face, but then she shook her head to let it fall away. "And whatever. I'll take it. And it'll be great because I know what I'm doing."

Naya rested her chin on her hand. O didn't say a word, wanting to let her continue without interruptions. "So many of the folks at MP are watching me closely. And I know most of it's just curiosity—not some Surya-esque grand scheme to see me fail—" Her nose wrinkled at Surya's name—"but I feel like I have a lot of eyes on me right now. And you obviously hate me saying it—" she said gently, nervously—"but you're the most *esteemed benefactor*. A legacy director. Like, you know they call you the *Golden God of MERAHPUTIH*, right? It's who you are."

O clenched his jaw. He bristled at the labels that separated them, his voice edged with sharpness. "No—it's not *who* I am. It's *what* I am, and it's only one small part of me."

Naya didn't reply.

Surya. Fuck—O hated that Surya's name was being mentioned in a conversation about their relationship. *He* started this, hadn't he? *He* was the one who put that fucking title in Naya's head.

O's shoulders tensed. "I do hate it, Naya. They feel like such awful words when they come out of your mouth. I hated it when Surya used them against you that day on the steps, but honestly? It feels like you're using them against me and I hate that even more."

Naya's shoulders drooped. She put a hand on his cheek and brushed her thumb along his eyebrow. "I'm sorry."

He nuzzled into her hand and kissed her palm. Her eyes stared off at nothing, recalling a memory. Slowly, her brows drew together and she gritted her teeth. "But it's opened up old wounds," Naya said—her voice haunted. Another pause as her eyes went red and glassy. "And it was all wrapped up in people accusing me of sleeping my way to the top... which was untrue." Naya closed her eyes. She looked so small as she crossed her arms and curled in on herself a little.

"Lovely one," he said softly as he wrapped his arms around her, landing a soft kiss on her bare shoulder, "Would you like me to send Endah's thugs to sort them out?"

A startled laugh bubbled out of her—such a wonderful sound to his ears. "I can just imagine what she's planning for Visser. I'm scared for him." She giggled as she leaned her head on his chest.

Her head angled slightly into his shoulder and she inhaled deeply, taking in his scent. Her body relaxed into his, and she looked at him, her face close. Naya lifted her chin and pressed her lips ever so gently onto his. O let her take the lead, her kiss slow and careful. It wasn't fervent like the times before; this was a request for comfort. She licked the inside of his lip, sighed into his mouth, and then pulled away. "If you had been some random gallery visitor hitting on me that day on the steps, I would've been in your bed that same night," she confessed, her voice sulky and wanting.

O got hard instantly at her admission.

"Those are my cards," Naya concluded. "So, show me yours. Tell me explicitly what you want."

Explicitly. O perked up. He reached for the forgotten bottle of red wine and poured them a drink. And then he gestured for Naya to lift her knees up, and moved over to the barstool in front of her. He gently lowered her legs back down, her feet resting on the tops of his thighs. He passed her a wine and they clinked their glasses together and sipped. Her round face looked so lovely from below as she watched him, leaning her head on her shoulder. Naya bit her lip as she smiled down at him, patiently waiting for him to speak, taking another sip. He loved the way her lips puckered together at the aftertaste of the pinot noir.

This *is what I want,* he thought.

She raked her fingers through his hair. His lids closed as he let out a soft purr. Naya bent down to kiss his temple. "You smell so nice," she whispered.

O couldn't help his laugh. He sat up to look at her, his arms resting on her knees, and asked, "Srinaya, how explicit do you *really* want me to be?"

At that question, the hollow of her neck flexed as she inhaled through her mouth and then swallowed. She took a massive gulp of her wine to steel herself. "*Explicitly* clear," she said. "Convince me."

O lit up at her last words.

She wanted this—*him.* She just needed a little push. "Alright," he said, taking an equally big gulp of wine and putting his glass aside. "You love the way I smell, lovely one? Where I'm sitting, I can smell that shimmery gold body oil you wear." She blinked and he clarified, "I was playing with your products in the bathroom before." He shrugged. "It was either that or jerk off, and the latter felt really dirty, and not in a good way." Naya's mouth fell open and she squeaked, turning bright red at his confession. He grinned devilishly as he continued, "But there's this spicy scent you have—that your skin has. Your natural scent. It's earthy and warm... almost like cinnamon." He took her wrist and pressed his nose to her pulse point, eyes closed to allow his sense of smell to take over. His brow furrowed in pleasure. "And on top of that vanilla, sandalwood, jasmine and cinnamon," he murmured, "I can smell how wet you are. How wet you've been this entire time." She stiffened a little—blushed an even deeper red, and her knees instinctively pressed together.

He shook his head and came forward. "Don't be embarrassed," he breathed. "It's the best fucking scent in the world." He carefully wedged his hands between her knees and pushed them apart slightly, his fingers sliding up her thigh. "Explicitly, Naya, I want to bury my face in every curve and crevice of you. You make it difficult to behave; I'm trying so hard. What I want is to know everything there is to know about you. I want to learn your favourite food, and songs, and movies... What pisses you off. What makes you cry. Who broke your heart. Who your favourite artists are. I want to get wasted and dance with you at Le Roy. I want to watch you paint and create... And now that I know what your pussy smells like, I want to know what it tastes like—*feels* like. What you sound like when you come. I want to do so many fucking filthy things to you, Srinaya. I want everythi—"

He didn't finish the sentence, his tongue thick and dry from his ridiculous confession. He swallowed and rubbed his face with both hands, hiding his embarrassment. "Shit," he muttered under his breath.

But when he looked up at Naya, her brows were raised in surprise, deep brown eyes turned black with arousal. She leaned her body towards him, hand pressed to her chest. She looked *heartened*. And then she whined his name and seized his shirt roughly to pull him onto his feet, barstool scraping back. O stood between her thighs and her legs opened wider to clamp against his hips. Her hands shook as she pulled his body to her, unbuttoning his shirt.

"Put me out of my fucking misery, Naya. Choose me. I'll be good to you. I promise."

Naya's breath was ragged, frantic, as she wrapped her legs tighter around his waist. Her fingers gripped his scalp, and she pulled his face down to hers and sucked on his bottom lip. O grunted in response.

"I want you right now. I want it all *right now*. That's the only answer I can give you. Please, Owen, help me forget," she moaned.

eighteen

Naya's fingers splayed on either side of Owen's jaw as their tongues twisted together, mouths hungry and breaths intermingling.

"Yes, yes. Anything you want," he vowed between kisses, the words said with a growl, his chest vibrating against hers.

Owen's shirt was unbuttoned and Naya desperately pawed at the stupid fabric to rid him of it completely, tossing it far, far away. A guttural laugh came out of him, and all of a sudden his long fingers were on her sides and sliding upwards heavily against her skin, taking her tshirt up with them. Naya's top was wrenched over her head and tossed away with his shirt.

They both paused to admire each other. He stood still, confidently, enjoying her slow perusal of him. Naya swallowed at the sight of Owen's lovely tanned skin, so very pleased to find freckles sprinkled over his shoulders and chest. She played connect-the-dots with the darker ones, tracing a finger over them.

That half-joking comment Ravi made at *Pak* Mudi's—about Owen looking like an Ancient Greek statue—wasn't far off. He was pure muscle; his broad shoulders framed well-defined pectorals that were covered in soft brown hair. She'd touched his stomach before under his clothes, but to see his golden skin, stretched tight over his abdominals, made her lose her breath. Her eyes lingered on the muscular vee that slanted down into the waistband of his jeans. Her brain short-circuited.

"You're beautiful," Naya blurted. She blinked up at him.

Owen's eyes darkened, and his nostrils flared. "Me?" he said with an incredulous look on his face. "Look at *you*." His head tilted as he studied her.

They were opposites; Owen was sharp muscular angles while she was all curves. He ran two fingers down her chest and between her cleavage. "So soft," he breathed. He caressed the swell of her breast with his knuckles, and Naya pulled her shoulders back in a silent request for more. "Jesus, Srinaya," he commented. "*Look* at you," he repeated.

He placed his palm flat on her chest and stroked her with a feather-light touch. Naya sighed, leaning her head back. He hooked his thumb under her bra strap and pulled it off her shoulder and did the same to the other. She flashed him a naughty smile as she asked, "Since you're all about fairness, would you like me to take this off?"

Owen's beautiful full lips curved into a wicked grin and he laughed again. "For the sake of fairness, yes please."

She reached back and undid the hooks, and pulled the emerald green fabric away from her, dropping it on the floor. She placed her hands on the counter, pushing her tits forward. Her nipples were painfully hard, and the cool air on her exposed skin made goosebumps appear.

Owen went completely quiet as he took her in. At the sight of her silver nipple piercings, he licked his lips and swallowed. His eyes flicked up to hers and he dipped his chin as if to warn her of what was to come. His hands swept over her tits, down her abdomen and around to settle under the waistband of her underwear just above her ass—and he pulled her towards him roughly, angling her pelvis forward. She whimpered at his heavy-handedness, at how she had to lean back because of the angle of her hips. She rested on her elbows and he bent over her, the waves of his hair falling over his face. She reached up to sweep his hair away, and he pressed into her touch.

She was caged under him *again*; the top of Owen's thighs pressed against the edge of her stone bench with her legs on either side of his hips. There was no mistaking how hard his cock was under those jeans, pressed against her pussy.

He brought his hand up to his gorgeous face to lick his thumb, coating it with his spit, and rubbed her nipple. She gasped as she watched him brush the soft pad in circles over the tip and then he blew on the cold wet of his spit on her skin, and her nipple hardened and pebbled even more, and her eyes rolled back as she let out a low moan. And then he bent his head down to take her other nipple into his mouth, sucking and licking, and the warmth between her legs got hotter and wetter.

Owen kissed his way up her chest—his rough stubble tickling and burning—and he nibbled on the delicate skin of her neck. His throat rumbled as he ran his tongue along her collarbone, and then, without warning, he sank his teeth into her shoulder. Hard.

Naya yelped as her spine went taut and tears formed instantly. She squeezed her eyes shut and the saltwater fell down her cheeks.

She couldn't think; forgot how to breathe. The pain pulsed through her—sharp at first, fading to a heavy ache that settled deep inside her pussy. And then Owen was sucking on her nipples again, and she didn't know what to do. She wanted to hit him and scratch him for hurting her, and beg him to fuck her and hurt her again.

When she opened her eyes, Owen's bright eyes searched her face, and she inhaled sharply, bringing air and his scent back into her lungs, her brain still aware of the waning throb at her neck. Naya was clutching him tightly—their chests pressed together. She felt strange—confused. She wanted to cry. She frowned—was she drunk? Her body was heavy, boneless.

"Did that help you forget?" he asked, breathing into the shell of her ear. Owen kissed her tears away and nuzzled the spot where he bit her, running his lips over her scorching skin. "Oh, Naya, you're so pretty when you're overcome," he whispered.

Naya blinked—tried letting his words sink in. "*Fuck*—Owen," Naya groaned, and she collapsed back on the cold kitchen counter.

Instinct took over. Her hand slid over her belly and down, into her underwear. She parted her pussy lips, slipped her fingers inside, arched her back and moaned. *"Please,"* she whined.

Naya registered a deep gravelly laugh as Owen pulled her hand away and said, "Not yet. I have more to explore."

He took her fingers in his mouth and sucked on them, moaning in approval. She watched on as he licked her fingers clean—as his whole body tensed. His lashes fluttered shut and he rolled his head back. His eyes snapped open—jaw set as he pulled her to sit up.

"Take me to your bed."

†

Jesus fuck—

Witnessing Srinaya writhe on her kitchen counter, unable to control herself as her hand explored between her legs was one of the hottest things O had ever seen. And finally getting to taste her sweet and salty juices made his pulse throb painfully in his cock, his balls feeling tight and full.

He helped her slide off the island, revelling in the jiggle of her tits and belly, and held her hand as they walked out of the kitchen and down her stairs. Her brain was fuzzy still; she leaned her shoulder against the walls as she walked down the steps carefully, giggling like she was drunk.

She led the way, looking up at him, those gorgeous apple cheeks ruddy. Her eyes and nose were still red from when he bit her and she had cried; as soon as he'd done it, he was terrified he'd made a huge mistake, but the way she bowed her spine, and the strong scent of her arousal encouraged him.

Naya pulled him into her bedroom and turned to face him. She stood by her beautiful carved bed, expectant—all golden-brown skin and tattoos and smooth curves, lovely tits heavy and round, and invit-ing. And those little nipples with silver bars through them. Fuck—what a wonderful surprise that was. And her tattoos, the mix of large pieces done professionally and the smattering of little stick 'n' pokes —some of which he would *definitely* ask her about later—made her so fucking beyond compare that he didn't know what to do with himself.

She still wore her black pants and underwear which was absolutely unacceptable. "I want you naked, lovely one."

Naya didn't question him. She shimmied out of her black pants, tossing them onto her armchair. She stood straight again, and O's breath caught at the sight of her high-waisted panties. She moved to take them off but O stopped her. "Wait," he said. "Turn around please."

She obeyed, turning her sinuous body away from him.

And then he saw it—the intricate tattoo in the middle of her lower back. Orchids. Eight of them. He *had* seen them that night in the hotel room. Still… it didn't mean anything. It wasn't proof they'd had sex.

But—*Fuck*. He had to stop. Tell her before there was no turning back.

"Naya…"

He came forward to pull her around, just as she looked over her shoulder at him, biting her lip. "Is it time to take these off yet?" she asked teasingly, her thumbs hooked under the waistband of her panties, pulling them down ever-so-slightly over the curve of her arse.

The blood pumping reason into his brain drained downwards into his cock. He shook his head. "Not yet."

O neared her, gently pushing her forward to bend her torso over her bed, arse up. Her breathing shallowed, and she pressed her cheek to the white linen sheets to look up at him. Her eyes were bright, excited, ready. He ran his palm over her smooth tattooed skin, and kissed her shoulder, and then her cheek.

"I've fantasised about you bent over like this so many times," he said quietly, his hand roving over her arse cheeks and under between her legs.

Her eyes closed and she widened her stance to give him more access. He was so pleased to feel how damp her panties were. "Don't move," O murmured, as he crouched down behind her and palmed her pussy over the wet fabric. "What a view, Naya," he commented, enjoying her scent, the sound of her ragged breath, and the sight of her arse covered in stretchy green lace.

And then he couldn't wait any longer—*had* to see her pussy. He pulled her underwear off, guiding them over her arse and down those brown dimpled thighs and they dropped to the floor. She stepped out of them, still bent at the waist. O took them and stuffed them in the back pocket of his jeans. "I'm keeping these," he declared, and Naya huffed out a sweet little laugh.

From where he was, Naya's lovely pussy, with its puffy brown lips and sprinkling of dark pubic hair was perfect—just like everything else about her. He didn't know why he was surprised. Or maybe it wasn't surprise at all, but utter awe that what he'd imagined wasn't even as perfect as the reality of her. And he said so under his breath, and she gripped her white sheets, blushed and said, "Thank you," ever-so-quietly.

He settled on his knees and stroked her with the back of his hand. Naya melted into his touch. He gently ran his finger between to part her lips, and exhaled sharply at the beautiful dusky pink of her clit and opening. "So wet and inviting," he purred.

He gently slid two of his fingers into her and she grunted. She was warm and slippery; his mouth watered. He took his fingers away and she made a sound of protest, and O appeased her by burying his mouth into her, running his tongue firmly along her slit. She gasped loudly as her body stiffened, and she moaned, breathy and low. Naya arched her back even more, stepping her legs wider, pressing herself against his face.

O sucked and nibbled and laved her cunt all while undoing his belt and the buttons on his jeans. He palmed his cock over his briefs; the fabric almost as damp as hers were. He spread her lips wider, dipping into her, reaching inside her as far as his tongue would allow.

Naya sighed as she rode his mouth, her little feet tiptoeing and curling in pleasure, but when he peeled himself from her to take a breath, she pulled away without warning, and announced, "It's my turn now," scrambling onto her bed and twisting her body to face him.

O stared at her from where he knelt on the floor—mind blank—his hands on the bed frame to steady himself from the sudden lack of a warm, wet body in front of him. Naya reclined on her side, knees together, looking all demure. She bit her lip and curled her finger at him to join her. She smiled invitingly as she strained her neck to see him over the edge of her bed. "Come here," she said huskily. "Let me taste you."

O pouted at her. "I wasn't finished."

Naya mirrored his pout but her eyes were full of humour. "Your tongue feels amazing," she purred as she stretched like a cat.

He loved the way she performed for him—how she raised her arms over her head and arched that back to encourage a reaction, to invite him to look his fill. Her lovely dark hair came loose as she lay back, and it fell down over her flushed chest and the rosy tips of her nipples. O peeked over the bed to get a better look at her lovely big belly. Naya curled up on her side, facing him, her little hands pressing her tits together as she continued, "But I've dreamt about sucking your cock since we met." She pushed herself up a little higher, ankles crossed. She looked him square in the eye as she said, "I've dreamt about kneeling in front of you and letting you fuck my mouth in your office."

O's brow arched at that, and he stood, wiping his mouth with the back of his wrist, the smell of her juices making him dizzy. She followed his face as he rose, eyes wide with surprise as if she'd forgotten how tall and big he was, and then she realised he was still clothed and pouted again. "For the sake of fairness," he sighed dramatically as he pushed his jeans and underwear off his hips, stepping out of them and tossing them on the armchair with her pants. "Tell me more. What else have you dreamt about?"

Naya sat up abruptly, rendered speechless, big brown eyes fixed on his very hard, very eager dick. Her pupils flared and mouth parted, her little pink tongue sweeping across her top lip. He stood a little straighter, lifting his chin with pride, and she took a breath to say something, but no words came out. *Hmm.* He smirked. Naya thought *she* was the only one who could tease—put on a show.

He let out a deep slow growl as he leaned his head back and raked both hands through his hair, one after the other. He flexed his biceps for good measure and ran his hand over his nipple, pinching it gently. Naya sat up even straighter, her fingers running over her mouth as she watched on. He widened his stance, brushing the other hand down his chest and over his stomach. He dragged his other palm over his tongue, coating it with his spit. And then, with his eyes on Naya's captivated face, O wrapped his hand around the head of his cock, twisting his wrist gently as he stroked to the base and back up to the tip. She made the tiniest little whimper. He growled, caressing his cock up and down and let out a low, "*Fuck,*" so thankful to finally touch himself with all the goddamned tension between them since his arrival at her door. Naya hummed with rapt approval. "What else have you dreamt about, Naya?" he slurred.

Naya's black eyes flicked up to O's face for just a second before focusing back on his dick, his hand pumping a little faster—pelvis tight. She crawled closer, and O stepped forward too, knees pressed against the side of the bed. Naya reached out her little hand and stroked his inner thigh, sweeping upwards. She shuffled nearer, sitting on her knees on the bed in front of him. She cupped his balls in her hand, making him grunt, and boldly looked up into his face as she said, "I've dreamt about you fucking my mouth so hard you make me cry. I've dreamt about you ruining my makeup."

O let out a deep moan as he jerked himself off harder. Naya looked down at his cock reverently, sitting back on her heels as if kneeling in worship. What a sight. He reached for her with his free hand, cupping her cheek, and she took his thumb in her mouth. Her breath quickened, chest rising and falling and O imagined coming like this—wanted to see his cum splatter over her chest and drip down between her tits.

Naya's thick dark hair swept behind her, her brown skin glowing with a sweaty pink sheen. He lifted his hand to spit in it again, but she caught his wrist and brought it to her lips, rolling her tongue in her mouth before licking the centre of his palm, her tongue flat and thick with her own saliva. "Jesus fucking Christ, Srinaya, you're the devil."

She knelt up, their faces closer. Her cheeks and the bridge of her nose were red, and she tilted her chin up, pretty eyes challenging. "I've dreamt about—" Her breath caught, brows drawn in pleasure, and he looked down and realised she was touching herself as she stroked his balls. He stroked himself even faster—"I dream about tasting your cum, drinking you in. About you overpowering me, making me take every-thing you give me. I dream about *you* taking whatever you want. Anything, Owen," she whined, voice going higher. Her head fell back, eyes shut—and that was it. *Enough.* No more teasing.

He gripped the nape of her neck and kissed her, his tongue rough and violating between her lips. He declared, "You can taste me later. I need to fuck you now," and he pushed her firmly so she fell back, and she let out a rumble that sounded more animal than human.

Naya pointed to her drawer, and O found the condoms. He ripped the packet open with his teeth and had the strongest urge to bite her—to make her cry again, to ruin her makeup, just as she said. He pulled out the latex and rolled it over his erection and she watched on, eyes wide and impatient. He could *feel* her need in the air, her excitement palpable. He knelt on the bed between her legs. "Please, please, please," she whispered.

O leaned over her wonderfully soft body, and Naya reached between them to *finally* touch his cock, wrapping her hand around him and stroking him gently. And then she guided him to her pussy, and O pushed the crown of his dick into her and she tilted her hips up as he slowly, slowly lowered into her.

nineteen

The feel of Owen joined to Naya so intimately—her pelvis pinned firmly against his—made her feel such a deep sense of rightness she couldn't explain. She huffed out a joyful little laugh. *"Mmm, yes,"* she purred luxuriously as she bit her lip.

Owen was sinfully beautiful—*everything* about him. Every fucking inch, and there were quite a lot of those… Seeing his cock—so long and thick and hard as he stood confidently by her bed made her heart thrum happily. And the way he preened at her very obvious approval, the way he squared his shoulders and flexed his muscles to impress her made her feel like a conquering queen. And *god*—was she impressed. His dick jutted out proudly, angled upwards. His foreskin was a darker gold than the rest of him, and when he wrapped his hand around himself and stroked down, revealing that gorgeous bright pink head, she was mesmerised. Fuck—she wanted to suck on it desperately, wishing she could take him all the way down her throat. She would enjoy trying.

And then he climbed on top of her—all hot and slippery and smelling musky and clammy with sweat and her juices, and Naya thanked the heavens he'd prepared her—had gotten her pussy so fucking soaked. She squeezed her eyes shut as he pushed his cock in, stretching her open. She couldn't breathe again, too overwhelmed by it finally happening.

Owen. Pressed against her, inside her.

He looked as lost as she felt—his eyes wide with surprise, pupils so big she could see her reflection in them. His lips were swollen and red, messy hair damp as he stared down at her. The only sound he made was a low gravelly hum; he didn't say a word as he sunk his thick erection into her—his whole body straining as he tried to control himself.

Naya's brows drew together as Owen's cock pressed against her cervix—touching the very end of her. It ached in the best of ways, and tears formed in her eyes. He blinked down at her, and Naya squeezed her muscles tightly around him. Owen swore. "You—" he said, all throaty and tense—"feel better than I'd imagined."

Naya's whole body softened at his words. "You as well," she sighed. He curved over her—his knees on either side of her hips, the fronts of his muscular thighs pressed against the backs of hers. She clamped her knees against his ribs; her own body curled under him—a shell tumbling under the break of a great golden wave. Pinned against him, by his legs, his giant boulder of a body, and by his cock buried deep inside her, she wanted to drown.

Intense affection for Owen washed over her. His hands were braced on either side of her head and she turned her face to brush her lips against his wrist. Something a little dark—*doubt, maybe?*—appeared on his face. She lifted her hands to stroke his cheeks and ask if he was alright, but he grabbed her wrists without warning, crossed them over each other and restrained them above her head.

She gasped.

"You made us wait two days." Owen pulled away to search her face. He admired the shape of her tits with her arms straight above her— back arching as she tried to protest against his hold, her clit throbbing as he overpowered her with very little effort. "Fuck—Naya," he breathed, his voice thick and heavy with yearning.

He finally moved his hips, hitting the deepest part of her again and again, over and over—long, fluid strokes. Her pussy burned with the friction building, and tears rolled down from the outer corners of her eyes and into her hair. He pressed his forehead to hers as he said, "We could've been doing this *two days ago*."

He sounded pained—affronted even, and when she blinked more tears away and her vision cleared, his slanted brows told her he really *was* hurt. "I know. I'm sorry," she whispered.

Every thrust made her lose her breath. She desperately wanted to put her hands on him—caress him and dig her nails into him, but he kept her pinned, his long fingers wrapped around both wrists while his free hand roamed over her belly, squeezing her flesh. Naya mewled as she tried to free her hands, twisting her wrists, but he was too heavy, too strong, and she didn't really want him to stop. Owen pinched her nipple firmly and she made a sound—high-pitched and eager. Was the pressure too much or not enough? Her brain couldn't decide. He nuzzled her cheek, and the smell of his spicy, salty skin mixed with her juices all over him made her wetter.

"I *should* punish you," he grunted—hot breath on her lips. "You disappeared..." He lifted his chin, lips parted. His hair, now tangled with perspiration, stuck to his neck and forehead. She watched as beads of sweat ran down the ridges of his shoulders and chest, dripping onto her tits and stomach.

Her breath was shallow, face hot, eyes glassy and stinging with his sweat and her tears. "Please," she begged, "let me touch you too."

He didn't slow his pace, didn't fuck her gently. "When you weren't there, Naya," he sighed as if he didn't hear her. He wrapped his hand around her throat—thumb and forefinger gripping her jaw. Such terrifyingly large hands capable of causing so much damage. Naya's whole body burned hotter at the thought. The grunts that escaped his throat were the filthiest sounds she'd ever heard. "I've wanted this for so long," he rumbled.

Maybe it was the hurt and desperation in Owen's eyes, or her own urgent need to comfort him, and be comforted *by* him, but all of a sudden something in Naya broke, and a wave of *too muchness* rose up from within her. "Owen."

He blinked at the sound of his name, at how her voice cracked as she said it, straining against his grip on her wrists. His face slackened as he slowed his thrusts. She sniffed, "Not letting me touch you is *horrible*. Punish me some other way."

✝

O released Srinaya's wrists at once. Such a sad and desperate sound... like the intake of breath before a wail. The sorrow in her eyes was worse than the reality of two lost days of pleasure.

He wasn't cruel; he understood her need for space. He understood he'd had so much more time to fall for her, his feelings flickering to life more than eight months earlier and then sparking even hotter only three weeks ago. She had some catching up to do. But when he'd driven his cock into her, and her body stretched and wrapped around him, all he could recall were the parallels between waking up in that empty hotel bed, and arriving at MP just two nights earlier to find her gone.

He felt wounded. Betrayed. It was ridiculous—he fucking knew that—and it had nothing to do with Srinaya and everything to do with him.

Naya rolled her wrists and sighed. "Much better," she said softly, and she wrapped her arms around his neck, pulling him down to bury her face in his chest, landing the softest kiss above his heart. She glanced up at him, the corners of her eyes crinkling happily at being unrestrained.

"Shit—I'm sorry. Are you okay?" he rushed. "I'm so sorry. Did I hurt you?" He nuzzled her hands and kissed her knuckles.

"Yes, I'm okay, and yes, you hurt me," Naya answered, "but I needed it. I *still* need it." She rubbed her eyes and then pulled her long hair out from under her, twisting it out of the way. "I just... didn't like not touching you, especially our first time together."

Regret lanced through him. "I'm sorry, lovely one," he repeated, planting little kisses all over her cheeks and eyes. He lowered his torso onto hers, and rested his chin on her chest, her heart beating fast. "I... I got lost in my thoughts... I think I took your offer of taking everything I give you to heart..."

She glowed before him. "I'm okay—promise. It was so good until it was too much." She cupped his cheek and lifted his face so he'd look at her. Naya smiled affectionately as she added, "And you stopped as soon as you understood."

O wrapped his arms around Naya's waist, forcing her to arch her back off the bed. She grunted and then exhaled a little giggle and said, *Ow*, at how tightly he squeezed. He bared his teeth in a grimace. "I may have been a little fixated on you strapped to Mistress… What was her name? Twila?"

Naya squealed and then laughed loudly, body shaking in his embrace. "It was Starla. And she is fictional," she answered, slapping his shoulder.

"Starla! Of course. Still though... You strapped to a St Andrew's Cross? You knew what you were doing when you planted that image." He lowered his voice to almost a whisper, and he took her nipple in his mouth, the metal clicking against his teeth.

A new wave of arousal swept across her face as her lips parted. "I did," she confessed.

O's cock, which had softened slightly when he stopped fucking her, came back to life, blood surging into him and he rocked his hips. She let out a little *Ah*, and then said, "You feel so perfect inside me, Owen." And then, with her pretty little hands free from his grip, she dug her nails into his back and pulled them upwards, scraping his skin.

He puckered his lips to exhale a slow harsh breath.

What a goddess she was. He pictured her earlier, kneeling in reverence on the bed in front of him, head bowed as she touched him adoringly. He had to do the same for her. Worship her. *Give*—not take. He was still kneeling between her strong thick legs, his thighs pressed against hers. With one hand braced on the bed and his other arm still wrapped around her waist, he said, "Alright, you're on top," and pulled her up as she squeaked, arms flailing like windmills to balance herself. His cock slipped out of her as he changed positions and she whined. "Soon, *sayang*, I just need to stretch my legs," he assured her and lifted his hips so she straddled him, her hands gripping his shoulders.

Her eyes went wide. "Jesus, you are strong," she commented, her cheeks flushing with approval.

Another swell of pride washed over him.

She looked beautiful sitting on top of him—all sticky, with finger marks on her hips. Her tits hung low, and O caressed and squeezed the folds of her soft dimpled belly and thighs. She twisted her hair up and tied it, chin up and eyes closed, and O remembered wanting to see her do just that a couple of weeks back when they sat under the trees at MP for the first time. Naya fanned her face—looking sheepish. "Your body's too hot," she commented, and O drew his brows together as he answered, "Thank you? Or sorry?"

His cock laid hard against his stomach, and Naya looked down at it, eyes ablaze again. He stroked himself, beckoning her. "It's your turn to take what you want," he said. "Anything. What would you like?"

Her mouth broke into the brightest grin, her tongue running along her teeth in excitement. And then Naya—the divinely filthy thing—rolled that lovely pink tongue in her mouth and spat into her hand and stroked his cock with a confidence that was downright wild and sexy. O stared up at her in wonder. An image of himself on his knees before her flickered to life in his brain, his forehead pressed to the floor in submission. He wanted to glorify her; she deserved all the praise. He sighed as he closed his eyes and rubbed his face.

O's hips flexed when a different kind of pressure encircled his cock, and his eyes shot open to witness Naya taking him between her lovely lips, the hollows of her cheeks drawn in as she sucked him.

"*Christ...* Srinaya," was all he could manage. Her hand squeezed the base of his dick as she worked her lips over the crown and down, sucking and licking, and then she took him as far down as she was able. She pushed his dick into the back of her throat, and when she lifted her eyes to look at him, they were bright with tears, and O's balls tightened, preparing themselves for release. He panted, his face burned, his head was heavy, and that familiar tingling in his pelvis very slowly appeared.

Naya pulled his cock out of her mouth with a smack of her lips and shuffled forward, positioning her body on his lap. She stroked him gently, guiding the head of his dick to her pussy's entrance again and then slowly seated herself, a low *Mmmm* escaping as her tight cunt enveloped him.

The way she said his name as if it was an exclamation followed by the second syllable—*Oh!-wen*—made his balls tighten even more. Naya rocked her hips, arching her back, hands resting on his sternum to prop herself up. Tits pressed together, those pierced pink-tipped nipples were right in his face. She lengthened her neck, chin up, and O just *had* to wrap his hand around her throat, holding her firmly. She opened her eyes.

"It hurts, Owen, in the best way," she sighed. "The way your thick cock stretches me, hits the deepest part of me, the way it—" She gasped as she tilted her hips forward, and O could feel the head of his cock reach her cervix. O let go of her throat and splayed both hands on her waist and bent his knees, and she smiled down at him, knowing what he wanted. "Yes, fuck me," she said, her voice sweet.

And so O did, with her permission. He pumped up into her, more gently than when Naya lay underneath, and with every jolting impact, her body bounced and jiggled. Fuck—she watched him so intently, smiling so generously at him.

He rasped her name.

Naya's eyes almost looked cruel as she began to move her hips in time with his. "Come for me," she purred, stroking his chest and abdomen, rolling his nipples between her fingers.

He shook his head. "Not before you. Or will you come with me?" he panted through clenched teeth, already at the precipice. *Oh god... so fucking close—*

She lifted her chin, looking down her nose at him haughtily, her hips grinding against him harder and faster. "You're going to come first." Her voice was soft yet edged with a finality that said she didn't want him arguing.

"No-no-no, I'll wait. I can wait for you," he ground out, and Naya laughed languidly.

She fucked him harder, circling her hips and leaning back with one hand behind her on his thigh, her gorgeous round tits bouncing as she moved. "Are you really saying no to me?"

He opened his mouth to explain, to tell her he'd been desperate to witness her come apart for ages, but she pressed her fingers to his mouth and bent over him. She murmured in his ear, "One day, you'll fuck me without the condom."

O's eyes went wide as he looked into her face with surprise and confusion and—did she actually say that? He was so close to coming his spine had stiffened in anticipation and he blinked—not quite computing.

She huffed out a playful laugh, quickening her pace as she lifted herself off his needy cock and drove her hips back down over and over again. She moaned, "I'd love to feel your cum dripping out of me..." and then she did that thing she loved to do where she arched that back and purred like a cat with her arms up like some fucking Hollywood femme fatale as she looked down at him and asked, "Wouldn't you love to see your cum dripping out of me, down my thighs, Owen?"

God damn her. God damn that dirty mouth. He would definitely punish her later. "Fuck, Naya, *yeees—*" was all he could utter before his pelvis strained and he bucked into her, and she bent down to kiss him, and he groaned and swore into her mouth as he came so hard tears formed in his eyes and white spots appeared in his vision, even with his eyes closed.

twenty

Owen called Naya the devil, and she basked in that title. She took pleasure in saying things that made his nostrils flare and full lips part, or inspired him to grip her a little tighter, causing a little more pain. Seeing him writhe and grunt and come so hard beneath her as she shocked him with her words made her feel like she had him wrapped around her little finger.

She sighed as he slowly came back to his senses, eyes focused, breathing back to normal. He pulled her in for a long, lazy kiss, tongue heavy and slow in her mouth, and then he lay back like some gorgeous work of art, one hand behind his head, the other resting on his stomach. If Owen was a bronze statue, Naya would title him *'Adonis Reclining,'* or *'Eros After The Throes of Passion'*—something befitting the *Golden God of MERAHPUTIH.*

"What are you thinking about?" Owen asked in a croaky voice, eyes bright but rimmed with red from the intensity of his orgasm. "You look like you're scheming," he commented, eyes narrowing in feigned distrust.

Naya flashed him a diabolical grin and waggled her eyebrows. "None of your business," she declared, which got her bucked off Owen's lap and pinned under him instead.

He kept her wrists free, she noted, instead using the weight of his body to sandwich her between himself and the mattress. Naya shrieked at Owen's strength and speed, and he nibbled at the sensitive spot under her ear, which made her giggle as she swatted at him.

"You're ticklish!" he realised, teeth bared, sounding far too delighted about this new piece of information he could use against her later.

Owen brushed his lips along her cheek and then nipped at her earlobe. He pulled away to look at her, his expression exuberant like a gigantic puppy with too much spring in its step, even after a play at the park. His fit body made sense—he probably had to run, and run, and run to get rid of all that energy trapped inside him.

Or fuck, and fuck, and fuck.

Well.

"Don't move," he said puckishly. "I'm going to do the whole unsexy post-coital-profalactic-removal-and-disposal, get us something to drink, and then you're going to show me how *you* come. Fuck, I can't wait. And after, we're going to go have a cigarette while you tell me about some of those tattoos you have—'*BACKSTREET BOYS 4EVA*', Naya? Really?—and then we're going to eat some *mie goreng*, and then we'll fuck again. A few more times, if that works for you. Back soon," he said in one breath, with the biggest grin he'd flashed her yet, and then he leapt off the bed like a spirited colt—all golden legs and torso— and disappeared out of the bedroom.

Naya was left with such fucking adoration for him that she covered her face with her pillow to muffle a squeal. She stretched her body, feeling that ache deep inside—recalling Owen's fingers inside her and his mouth pressed against the folds of her, and that beautiful bright pink cock head sliding in and out of her pussy *and* mouth. Naya hummed happily at the thought. What a great, productive day. *Did some work, got fed, got thoroughly fucked.* She checked the time. Only 3pm! *So productive.* She curled onto her side, closed her eyes and waited for Owen to return.

When Naya opened her eyes again the sunlight in her bedroom had softened. She arched her back, feeling that welcome throb between her thighs as she stretched. She murmured Owen's name but there was no reply. She looked at the clock. *Shit—almost 5pm.* She stumbled out of bed, pulled on clean underwear and a singlet, and made her way upstairs, afraid to discover her home devoid of his presence. She steeled herself as she climbed, expecting to find him gone, telling herself he shouldn't have had to wait—that he was an important man with important things to do, and that even if he had left, it didn't mean anything bad, right? But halfway up, his warm Australian accent floated down to her, and Naya exhaled a long breath of relief. She followed his gravelly voice through her now tidy kitchen—his shirt, her tshirt and bra hanging neatly on the back of one of the stools, and food cleared away—to the balcony.

He paced back and forth; he was on a call, his earpods in, hands gesticulating as he spoke. He wore only his jeans, sitting low on his hips without his belt, the light creating bright ridges and shadowed valleys over his naked torso. She felt a spark of need when he inter-locked his fingers and raised his arms straight above his head to stretch, his powerful body looking like *Pemuda Membangun*, the immense terrazzo statue that posed defiantly at the roundabout on Jl Sudirman, with his flaming bowl held up to the heavens.

Naya stepped out onto the balcony and he turned. His face softened instantly, and in two strides he was pressed against her, his fingers in her hair. In his controlled *business-voice*, he said to the person on the phone, "Tom, get it done, please. I have to go," and pulled out his earpods and shoved them carelessly into his pockets. And then Owen Jameson—*Owen Jameson*—curled his spine in some kind of reverent bow to nuzzle her shoulder and inhale her scent, and in his breathy *only-for-Naya-voice*, said, "Yay, you're awake."

"I'm sorry," Naya murmured in his ear.

"Don't be. You needed rest and I kept myself occupied."

"I thought you might've left."

"I would never."

She sighed at his sweet words. He slanted his mouth over hers, his lips heavy and impatient and Naya's whole body opened like some fucking blossom welcoming the sun. The image would have been ridiculous if it didn't feel so good.

He led her to the sofa, sitting her down and kneeling on the floor between her legs to kiss her some more, and when he spied his finger-prints on her hips and thighs he made a sound of regret, but Naya captured his mouth with hers to silently reassure him.

They sat on the floor of the balcony, smoking and drinking, listening to music and making out. Owen shared stories about what MP was like when he was a kid, and his life in Melbourne, making a pointed effort to not talk about his family. Through all his stories, he smiled and laughed, and Naya basked in his loving and open energy.

He asked questions with child-like curiosity, captivated by the tattoos that covered her body, and the stories behind them. He admired the large pieces, especially the Batik-inspired sleeve, and the large snake that curled around her forearm, but her stick 'n' pokes fascinated him the most. He lifted her tank top and pointed to a wonky drawing of a slice of pizza on her ribs, tattooed by an ex-girlfriend during a drug-fueled night in New York in her mid-twenties. Naya smiled at the memory. And then Owen pointed to the pineapple wearing sunglasses that floated above the slice of pizza. Naya shrugged and explained, "I love pineapple on pizza."

Owen stared at the tattoo for a *really* long time, and then looked at her. "Srinaya Matthews, you're officially flawed." She gasped in mock-offence as he exclaimed, "You disgust me, Naya. *'BACKSTREET BOYS 4EVA'*—" He poked the text on her right side and she squealed as she flinched away—"and now I find out you like *pineapple* on your pizza?" He shook his head. "Who *are* you?" he accused dramatically, "NSync—*maybe*. But Backstreet Boys? Gross."

Naya laughed so hard she couldn't catch her breath when he grumbled about sticking his dick into a Backstreet Boys groupie.

Owen pointed to other little pieces and Naya shared their meaning: the Lilith insignia Arum tattooed on her, the ink blessed under the full moon—for protection, one of those '90s *S* thingies that every '90s teen drew on their school books—an ex-lover had been feeling nostalgic, a microphone—for her mother, who she didn't want to talk about, a sprinkling of stars and hearts by friends and lovers, the little takeaway coffee cup—an ode to Melbourne, the Venus of Willendorf in all her fat and fertile splendour—an ode to Naya herself.

Owen's hands moved over her body, inspecting them carefully. "I saw one earlier," he growled and gently pushed her back onto her elbows. He opened her legs, pointing to the little *'EAT ME'* candy heart on her inner thigh. "This one," Owen said, freckles standing out against his flushed cheeks.

Naya bit her lip. "No story there."

"Just a request then?"

Naya saw that familiar dip of his chin. She held his gaze. Her devil scratched at her bones, and she slid her tongue over her teeth. "More like a demand."

Owen silently watched her, thumb circling the tattoo on her inner thigh. Naya canted her head as she watched the grey fall off the edge of his irises to make room for the black pupils expanding. She'd never get used to that.

Her devil was done waiting so Naya spoke plainly. "It's my turn to come, no?" She placed her foot on his shoulder as she tilted her pelvis up, and she nodded her chin to the tattoo which was now closer to his mouth. A feral smile appeared on his face—all pretty white teeth—and he moved, but Naya spoke up quickly. "You should know," she said, "that I need my sex toy to come. But it'll feel so good with your help."

Owen's smile softened and he brushed his lips over the bridge of her foot, and then planted a kiss on her calf. He settled onto the floor on his belly, face between her thighs as he dragged his tongue over her tattoo. When his eyes flitted up to her, Owen purred, "Show me."

†

From the moment O spotted Srinaya from across Chidori, he *knew* her sweet and placid exterior hid something restless and wild underneath, and he was deeply honoured to be someone with whom she'd let that quiet facade fall away, leaving this brazen, passionate and needy goddess in her place. Every facet of her enthralled him—he would love all the new sides she hadn't yet shared.

"Taste me and I'll show you," Naya said with a twinkle in her eye, chin held high and unashamed.

O kissed the soft curves of her belly and moved down over the black curls of her pubic hair. Running his palm over her lips, the darker skin swollen and inviting, her breath hitched as he parted them and brushed his thumb up the centre, from the opening of her pussy to her clit. She glistened—so wet and smelling so salty-sweet—and he dipped two fingers inside her. She flinched in wanton delight, and her pelvis curled upwards. Naya reached down and moved his hair off his face to watch him, their eyes meeting, and repeated herself, "Taste me," this time her voice more desperate, and so he did—with absolute pleasure.

He spread her open and pressed his mouth to her, planting soft kisses, brushing his lips over her delicate, slippery skin. He hummed against her clit, his hot breath making her whimper. "Fuck, Owen, more..." was her response, one hand raking through his chocolate waves while the other caressed the crease where her thigh met her hip, right where her pubic hair began.

He licked more firmly—sucked harder. He pushed his two fingers deeper—so deep that his knuckles pressed against her pussy's opening. O had never been so grateful for his big hands—how his long fingers could offer her so much attention. He rubbed her G-spot as he laved her cunt and her spine bowed.

The sounds that came out of her throat as she abandoned all politeness and control were nothing short of bestial. She was dripping wet—his hand soaked with her juices. Fuck—she was delicious as if she had been designed for him to taste, her biology perfectly compatible with his. He couldn't explain it—it just *was*; he wanted to lap her up—drink her in. Her thighs trembled and her toes curled when he started fucking her with his fingers. "Yes, yes, yes," she mewled.

She squeezed her tits and pinched those gorgeous little nipples—so hard and prominent under the fabric of her white singlet. The sight of her writhing against his mouth and hands, and moaning so deep sent a jolt of pleasure to O's cock. His erection strained in his jeans, the thick denim uncomfortable against his sensitive skin. He pulled away to undo them, and Naya went still as she watched him with intense focus, like the first time she saw him undress. She sat up hurriedly to help with the buttons, biting her lip harder with every *pop-pop-pop* of the fly opening, and when his cock sprung free, she made a high-pitched sigh of approval. "Jesus, Owen," she breathed, big black eyes hungry. "Take these off, *please*."

He stood, removing his jeans, the crown of his dick wet with his own need for her. He cast them aside just as Naya removed her singlet, standing naked and ready before him. With eyes hazy, she murmured, "You make me feel so good." She grabbed a fistful of his hair as she kissed him hard, standing on her tiptoes.

He loved the way she ended each caress of her tongue with a flick along his. It sent a pulse of pleasure through him—made him want to grab her and hurt her in all the ways he knew she wanted. O leaned down to meet her halfway and placed his hand on her chest, right at the base of her throat like he had two days earlier. She bit her lip, remembering as well, and he dipped his head to kiss her slowly.

Naya broke the kiss, tugging him forward as she knelt on the couch, her hands on his waist to manoeuvre him to stand in front of her. She stroked down the fronts of his thighs. Her grip was firm—demanding —and she pulled him closer, lips parting to take his dick into her mouth. "But this is supposed to be all about you, lovely one."

Something like surprise or confusion flashed across her face, and then she laughed as she said, "This *is* all about me." Naya's beautiful dark brown eyes, with those flecks of gold, were wide and serious. "I want to suck your gorgeous cock, and it's a little bit for you, but *all* for me." She said the last three words as a moan and his erection became unbearable. "I'm very selfish, you know," she purred, and then without taking those expressive eyes off him, she took the head of his cock between her pretty pink lips and gently sucked.

Srinaya Matthews. Kneeling before him with those magic hands— so wonderfully capable of creating stunning works of art—wrapped around the base of his dick, licking and sucking and *moaning* in utter delight. O couldn't believe it. She'd sucked his cock with the condom on earlier, and that had been fucking incredible. He didn't imagine it would get that much better without one. His body sagged a little as he submitted.

Her eyes shut as she licked the sensitive crest underneath, and then took more of him into her mouth. Her hands stroked as well, following the rhythm of her lips, and O's head fell back as his hips started to move of their own volition. He swore under his breath. "Fuck—Naya, please," O whispered, and he didn't really know why he was pleading. It was all so perfect. He stroked her brows, and swept some hair away from her eyes, and Naya pushed him deeper—opened her mouth wider to accommodate him. Her eyes went bright with tears, nose and cheeks going red. Her sighs got louder and more fervent. God, he wanted to cover those lips with cum, watch her lick it off. O's eyes rolled back, his lips parted, chest feeling heavy as he tried to catch his breath. The pressure in his pelvis was too much to bear. "Naya, love, stop," he ground out.

She released him immediately. "I'm sorry—was I too rough?"

O could only laugh and run his fingers through his hair in frustration. He shook his head. "Jesus—no. I was close to coming and, *fuck*—you're supposed to be showing me how *you* come."

Her swollen lips curved up in relief. "I got carried away..." she said and blushed. "But look at you." Naya nodded her chin at O's dick, saying, "How could I not?" and then kissed the tip, flicking her tongue against it playfully, making him shiver.

She sucked on her bottom lip and stood, bracing her hands on his stomach. She tilted her head to the side as her gaze roved over him from his head to his feet and back up again.

"You're beautiful. I want to draw you," she said, voice distant as her eyes flitted over his face and torso like she was figuring out how she would go about translating his form onto paper. "And you feel so good." Her lids closed and her lashes cast pretty wing-like shadows on her cheeks. Her eyes snapped open as she continued, "And you smell amazing. So familiar. I can't explain it—" nuzzling his chest and inhaling deeply. "And Owen, you *taste* so good—my god," she whined. She pulled him close, her belly pressed against his cock. Her nails dug firmly into his flanks, making him shudder.

Jesus Christ—she had a way. With words, with her fingers, with those fucking big brown eyes. He cleared his throat to keep some semblance of control given Naya had him practically falling at her feet.

"Right. Your vibrator's in the bedroom?" O asked in the most authoritative voice he could muster.

"Mm hmm."

"Right. Off to bed then," he murmured, and intertwined their fingers to lead her through her darkened home, turning on the lights as they passed.

O pulled her into the darkness of her bedroom. Naya sauntered in behind him, switching on the lamp to cast gorgeous shadows over the curves of her body. The amber light seemed to bring out the darkening bruises on her hips, and as he sat at the end of her bed and pulled her to him, O ran his thumb over his fingerprints. His brows knitted. "I'm sorry about these," he said, and he meant it.

She didn't even look at the bruises, completely unbothered by them. She stood between his legs, her face slightly higher since he was seated, and ran her warm little hands over his cheeks and then raked her fingers through his hair. "I'm not," she sighed into his mouth before sealing her lips over his.

In between kisses, her hands found their way around O's cock again, and he grumbled at her. "Srinaya," he warned.

Naya huffed a little laugh and pressed a finger over his lips. "Shush," she whispered.

She pushed him roughly so that he fell backwards, O's cock excruciatingly hard against his stomach. And then his brows shot up, because Naya was rolling a condom down his shaft. "Where the fuck did that come from?" he asked, voice high, grinning. O was genuinely confused, and very fucking impressed. "When the fuck did you unwrap that?"

Naya grinned right back as she climbed on top of him, straddling his thighs and twinkling her fingers. "I also have magical tricksy ways," she said, eyes narrowed mischievously.

O drew in a long breath and reached for her, and she scooched forward, the slippery folds of her pussy rubbing along the length of him as she did so. He took in the sight of her, gently rocking her hips back and forth, leaning forward, supporting her body with her hands on his chest. She was all soft folds of flesh and smooth, slippery, shimmery skin. He ran his thumb over her lips—that pouty mouth that said and did such filthy things—and she took him in and sucked, her tongue running firmly along the pad.

"Naya, come for me," he said in a wavering voice, surprised at how needy he sounded. He gave in then, decided to drop the pretence of control. "I need it—I do. Please. Show me."

Her face softened, and she kissed him gently, almost chastely, and when she sat upright again, a sleek vibrator with gold buttons and a dome-shaped head made of soft silicone had appeared in her hand. O held his palms up as he laughed. "You *are* the fucking devil! That's devil-magic right there," he exclaimed and she gave him another impish smile.

Naya climbed off him and lay on her back beside him, and said in the softest, breathiest voice, "Fuck me, and I'll come for you."

He rolled onto his knees swiftly and nestled his thighs against the backs of hers. He slowly pushed in, and the beautiful Naya tensed—stopped breathing. Her eyes squeezed shut, and she finally gasped for breath, and then moaned when O pulled out and thrust back in. She opened her eyes, and those perfect little tears spilled down her cheeks again. "Lovely one," he murmured into her neck, "is this what you need?"

Naya dipped her chin as she gasped again. "Please, more."

And so O began to fuck her harder. Long strokes in and out, as she brought her knees to her chest, tilting her hips forward, giving herself over to him. Her one hand was above her, bracing the bedhead as he impaled her again and again, the little opals in her nipple rings catching the light. What a beautiful offering—Naya sharing her pleasure so openly with him. It was a revelation, a declaration of trust. He wrapped one hand around her waist as she arched her back, needed to be as close to her as possible. She whimpered, her hand stroking the back of his neck and then gripping his hair.

Her spine began to stiffen, skin clammy and eyes rolling back. She moaned his name, and fuck—his name sounded like music when she said it. He couldn't imagine ever tiring of hearing it come out of her mouth.

She turned her vibrator on high and licked the head to get it all slippery and wet, and O's breath caught. He watched, utterly enthralled as she pressed it to her clit, and then angled it to a secret spot only she knew, and she purred so low and guttural that O quickened his thrusts. Her arse cheeks flexed, her pussy muscles tightening around his cock.

He gripped her soft thighs as he fucked harder, as deep as he could go, hoping to god it hurt her and she loved it. He could feel her hips begin to shake with every thrust, and she started to pant, brows drawn together, and eyes glassy with tears again. This was it. It was about to happen. Her muscles tightened around him, and for five slow seconds she went still and silent. O leaned in close, never breaking his rhythm.

He whispered, "Please, love."

Naya's spine arced. She cried out—hips lifting off the bed. O fell in love all over again. Her whole body bucked against him, legs clamping around his waist. She squirted her juices over his cock and brought him to the brink of his own orgasm. Naya sobbed, eyes scrunched shut for just a moment and then she dug her nails into the swell of his arse and a rumble escaped her throat.

"More," she mouthed in a gasp, and O—so desperate to give her everything—picked up the pace and pressure, pounding her mercilessly, and then sank his teeth into her shoulder, right next to her first bite.

She yelped. "*Yesyesyes*, come with me, Owen, I'm going to—"

Srinaya's chest heaved, and then she came again, the gold in her wide eyes sparkling. She sobbed with every buck of her hips and this time, O roared as he dived over the edge to join her. "Naya, I'm yours," he croaked as his hips flexed and his body trembled, his orgasm making his ears ring, and those stars from earlier reappear, but this time they were multicoloured.

twenty-one

When the lust-fueled fog in her head cleared, and all that was left was the glaring reality of what just happened, Naya was taken back to the night in Purnama when she'd first received official approval to curate *Heartbreak*. She remembered leaning against that bare white wall, the almost-blinding downlight pointed at her. She'd felt exposed that night, the weight of everyone's expectations heavy on her shoulders.

She felt exposed again in the dim lamplight of her bedroom.

Laying next to Owen, tucked into the warmth of his body as he caressed her, something uncomfortably familiar emerged. Underneath the smell of sex and sweat, there was a hint of something—a scent she noticed the first time they met—the warm, sweet smell of summer in Melbourne. Her chest ached—yearned.

Melbourne. Comfort. That moment when the plane hit the tarmac and she knew she was finally home—that's what Owen felt like: *Home, finally.*

No. He couldn't feel like that. He couldn't *be* that. He wasn't just Owen—he was Owen Jameson. Son of Edward Jameson. Grandson of Rina Candrawatih. So much came after his name.

Naya looked up at him, with that perfect straight nose and those pillowy lips. He kept his face relaxed, but his gaze was intensely focused on her. His eyes were the colour of the Melbourne sky before a downpour. Something in them spoke of deep vulnerability.

She should've revelled in this shared moment, knowing he also felt exposed in his own way, but a small part of her resented him for it. What did he have to feel vulnerable about? What did he have to lose, really?

He clenched his jaw. He must have sensed her growing doubt. She swallowed, looked away and pushed up to sit. Owen did the same.

"Talk to me," he said quietly, shifting to face her.

Naya was tempted to slip out of bed and hide in the shower to—she didn't even really know. Scrub herself clean of him? Forget it ever happened? *Absolutely not.* It had been a wonderful afternoon—more wonderful than she'd expected. *He* was more wonderful than she expected, which was the fucking worst, because now she would feel the void left in his wake when this ended. She frowned at the thought of exchanging goodbyes.

Owen reached for her hand and pulled her to sit in front of him. "Do you regret this?" he asked, voice calm, although his Adam's apple quivered as he swallowed nervously, and it broke her heart to see the worry written on his face. "You asked me to convince you, but did I cross a line?"

Oh god. No. She didn't like where his thoughts took him—as if her silence was due to some belief that Owen had taken advantage or manipulated her. She slumped. "You did everything right, you utter shit," she grumbled as she covered her face.

He let out a chuckle and called her a *Backstreet-Boys-loving-harpy* under his breath, and then his arms were around her waist as he pulled her close again to sit between his thighs. He nipped at her earlobe and she pouted.

"You're unhappy," he said softly. "Come on—lay your cards out on the table."

She pressed her face into his shoulder and grumbled, "You've made me the opposite of unhappy. You're so fucking lovely—it's the worst."

He huffed. "I'm sorry," he said, and although Naya wasn't looking at him, she heard the grin in his voice. "Are those your cards then? You're happy and I'm lovely? Because those sound like good things, yet you're sulking."

Naya faced him, her legs crossed, knees resting on his thighs. She ran a finger over his collarbone—created new constellations with the freckles on his chest. Owen's giant hand rested on her thigh and the other swept her tangled hair over her shoulder. "I still worry about what people will say if they find out." He nodded but didn't respond. "I —" She rubbed her temple as the memory of getting doxxed by her former uni friend and the harassment that followed replayed in her mind. "I worry about people showing up at my house."

Owen stiffened. "Is that what happened? You had a stalker?"

Naya gave a half-shrug. "I got mail hand delivered, late-night banging on the door, prank calls."

There was a sharpness to the set of his mouth, as if revenge lurked just underneath the surface, desperate to be set free. She wanted to bask in that rage, to coax the beast out and witness the kind of damage he could do to those who'd hurt her. She adored his sweetness, but those moments when Owen morphed into the untouchable esteemed benefactor—flinty eyes bright and terrifying, and that commanding swagger that made people move out of his way? Naya let out a quiet breath. It was hypocritical to think those things, all the while using them as a reason for it not working out between them. She couldn't have Owen without his last name. Besides, he wouldn't be the same person without the titles trailing behind him.

She considered her predicament. What was growing between them wasn't at all the same as the Reginald Muse thing. There was no cash prize, no panel of judges. She hadn't fucked her way to a win then, and she certainly hadn't done it this time. She won the curator position and the exhibition on her own, *and then* fucked an incredibly sweet, handsome man. Granted—this particular handsome man also happened to be the golden prince.

She couldn't keep leading him on if this wasn't going anywhere. Naya exhaled sharply, raised her chin and sat up straight. "If people find out, is there a chance I'll get fired or that *Heartbreak* will get taken away?"

"Absolutely not," Owen answered firmly.

"Is that because you'll pull some strings or because this isn't considered a breach of company policy? I don't want any favours."

A vertical crease appeared between his dark brows. "Do you think I've done you a favour?"

"You tell me. The new offices. Was that a little bit about me?"

He hesitated and then winced. "Yes and no. When you said you worked from home because of your cubicle, I was worried I'd never see you so I did have a personal stake in getting you an office. But as a senior curator you *were* supposed to get one. If Gunawan had mentioned it I would've done the same. It just so happened I spotted you and that hot arse of yours talking to Yanto that day. It felt good to see you so pleased though, and you can't make me feel bad about that." Owen brushed his thumb over her bottom lip.

Naya took in his words. She shifted closer. "And what about approving the extra rooms for *Heartbreak?*" she asked, thrumming her fingers on his forearms.

He rolled his wide shoulders like a gentle ocean wave. "Extra space equals more artwork, equals more visitors, equals more money. And all of that equals more funds for community projects. Nothing—especially Surya's fragile ego—gets in the way of supporting the community. That's why MERAHPUTIH was founded in the first place." His mouth curved downwards in annoyance. "Everyone's forgotten my grandmother's vision."

More questions swirled in Naya's mind, but she didn't have the clearance—or the energy—to ask them. "Alright," she conceded. "Just—please. No preferential treatment, okay? No favours."

"Done." he said, all business-like, as if he was closing a deal. "But just so you know, *Endah* called me back here for you. She said the new curator was having a hard time." Naya flinched at that revelation, and Owen stroked her arm as he continued, "When Endah asks something of me, I do it. *Endah* did it for you. I did it for her. *And* you."

Naya took that all in. She couldn't help feeling like she was more trouble than she was worth. She looked down at her hands but Owen lifted her chin to meet his eyes. His chin was raised too. He looked powerful—uncompromising. *There you are, Mr Jameson.*

"Would I have done it if Endah hadn't asked me to, though? If I had been here and knew it was happening, yes. Because I fucking hate bullies, Naya, and I won't tolerate them in *my* house. There's a reason why they call me the *esteemed benefactor*," he said, although his lip curled at the title. "I bring in *a lot* of money. The most money. The directors *may* have equal claim and the board members *may* have their say, but they all know MERAHPUTIH is a little bit more mine."

Oh god—Owen wasn't the golden prince. He was king.

His voice softened. "I won't tolerate you getting hurt again if I can help it. I wouldn't call that a favour. I'd do that for any of the staff, and especially my friends. We're at least friends, aren't we?"

The way he looked at her—so vulnerable and hopeful, especially after learning he was *at the very top*—touched her. "Yes, of course we are," she assured him. She took his hand that held her chin and nuzzled it. "Endah asked you to come here?" she murmured. She had to buy Endah flowers or something.

Owen grinned at that. "She mentioned something about you *not being Indonesian enough*—" He used air quotes—"and told me to get my white arse back to Jakarta to show them all what a *not Indonesian enough* person was capable of. I think she has a soft spot for us poor *bules*."

"We're not the same though."

"I know. You're better."

Naya frowned at that ridiculous comment. "What?"

"I didn't earn my position. I inherited it and, let's be honest, I was the only choice. MP probably would have gone to Gem if she were here," he said, and the tiniest flash of hurt appeared on his face. "*You* earned your position here. And your work is impeccable, Naya." Owen touched a lock of her hair and twisted it between his fingers. "You haven't done anything wrong. You got the job through merit alone, and we met after you got the show." Another flash of *something* appeared as he said that, but Naya couldn't name it. He cleared his throat. "Anyway, I'm more than happy to throw my weight around in support of the show. I'm good at ruffling feathers."

"Yes, you are," Naya commented, biting her lip.

"So are you," he said with a smile.

He kissed her gently, his playful tongue caressing hers. She couldn't imagine not kissing him again. Maybe this really could work. She wanted it to... She flushed all over, but before it got hot and heavy, Naya pulled away and blurted, "Don't take on Surya for me."

Owen bristled. "He's being a cunt to you and I won't have it."

"That's really gallant of you, Sir Lancelot, but I don't need you saving me."

"Naya."

She placed her hands on his shoulders to reason with him. "Okay, look. There needs to be equal treatment between all of the curators."

Owen arched an eyebrow at that. "I mean, Ravi and Chris are good looking guys. I'd give them a go. Foursome?"

"I mean, at work, you fucking perve."

He smirked. "A foursome in my office? Is this a new fantasy, Srinaya? I'm happy to oblige."

"Oh my god—during office hours! *Ugh*, you know what I mean," she said, smacking his arm, before he could make yet another smart-ass comment. The laugh that vibrated in his chest made her clit tingle. "If you ever witness Surya say something shitty to me, be there for me but let me handle it." Owen thought about her words, eyes narrowing. "Please, Owen. He'll think I'm hiding behind you. I'm not weak," she said defiantly.

"No, you're not." Owen still didn't look convinced though. "If I ever hear him say anything behind your back—"

Naya nodded her head quickly, "Oh, by all means. Defend my honour. But as someone who hates bullies and would defend Gunawan or Tini in the same way—not as someone who's deep-dicked me."

Owen barked out a laugh, beautiful teeth sparkling. He squeezed her tight and ran his lips over her neck. "Speaking of deep-dicking..." He pushed her down, parted her thighs and pushed his fingers into her, and she squeaked. "Still so wet," he murmured, pinning her hips down with a heavy hand on her lower belly. She brushed the back of her hand against her mouth as she watched his freckled cheeks turn pink, offsetting that lovely golden tan perfectly. Owen twisted his wrist, as he slid his fingers in and out, and Naya purred.

"As much as I'd love to play again, we have a cocktail party to go to." His fingers slowed.

Naya blinked. "What?"

Owen shook his head, tsking at her. "Cinq-Huit, lovely one."

Naya groaned and crossed her forearms over her eyes. "Must we go?"

Owen made a face as he said, "I hate to pull rank while I have my fingers inside you, but yeah, we need to be there."

Naya raised up onto her elbows and swallowed. "Would it be ok if we go separately? Or at least *appear* to go separately? I don't want people gossiping."

Owen's eyes showed no hint of offence as he nodded. "I'll meet you there. Will you come and talk to me though?"

They showered quickly, kissing and caressing each other under the warm water, washing away the sex and sweat, but no amount of scrubbing could erase their desire.

Before Owen left to change at his place, he held her tightly, and even though he used her soap, she still noticed the scent that brought her back to Melbourne. *Home.* Still disconcerting, but now, maybe a little less so.

Naya stared at her reflection. She ran her hands over the bruises on her hips. She wanted to tattoo Owen's fingerprints to her skin so she would always remember their encounter. Shit—that was a sign, wasn't it?

She DMed him.

SNMXX:

Could we go all in this weekend and see what happens? Would that work for you?

Aud Pitch

Owen reacted with a heart emoji.

OH.EM.JAY:

Yes, I'd love that. Thank you for today.

I miss you already. Can't wait to see you in a bit. x

twenty-two

O's heel tapped restlessly against the metal wall of the elevator as he waited for the doors to open onto Cinq-Huit, the popular rooftop bar he co-owned with Mario. He focused on the whir of the lift as he steeled himself for loud music and too many bodies, his pulse racing and palms slippery. He should've been blissfully happy after the day he'd shared with Naya. God—he wished the cause of his panic was simply due to being far away from her, and maybe that was part of it, but this dread was older than their budding relationship—more familiar.

He should've taken a Valium.

He buttoned his suit jacket as he exited the lift, fixing his shirt cuffs and striding out through the corridor leading to the large main bar. He made eye contact with partygoers, smiling and nodding politely as he walked past but refused to stop and chat with anyone, instead heading straight for the bar.

Fuck, he didn't want to be there. He didn't want to be out at all. If it wasn't for Endah requesting his attendance, well... Srinaya had to be there since Endah planned this party for her department, so he supposed he would've turned up anyway. What else would he have done after spending the afternoon and early evening hearing her make the most wondrously dirty sounds, all rosy and brown and shimmery?

He exhaled, counting his breath, counting five things he could see, four things he could hear…

His heartbeat slowed just a little.

The bartender served up his whisky and he downed it, needing the biting heat in the back of his throat, and ordered another. He mindlessly scrolled through a random feed on his phone, looking too busy to socialise, and waited.

A hand touched his back and he spun around, expecting to come face to face with Naya, but it was Endah, a warm smile crinkling her eyes. His unease faded as he kissed her cheeks. She fiddled with the lapels of his suit jacket, brushing invisible lint away. "Owen, *sayang. Ganteng banget kamu.* Just like your father," she said in her soft sing-song voice.

O squeezed her hand and ordered her usual—a very dirty martini—and then turned back to her. "And you look stunning, *Tante*," he responded. He nodded at her outfit. "Are you looking to start a bar brawl? I'm going to have to fight off a lot of men with you in that dress." He grinned at her and winked, and she smacked his arm.

"*Aduh, kamu,*" she muttered, although she was smiling too. "Such a shameless flirt. You do like to cause trouble."

O shrugged. "All the better to keep you on your toes." He tiptoed and raised his arms above his head. "*En pointe, non?*"

Endah elbowed him and laughed.

They rested against the bar taking it all in. The celebration was well underway, and the MP staff's smiles and excitement would've been a lovely thing if he didn't feel so… *wrong.* The cacophony of laughter and spirited conversations grated on his nerves. It was all too much—the music and voices too loud, the lights too bright. He frowned as he searched for Naya in the crowd of guests.

"I haven't seen her," Endah said, carefully studying him.

O didn't have the energy to feign innocence. "She's coming."

Endah looped her arm into his elbow. "Of course she is. *You're* here." Endah winked as she took a sip of her cocktail.

O's heart cracked open, unable to contain the affection spilling out. He combed his hair with his fingers and sighed. "She's fucking wonderful, Endah," he confessed, and Endah lit up hearing those words, and then—god love her—her eyes went slightly glassy as she said, "Look at you, *nak*."

The beautiful old woman reached up to touch his cheek. "It makes me happy to see you happy. You deserve it."

Endah and O toasted. "To MERAHPUTIH," Endah said.

O added, "And a particular senior curator."

They sipped. Endah said, "So, you've reminded Srinaya of how you two met back in Melbourne? She doesn't seem like much of a romantic —too logical to be whimsical—but I bet even *she* thought it was a bit serendipitous, no?"

O stilled and cleared his throat uncomfortably. "Um, no. She doesn't know, and I'm not going to tell her."

Endah's eyes hooded in confusion. "I don't understand."

"It doesn't really change our current situation. Even if I hadn't met her back then, you still would've summoned me, and I would've shown up and fallen for her, and we'd be exactly where we are," he said, although he wondered if he would've scared her away with his intensity if he *had* just met her for the first time on those steps. He had a habit of swan-diving into things. Just like Naya, he didn't do things half-arsed.

Endah eyed him, the gentleness in her gaze replaced with shrewdness. "What's that *bule* phrase, Owen—*lying by omission?*"

An unwelcome prickle crept up his neck. "Hang on a minute," he said defensively, "we shared a moment eight months ago. She doesn't remember, so it doesn't matter."

"Oh please—*a moment*," she echoed derisively. "It was an entire night. And it matters to *you*, Owen. You said you never stopped thinking about her."

"She doesn't need to know that."

"You are *not* this selfish, Owen."

O couldn't stop the voice of his sixteen year-old self from coming out. "Maybe I actually am," he flung back.

"Owen," she said, exasperated.

He hated when people repeated his name to chastise him. "Stop,

Endah," he snapped. "It doesn't change anything. Besides, she wouldn't take the news well, and I'm not going to risk it when it *really doesn't matter.*"

Endah's brows slanted. "Think about what you *just* said, *sayang.*"

O rubbed his eyes in frustration with a sprinkling of shame. "*Tante,* please."

Endah nodded, lips pressed tightly together. Oh god, O loathed that look. If that wasn't a disappointed mother look he didn't know what was. A bloated awkwardness emerged between them. He counted his breaths.

He opened his mouth to try to explain himself but Endah's husband appeared at her side. O hugged him affectionately. After a brief catch up where O and *a date* were invited over to Endah's and Agung's place for dinner—and a request for a quick conversation about Surya before O inevitably slinked out without saying goodbye—Endah was whisked away to mingle with other guests. He squeezed her hand in apology before she disappeared, and her dark eyes softened.

He huffed. Naya never had to find out about Chidori. *It really doesn't matter.*

He needed to see her. Her pretty smile would be a soothing balm for the scratchiness in his brain. O checked his watch. *He* had been fashionably late. If Naya hadn't arrived yet, she was *obstinately* late. His fingers tapped restlessly on the bar.

He took out his phone.

OH.EM.JAY:

Where are you? I need a smoke and you're my hookup.

Naya replied straight away.

We finished them this evening and I didn't have time to buy more, I'm afraid.

You look very handsome btw

Yes—she had arrived.

O craned his neck in search of her.

SNMXX:

I'm not the only one to think so either. I've heard a zillion comments about the sexy bule director and his gorgeous surfer hair and broad shoulders

They're wondering if you have a superhero costume under your get-up.

I think I'd like to see you in spandex...

OH.EM.JAY:

Shut it.

SNMXX:

Bet you'd look amazing in a cape

O snorted, his anxiety plateauing.

SNMXX:

Was planning on bumming smokes off you for once.

OH.EM.JAY

Cannot believe you didn't bring any! Unforgivable. How will you make amends?

SNMXX:

Clutches are fucking stupid and I don't have pockets in this dress! Holding my phone and have cash and cards in my bra

OH.EM.JAY

One of the MANY upsides to having big tits.

Condoms?

SNMXX:

Those perforated edges are itchy

OH.EM.JAY:

You're adorable. Where are you???

SNMXX:

Around. Charmed a server into going downstairs to buy some cigarettes. You have pockets. You're holding them.

You look upset. What's wrong?

OH.EM.JAY:

I'm feeling a little anxious—that's all.

Come here, lovely. I need to see you

SNMXX:

But I'm so enjoying watching you from where I am!

You are wearing the fuck out of that suit, Owen. You look so sexy.

OH.EM.JAY:

I'm glad you think so. I chose it for you

SNMXX:

I have a few ideas for that tie. We could find a bathroom and I'll make amends

OH.EM.JAY:

Srinaya Matthews.

SNMXX:

Owen Jameson.

OH.EM.JAY:

You're fucking filthy

SNMXX:

I am.

OH.EM.JAY:

When you were riding me this afternoon, you said some very filthy things.

SNMXX:

I did.

OH.EM.JAY:

You said you wanted me to fuck you without a condom, that you'd love to feel my cum dripping out of you

SNMXX:

I would.

OH.EM.JAY:

Maybe it's time for a discussion then? I'd prefer to do this face to face but since you're being a fucking tease and I'm not in the mood to talk to anyone else, this gives me an excuse to look busy and keep DMing you.

I didn't bring condoms either (would like to say I was being a gentleman or some shit but tbh I was running late and forgot them) and I don't plan on charming a server into buying some for us.

SNMXX:

"OH.EM.JAY: Cannot believe you didn't bring any! Unforgivable."

That totally makes us even. I take back my offer of making amends.

OH.EM.JAY:

Noooooooooo

SNMXX:

😩 Alright. Let's have this discussion.

OH.EM.JAY:

Sure? I know it's very early days between you and me... and despite this raging hard-on I can wait until we get back to yours. Or mine. Wherever. I may need to go into the bathroom and have a wank to get through this evening though.

Ooh. Maybe you could send me an inspiring photo. Ooh! That's an enticing thought

SNMXX:

Happy to send you some snaps later but let's get the talk over and done with, because it's unsexy but necessary and I was very serious when I said what I said but only if you want to

I'm enjoying watching you squirm over there by the way. Very smart wearing black

OH.EM.JAY:

I know. Harder to see the erection.

Ok. So, I got tested a few months ago. All clear. You're the first person I've had sex with since.

Aud Pitch

O forced himself to slow his steps as he climbed up to the mezzanine that led to the large rooftop section. Most of the guests ended up outside, the open air platform lit by warm lights and decorated with huge palm trees, ferns and other tropical plants. People mingled on outdoor couches and cushioned benches, enjoying the warm breeze.

He flashed a smooth smile to a gaggle of people from the advertising department, held up his empty glass as he apologised for not staying to chat, and they waved him through.

And there she was, her back to him as she rested her forearms on the railing. She looked out at the city, smoking a cigarette, wearing a forest green silk dress. The shade was deeper than the lacy bra and panty set she wore earlier that afternoon, and O's trousers started to feel more restrictive at the memory. The dress started midway down her back, with thin straps that showed off her shimmery brown skin and tattoos. The green fabric cinched in tightly at the waist and flowed over the curve of her hips and arse, ending at her calves. She turned to look over her shoulder and spotted him and her eyes lit up, although she kept her smile tight-lipped. Naya nodded her head in greeting and brought the cigarette up to her mouth again. O swallowed down a curse when the hollows of her cheeks appeared as she sucked. She turned away to exhale and played with her phone, and O walked past her to the bar.

O counted five things he could hear to slow his racing heart. He was as tense as a coiled snake; he wanted to shred that fucking dress in front of a balcony full of witnesses. He ordered himself a drink and then Naya's sweet breathy voice said, "Hello, Mr Jameson."

She smiled placidly and held out her hand. O took it, and they shook. He glanced down at the low neckline of her bodice, and the split that showed an almost-inappropriate amount of leg. And those black strappy shoes with the clear block heels that showed off her adorable little toes… "You look—" He cleared his throat—"you're forgiven."

Her hair was curled and swept to one side loosely, and she shrugged her bare shoulder. She fiddled with one of her long sparkly earrings as she waved at a colleague on the other side of the bar who called out, "Well done getting DEWI to finally exhibit with us!"

Naya thanked them and turned back to O to murmur, "I'd still like to make amends."

O blinked at her. "Wait a sec. DEWI confirmed?"

"Yes. They've got something that'll fit the theme. It's one of their first-ever pieces."

Pride pinged through O's ribcage like a pinball hitting all the targets. "You're amazing," he breathed, and then he realised he was gawking at her on a crowded rooftop filled with nosy people, cleared his throat and looked away. "What's your poison, Ms Matthews?" he asked breezily, and then for good measure, added, "Maya, right? Your name is Maya?"

Her mouth went tight as she tried to stop herself from laughing. "It's Naya, *Mr Jameson*. Srinaya. Double whisky neat, please. And if you're free now, I'd appreciate a quick chat to ask your thoughts about one of the artworks."

They took their drinks to the railing as they made small-talk far enough away from other people without making their wish for privacy too obvious and looked out at Jakarta. Cinq-Huit sat upon one of the tallest buildings in the area, and the glittering lights below them made up for the lack of stars in the sky.

O stuffed a hand in his pocket to not only stop himself from reaching for her, but to hide his ridiculous hard on, which would not bloody go away.

"So," Naya said with a pleasant smile. Her back was straight, one hand clasped around the wrist of the other. At this moment, she was Srinaya Matthews: art curator, not Naya: lover.

Someone interrupted them to respectfully shake O's hand and congratulate Naya on the DEWI addition and she waved away the compliment, claiming it was a team effort. He wanted to spank her for not accepting the praise she deserved.

He felt self-conscious about his body, as if muscle memory had flown over the railing. What did he normally do with his feet and face when he was talking to someone he hadn't seen naked? He took small sips of his whisky to keep his hand busy and ran his fingers through his hair.

"You look so stiff," Naya commented airily with a slightly distant smile. She took a sip of her drink too. "Your shoulders and spine, I mean. Relax. You're doing a terrible job of playing it cool."

O swore under his breath. "I've forgotten how to stand like a normal person."

She let out a little controlled laugh as she looked around at all the guests and waved at someone. O noticed a few people looking their way. He gave them a legacy director smile—reserved and not reaching his eyes. "Right," she said, her hand gesturing in a commanding way as if she were giving a presentation. Her eyes looked up at him—all business. "Did we come to a mutual decision about you fucking me without protection?"

O sputtered and his eyes darted around to make sure no one heard. He took another sip of his drink and nodded. "I would *very* much like to, if you're game."

"Oh, I am absolutely game. Where should we go?" Her face was impassive even though her chest flushed. O's body went hot. "I want you to fuck me hard and come quick. Could we? I want to taste your cock after you've—" Naya's eyes flitted to the right—"already assigned spaces that will be used for the larger installations, especially that beautiful piece we discussed on Wednesday with the tree? That's going to go in the newly renovated north wing. Gunawan has contacted the audio-visual techs to have them set up that room for *only* that piece, since we all believe it is the title work of the exhibition..." She put on a tone that matched her presentation stance.

O bit the inside of his cheek as four femmes walked past, one of them eyeing Naya up and down and then flicking their eyes to him before heading to the bar. When they were out of earshot, Naya's voice trailed off and O snorted into his drink. She pursed her lips and held in a giggle.

"The fucking devil, Srinaya," he muttered, looking down on *Jl Sudirman* and the traffic that was only starting to ease. "Fucking hell." He pinched the bridge of his nose.

This was stupid. Why had he insisted on coming here? They never should've left her bed.

He drawled, "Past the bathrooms downstairs by the bar, there's a door around the corner that says *Private*. Knock on that door in ten minutes," and then he downed the rest of his drink, nodded crisply and walked away.

twenty-three

THE DJ DOWNSTAIRS SPUN LOUDER, THUMPIER TRACKS AS NAYA MADE her way past the dancefloor, spotting the hallway that led to Owen, waiting impatiently, all hard and hot. Hopefully half naked.

Tini emerged from the mass of sweaty MP bodies wearing an impressively short gold sequined dress paired with gold platform heels. She swayed drunkenly as she blocked Naya's way. "You look damn hot, *Mbak* Naya. I know you're my boss, but tonight, you're just my friend. Your boobs look *mm-mmm-MMM* in that dress."

Tini fussed over Naya's hair, sweeping the waves off Naya's shoulder, and spotted the bite marks. Her eyes went huge as she squealed, "Oh my god!" and clumsily pawed at Naya's hair to cover the bruises again.

Shit, shit, shit.

Naya raked her fingers through to smooth it back down, face burning. Tini grabbed Naya's shoulders and pulled her in to speak under her breath. "Please tell me he did that. *Puh-leeeeeease* tell me you gave enthusiastic consent because *did you see him in that suit?* Does he look as good without clothes? Oh my god I can't even imagine—" Tini made a very inappropriate high-pitched orgasmic *uuuuuuugh,* and Naya shushed her.

Tini jumped up and down. Naya had no idea how she didn't break her ankles in those ridiculously high heels.

"Tini, Tini—*Tini!*" Naya hissed to get her attention. "Please. Please *stop.*" Tini got ahold of herself. She looked around and smoothed her own sleek chin-length bob with her hands. Naya said, "Please. Please don't say anything. To anyone."

Naya's face must've clearly conveyed fear, because Tini grabbed both of her hands and said quietly, "I promise I won't say a thing."

Naya squeezed Tini's hands firmly. "Not even to Edhi."

Tini rolled her eyes. "Well, *duh.* I love Edhi but he'd tell everyone. I won't repeat this. I promise."

Naya exhaled, and nodded her head in thanks. "Let me get you a drink."

She took her time making her way through the crowd of colleagues with her quadruple whisky neat to share with Owen, waving and chatting to people as she meandered towards the private room. The dark corridor was thankfully empty, and she hurried past the bathroom doors and around the corner before someone could walk out and corner her for a chat, or wonder where she was going and try to follow.

She knocked on the door marked *Private*, straightened her dress and hair, and a wave of giddiness flowed through her as she waited. The door swung open, light pouring out from the room, and Naya came face to face with Endah.

Naya paled.

Owen lounged on a couch, one leg crossed over the other. His mouth curved into an apologetic smile and he beckoned her to come in. Naya froze, eyes darting between Endah and Owen, her feet refusing to take her into the weird, fancy looking green room with sofas, a massive tv, a kitchenette and dining table.

Fuck—she'd been caught red-handed.

Endah spoke, "Naya, it's okay. I know about the two of you. I'm happy for you. Please, come in."

Naya's eyes flicked to Owen, cheeks burning, and he nodded reassuringly.

Naya felt naked in front of *Ibu* Endah. In the harsh light of this living room or whatever the hell it was, her dress was gaudy and revealing—inappropriate. She wanted to cross her arms over her chest, but that would push her tits together and highlight her cleavage even more. She took a tentative step inside, and then another.

"What is this?" she asked in a small voice.

She couldn't help but feel ambushed—betrayed. Owen stood, reaching for her. "It's alright, love."

She stared blankly at his open hand, and then up at his face. "What *is* this?" she repeated, refusing to touch him in front of Endah.

Endah stepped forward. "Owen and I were talking about Surya."

That name snapped Naya out of the blur of confusion. "What about him?"

"We're discussing removing him," Endah said, clasping her hands together. "His conduct at MERAHPUTIH is unacceptable."

Owen nodded. "He's unfit to be on the board." He stepped away from Naya and leaned against the wall to her right, burying his hands in his pockets.

The cogs in Naya's brain that had screeched to a halt at the sight of Endah began ticking over again. "But he *was* voted in," Naya argued, glancing back and forth between the two directors.

"It's just business," Endah answered dismissively.

"And… nepotism," Owen added with a cringe.

Naya arched her brow.

"His family," Endah continued, "owns the textile company that manufactures our products for the design stores. By giving them a board seat, they give us significant discounts on production."

Oh for fuck's sake.

Owen crossed his arms, his pristine suit jacket creasing. "We're still paying an exorbitant sum though, aren't we? And the more I hear about his shitty attitude, the more I want to tear up the agreement."

Naya bristled at how flippantly Owen spoke, as if ending the contract was some easy thing that didn't mean trying to find tens of thousands of dollars to make up for the difference in cost.

"So, an advantageous business deal, and preferential treatment due to family ties. Got it." Her tone dripped with loathing and she didn't care. "And what will be your reason for removing the nephew of *Bu* Tuti then?"

Owen widened his stance as he declared, "His prejudice against you."

Get totally fucked, she almost spat out, but instead, she enquired, "Did someone make a complaint on my behalf?"

Endah pointed to herself. "I did."

Shit—more unsolicited favours from Endah. Naya took a deep breath and lifted her chin. "You can't use that as grounds for his dismissal."

Owen blinked and his nose wrinkled. "What do you mean?"

Naya finally crossed her arms, not giving a shit about her cleavage anymore. "I'm not going to be the reason he gets kicked out."

Owen looked confused. Annoyed. "But-But— he's been awful to you," he sputtered.

Naya half-shrugged. "He's awful to everyone."

Owen pushed himself off the wall and straightened to his full— usually unnerving—height. This time, Naya was *not* intimidated. "But he's extra awful to *you*." he argued. "Naya, he emailed Bakti and Tuti to get '*I Am Just Waiting To Join You*' blocked from the show."

Naya gasped. "He *what?* Can he actually do that?"

Endah held her hand up to silence Owen, who was about to answer. "No, he can't. It's sorted and everything is going ahead as you planned," she said firmly. "But, surely you understand that I couldn't condone what I witnessed in that meeting. I had to go to HR to report him."

Naya rolled her eyes internally. Like that meant anything to a member of the board, let alone someone related to the last living founder. She held her ground. "I wish you would've asked for my consent first, *Ibu* Endah. I wouldn't have given it. I'm not going to be that person."

"What person, dear?"

"The person who causes a fuss. Who ruffles feathers."

Owen's jaw ticked; he obviously remembered their earlier conversation when he claimed she was good at ruffling feathers, just like *he* was, that he took pleasure in how she ruffled his. Naya nervously ran her fingers through her hair to make sure it covered her bruises.

Endah reached for Naya's hand and gave it a squeeze. "You aren't causing a fuss at all! No one thinks that."

"Please don't involve me in this. I don't want to be known as the person who caused the relative of a legacy director to be ousted. You can't honestly expect me to go along with being the reason why MP ends a business arrangement that's over a decade old."

What were the flow-on effects of this? Signing on another manufacturer, sans discount, meant higher retail prices on products. What if visitors stopped buying items? Who would pay for losses in revenue? Who would lose out? Certainly not the board. What if people lost their jobs as the company tried to tighten the purse strings? How could they expect her to say yes? Fuck—when could she go home?

She closed her eyes, weariness overtaking her. She was the newest employee; the rest of the staff had been dealing with Surya's shittiness for years. And Naya's point of difference—her whiteness… Wouldn't it look like her being half white gave her more clout than the local staff, who had put up with Surya for so much longer? And now that she was sleeping with the king, it was like a trifecta of borrowed power that she didn't ask for, or deserve…

"I don't want you to think I'm ungrateful, but I don't want the attention." Owen's nose flared and his mouth flattened into a thin line. She continued, "I do want him gone, but not *because of me*. Please don't drag me into it. People will talk."

Endah leaned on the edge of the console table. "Alright. But if someone else makes a complaint against him?"

"If people *who are not members of the board*—" Naya stressed—"make complaints against him for how he speaks to me, I can't stop that. And if I'm questioned, I'll tell the truth." She shifted on her heels. "If two or more people complain about how *they've* been mistreated, then I'll be happy to make an official complaint to help. But—" She swallowed, and her hands began to tremble. She closed them into fists—"until that happens, I'm fine with sticking up for myself." Owen exhaled a frustrated curse. "Look, if he knows he's in trouble, he'll probably back off now, anyway, at least in front of other people."

Owen came near, reaching for her again. "I hate the idea of you being alone with him," Owen murmured, concern marring his face.

Naya closed the distance between them and his slender fingers stroked her upper arm. She repeated her words from earlier that evening: "I'm not weak."

Owen gazed at her, his face soft with affection. "I don't have to think you're weak to hate it." He curled a lock of her hair around his finger. Naya was keenly aware of Endah watching them. He carefully said, "Let's just tell people we're together, Naya. If everyone knows, he'll back off." He chuckled awkwardly. "I think tonight proved I'm terrible at playing it cool in public."

A fresh surge of annoyance flooded through her. "I said no," she snapped, jerking away from him.

Owen recoiled as if stung. "Why?" he demanded.

Was she doing a terrible job of explaining herself? How could he be this fucking obtuse?

She exhaled a sharp breath. She turned to Endah and said in a barely controlled tone, "You have my answer, *Bu*. I'd like to have a word with Mr Jameson in private."

Owen clenched his fists at the sound of his last name. Endah nodded silently and floated towards the door. As she passed, she gave Naya's arm a squeeze. "We will think of another way to get rid of him that doesn't involve you. I'm sorry I went to HR without asking you first." And then Endah left the room, the door closing behind her with a loud click.

Naya seethed—resentful of being asked to go along with being a pawn. Owen collapsed on the couch, rubbing his temples. He looked hurt, as if she had struck him, and she didn't understand why.

She answered his question with a trembling voice. "*Why?*" She took a gulp of whisky and breathed out the biting heat from the back of her throat. "Because of what happened to me in the past," she said in a patronising tone. "Because I'm a private person. Because this is our *first day* together and I *told* you only a couple hours ago that I wanted to go slow." She faced him, hands wildly gesturing between them. "Because I'm enjoying whatever this is, Owen, and maybe this thing between us could be something really great and I'm not going to-to-to *cheapen* it by using it to protect myself from the likes of Surya!"

It was all too much. She glared at him, begging him to *just fucking get it.*

The furrow in his brow deepened, Adam's apple quivering. He nodded slowly, and it seemed like her words had finally landed.

†

O hurried to the VIP room with a bottle of whisky he swiped from the bar when he bumped into Endah exiting the suite. "I've been looking for you. We're about to leave but I want to speak to you quickly. Come in."

O winced internally. Endah being there was like a bucket of ice cold water straight to his groin, but he was at least grateful for the opportunity to apologise for his behaviour earlier. "*Tante,* I'm sorry for snapping at you. You know I love and respect you. Your opinion matters, but I've made my choice."

Endah waved him off. "It's fine. You're old enough to make your own decisions. And mistakes." She crinkled her eyes at him. "I won't say anything. Anyway, that's not what this is about. I have more Surya gossip."

If Endah was like a bucket of ice cold water, Surya was a swift knee in the balls. "*Ugh,* what now?"

Endah smiled conspiratorially. "He emailed Bakti and *Bu* Tuti to raise concerns over some questionable works that could sully the reputation of the gallery if they were permitted to be exhibited in *Heartbreak.*"

O saw red. His body burned, at first from desire but now from displeasure. He took off his tie and undid the button on his collar. "For god's sake," he growled.

"Mm hmm. He also said—" Endah raised her phone to read from it — "*it is my duty as someone close to one of the co-founders of MERAHPUTIH to uphold* Indonesian *traditions by preventing controversial western views to pervade our prestigious institution."*

"To fucking *what?*" The silk tie he'd been holding was now a crumpled ball in his fist. "I know what piece he's offended by. It's so moving, I almost cried. Also, we've had *'Piss Christ'* hanging in the Purnama, for fuck's sake! I clearly recall Surya getting his photo taken in front of it. Wait—did *you* get an email?"

Endah shook her head. "I pushed for *Heartbreak* in the first place, so of course I didn't get it. Bakti forwarded it onto me with a laughing emoji. He told Surya he disagrees with the accusations and trusts Naya's judgement."

"And Tuti?"

"Not sure. But she's never baulked at controversial works."

Naya feared everyone accusing her of hiding behind O, while this pipsqueak hid behind the skirts of his powerful aunt?

O's anger *actually* caused him to vibrate. God he needed more than alcohol. He needed his Valium. He needed Naya. "It isn't even controversial. It just has nudity. *I* didn't receive an email, obviously, because —" He gestured to his face, his very *western* face.

Oh, he wanted to break something. So, so badly.

"Let's remove him," Endah said with a wink.

At first, O assumed Naya's refusal to announce their relationship was fueled by embarrassment to be seen with him. He'd felt rejected— feared she saw him as unworthy. Srinaya was a bright spark—so fiery and full of life, and O really... *wasn't.*

Many past relationships ended because his partners found his reserve tiresome. They liked his name and all the perks that came with it, but they weren't interested in his brooding—that sometimes, the anxious thoughts were too loud, and too much, and made it hard for him to leave his house. Sometimes, he couldn't put on the easygoing smile and pretend to be okay.

One ex said he was *lacklustre under the pretty package.* "Great sex, great body, *such* a pretty face," Andy had said—his tone so cutting, "but you're such a bore when you're being a headcase. I can't handle it anymore."

O never forgot those words.

Naya stood by the door of the VIP room, rubbing her arms to self-soothe, her disappointment a horrible, ugly thing.

This wasn't a problem O could fix for her. He *knew* she was perfectly capable of solving her own issues, and he admired her for it, but he'd presumed it would still be his to handle because he was good at getting things done. Just because she could do it all on her own, didn't mean she *had* to. Owen Jameson: the fixer, the man with the answers. It was who he was. He wanted to do her this favour... but then he remembered her clearly insisting she didn't want favours from him.

Christ—he hadn't listened to her when she told him to leave well enough alone, and then he projected his own self-loathing onto her by getting angry at her.

He held out his hand. "Hey, will you sit next to me? I'm sorry... that I got my back up. I was offended. Honestly? I thought you were ashamed of me."

Naya watched him, and he blushed under her careful gaze. Then she moved forward, her heels clicking on the polished cement floor as she sat on the couch next to him and covered her face with her hands. "No, Owen. I'm ashamed of *myself*," she said, voice trembling.

"I didn't understand before, Naya, but I think I do now." He intertwined their fingers. "You achieved something—a promotion maybe?—that made people jealous enough to accuse you of sleeping your way to the top." Naya's pretty dark eyes flicked up to him. She nodded. "You were harassed online, on the phone, and at home. You were traumatised. So much so that you don't want to *cause a fuss* now—even though you're actually being bullied by someone with power—because you are now sleeping with someone who is at the very top." He gestured to himself. "You're worried that if you come forward, people will find out you're sleeping with me—running the risk of once again being accused of sleeping your way to the top—instead of focusing on the fact that you helped the company get rid of a toxic person who has caused you and others harm."

Naya laughed mirthlessly. "All I wanted at MP was to keep my head down and do good work. Prove myself. This thing between you and me came out of left field." She sighed as she moved closer. "And I'm so touched that I have your support, and Endah's, and Bakti's, but the others don't have that privilege. I want to be recognised for what I've done—not who I know."

O nodded slowly, taking his time to absorb her meaning. He tipped his head in thought. "But—and please hear me on this, and understand that I'm not trying to accuse you of anything or make you do anything you don't want to; I just want you to see another point of view, okay?"

Naya nodded but held her breath, as if she was bracing for him to say something terrible. He stroked her arm. "Do you not see that your connections mean *you* have power too, and you can help those people who don't have as much power as you?"

She shut her eyes tightly—brows slanted with hurt. "I understand what you're saying, but I just can't, Owen. I *can't*. I *won't*. There's more to the story but I'm trying so hard to put it behind me. I *had* put it behind me before you."

A stab of remorse rushed through him. "Naya, I care about you so much, but I don't want to be the cause of even more complications." O enveloped her waist and pulled her onto his lap and she pressed into him, wrapping her arms around his neck. He said his next words carefully, *hating* them. "If you'd prefer to go back to being colleagues, to uncomplicate things, I'll understand. I'll… stay away."

Naya clung to him tighter. "I don't want that. Remember what I said this morning? That I was scared *and* I should have stayed late to meet you?"

"*Both things can be true*," he said.

"It would be easier if you stayed away, *and* it's not what I want."

He pressed his cheek to hers. "I'm very sorry."

Naya made an adorable little throaty chirp as her eyes closed. She pulled her long hair from between them, flicking it behind her. O saw bite marks on her gorgeous brown skin and gasped. "*Sayang*, your shoulder," he murmured in apology. She buried her face into his neck and chirped again, not caring.

O finally saw his heavy-handedness—how he continued to assume he knew best when she shared what she needed in order to feel safe.

"Naya," he purred into her ear as he nipped her lobe, "I need you to tell me one more time, explicitly, what it is you want and don't want. I don't want any misunderstandings about this. I got so excited about the *potential* of us that I wasn't paying close enough attention earlier today and I'm sorry about that. Could you tell me again?"

Naya rubbed her eyes. "Take me home. Yours or mine—whichever. Let's talk at home."

twenty-four

What a sour note the Cinq-Huit party ended on.

Naya cringed at the thought of coming face-to-face with Endah in that suite. God knows what Naya's face gave away when the door opened. She was so excited; had been so aroused. She adjusted her tits before she knocked, for god's sake.

Owen had compromised her judgement; she couldn't help herself around him. Making out with him against a tree right around the corner from their workplace? Talking dirty to him on a crowded rooftop full of colleagues?

She'd always been great at compartmentalising; she never allowed her feelings and sexual needs to get tangled with her work, and since the incident with Sal, Naya *never* slept with people with whom she collaborated until their projects were well and truly over, and only ever fucked her so-called betters when there was no chance of professional overlap or expectations outside of having a good time.

Two years ago, she'd spent eight glorious weeks in the arms of Gabe Travers during an art residency in Toronto. Gabe was a *very* big fish; they were a world-famous sculptor whose work graced public parks and town squares all over the world. They held more power than Naya but that didn't matter since their professional lives didn't overlap. The pair drunkenly met at a bar down the street from Naya's studio. She welcomed their advances, and the two of them laughed, and explored, and fucked almost every day for the entirety of Naya's residency. And when it was time to leave, Gabe drove her to the airport and that was that—a beautiful time with a beautiful human.

But Owen.

Well, he may not have been well-known like Gabe, but Owen was the biggest fish of all, and more beautiful. He somehow got through her resolve to keep everything separate, and now she had to contend with her ridiculous feelings and sexual needs getting very tangled with her work, and for once, she wanted to rebel against herself.

Her day glimmered all the more brighter when she saw him at MP. Since moving into her new office—fortuitously situated with a perfect view of his fancy suite—Naya spent a great deal of time distracting herself by watching him stalk around, earpods in, talking on the phone. He was stony-faced and straight-backed when he played the part of JP CEO and MP legacy director, with his arms crossed over his broad chest. And then, Endah would visit him some afternoons and he would pour her a cup of tea and he transformed into just Owen—*her* Owen, leaning back casually on his couch with his giant fancy shoes crossed on the coffee table, joking with the fiery old dancer. Naya even heard Endah squeal and cackle and the cheeky smile on Owen's face was such a welcome sight.

Owen sat on the couch in Cinq-Huit's private room now, that devilish charm nowhere to be found—replaced instead with child-like hurt as he held her gently in his arms and apologised for getting so wrapped up in the excitement of being together that he hadn't taken her concerns seriously.

Naya understood. She was excited too. When Owen told her what he wanted, Naya had been moved; he'd cracked open her heart so much wider. *What I want is to know everything there is to know about you. What pisses you off. What makes you cry. Who broke your heart.* His openness inspired her to reciprocate. But mixed with that openness, excitement was inadequacy and fear. Naya was so fucking tired of the fear, but being tired of it didn't make it go away. Being tired of Surya definitely didn't make *him* go away, and at this moment her fear of being accused of seducing Owen to climb to the top loomed larger than the pleasure of Owen's arms around her.

Nevertheless, she'd shared her intentions aloud and wouldn't take them back now. He just needed to understand that she refused to be pushed.

"Home—yours or mine," she said in the private room at Cinq-Huit. She needed the quiet, the safe little bubble that was filled with only the two of them, and Owen obeyed immediately. He led Naya to the service elevator and down to the basement where his driver waited for them. Owen introduced her to *Pak* Ibrahim, who gave her a quick smile and tight nod, and then she was ushered into the back of the sleek black car, Owen holding her close.

They snuggled together silently, Naya's back pressed into his side with his arm around her, her head resting on his shoulder. Owen draped his jacket over her front to keep her warm, and she murmured thanks. He kissed the top of her head and stroked her arm.

"I'm taking you to my place. I hope that's okay," he rumbled in her ear, and Naya nodded, enjoying the darkness of his car and the weight of his forearm crossed over her torso.

"Oh wait—I didn't bring a change of clothes," she said, twisting her neck to look at him.

Owen stroked her hair. "I have tshirts, and I stole your sexy lacy underwear this afternoon, remember? So, unless you went commando to a company party…" He reached under her dress and ran his hand up between her thighs. "Oh, yes. Very professional of you to put on under-wear, Ms Matthews. Smart thinking," he said playfully, and Naya squeaked as his fingers tickled her. She leaned her head back onto his chest to smile at him, and Owen's fiery eyes stared down at her. He ran his lips over her brow. "You'll sleep naked tonight and have two pairs of clean underwear in the morning."

They didn't speak for most of the journey to his place, Owen humming a tune under his breath. Naya's mouth curved. "Are you singing 'Close to Me'?"

She heard him smile, his breath warm on the top of her head, but he didn't answer.

✝

Owen's home was magnificently small. Or rather, the house itself was. Naya couldn't tell for certain in the dark, but the property looked like it was at least four times larger than any of the neighbouring homes in the secure complex in which he lived. His house, situated at the back of the block, was hidden out of view by trees. So many of them—like a small forest in the suburbs.

The driveway up to the house was dimly lit. Tropical plants grew big and wild on either side. And then, as they drove further in, the house came into view—a beautiful modern structure that was all concrete, natural stone, carved wood and glass. Hanging vines fringed the floor-to-ceiling concertina windows at the front like a natural curtain, and the huge trees that stood tall and proud looked old and established—much older than the building.

"Owen," Naya breathed, her eyes wide as she stepped out of the car and was led up the curved stone walkway flanked by more vines that protected them from prying eyes. "This is incredible," she murmured. "This feels like you."

Owen smiled down at her as they reached the massive wooden doors, intricately carved with a traditional Indonesian motif. He opened the door and let her in. "How do you know what feels like me?"

Naya placed her shoes by his front door and he did the same, and then he pulled her into the living room. "Well, it's beautiful like you. Quiet. Unassuming. Balanced—like mine, but in a different way."

As he sat on the arm of a big dark teal couch, she followed the long wall of windows and looked out. Some of the trees were lit from beneath. Her eyes scanned upwards into the branches. "The way it works *with* the landscape... you built it around the trees, right? And it looks so wild out there..." She gestured outside. "I can't wait to see it in the daytime." She craned her head to see around the corner. "That is a gigantic pond," she commented. "Does *Pak* Yanto feed the giant fish there? No pet cats, I'm presuming?"

"No fish," Owen answered. "It's a swimming pool. Outside the bedroom."

Naya's mouth dropped open. "One of those natural pools? Really? Can we swim tomorrow? Please?"

"Whenever you want, lovely one. We can swim tonight if you'd like."

"I don't have a swimsuit."

He shrugged. "Then I won't wear mine."

Owen sat barefoot in his white shirt and black suit trousers. There was something different in his demeanour, as if Naya standing in his home was his way of sharing something far more intimate than his body. The way his hands were buried in his pockets with his shoulders hunched—he looked exhausted... defeated.

"Are you okay?"

He gave her a tight nod. "My anxiety... I've been feeling this way since I first arrived at Cinq-Huit. It's... been a big day."

Naya went to him. With Owen sitting on the armrest of the most comfortable looking couch she'd ever seen, they were eye to eye. She stepped between his knees, and his hands gripped the sides of her dress. He looked... ashamed. Scared, even. Did he think this thing between them was coming to an end? Naya cupped his face in her hands and kissed him, and he kissed back gently, following her lead. She unbuttoned his shirt, sliding her hands underneath the fabric to ground him.

"What do you need?"

"Just you."

She didn't want to push him to say more. "You know," she said, as she ran her fingers along his jaw to comfort him, "I was worried your house was going to be like one of those Pondok Indah monstrosities."

Owen wrinkled his nose. "All columns and marble like the Pantheon?"

"Exactly! I don't think I could have taken you seriously if your place was like that..." She wrapped her arms around his neck. He enveloped her waist tightly, as if he never wanted to let her go. "But this?" She looked around at the high ceilings, gauzy curtains, and wooden floor with rugs and big comfortable furniture in light grey, dark teal and bronze. "I see you. Hard and soft. Straight lines and twisting overgrowth. Strong and unyielding *and* so vulnerable. Your first name and your last name..."

Owen's eyes snapped to hers and his brow furrowed as he searched her face. "What are you saying?" he asked with trepidation.

Naya kissed him again. Slowly and heavily, taking her time to explore his mouth. He sighed. "I've been unfair to you," she confessed. "You'll never be just Owen without also being a Jameson. Your last name and your family legacy are as much a part of you as those big hands and beautiful eyes and adorable freckles—have I told you how much I love your freckles?—and I wouldn't want you to change, just as I refuse to be changed."

Naya's brows knitted together, and heat swept over her face, but she forced herself to look at him. "I'm practical. I wouldn't really call myself much of a risk-taker, or a romantic. When I make big decisions, I weigh up all the options. I'm an immovable object." She shrugged, unashamed. "I'm not the kind of person who jumps in quickly when it comes to serious relationships."

Owen was silent, expectant. He nodded his head, hanging onto every word. Naya ran her hands over his warm chest—the hairs under her fingers soft. "I've never felt this way so quickly. It's—" She swallowed—"wonderfully unexpected, but also terrifying... Since you asked me to be absolutely clear so there are no more misunderstandings..." *Shit*—she cleared her throat and jumped in with both feet. "I'd like to give this a real try... if you're still interested."

Watching Owen's eyes light up in surprise and pained pleasure all at once was a fucking gift. He looked like he might cry.

"Really?" he asked, voice strained. He stroked her hair and leaned in to kiss her again but she flinched away.

"But you can't rush me, Owen," Naya said sternly. "I don't want any more of the staff finding out until I'm ready. Endah knows, Arum knows. I'm assuming Mario knows?"

Owen nodded.

"Bakti probably knows—I'm not sure."

"Wait—why would *Bakti* know about us?"

"He's Arum's dad."

Recognition dawned on Owen's face. "Of course. *That's* why she looked familiar. I met her at some event a few years ago."

Naya smiled. "I know. Arum remembers you and said it was disgusting how lovely you were." Owen looked pleased to hear he'd already won over her best friend. She continued, "And god—Tini knows..." Owen blinked at her. "She saw the bite marks tonight," Naya explained.

He grimaced. "Oh *no.*"

Naya rubbed her temples. "I know. Although she's been Team Owen since you had lunch with us. She told me to give *enthusiastic consent to that dick.*"

Owen howled at that, holding his belly, and Naya revelled in his joy. As his laughter faded, he cupped her face. "No one else connected to MP will find out about us from me. And I understand that you want to go slow, but I do have a request, Naya." She lifted her chin a fraction in question. "I can't be a secret forever. I won't be hidden away, and I don't want to hide you. Could we negotiate a time frame? I know you're scared. If we have a date to work towards, we can work through it together."

She pursed her lips. Her main focus at work was, of course, getting through the planning stages of *Heartbreak* with as little Surya-drama as possible. She had another two months before the show started. "The *Heartbreak* opening. Would that work?"

Owen did a terrible job of tamping down his excitement. "Really? Opening night?" He asked, not casually at all. Naya winced internally but nodded. "That's perfect!" He exclaimed. His upturned eyes crinkled. "I've been smitten for fucking ages, Naya."

She huffed, and rolled her eyes as Owen pulled her to him roughly, face buried in her neck. "Don't be dramatic. Three weeks is not ages."

twenty-five

O awoke in the middle of the night to Naya's warm body curled in his arms. She slept soundly facing away from him, her hair a tangled mess in his face. He smiled at how perfectly domestic it seemed—waking up to hair tickling his nose and mouth. He brushed her long tresses away gently and wondered if there would come a day when he'd find it annoying, wishing she'd put her gorgeous hair in a plait.

He remembered his dad hating how his mum never put the toothpaste cap back on the tube, and how there would be water splashed everywhere in their bathroom after she finished getting ready. *How can such a tiny woman create a flood from washing her hair? There's water on the ceiling, Molly—what the fuck.*

The same went for his father's nervous habit of chewing on pens and crunching down on peppermints instead of sucking on them like a *civilised human.* His mum hated the sound. *I swear you'll break a tooth and you'll get no sympathy from me,* she would say in Indonesian.

O wanted that for him and Naya—wanted to get to a point where they would annoy the shit out of each other and grumble and argue but kept on being deeply in love anyway because there was no other possibility but to be together.

But even after Naya had been unmistakably clear about wanting to be with him, their relationship was precarious—a house perilously close to a crumbling cliff's edge—because of his stupid Chidori lie.

Endah's words about lying by omission hurt him. Scared him, even. O had mentioned to Naya too many times that their first meeting had been on the steps of MP. There was no going back now, and fuck—what would she do if she ever found out?

He kept insisting to Endah and Mar that *it really didn't matter.* None of them believed that. It could have been so much smaller though—a burden he carried alone—but he'd made it so much bigger and heavier by bringing them into it.

He'd called Mar in that hotel room, his head pounding and stomach lurching, prattling on about how he'd slept with—and *maybe* fucked—the most beautiful person ever. "But when I woke up, she'd gone. She left a thank you note: *Thanks for a night I wish I remembered, xox N.*"

"No phone number?"

"Nothing."

"Okay," Mar said with finality.

But it wasn't okay. That couldn't be it. "You know everyone, Mar," he pleaded. "Her name starts with N. She's average height, maybe? I don't fucking know, everyone's short to me," he complained without taking a breath. "Early to mid-thirties. Part-Asian, tattooed. Dressed a bit...I don't know—grungeish, I guess. Ripped jeans and tshirt. Long dark hair. Plus-sized, big tits, amazing arse—oh my god. Hard to miss."

Mario's eyes went wide on the video call, amused by his frazzled appearance. "Calm the fuck down. You're going to have a stroke. O, breathe."

O collapsed onto a chair, closed his eyes and breathed deep. A gaping emptiness appeared when an image of his parents holding hands played behind his closed lids. Mar's voice grew serious. "Owen. Jesus, are you okay?"

O buried his face in his hands. He didn't speak for a long time. So much loss. So much fucking loss. "I know this seems crazy, mate, but my dad used to tell us the story of how when he met my mum, he knew—he fucking *knew* instantly that they'd be together. And you know, I always thought he exaggerated it a bit to make it seem way more romantic than it actually was but—" His chest hurt and he fucking hated it—"if this is even a tiny bit like how he felt... shit. Mario."

Mar calmed him down, and promised to ask around, but no one knew her. And now, due to a stroke of good fortune, Naya was in his bed, all soft moans and sighs, and long dark hair in his eyes and up his nose. He had to keep her there, which meant he needed to keep this lie, and ask Endah and Mar to do the same. It made him feel like an utter piece of shit, but they'd do it for him, because they were his family.

He tightened his arms around her, and she moved slightly under his grip. She purred, rubbing her feet against his.

O stilled. He hadn't meant to disturb her. They'd stayed up late listening to music and snuggling naked on the couch (*for the sake of having clean underwear in the morning*, O assured her, and she rolled her eyes). She craved nothing but his kisses, which felt far more intimate than their intense afternoon of sex. She was nervous and shy—so different from the unashamedly dirty woman who appeared before the mishap in the VIP room.

Her breathing deepened as she roused. Naya arched her back, her arse pressing against his pelvis, and murmured sleepily. He inhaled that spicy cinnamon scent from her neck and she shuddered as he blew a breath along her shoulder. Reaching back to cup his nape, she pulled him closer and twisted her neck to brush her lips on the corner of his mouth.

"*Sayang*," he whispered in her ear. "I'm sorry I woke you."

Naya sighed. Her eyes fluttered open, and she placed a hand behind her on his hip, sweeping it across the crease where his stomach met his thigh and over his hardening cock. Naya wrapped her soft fingers around him and stroked gently, and O growled into her ear.

"Make amends then," she moaned, voice sleepy, and O smiled and nipped at her neck.

His one hand wrapped around her throat as he slid his tongue into her mouth. She whimpered when his other hand reached between her thighs to part her pussy lips. "Already so wet, Naya. Is this for me?"

Naya flinched as O dipped two fingers inside her and then brought them to her mouth. She sucked on his fingers, her tongue tickling the webbing, sending a delicious jolt of pleasure straight to his cock. She hummed as she licked him clean and finally answered him, "Always. Always so ready for you." She twisted around to look up at him, eyes hooded and bleary. "Please—no teasing."

His cock rested against her swollen lips. She tilted her hips slightly and positioned the crown to her entrance. "Wait, Naya. Condoms? I have some here," he asked. He could hear the strain in his own voice, trying so hard not to drive into her yet.

She shook her head. "It's just you and me now, remember?" she breathed, and those words coming out of her mouth were like the most beautiful poem.

He swallowed down a sob, and repeated her words as he pushed into her warm tight cunt: "Yes, it's just you and me now, lovely one." He swore as he slid all the way in, and she gasped. "Fuck, you feel wonderful," he sighed.

He circled his arms around her body and found a slow rhythm, sliding almost all the way out and then back in, her silky juices making it feel like velvet—so luxurious and warm. The sensation of her welcoming him without the thin latex barrier—a declaration of trust and commitment—made tears form in his eyes. "You and me, you and me," he whispered.

He wrapped his hand around her throat and she lifted her chin in submission. He drew her closer, her back pinned against his chest as they spooned. Naya bent her leg to allow him to slide in deeper, and when O deepened his thrusts, she moaned, "*Yeeees*... like that, yes."

He wrapped her silken hair around his hand and pulled firmly, and she gasped, her voice high and desperate as she urged him on, "Just us, Owen, please."

O's breath hitched. He'd been needy since the rooftop bar, so many hours ago. His toes curled and he panted. "Love, already close. So fucking close. Can I?"

Naya answered instantly, "Inside me, yes. Come inside me," she sobbed, as he fucked her harder.

A guttural sound came out of him. "I have you now, Naya. Fuck, love—" and then he came, hips shaking as he emptied into her, and

Naya rolled her pelvis in the most delicious way that made him buck until he hissed because it was too much. He bit the inside of his cheek to stop himself from saying the words on the tip of his tongue: *I love you. I've loved you for a very long time.*

She looked over her shoulder at him in the dim light of his bedroom, smiled lazily and sighed. God—she was so beautiful. He kissed her brow. "What about you, *sayang*?"

Her voice was sleepy again as she answered, "I'm good. I'm satisfied."

"Are you sure?"

"*Mm hmm.* Don't keep score," Naya whispered.

O cleaned her with a warm washcloth. She was compliant—limbs heavy as he caressed her between her legs—more asleep than awake. When he slid under the sheets next to her again, she draped her arm over his torso, nuzzling into his shoulder. She purred quietly and then went silent.

O drifted off soon after.

twenty-six

THE LITTLE FOREST THAT PROTECTED OWEN'S HOUSE WAS MORE beautiful in the daytime than Naya imagined. The colourful foliage was cut back in a way that made the gardens still look untouched—a wild oasis that hid them away from the outside world. The ferns growing at the base of the trees reminded Naya of pictures of the Kalimantan rainforest. She had even seen a monitor lizard scurry under the bushes and shuddered.

He had fruit trees—*rambutan*, durian, *jambu*, and mango. The green mangoes were in season and she could smell their sweet aroma when the breeze blew through the house.

Owen acted less burdened than the night before. He made coffee and grilled ham and cheese toasties while Naya peeled *salak* and mangoes for breakfast. He bounced around his kitchen laughing and teasing, stealing kisses and demanding snuggles, and she was more than happy to accommodate him. The day before was trying for both of them—highs and lows, mind blowing pleasure, joy and fear. The way their evening's mood dipped to expose some of their insecurities—in front of Endah, no less—before shooting back up to end on a very happy note meant they went to sleep feeling emotionally bruised.

They'd slipped into the pool early in the morning after a restless sleep—both too anxious about their blossoming relationship, as if they'd wasted far too much of their lives not being together, and had to make up for lost time by learning everything they could about each other.

She made every effort to be unguarded with her words. She'd only ever been honest about her deepest fears with friends who'd known her for decades. And really, Owen didn't know her well at all. She was following her intuition in choosing to be with him, something she'd done less than a handful of times since Sal over a decade ago, and that was a terrifying thing.

Sure—she was an immovable object, always taking her time, checking all available options. But after yesterday, she realised not being with Owen *wasn't* an option. Owen had a way of getting past her defences, not from always pushing but from being the first to be vulnerable.

He finally opened up about the day his family died—how Endah delivered the news since his dad's brother, who had inherited him, was on military deployment. His parents flew to London to visit Gemma during her second term break at uni. They were in a car accident on the way to dinner. All three died before the paramedics arrived.

Endah flew to Australia to tell him. He was angry and mean for months, self harming and getting into fights, and yet Endah and Agung had been there, patiently waiting, absorbing as much of his hurt as they could bear.

Endah saved him. Owen didn't say it, but Naya could see the look on his face as he recalled the part she played in the story.

Naya shared the history of her own difficult upbringing—how she didn't talk to her mother anymore and didn't see her dad much, although they had a good enough relationship. As a teenager, she asked her dad to send her to school in Melbourne so she could get away from her toxic mother. Her parents never married, and their relationship hadn't worked out, and her mother's resentment for having to care for a kid she probably never actually wanted, especially without a husband, made Naya the target of her rage. "I haven't talked to her in six years, and have no idea where she is, and I truly don't care," Naya said with a shrug, and then she'd quickly kissed Owen and asked him to fuck her again, and to make it hurt, and he did, a silent understanding between them that she *did* care very much but accepted that this was just how it was.

"You have me," he rumbled into her ear as he thrust into her over and over again, the intensity of her pleasure chasing away her sadness. "We have each other now."

⳨

In the afternoon, after napping together on the daybed out on the deck, Owen picked mangoes from his garden. The tree sagged from all the ripened fruit, and as he picked them, the smaller branches sprung upwards, shaking with delight at being unburdened. Naya gave her shoulders a little shake as well.

She snapped pictures of him on her phone. Standing barefoot in his lush little jungle, Owen was a mythical forest deity with that golden-tanned body and that wavy gold-streaked hair half tied up, wearing only a batik sarong... If he was walking around nude he would have looked like Adam in the garden of Eden. Naya sniffed at the thought of being Eve. Being the devil appealed to her though, slithering over Owen and tempting him to do sinful things.

He rose onto the tips of his toes as he reached up into the tree, holding onto a branch for balance, his movements surprisingly graceful for someone so broad. She'd draw him like this. This was Owen at his most beautiful, in his element at home. Quiet and calm. No responsibilities, no problems to solve. God—maybe she had it all wrong. Maybe she *was* Eve, but Owen was the fruit.

She remarked, "You're very distracting, you know."

He snorted but didn't even look back at her. "You're one to talk, sitting there in only your undies and my tshirt, looking like trouble."

She pulled at the tshirt—a grey marle fabric that almost matched the grey of his eyes. "I've never dated anyone whose tshirts fit me. This is a whole new experience. I can't wait to see your tshirt collection," Naya commented, sitting cross-legged on the daybed. "You know how in movies and tv shows, you always see women swimming in their boyfriend's clothes and they look so adorable with their hair all mussed up? I've always wondered what that feels like." She looked down at herself. "I mean, I'm definitely not swimming in this, but still."

Her tits filled out the chest, although the sleeves were far too big and long so she'd rolled them up. It was very tight around her belly and hips of course, so she knotted it to sit higher on her waist, not caring if it stretched. "It's mine now," she said cheekily. "Consider it the first item of clothing I'll leave here. Aside from the underwear you stole." She felt fizzy at the thought of leaving some belongings at his house.

Owen turned around to look at her with a quizzical expression. "Uh oh—are you upset because it's going to be stretched?" she asked, pointing to the knot.

He dismissed that with a wave of his hand while his other arm cradled the mangoes. "Fuck the tshirt. Stretch them all—I don't care. Did you just call me your *boyfriend?*"

"I mean..."

"You did! You called me your boyfriend," he teased, mouth open wide in mock surprise. He looked ridiculous, standing there with an armful of fruit.

Oops. *Too late to walk that one back.* She was totally blushing. She couldn't help being unguarded around him, and it made her run her mouth off. "You're too old to be a boyfriend."

Owen feigned offence, gasping. "Harsh."

"You could be my Daddy."

Owen guffawed and Naya grinned at him. She felt proud whenever she made him laugh like that. When he caught his breath he asked, "What does the role of Daddy entail, then?"

Ever the wanton performer, Naya made her voice all sulky and let out a whine, leaning back against the cream cushions on the bulky hand carved seat. Owen went still as he watched. "Telling me what to do, punishing me when I misbehave..." She ran her hands down her chest and the sides of her tits, and pushed them together with a sigh. Owen stalked closer, right to the edge of his pool which blocked his way to her. "Taking care of me, praising me and rewarding me when I'm a *very* good girl..." Naya arched her back off the daybed, toes curled, and she dragged her fingers between her thighs. She whimpered again, and pouted at him.

Owen hissed in a breath, baring his teeth and shaking his head at her. "You are a very good girl," he said, and then his smile went practically satanic as he added, "Such a *very*... very... good... *girlfriend.*"

Naya let out a very loud, *uuuugh,* and buried her face in the cushions, and Owen laughed, eyes crinkling mischievously. She grabbed her phone and snapped a photo of him grinning while holding the mangoes against his chest, and sent the photo to Arum.

Arum responded instantly.

ARUM:

!!!!! UM WHAT

NAYA:

I know

ARUM:

WHAT

NAYA:

I know

ARUM:

Fuck—that bod

NAYA:

I KNOW

ARUM:

but also LOL juicy mangoes

Where are you? Are you in Puncak or something?
Looks like you're in the mountains.

NAYA:

I'm in fucking MENTENG. He lives in a jungle in the suburbs!!

ARUM:

Mar's with me! INVITE US OVER PLZZZZZ! We will bring weed and wine! I must re-meet him!

"Arum is with Mario and she wants you to invite them over."

"Invite away," he said as he strode towards the deck that led to the living room and kitchen. "Are you okay with walking around in just a tshirt and underwear?"

His tshirts may have fit her but her big belly and huge ass would no way fit into any of his pants. Naya nodded. She felt no shame about her body; there were enough naked photos of her on the internet if one were to look hard enough. She asked him, "Would it bother you though?"

"Not at all. You might be mine but your body is yours."

Naya couldn't help how wide her smile went. What a perfect fucking answer that was. He was full of perfect fucking answers.

NAYA:

He said come over!

But do you think you could stop by my house on the way and get me a weekend's worth of clothes and my sandals?

And bikini.

And maybe work clothes for Monday?

AND MY VIBRATOR. And the charger. Please!

Literally just in his tshirt and my undies. I hope Mario doesn't mind.

ARUM:

Like he has a choice. Give us 2 hours. But also, HOLY SHIT YOU FUCKED OWEN

"They'll be here in a couple of hours," Naya called out.

"No worries," O answered.

He rushed inside, gently dropped the mangoes in the kitchen sink and quietly raced around the house trying to find his phone to send Mario a message.

OWEN:

Hear you're coming over?

MAR:

DUDE I HEARD! YOU AND NAYA ARE A THING!
FUCK YEH

OWEN:

Yeah yeah it's great

really happy but listen

you didn't tell Arum about the whole me knowing her
for 8 months did you?

MAR:

No?

OWEN:

Please don't say anything about that ok?

MAR:

Ok I won't. Why tho?

OWEN:

Because I'm not planning on telling Naya

MAR:

Ok...

OWEN:

Look I know ok? I'm a piece of shit, I know.

MAR:

I didn't say anything

OWEN:

But I know. and I'm sorry for making you lie but please
don't say anything

MAR:

It's ok dude. I understand.

OWEN:

Really?

MAR:

I mean I don't agree

OWEN:

ffs

MAR:

We're on the way to pick up some clothes for her and then we'll be over and I won't say a thing

OWEN:

ok I'm sorry for making you lie

MAR:

It's fine. Can't wait to meet her.

OWEN:

You're gonna love her.

MAR:

If 2 rad people who I care about love her then I'm sure I will too.

OWEN:

3—Endah loves the shit out of her as well

MAR:

Sure you want me to meet her then? She may fall in love with me. You know I'm the one with the personality

OWEN:

Fuck off. Hurry up.

twenty-seven

They were notified of visitors by the security guards at O's front gate and a moment later, Mario parked his car at the end of the walkway.

Naya stood by the door, bouncing on the balls of her feet. "I can't wait for you to meet Arum properly. I'm sure she would've been much more reined in since you met her with her parents around."

And then, Arum—cropped bluish-silver hair glinting in the afternoon light, wearing flared ripped jeans and one of Mario's tshirts, *that she was swimming in*—jumped out of the car. Mar's gaze was locked on Arum; his best friend was besotted—it was blindingly obvious.

The four of them stood in the foyer—old and new friends. Arum spoke first, sticking out her hand. "Owen Jameson. So we meet again," she said.

"Arum Handoko, codename Pixie-Goth," O answered.

They shook, eyes boring into each other.

Naya and Mario glared at each other like two gunslingers in a western. "The infamous Trout Pout."

"Ms Tits McGee," Mario responded, stressing the *Mizzzz* with a very evil sneer, and then Naya giggled and pulled him in for an embrace, and kissed his cheeks as if they'd known each other forever, and Arum did the same to O.

O sulked, "I feel left out because I don't have a codename."

Arum scanned him from head to toe, her thickly lined eyes scrutinising. A few inches shorter than Naya, she only came up to O's underarm. Standing in front of him with an arched brow, she lifted her chin high to look up at him. "Big Moose," she commented.

Mario piped up instantly, "Biggest Whiney Bitch."

"I called you Daddy earlier." Naya said *Daddy* in the breathiest porn voice he'd ever heard. She pouted. "Did that not please you, Daddy?" Shit—she did it again, the copper flecks sparkling against the dark brown of her eyes.

Arum cackled like some evil witch while Mar howled, and O covered his face, his cheeks burning. "Uh-I—" he sputtered behind his hands.

Naya pulled his hands away and went onto her tiptoes to murmur, "*My favourite*—that's your codename," and nuzzled his cheek, and he wrapped his arms around her, kissing her neck.

Naya and Arum went to the bedroom to unpack Naya's things while O and Mar stayed in the kitchen, slicing fruit to serve with the charcuterie board they prepared.

"You and Arum," O commented. "I'm happy for you."

Mario grinned. "She's fucking adorable."

"She is. Adorable with bite. Absolutely your type."

"And Naya. Jesus. She's here. Looking amazing in your tshirt. And not much else."

"I know." O closed his eyes for a brief moment, smiled and sighed.

Mario leaned over the kitchen counter, resting his chin on his hand. "Why won't you tell her about Melbourne?"

O craned his neck to the bedroom door just as Arum cackled loudly at something. He played music through the Bluetooth speakers so he and Mar wouldn't be overheard. "I don't know the full story, but there was some incident in the past where she was accused of sleeping with her boss or something, even though she hadn't. Sounds like the bullying got bad and somehow the police got involved."

"Whoa."

O peeled the mangoes, slicing chunks of the sweet and slightly savoury flesh. "She might think I slept with her and then kept tabs on her. And then followed her to Jakarta, which—yeah, I kinda did… but only because Endah asked me to." He grimaced. "And when she got the show, I showed up around the same time…"

"What—you worry she'll think you pulled some strings on top of stalking her?"

O nodded.

"But you didn't, right?"

"*No.* I didn't even know she was living in Jakarta, let alone being hired at MP."

"Seriously, that's some destiny shit right there."

O smiled weakly. "But now we've got some dramas at MP. Surya has it in for her, because she had the audacity to stick up for herself when he was being a prick, and I can't do anything because she doesn't like the optics of me stepping in to defend her."

Mar winced. "Oh, you must be *hating* that. Mr Fix-it Protector Man."

"Oh, shut up."

"Mr Knight in Shining Armour."

"Yeah, alright." O threw a little bit of *salak* at him. Mar caught it and popped it into his mouth, grinning like an arsehole. "Anyway, I'm trying to figure out a way to oust Surya without getting her involved, because she doesn't want to be the reason someone is fired, even if she's also getting hurt by the fucker and has every right to want him gone. It's infuriating, even though I get it." Mario nodded slowly, taking in the story. "Also, we're keeping our relationship quiet until opening night, and I'd normally be really happy about quiet nights in together—"

"Because you're an antisocial fuck—"

O pointed a finger at Mar. "Exactly, but this time I feel like I'm being hidden away and *that* doesn't feel good."

Mario rubbed his face in exasperation, looking to the heavens. "Owen, you insecure, brooding gorilla." O put down his knife and stepped back from the counter just in case he accidentally threw the very sharp blade at his best friend's face. *"Compromise,"* Mar said.

"You're hiding something from her. You don't think it's a big secret. And yeah—maybe it *wasn't* a big one. But you made it huge by keeping it, instead of letting her see it for what it was—a serendipitous *pre-meet-cute*. And," he added pointedly, "I'm keeping it for you too. From *Arum.*"

Oh shit—this was a mess.

Mar continued, "You don't have the right to be angry when she's at least going public soon. And people *will* talk, O. They'll have opinions, and she's willing to face that."

O rubbed his chin. Mario was right. Again. Of course he was right. It was selfish and stupid for him to feel insecure about this at all. "Shit. Yeah. Okay. Thank you. I'm sorry."

Mario shrugged dismissively and crunched down on another bit of *salak*, and then his eyes softened. "Enjoy getting to know each other. Enjoy the privacy. Stay in bed as much as possible. If she's anything like Arum, the sex is fantastic and she just wants to be fed chocolate and cake and drink lots of expensive wine."

O's eyes rolled back into his head as he groaned, "Oh my god, the sex."

†

"What-is-going-on-with-you?" Arum asked, punctuating every word with a smack on Naya's arm.

"*Ow.*"

"You went from not wanting to get involved to spending the night at his house? The fuck?"

Naya nervously tied her hair up into a bun. She shrugged, trying to make it look flippant. "I couldn't help myself," she mumbled.

Arum crossed her arms as she paced around Owen's huge bedroom, admiring the opened concertina windows that led out to the deck and pool. She turned to Naya, hands up in the air. "Cannot compute, Sri."

"It's all your fault! He was supposed to meet Mario for brunch yesterday morning, but Mar was a little *busy.*" Naya glared at Arum, brows raised. Arum grinned unapologetically. "He found my username after seeing the posts from Le Roy, and we DMed and then he came over, and... we talked."

Arum looked at her without blinking, waiting for more. Naya massaged her temples. "Look, something happened at lunch on Wednesday. We were sitting at *Pak* Mudi's and we were having a meal with the team and he was so lovely and unpretentious and—well *hello*, you have eyes. Look at him!" Arum nodded her head slowly, knowingly. "But something clicked as we talked. I don't know what it was. But then I got scared because he's *bigger* than Sal and Reginald Muse, and Surya is a bigger bully than Melinda. But he asked me if we could try and work through it so he came over. *With food.* Croissants, and bagels with cream cheese and bacon, and fucking *martabak* and *mie goreng*. And wine."

Arum groaned in pleasure. "God—these boys know what the fuck they're doing."

"And the sex, Arum. Oh my god." Naya sighed, brows drawing together. Arum's eyes sparkled. "But even before the sex. He was so vulnerable, and open, and kind, and I couldn't keep using his status at MP against him. I just *couldn't*." She took a deep breath in, and then exhaled. "You know me. I can't just jump into things like you. I wish I *could* be more like you." Naya swallowed and sat at the end of the bed. She shook her head as if she was trying to shake herself awake. "But not trying with Owen feels really... *not good*."

Arum sat next to her, hugging her knees. "I've never seen you like this."

"I know."

"Not even with Sal."

"I know."

"You planning on telling him *everything?*"

"I think so."

Arum's eyes went wide, and her brow's shot up. "Jesus."

"I mean, not right away. I'm a little terrified."

"Don't be," Arum encouraged. "I'm so happy for you. And proud of you too. I know this is a huge deal." Arum stroked Naya's arm, and then tucked some unruly strands of hair behind Naya's ear.

"Remember, bud, you are not doing anything wrong. You're both grown adults."

"I keep telling myself that. But I've still asked Owen to keep this quiet until the show's opening, because Surya is causing trouble and I don't need any extra—" She gestured with her hands in an effort to show how overwhelming it all was.

"That asshole."

"You never told me he's Ibu Tuti's nephew."

"Is he? I didn't know that."

"That's what Owen told me." She shrugged. "I want to enjoy what we have, and not get dragged into office politics. Owen and *Ibu* Endah asked me to come forward to make a formal complaint against Surya, but I don't want that kind of attention. Especially now that Owen and I are a thing. Is that selfish of me? To not want to help?"

Arum patted Naya's thigh. "Kind of? But I get it. Look. Just enjoy Owen this weekend. God—he is so pretty I don't know how you can stand it. You should be all blissed out."

Naya closed her eyes and sighed. "Don't worry—I am. Are you?"

"Oh, absolutely. Believe me. Mar's a fucking dream." She sighed happily, and then linked her arm to Naya's elbow. "Look at us—two best friends fucking two best friends. We should just get it over and done with and have a foursome."

Naya giggled and rested her head on Arum's shoulder. Arum reached into Naya's overnight bag, pulled out some lounge pants and shoved them in Naya's face. "Put some goddamned pants on, will you? When you said you were in your underwear, I wasn't expecting see-through lacy ones. Cover your ass before it steals Mario away."

⊥

They ate, and drank, and smoked, sharing stories about life in Melbourne, all the haunts they visited and whether or not they'd ever crossed paths. Arum and Mar knew many of the same people, while O and Naya found that their connections in the art world meant they also travelled in similar circles, although it seemed they always missed each other.

The sky got darker—the almost-white turning to dark purple with patches of grey, and a warm breeze came through as the sun disappeared. Lamps were switched on, and the tangy citronella candles lit to ward off pesky mosquitoes that only seemed to attack O's ankles.

While Srinaya and Mario walked through the illuminated trees, sharing a joint in the semi-darkness, Arum and O sat on the deck arguing about music. O turned to her as she smiled at her new lover and best friend giggling like teenagers.

"So," O said, "aren't you supposed to be interrogating me or something?"

Arum sniffed a laugh as she lit a cigarette. "Feel like I've learned a lot about you by your taste in music. Approve of your love of UMO and Surprise Chef, but am disgusted by your hatred of Portishead and Whitney. Either way, I'm a little too drunk to think of difficult questions to ask, and I can tell you make her happy." O chuckled as he poured the last of the wine. "Thing is, Moose, she's been through a lot. And she keeps things really light and fun with most people because she doesn't like bringing them down with her heavy shit, which is ridiculous since she's amazingly good at being there for others, and people can't help but want to reciprocate."

O grinned at her praise for Naya and nodded in agreement. "You should see the way her team looks at her."

Arum shrugged, unsurprised. "If they have a heartbeat, she'll charm them. And if she can't charm them, they're cunts."

He lowered his voice so that Naya couldn't hear him. "Arum, please tell me. How bad was this bullying incident?"

Arum's smile disappeared. "Bad. Her first solo show got cancelled, mail was dropped off at our door... I can't prove it but I *know* someone broke into our place and moved things around. I'd had enough and called the police. They weren't able to do much, but it calmed down after that. The mental toll it took though... and she lost someone very important. He walked away. Kind of. It's complicated."

Oh. That was new information.

"And then she had to start from scratch. She almost gave it all up. But look at her now."

Arum leaned back, hands braced behind her, legs crossed at the ankles. She still watched Naya and Mar—Naya screeching with laughter at something Mar said—and her mouth curved upwards with affection. "Did you feel it straight away?" she asked.

The question caught him off guard. If they were closer friends he would have used the most poetic words he could muster to explain how intense the feeling was—tell Arum that he had no fucking choice in the matter, and was absolutely fine with that, because even if he did, he would always choose Naya. "Yeah. The moment I saw her, I knew."

Something akin to relief passed over Arum's face as she watched Mar gesticulating wildly, sharing a story that made Naya double over in a fit of giggles. Arum leaned into O as she mused, "I think that's what I feel."

Right. He didn't know Pixie-Goth well but assumed the alcohol and weed relaxed her enough to dull some of her sharp edges. It was his turn to say something about *his* best friend. "Be kind to him, yeah? He's my family," he said as he put an arm over her and kissed the top of her head, taking the cigarette from her fingers to have a drag.

Naya and Mario were slowly walking back towards them, Naya clinging to the crook of Mar's elbow, still deep in conversation. Arum rushed her final words quietly. "I've never seen her like this. It's beautiful, like you've known each other for way longer than three weeks." O swallowed—kept his breathing even. "Listen, Naya is good at a lot of things. She's very good at loving. But god, is she terrible at letting go. It's why she doesn't give herself the chance to lose herself in relationships often. So don't fuck it up, Owen—I swear to all the deities I work with I'll fucking hurt you if you do because Naya doesn't realise it yet but she's falling. Hard."

twenty-eight

Over the next few weeks, Owen and Naya settled comfortably into each others' lives; she had her own section in his absurdly large walk-in wardrobe, and she moved half of her clothes to his so there'd be room in her much smaller closet for Owen's belongings. She liked seeing his clothes hanging next to hers—enjoyed looking over to *his* side of the bed. He'd already commandeered the bedside table, covering it with his charging dock, medication, and books. Her bathroom storage held his grooming accoutrements and a bottle of that delicious summery cologne he wore, and they had one of those soppy *his* and *hers* attachments for her electric toothbrush.

Owen bought her the exact same sextoy for his place, vowing to buy a dozen more and stashing them everywhere so they'd never be without one.

The whole thing was so fucking *domestic,* she should've shied away from it but found herself relishing it instead. She didn't think it should feel so easy. Things that mattered were never easy, but being with Owen was the easiest thing in the world. It felt brand new and exciting, *and* so comfortable and predictable.

She asked him to stay away from the fifth floor to give her time to adjust without distraction—try to find her footing in their new dynamic. She frowned whenever she glanced at his empty office. Owen was a bright golden light to everyone on the fifth floor, who perked up when he was there, not because he was their boss and the staff felt the pressure to be more productive for fear of getting into trouble. In fact, it was the opposite—Owen cared for the staff and they cared for him right back; they were relaxed in his presence and they worked *better* because of it. He wasn't like Surya, who loved his board member status but loathed the employees, and who basked in the way the staff stopped talking when he stalked through the open space. Surya probably believed it was a sign of respect when it was really hatred mixed with fear.

Naya longed for Owen's touch all day. He was no less needy; every reunion was desperate and rough as if they hadn't seen each other for weeks instead of hours. She ran into the protective warmth of his arms, allowing him to hold her tightly, kiss her until her lips hurt. She lost herself in him and loved it.

By Thursday, Naya couldn't stand it any longer.

NAYA:

The staff miss you here

OWEN:

That's sweet, but as much as I miss the staff, I've been banned from setting foot on the fifth floor until further notice.

NAYA:

This is your official notice then. I miss you here too

OWEN:

Be sure, because you can't take it back! I've been climbing up the walls working from home.

NAYA:

God you're dramatic.

OWEN:

Currently texting you from my rowing machine because I can't stand the sight of my fucking office. I've done an hour of work today

NAYA:

Then come and work here. x

He showed up after lunch, the happy voices of the juniors greeting him such a sweet sound that she couldn't help her smile. He caught her eye as he sauntered into his office on the opposite side, his face not giving anything away, except for a friendly nod and a lick of his lips. She crossed her legs under her desk.

Tini, sitting on Naya's couch, chuffed. Naya jumped at the sound; she'd completely forgotten Tini was there. Naya's ears grew hot and her eyes widened, but she was too happy to be annoyed.

"Busted," Tini said, and Naya kicked her out with that comment, all the while giggling as the door shut in Tini's face.

Naya transformed into a machine over the following week, the clarity a refreshing change from the fog of missing him, and the guilt for keeping the *Golden God of MERAHPUTIH* away. By the end of their second week, the final artworks had been chosen. Eighty-eight pieces would be exhibited. Some were already trickling in.

There had been more setbacks with the renovations; the scheduled date of completion was moved to only two weeks before the opening. She thrived under pressure but with so many variables to consider, and the many scrutinising eyes on her, the pressure was more oppressive than ever. No matter. It would all work out because Naya trusted the Bevy and knew they'd find a path through any roadblock together.

$\perp$

Late on Monday morning, caught up and in control, the Bevy congregated in Naya's office, going over their tasks for the week ahead. Gunawan and Ravi were talking them through the product designs for the gift shop when Naya received a DM from Ruben back in Melbourne.

RU:

Ahoy ahoy boss, are you planning on doing the second piece for MP? Need to know so I can call in reinforcements

NAYA:

??

Aud Pitch

RU:

The mural

NAYA:

??

RU:

Did you not get the email?

NAYA:

YOU check my emails.

RU:

🙂 Do you know someone called Suryadharma Ali?
He's a board member at MP or something.

NAYA:

Yes. I know him. How do you know Surya?

RU:

He sent an email on Saturday

NAYA:

Why?

RU:

He's asked for a second piece.

NAYA:

Bro I'm so confused rn

RU:

Sri

Pay attention

This Suryadharma guy emailed you 2 days ago.
Saturday.

asking for a mural at MERAHPUTIH.

NAYA:

Wait.

Wait wait wait. WHAT

RU:

Jesus Sri, check your fucking DEWI email account more

NAYA:

I DON'T CHECK MY EMAILS ON THE WEEKEND AND IT'S BEEN A BUSY FUCKING MORNING OK

WAIT.

Jesus let me read the email. Gimme a bit

Naya frantically logged into her DEWI email account and—yes. There it was. An email to DEWI from Surya. She interrupted Rav as he was showing the team some designs for tote bags, journals and tshirts, and talking about licensing. "Rav, so sorry. Urgent personal business. I shouldn't be too long."

Rav nodded and Gunawan asked, "Everything ok?"

She grabbed her cigarettes and mumbled, "Yeah. Um-uh-just have to make some calls. I'll be back soon. Love the designs so far."

And then she rushed out of her office, down the elevator and out the front door, speed walking to the rear of Purnama.

She sat on the steps leading to the back entrance and tapped on the email:

Subject: MURAL AT MERAHPUTIH

Dear DEWI and Team,

The directors of MERAHPUTIH are delighted to hear of your involvement with *Heartbreak*, the exhibition reopening our prestigious Purnama gallery. The unfortunate cancellation of Alex Visser's show makes it all the more imperative that this new show is a success, and your contribution will distract from an otherwise humble event that has been curated with works by unknown artists, since it has been planned at the last minute.

Aud Pitch

To garner more media attention for this small exhibition, we would like to
offer you the exciting opportunity to create a mural in our prestigious
complex.
Please see the attached photos with all relevant technical information.
We have heard from others with whom you have worked that your murals
are created pro bono, with the exception of material costs. Is this the case?
If so, and if you are interested in creating a piece for us, is there time to
have the mural finished while the exhibition is running? We are unsure of
your schedule but it would certainly be a wonderful PR opportunity for our
esteemed foundation.
We do hope you will work with us on this project.
Should you have any questions, please feel free to reply to this email.

Kind regards,

Suryadharma Ali
Board Member
MERAHPUTIH

twenty-nine

Holy Shit.

Naya's mouth gaped as she reread the email three more times.

Holy fucking shit. Surya was offering her a mural. At MERAHPUTIH.

Did Owen know about this? No—Owen stanned DEWI like a Backstreet Boys groupie; he wouldn't've been able to keep the news to himself. *Which means Surya's gone rogue again.*

Naya shook her head in disbelief.

The directors would be crazy not to greenlight the opportunity to have a DEWI mural. The uptick in social media posts alone would be worth it, not to mention licensing the image to use on items they'd sell in the design store, which of course she'd agree to. Anything for Owen —for MP.

Her DEWI email inbox constantly overflowed with invitations to create works for commercial and private spaces, but she had carefully cultivated an attitude of being picky—so picky DEWI was considered a bit of a dick—about which commissions she accepted. As DEWI, Naya only took on the work she wanted—opting to create three or four major murals per year, and maybe a gallery show if she could be bothered—which meant *everyone* wanted a piece of her alter ego.

Aud Pitch

Naya opened the attached photos and squeaked at the image of the south wall of the Purnama Gallery. Her hallowed ground.

God—the symmetry of it all was beautiful: DEWI's first ever piece within the walls of Purnama, DEWI's latest piece on the outside, like a tattoo—a permanent mark on MP's skin—and around it all was Naya, hiding in plain sight.

Ha! Naya hated professional favours, but this was just too delicious —Surya trying to cause damage when he'd actually given Naya a beautiful gift.

What a fucking idiot.

NAYA:

Right.

Ok.

This is all a bit exciting.

RU:

So what's the go? "In Repair" is packed and ready. Leaving tomorrow. Should only take 2 days

ETA Thursday

Or are you planning on just doing a mural there and not bothering with "In Repair"?

Need to know asap since it's getting picked up first thing.

NAYA:

Send "In Repair" please.

RU:

Done.

And the email?

NAYA:

One sec. Let me think.

Ok I need 2 things.

From the DEWI email account, reply to Surya and tell him DEWI is confused by his email because DEWI approached Srinaya Matthews on Thursday asking about doing a piece at MP

And then send me an email asking if I ever received the email that DEWI sent on Thursday offering my services, because DEWI is confused.

RU:

Ruben is also confused...

NAYA:

Fuck. So is Naya

I'm not explaining this right...

Basically I need it to sound like DEWI offered to do a mural BEFORE Surya offered the opportunity, get it? But Naya didn't receive the original email, which is why Naya didn't respond to DEWI.

Jesus this is convoluted.

RU:

OOOOOOH Ok. No I get it

And since there actually is no first email, we're pretending that one got lost somewhere, so DEWI is writing all like, "Hey, so I got this weird—and kinda neggy btw—email from some arsehole higher-up where you work offering me something I already offered you 2 days earlier. Did you not get the email or something? Either way, I'm still interested in working with you, Naya, since you've helped me out in the past, but if that other guy is gonna get involved, no thanks."

And then to Suryadharma DEWI can say, "Not sure what's happening over there at MP but I offered Srinaya Matthews a piece on Thursday, so I'll be working with her, tyvm."

NAYA:

Yes! Exactly. You're the best.

ASAP please, Ru. Am going to have a cigarette to calm my nerves and then will go straight to one of the directors to tell them.

Fuck. This is big.

RU:

Feels like sexy corporate espionage type shit.

Got a boner rn

NAYA:

RU:

Ok. I'm on it.

NAYA:

Thanks 

RU:

What's up with this Suryadharma guy?

NAYA:

He hates me.

RU:

LOL. Sure you don't want to ask him to pay?

NAYA:

If he was the one paying I absolutely would. But he's not—the gallery is. Anyway, having a mural on the side of the building is payment enough.

RU:

You gonna tell him who you are?

NAYA:

One day he'll find out.

RU:

Sounds like a cunt. Can't wait to ignore him to his face.

Ok. Figure out dates so I can contact local artists and other peeps that will want to help. I'll get more people involved since you're gonna be running the show as well.

Get cracking on a design. Will book my tix too.

NAYA:

I've already got an idea. I just need to figure out how to plan it all. Fuck.

RU:

Happy to help. We'll do it like the one in Sydney. Send me the drawings. I'll contact the paint suppliers

And Sri... congratulations.

This is massive. I know you love that place. You're gonna have a piece ON your fave gallery

Go out and celebrate yeah? Take Arum with you.

God I miss that saucy bitch.

Naya couldn't stop the laugh that snorted out. She wanted to call Arum and Stefan to scream in their ears. She wanted to tell Sal.

Was it the time to tell Owen? Was she ready for that? The people who knew Naya's secret were a very tight group of friends who'd known her from the beginning—from the drama of the Reginald Muse award and the false accusations of her sleeping with a judge to win. No one *new* knew. Owen would be the first person in almost a decade to be brought into the circle. And, she realised, as she made a mental pros and cons list, telling Owen about DEWI meant telling him the whole story of Sal and Reginald Muse, and she didn't know if she had the spoons to deal with all of that *on top* of planning a show as herself, and a mural as DEWI. There'd be too many questions, too much to explain, too much pain to dig up. But she would. Later. When she had time to gather her thoughts.

She waited for the DEWI email from Ruben and then walked back around the building, running her hands over the rough concrete of Purnama's spartan exterior walls—*DEWI's canvas*—and returned to the fifth floor.

She rapped her knuckles on the glass door of Owen's suite. He sat on his couch, brow furrowed in concentration as he tapped away on his phone. He lifted his chin in acknowledgment, beckoning her. Naya strutted in and flopped down on the adjacent couch, the wall of glass behind her. Worry marred his handsome face, his usually tanned skin looking pale in contrast to the dark week-old beard he'd let grow.

"Are you okay? You rushed out and looked worried. I was about to text you," he asked.

She wanted to rub her thumb over that little wrinkle between his brows, brush it away with a kiss. She shuffled her ass forward on the seat to lay back more comfortably with her knees crossed. She lounged rather unceremoniously, like a rebellious teenager; anyone looking in would think she was being far too familiar with the legacy director, but she didn't fucking care today.

Besting Surya—without even making a move—made her feel like throwing all her ridiculous relationship rules out Owen's windows. She probably should've approached Owen when Endah was around because now that she sat in his office, all she wanted was to feel that beard against her cheek and between her thighs. She sighed his name and Owen's eyes flickered at her tone.

"God," she gritted out. "I remember when you told me a couple weeks ago that I make it difficult to behave." She arched her back a little as she stretched, purring, "Ditto."

Owen cleared his throat and Naya watched the corded muscles of his neck flex. The honey of his eyes went bright, and as he clenched his jaw he clasped his hands together and crossed his own legs. His eyes flicked upwards to track someone as they walked past the glass and he gave them a tight-lipped smile. When his eyes met hers again, that lovely tongue of his darted across his lips, bright pink against the darkness of his beard. She let out a little *Mmm* and then rolled her hips, pulling her skirt up a little higher. She uncrossed her legs and parted her knees a touch, murmuring, "I want to be spread open on your desk right now."

Owen looked like he almost swallowed his tongue, and Naya smiled innocently at him but Owen was dead serious now, predatory eyes on her. "You fucking little devil. Describe it to me."

She closed her eyes and brushed the back of her hand over her sensitive lips. She thought of all the different scenarios she'd conjured up in her mind. Which one to choose? She wanted them all. "You behind that fancy desk of yours." She jerked her chin in the desk's direction. "Me sitting on it, wearing nothing, my feet resting on the arms of your chair as you lick me and fuck me with those beautiful fingers." She gazed at his hand, at the slender interlocking digits resting calmly on his lap. "Wearing your most expensive suit."

Owen moved ever-so-slightly, his pelvis involuntarily flexing. "And then?" he asked, voice as rough as ever.

Naya shrugged carelessly, and gesticulated, as if she were telling a wild story instead of saying dirty things to him. "So many options. Do I get down on my knees and beg you to fuck my mouth, *ruining my makeup*—" He growled as she said that—"or do you bend me over your desk and fuck me from behind like I've wanted since the first time I saw you in this office?"

Owen let out a sharp little breath, spine straightening as he squirmed some more. "You're a menace," he rumbled, and a powerful jolt of deja vu crashed into her. Another pang of *Home, finally.*

Naya said, "I feel very lucky to be placed right opposite your suite. Such a wonderful view. Did you do that?"

He let out an amused huff. "Endah," he admitted, and Naya just shook her head and smiled. *Of course.* "I'm surrounded by femmes with tricksy devil ways." He winked as he rubbed his scratchy beard with his fingertips.

It was definitely time for Naya and Indonesia's mother of ballet to get to know each other a little better, since every path to Owen seemed to be paved by Endah. Naya didn't know what to make of it, but she let the thought slip away—didn't want to think too deeply about it at that moment. She wanted to bask in the knowledge that Surya's hatred of her had moved the game pieces in her favour.

The sweetest thing of all was that Naya achieved the victory on her own, without the esteemed benefactor ruffling feathers on her behalf. Ever since Cinq-Huit, when Owen finally understood her reservations, he'd been supportive and kind, allowing her to take the lead, especially at work.

She studied Owen's face and he watched her right back, radiating a quiet kind of power. He always looked a little on edge whenever they were in public, as if he was afraid he'd give something away, and everyone would find out and she'd blame him. She realised then how tiring all the pretending was. The constant second-guessing, the avoidance, denying him affection. Denying *herself* affection as well.

She hated how often she made him frown; those wrinkles between his brows were going to deepen and become permanent and it would be all her fault. His *Naya lines*, he would call them.

A familiar feeling appeared—something she hadn't experienced in a very long time and, even in the past, she didn't think she'd felt it quite so strongly—not even for Sal. *Oh.* Naya cocked her head and her lids fluttered as she frowned right back at Owen. Something else clicked into place. *I know this feeling.*

She opened her mouth to speak. Owen's brows shot up in question.

No. Not the time for weird romantic realisations. Not at work. She closed the door to that line of thinking and feeling for later.

She put on a cheery smile instead as she said, "I have some pretty exciting news about the exhibition." Owen rolled his eyes, as if he knew she'd changed the subject but didn't question her about it. Thank god. "Surya's been scheming again."

His face went from aroused to angry in an instant. It was exhilarating to witness. "What's he done now?" he asked, voice sharp.

"He emailed DEWI on Saturday."

"What the fuck for?"

"He offered DEWI the opportunity to paint a mural here."

Owen raked both hands through his messy hair and rubbed the back of his head with his fingers in annoyance. His sleeves tightened over his biceps. "Did he now," he growled.

She nodded. "As ideas go, it's not a bad one."

"*Hmm.*"

"Did he ask for approval?"

Owen shook his head. "He definitely doesn't have the power to be making those kinds of big offers, but he obviously knew we wouldn't turn it down which… makes him look good. Slick."

"I know. I'm actually impressed with how underhanded it was. Didn't think he had it in him."

"You'd be surprised," he muttered.

She shrugged lazily. "Thing is, DEWI emailed *me* last week offering to do one, but I never received it. Not sure what happened."

Owen made a face. "How'd you find out then?"

"*Well*," Naya explained with a gleam in her eye, "in an attempt to butter up DEWI, Surya kind of said some not very nice things about *Heartbreak*. Basically told DEWI all the unimportant emerging artists would be riding their coattails since they're being gracious enough to lower themself to be part of such a *small exhibition*." The utter disdain that flashed across Owen's face was *the best*. She continued, "DEWI didn't appreciate Surya's attitude, so they sent me an email saying they're still interested in doing a mural if we're keen as well, but not if Surya is part of the planning team."

"Wait. Let me get this straight," Owen said, chuckling. "DEWI approached you last week, asking if you'd like them to do a mural, but you didn't receive the email. Meanwhile, Surya went over our heads, trying to leverage himself by getting DEWI to agree to do a mural, but bungled it up—because he's a dickhead—and DEWI says they don't want to work with Surya."

Naya nodded and waggled her brows. "That about sums it up."

"But DEWI wants to work with *you*," Owen said. Naya shrugged lazily again. "We're getting a DEWI mural—" Owen stated in a voice tinged with awe—"because of *you*."

Naya just smiled. Owen smiled right back—a smug little curve of the lips, and nodded his head slowly as if to say, *that's my Naya*. He was going to reward her handsomely when they got home. She clenched her thighs together. And then Owen's eyes narrowed again, assessing her from head to toe and back up, deep in thought. "You changed the subject before. What were you going to say?"

Naya flinched at his question and sat up a little straighter, fidgeting. "Um-I-this isn't the place to discuss it."

"Why?"

Naya pointed to the wall of glass behind her. The building was beautifully designed to allow for maximum light, but fucking terrible for trysts.

"It's about you and me? Is it important?"

Naya didn't really know how to answer that. She was out of her depth when it came to matters of the heart. "I mean, I guess? Yes. But it can wait."

Worry darkened his face. "Come on," he said and stood.

They walked to the lift, Owen casually talking about random shit as they passed the other staff. He led her into the quiet south wing of the Purnama, without saying a word. His pace quickened as they continued down the hallway, Naya taking almost three steps for every one of his to keep up. He unlocked a door with a *No Entry* sign on it and pulled her into the storage room, filled only with a dusty meeting table and some wonky plinths. Owen closed the door behind them, making sure the lock clicked, and turned back to her, eyes expectant.

Naya swallowed as he stepped closer. He'd touched her so many times over the past few weeks, in a myriad of intimate ways. Being naked with him was easy. *This* was shedding layers of skin and flesh and even bone, baring the deepest parts of herself, exposing nerves, the bits that were easiest to hurt. This was putting all her faith in someone else when so many of her life lessons had taught her that independence was the key to safety and self-preservation.

Owen didn't speak. He just waited, forehead wrinkled, brows furrowed into dark diagonal slashes. So worried. It ached to see him like that. She reached up to rub his Naya lines with her thumb and then cleared her throat nervously. She leaned toward him, his big body looming over her, making her feel small and cherished. *God—speak first. Say something*, she pleaded silently.

But maybe Owen had done enough of that, of always being the first to show vulnerability. Maybe it was Naya's turn to expose a nerve, to give *him* a gift—a clear message that Owen was worthy of her trust, and more.

Naya ran her hands over his chest. He looked anxious as he swept gold-tipped hair away from his face. "I—" She swallowed and squared her shoulders—"I think I love you."

thirty

O HELD HIS BREATH, HIS HEARTBEAT POUNDING IN HIS EARS. HE STARED into Naya's eyes, holding her chin to search her face to see if she was mocking him. She looked surprised by her confession, dark eyes wide, as if her brain was trying to catch up with her mouth. "Really? Do you really?"

He felt helpless, didn't want to get his hopes up, and then cursed himself for thinking she would ever admit to something so important without being sure first. This wasn't like that time she blurted out that thing about dick-sucking on a whim. She would've weighed up her options. *I'm an immovable object*—that's what she'd said a few weeks before.

She stared up at him and nodded, and then she pressed and rubbed her sternum as if she felt a jolt of pain there, just like O did whenever she said or did something so fucking endearing it ached.

"I—" She thought carefully about her words—"I haven't loved anyone in a really long time, and this feels bigger than when I last felt it. So it must be love, right?" Her eyes flicked back up to him and she nodded once, like she'd officially decided—committed. "I do. I love you." And then her mouth curved into a smile that grew bigger and bigger until she let out a shy little laugh, and she repeated it: "I love you?"

She blushed, and O's whole body was electric. He could've powered the city with how strong, and bright, and right this was. He threw his head back and laughed with her. "Jesus fucking Christ, Naya, if you were anyone else, I'd say that was the most unromantic overture anyone's ever given me."

She groaned apologetically—her adorable little ears turning red with embarrassment—and covered her face with her hands. He pulled her fingers away, kissing her knuckles and added, "No, but listen. Because I know you, and I've learned that you take your time, that you won't ever be pushed, and you wouldn't say something so important without making sure and *truly knowing*... Naya, it was the most beautiful fucking thing I've ever heard."

He pulled her firmly against him and kissed her hard, mouth and tongue desperate and demanding, and she melted into him, opening herself to be thoroughly tasted, rising up on her tiptoes to wrap her arms around his neck. And then he pulled away because he realised he hadn't said the words he'd been biting back for months.

"Naya, I've loved you for so fucking long. Since the first moment I saw you. You're brilliant, do you know that? Clever and kind and—god," he said, and closed his eyes as he sighed. "So beautiful."

He couldn't help but murmur all the adjectives he could think of in her ear as he led her backwards to the table. "So talented, so sexy, *I love you*, I love everything about you. Fuck, I need you all the time. I need you *right now*." All the words he'd wanted to say to her for almost a year came tumbling out; he wanted to shower her with praise, needed to slide into her, as if fucking her would turn this into an unbreakable covenant between them.

She sighed as he whispered dirty things into her ear, of how he needed to feel her lovely cunt stretch around his cock, feel her body shake and her hips press against him, watch her lips swell and redden to turn the same shade of pink as the soft inner folds of her pussy. Her brows slanted; she looked overcome and her eyes went glassy. O kissed her face, little kisses all over, murmuring, "Srinaya. *Aku sayang kamu*."

She shuffled back onto the table, her legs parted, and she pulled him to stand between her thighs. A dusty storage room with people walking past outside wasn't the place for something slow or sweet. Thank god Naya wasn't interested in that either. She hiked up her skirt and pulled her briefs off just one leg so the pretty lacy fabric still wrapped around her other thigh, and he pushed the straps of her singlet and bra over her shoulders and down her arms, her clothing bunched around her middle. Tits exposed, nipples hard and rosy, she looked wild and filthy. She had never looked so beautiful.

Naya, all smiles and breathy laughs, quickly undid O's belt and the fly of his trousers. Hooking her fingers under his jocks, she pushed his clothes off his hips, freeing his cock. She stroked him with those lovely little hands, staring up at him, inviting more kisses. And then she leaned back, guiding O's cock to her pussy's entrance, and she asked in the sweetest voice, "Say it again?"

O pushed his cock all the way into her as he said, *I love you*, and Srinaya—the sneaky and gorgeous fucking thing—said it too, *at the exact time*, her mouth turned upwards in a beautifully joyous smile, eyes black pools of pleasure, and O couldn't help but let out a noise that sounded very close to a sob. She leaned on her elbows as O grabbed the dimpled folds of her belly, squeezing her. She bit her lip, fingers reaching for the buttons of his shirt. He unbuttoned quickly so she could touch his skin, pretty magical hands exploring his stomach and chest.

She lay back with her knees clamped tightly to his sides and O leaned over her and nibbled her ears and shoulder and rosy nipples. He fucked her with intent—not losing himself in the moment. His strokes were focused, purposeful. It had to feel different from all the other times. His hands spread over her waist, pulling her to him, meeting his thrusts. Naya moaned, eyes bright and alert. He fucked her harder and her fingers circled her clit as her other arm wrapped around his neck and fisted his hair, and then her eyes rolled back as she mouthed another *love you*, spine curving off the table.

It was enough to send him over the edge and he huffed, and groaned, and came—trying to stay quiet which made it all the more hotter—pelvis straining as he emptied into her, convulsing against her pussy and thighs.

O caught his breath, still mindlessly whispering words of care and praise. He braced his hands on either side of her and planted more kisses over her face and shoulders and chest. "I'm so happy," he murmured. She hummed in agreement. He commented, "I don't like you not coming. I'm going to start walking around with a vibrator hidden in my pocket so I can help you come whenever you want." He rested his weight on her, chin resting on her heart.

She stroked his hair. "Maybe that could be your next business investment—inventing a sex toy the size of a lipstick but with the vibrational *oomph* of a tractor."

He shouted out a laugh and then covered his mouth, grimacing. Naya giggled, and then tilted her head and brushed his hair behind his ear. "I'll come when I get home and you'll help me with your beautiful fingers and it'll be amazing. Please... don't keep score. How much you want me, how hard you fuck me, feeling you come inside me... it's perfect." She sighed and clenched her pussy muscles, and his softening cock inside her stiffened a little.

"So the means outweigh the end?"

She stated, in some put-on maudlin tone, "It's not the *destination* that matters. It's the *journey.*"

O snorted and tickled her, and she yipped. She leaned forward to kiss him, chastely at first, and then her tongue explored the seal of his lips and he opened his mouth. His tongue pressed gently against hers, and then she pulled away to look into his eyes again. "I'm scared of what this means. But it's a beautiful feeling to love you," Naya confessed.

"I know it is. I've had the pleasure of loving you for so many months —" He faltered—"well, what *feels* like months." He cursed himself silently for the slip-up but Naya just smiled at him, love-drunk. "Don't be scared," O murmured, "I won't let anything bad happen."

✝

They left the gallery complex early—couldn't bear to be away from each other. They went back to Naya's house and had sex again, Owen helping to coax two orgasms from her, body trembling and muscles taut, murmuring the sweetest things into her hair, and neck, and mouth. It was like he'd been holding back for a lifetime and now that he'd loosened his tongue he couldn't stop the loving words from spilling out.

She felt boneless and weak, and couldn't remember the last time she experienced this level of euphoria that wasn't due to illicit drugs. They lay in bed after, bodies all sweaty and sticky and limbs all tangled together. He couldn't stop smiling. He walked his fingers across her belly and up between her tits as he hummed a happy tune.

"I think I want to go out," Naya said as he rested his head on her shoulder. She stroked his hair, pushing it off his sweaty forehead.

"Okay. Want to meet me back at mine after? You can ask Ibrahim to drive you if you want," Owen said.

Naya frowned at him.

She'd never been the sort of person who liked feeling tethered to someone else, but in that moment, she couldn't imagine being away from Owen ever again, and there had been plenty of instances that hinted at *his* clinginess.

When they were at home together, he stayed close; they were almost always in the same room, unless she worked in her studio and asked for privacy, or he went to work out in his gym and she stayed away because they always ended up fucking each other senseless since he couldn't keep his hands to himself when she did her downward dogs and pigeon poses and—truth be told—she couldn't handle seeing him do his own workouts on the mat either. The way his arms bulged, and those rugby player thighs tensed. God—and he got so fucking sweaty, and his sweat smelt and tasted *so good*. So for him to assume she wanted to go out *without* him, on the day she'd told him she loved him, made her feel an overwhelming desire to cling to him forever for his generosity but also fucking smack him over the head for being so obtuse.

She shook her head and held him tighter. "No, I mean *with you*. Let's go out."

Owen rolled onto his belly, pushing up onto his elbows. "Really? Out in public? As a couple?" His brows were raised, looking hopeful.

Naya tilted her head from side to side. "Well, I say *with you* but I was thinking we could both go solo. I'll take a taxi and you take *Pak Ibrahim*. I'll go in first and you walk in ten minutes later. We'll sit on separate tables on either side of the room and text." Owen *tsked* and rolled his eyes. "Okay, how bout we wear our earpods and talk on the phone?"

"Yeah, yeah, alright."

"Maybe we can signal using flags like on ships. What's that called again?" She waved her arms about.

"Settle down, you harpy," he grumbled as he climbed onto her and pinned her hands next to her head. Naya yelped when he bit her earlobe. Owen loomed over her and commented, "So this will be our first time out as a couple. Our debut. Coming out into society. Feels very Jane Austen." He batted his long, dark lashes.

Naya sputtered and then laughed loudly, her shoulders shaking. "I would *not* feature in an Austen novel. Too much of a harlot. Damaged goods. *NSFA—Not Safe For Austen.* I'm like a penny dreadful. Or a Dickens novel."

Owen nodded. "Dickens… okay then. Well, *I'd* take you in. I'd bear the shame to be with you."

"Aren't you sweet."

"That's how much I love you. I'd ruin my good name for you—a woman of ill repute. Filthy. I wouldn't have it any other way."

She pulled him down to slant her mouth over his and then nuzzled his cheek. "I love you too. Let's go to Le Roy. I'm close with the owner so it's a great place to start, I think. I've never bumped into any MP staff there, but if someone sees us, that's okay."

Owen's eyes softened. He was holding in his excitement, but seeing him so happy made her heart do stupid things in her chest. "As long as you're sure," he said quietly, trying to stop a huge smile from appearing on his face.

It warmed her to see him look so excited. But then her smile faltered and she bit her lip.

Owen and Stefan were going to meet. Which meant… she should probably…

She swallowed and sat up, and he followed suit. "Doubting our debut?" he asked.

She leaned back against her headboard and took a breath. "That night at the office. When you asked if you could touch me, and I said no."

Owen nodded. She rubbed her eyes as she recalled it. "I was so angry that you asked for permission, even though I loved that you did. I wanted to say yes so fucking badly, but honestly, I wished you'd just kissed me. I wouldn't've stopped you." She shook her head. "You have no idea how much I wanted you to just fuck me on your couch," she sighed. Owen rubbed his jaw restlessly as his cock thickened. His eyes went dark, but he sat quietly, patiently. The memory of that night made Naya flush with heat all over again. "I had sex with someone that afternoon, and then again the next night because I needed the distraction."

Owen shuffled to face her, eyes unreadable. "Did you now." Naya nodded. "Did it work?"

She shook her head. Her eyes travelled over the lines of his strong body with deep appreciation, and she let out a little sound at the sight of his now fully erect dick.

"Why not?" he asked.

Naya squirmed. "Because the fantasy of you was better than the reality of him."

His brow twitched at her admission. He pulled her closer as if to soothe her. Shuffling forward between his legs to hide in his arms, she smelt Melbourne in the crook of his neck. Naya stroked his jaw, swept her hands down over the ridges of his chest and stomach, and wrapped her hand around his dick. Owen let out a slow breath. She continued, "It felt wrong to get pleasure from someone else when you were the one I wanted it from."

She stayed silent, waiting, dragging her fingers ever-so-lightly up and down the length of him. "I'm assuming it was the bartender," he commented.

She gasped. "How did you know that?"

He lazily shrugged, running his big hands over her hips. "I watched the videos on their socials. I saw how you danced with him, and the way he looked at you."

He didn't look upset, which turned Naya on even more. He wasn't jealous—he was curious, wanted to understand. He twirled a lock of her hair around his fingers. "Will you tell me what you fantasised about while he fucked you?"

God—his voice was so low.

A bead of sweat trickled down her temple. She swallowed as she answered, "All I kept seeing was you standing close to me by your meeting table, bending down to kiss me. Taking it. Not asking for permission. Such a simple, innocent image but I came so hard thinking about it, and I fucking cursed you every time you popped into my head, because Stef deserved all of my attention but I couldn't give it to him."

Owen's mouth curved into a proud and devilish smile. He was so pleased with himself as he circled a finger around her nipple.

"Anyway," Naya added with a sigh, "I'm telling you this because he'll be at Le Roy tonight. And because Stef is my friend. I know you and I are exclusive but he'll always be important. I care about him a lot."

For some strange reason, Naya's defences rose, as if she was ready to argue, to fight for her friendship. She expected a leash to appear and for it to be tight—to be told that she wasn't allowed male friends, especially ones she'd had sex with, which meant she'd have to break it off with Owen, and it would hurt but she would do it because she wouldn't be controlled. And if he did all of that, she would know once and for all that romantic relationships were stupid, and a waste of time, and she could go back to being single and independent, not having to answer to anyone but herself. She could handle the loneliness. She had all her loving friends and her work to distract her.

But he didn't chastise her. He just smiled—stretched his big boulder of a body over hers to kiss her slowly, tasting of chocolate and mint, and then he bent his head down to take her nipple in his mouth. The click of metal against his teeth mixed with his hums as he suckled were such sexy sounds.

Owen manoeuvred her to straddle his lap as he lay back on her pillows and pushed his delicious cock into her, her nerves sparking back to life. And as she moved against him slowly, feeling his heart beat fast and strong under her hands, she moaned his name.

He murmured hers back and said, "I hope Stef likes me. I hope all your friends like me."

thirty-one

O STOOD OUT THE FRONT OF LE ROY GAPING AT DEWI'S HELLSCAPE mural. It was gigantic—about ten metres tall by fifteen metres wide. Lights pointed down to illuminate the piece, highlighting the more dramatic parts: a man bitten in half by a four-legged demon-dog, a cage full of people being lowered into a bonfire, a giant snake wrapped around a person, their head in its mouth. The mediaeval-looking tableau wasn't particularly gory. No blood spurted out of anyone, and no one was naked, but there was something about the piece that made you feel sinful for staring at it, as if you were looking at something forbidden.

DEWI was a fucking genius, and MERAHPUTIH was getting a DEWI mural, all because of Naya. He glowed with pride.

It was the most exciting thing to happen at MP in ages. O was bored of the offerings at the gallery; they booked the same big name artist as everywhere else—always tame and predictable, never anyone who even brushed up against boundaries, let alone pushed them. It was why he'd been happy to stay away, leaving it all up to the other three directors, only getting involved when a serious decision had to be made.

But *Heartbreak* was different. It was a little bit scary. The whispers from the board were mixed; most were looking forward to their bold new direction, while others would've preferred to play it safe. *Safe* still brought in crowds and money. All O knew was that *safe* kept him away. This project brought him back—had brought them DEWI, and it was all thanks to Srinaya Matthews.

Naya broke his reverie when she tugged at his arm, whining, *"Feed meeeeee... Corn Jaaaaaaacks,"* and stuck out her bottom lip.

"Alright, alright," he said.

Abandon all hope, ye who enter here was painted above the entrance. Hopelessness was a foreign state of being when someone like Naya led the way. He grinned down at her as she pulled him through the barn-like wooden doors, nose wrinkling playfully. She wore her oxblood trousers with a well-worn vintage black *Barbie* logo tshirt with holes in it that looked fitting *and* so strangely out of place. Barbed wire hoops dangled from her earlobes and she wore black flip-flops. She'd thrown the outfit together in five minutes but she looked so perfect, her fat arse swaying from side to side as she sauntered in without a care in the world, like she fucking owned the place. People called out to greet her and she waved at them, never letting go of his hand.

It was packed for a Monday. They went to the bar to order drinks while they waited for a table. He looked around at the space—a little divey, a little reminiscent of the local pubs in every Melbourne neigh-bourhood, the ones named after the suburb with the word *Hotel* added to the end.

Naya squeezed O's hand and pulled him down so she could speak in his ear, "Is this okay? I know you don't always like crowds. Will you tell me if it gets too much? We'll leave straight away." She looked up at him with care, her eyes black under the red of the bar's downlights.

"Thank you," he said. Naya, his little devil, and goddess, and safe harbour. He pulled her close and lifted her chin to steal a deep, slow kiss from her, and she let him... in front of everyone. He needed it—needed people to witness them. Maybe, in a small way, he needed Stefan to see too, wherever he was.

And then the man appeared—slithered right up to them. "Hello, gorgeous Sri. Where have you been? We've missed you," he said sulkily.

"Hey you," Naya said as she rushed to him.

Stef's lips parted and gave way to a grin that was curious and full of mischief, the red lights reflecting off his shiny jet black hair like a bloody halo. O already knew Stefan was beautiful from the photos of him on the bar's socials, but those pictures did not do the man justice. He was all lean muscle and smooth British accent—and had a leisurely, good-natured way about him that reminded O of Mario, but with an extra side of something wicked. The mural outside made sense with him as the publican.

Stef and Naya kissed on the lips—a quick peck—and hugged like old friends. It warmed O to see the care in the other man's gaze, the way he closed his eyes to savour their embrace, taking and giving comfort in equal measure.

"I've come bearing gifts," Naya exclaimed to Stef, and then stepped back to O and wrapped her arms around his waist, tucking herself into his side with her cheek pressed against his chest. "Well, just one very big—very *pretty*—gift. I've brought you a new friend. This is Owen. Turns out I *love* him. It's very inconvenient. It's taking up so much of my time."

O's heart burst at her public declaration in front of such an important person. He stroked her hair before giving Stefan one of his own dazzling smiles—the one he used when charming people to sign million-dollar deals or donate hundreds of thousands of dollars at fundraisers. Stefan blinked at him—disarmed. O wanted to preen; it felt good to beguile someone like Stef. O stuck out his hand and said hello, and Stef shook his head. "Oh no. No no no. Friends of Sri's don't shake hands."

Stefan hugged O tightly, kissing him on both cheeks, and O was so taken aback by Stef's open affection that he giggled awkwardly. Stef cocked his head as he studied O, his curious almond eyes roving over O's body, silky straight hair falling off his shoulders, and he said, "So *this* is why we haven't seen you round these parts." His eyes flitted back to Naya. She just pursed her lips and arched her brow. And then Stef looked back at O and commented, "I get it," in an appreciative tone.

O enjoyed Stef's drawn-out perusal; his cheeks flushed and his dick stirred. Stefan instantly broke the spell by clapping his hands, rubbing them together. "Right, then. Drinks to toast new friendships and new love. Let me go get us some shots," and then he slinked back behind the bar.

"Fucking hell," O murmured in her ear when he kissed her temple.

"I know," Naya said with a roll of her eyes and a shake of her head.

The fantasy of O was better than the reality of Stefan Wardhana? What a compliment that was.

⸸

"DEWI's coming for a visit, I hear," Stefan said as he slid into the booth next to Naya during a lull in drink orders.

Naya waggled her brows. O chuckled. "Word travels fast," he commented.

"Well, I heard it straight from the horse's mouth," Stef said.

O looked at Naya. She pointed to herself and shook her head. O was confused. "Wait—if not Naya… *DEWI* told you?"

Stefan shrugged as if he was bored.

O gaped. "You actually *know* DEWI?"

Stefan looked at O as if he had asked the most absurd thing in the world. "'Course I do."

"So, like, you have them in your contacts? You have their number?"

Stef ran his tongue along his teeth and said, "I have their private number that only very special people get."

Naya chimed in. "He'll never tell you who they are. Believe me. *So* many people have tried."

O put his hands up. "Oh no, I'm not interested in finding out who they are. I mean, they obviously have a good reason to keep their identity a secret. I don't know if they've ever done anything actually illegal but I know they've pissed off a lot of people."

Stef said, "But the best things they've done, no one even knows about. It's the long con. They're waiting for someone to notice, and even if no one does, it doesn't matter because *we'll* know."

Stef quietly shared the story of how one of DEWI's earliest pranks was donating couches and beanbags to conservative, strictly straight and all-white fraternities at Christian universities in the US. Some of the members from the Birmingham, Alabama chapter were involved in a horrific gay-bashing incident but, of course, they weren't arrested or even expelled.

"So," Stef said scandalously, "these beautiful new couches appear on their doorstep to replace their cum-and-beer-stained furniture. Definitely classed up the place. The upholstery motif was this really expensive looking floral design, but if you looked *really* close, underneath the flowers in a darker shade—" He pursed his lips trying not to laugh—"were images of men fucking and sucking." O roared with laughter and had to catch his breath. "Arseholes and dicks everywhere!" Stefan squawked.

O leaned his forearms on the table, enthralled by Stef's stories. "What are they like though?"

Stef rested his pretty head on his fist. "Kind. Self-critical. Very fucking angry. Very angry fucking too, actually," he said thoughtfully.

Naya burst out laughing then. "You're an idiot," she said in between giggles, elbowing him affectionately.

Stef pouted. "You're so mean, Sri."

"Sri," O repeated quietly as he looked at Naya. "That's a pretty nickname."

Stef nodded in that ridiculously sexy smug way of his. "Isn't it? After the goddess," he said pointedly, and there was a gleam in his eye. "You *are* a goddess aren't you, *Sri*?" He teased, resting his chin on her shoulder, face close to hers.

Naya pushed his face away and said to O, "Ignore him. He's showing off for you."

Stef dismissed her friendly jibes. "You'll find that her oldest and closest friends call her that, Owen. And, since you're the *closest* one of all—*lucky girl*—you should definitely start calling her that too." He lifted his chin to O, winked, and flashed a smile. *Jesus.*

O watched Stef closely, and Stef stared right back, dark eyes full of bad thoughts—O could tell. "You, *Sri* and Pixie-Goth," O murmured. "What a fucking troublesome trio you must be."

His pelvis ached.

Stef's eyes went wide. "Pixie-Goth! Is that Arum? I love it," he said, tipping his head back to laugh languidly.

$$\perp$$

On the way home, O said, "So that's Stefan."

Naya smiled. "*Mm hmm.* That's Stefan."

"Fucking hell."

"I *know.*"

"He's like MDMA on legs."

She chuckled, breathy and gravelly. "Sex, drugs, booze, laughs. Stefan's my pleasure pusher." She moved closer to snuggle O. "You ruined me for him."

thirty-two

"Isn't this an interesting turn of events," Endah said when she was updated. "I ask you to invite DEWI to show at your exhibition and now we're getting a permanent art piece."

She sat with her back straight—all prim and proper—on the edge of Naya's couch. One ankle was tucked behind the other, and she held a fancy white and gold teacup to her lips and sipped silently before placing it back on the saucer. Naya felt like an uncouth piece of trash sipping her green tea from a hot pink mug with *UNT* printed in big yellow letters on it, the mug's handle also painted yellow to look like a C. She turned it around so that Endah couldn't see the rude word, holding it close.

Owen had been called away to a lunch meeting across town. His absence gave Naya the chance to finally talk about personal matters with Endah. She spun the silver ring on her thumb edgily.

The last time they spoke, Endah had witnessed her and Owen having a heated disagreement at Cinq-Huit, and then Naya ended up politely kicking Endah out so they could continue in private. Things were better now—*better* than better, but there was a sharpness in Endah's gaze which Naya could take if it was about DEWI, but couldn't if it was about her relationship with Owen.

"A mural. On *Purnama*." Endah's lips pursed. She didn't sound very keen on the idea. She put the teacup and saucer on Naya's coffee table and clasped her hands on her lap.

"Would you prefer it was done somewhere else?" Naya would be completely fine with *any* wall within the complex. The rear of the archive building would do, for all she cared.

Endah stayed quiet for a moment, and then she let out a sharp breath. "I'm being sentimental. It's hard to imagine the Purnama—" She tilted her head—"*defaced.*"

Naya didn't take offence. She sympathised, in fact. The sight of it covered in paint would be confronting, like going back to your childhood home to find a different family living there—some random kid in your bedroom and the walls a different colour.

Endah sighed again and gave a quick little shake of her head as if trying to come to her senses. "I'll talk to *Pak* Bakti and *Ibu* Tuti about it but I doubt they'll have much of an opinion. Bakti and *Ibu* Tuti aren't quite as attached to this place as Owen and me. We'll tentatively approve the south wall." Endah fiddled with her hair, sweeping her hands up to catch invisible flyaways. "But Naya, make sure the piece you do shows how important this place is to us," she said.

Something in her voice gave Naya pause. The fact that she didn't even say DEWI's name, and the shrewdness in her eyes as she glared at Naya was... *consequential.* Endah tilted her chin down ever-so-slightly— her gaze never leaving Naya's. "Yes?" Endah asked, her tone even more clipped than before. She arched her brows.

Did Endah know?

Naya's lip twitched. Could that be why Endah mentioned DEWI right at the beginning of all of this?

No. Not now. Not yet—not when Naya wasn't ready to tell Owen the truth.

"Yes," Naya answered. "I'll make sure DEWI creates something you'll be proud of."

Endah nodded her head in approval and she smoothed her pretty skirt as she relaxed a little. She glanced at the closed door and asked, "And how are you and Owen doing?"

Naya couldn't stop the huge smile from appearing. "Good," she said brightly. She pointed to her flushed cheeks. "*This* is what he does to me."

Naya moved from behind her desk, which felt protective when they discussed DEWI, but too cold and distant for a conversation about Owen. Endah shuffled over to make room for her on the sofa. "Owen told me you were the one who asked him to come here. To help me—to show his *bule face* and throw his weight around in support of *Heartbreak*."

Endah's sweet laugh reminded Naya of the way wind chimes made her feel. "He does enjoy fixing things, doesn't he?" Endah asked. "He's mastered the art of using his presence to *inspire* people to get things done. He doesn't have to do anything but smile. Sometimes he shows extra teeth if people hesitate."

"And you have him wrapped around your little finger, *Ibu*."

Endah's mouth dropped open. "Owen said the *exact* same thing to me when he first came home."

Naya placed her hand on Endah's. "I want to say thank you. You've been an amazing ally to me. You know, I don't usually like it when people *manage* me. I hate it when people withhold things from me and think they know better, but you seem to make very good choices on my behalf so I'll defer all my decisions to you from now on. What should I have for lunch?" Naya grinned cheekily.

Endah blinked and let out another lilting laugh. "My goodness. You and Owen are a pair, aren't you?" she said, eyes crinkling. "Charming and disarming."

Naya let herself be vulnerable. It was the least she could do for the woman who'd somehow orchestrated the events of the past few months, and if she was the only mother-figure in her lover's life, Naya wanted to explain her intentions. She looked at her hands as she said quietly, "In all honesty, I love him. So much. It's disconcerting." She fidgeted. "And... I hope I'm not crossing a line by saying this, *Ibu*, but you did a beautiful job with him. He's—" She couldn't think of any words to even describe Owen—"*surprising*. Unexpected. So kind and caring. And he loves you very much."

Endah put her hand on her heart, taken aback. Her eyes softened, although there was sadness there. "*Aduh, Naya.* What a sweet thing to hear." She took both of Naya's hands in hers and squeezed gently. Endah paused for a moment, her eyes narrowing in thought. She squeezed Naya's hands a little tighter. "Remember how much you love him when you find out he's *managed* you, as you say, Naya. He really can't help it—he's learnt from the best," she commented and pointed to herself.

┼

Three days later, Endah emailed Naya—ccing Owen, *Oom* Bakti and *Ibu* Tuti—to give official approval of the use of the south wall of Purnama for DEWI's mural.

Gunawan—ever the dad of the group—said, "I'm so proud of you *Mbak* Naya. And I'm so proud to be part of this exhibition. We've accomplished so much in such a short amount of time."

Ravi shocked everyone by getting teary which, of course, got Naya's eyes prickling. "Goddammit Rav, I have sympathetic tear ducts. Stop it," she sniffled, which made Rav blub even more.

┼

Surya arrived in the early afternoon. He'd been absent for the past week, but his reappearance was heralded by a sudden spike in bad vibes out in the open office. All friendly chatter stopped dead, the silence so jarring that Naya looked up from her work and caught the crestfallen faces of the juniors as Surya marched past them to his suite.

She looked at her watch and grimaced. Her meeting with him to discuss the items his company would manufacture for the show was only a couple hours away. Checking and rechecking the final designs before emailing them for Surya's perusal was the team's biggest headache of the day—aside from the man himself.

Naya watched on as Surya unlocked his office door, making a ridiculous racket, as if he had every right to be disruptive while others worked. His door swung open and banged against the wall. He headed inside, dumping his bag on his desk. He turned on his computer monitor before stomping to the window to pull his roller blind down so roughly it closed with a loud thud.

Nur—who sat directly outside Surya's office—startled at the sound.

Ravi's usually gruff voice gentled. "Don't worry, Naya. We'll go to the merch meeting with you." He flicked his thumb between himself and Gunawan. "Buddy system."

"Buddy system?"

Gunawan sighed. "No one is left alone with him. We decided."

"Who's *we*? The Bevy?"

Rav shook his head. "Everyone."

Oh shit. "What happened? What did he do? I mean, y'know, besides all the shit he normally does."

"He's cast a wider net, Mbak Naya." Gunawan said, scratching his neat moustache. "You're not the only target anymore. Of course, it was always unfair that he had his sights set on you, but you seem..."

"I seem to be more... immune to it?" she asked with a rueful smile.

He laughed weakly. "I was going to say... brave enough to bite back?"

Rav said, "He made Nur cry last week. And he said some shitty homophobic things about Edhi's clothing."

"Clothing critique from the Andy Warhol wannabe?" Seriously. She wondered how many black mock turtlenecks the man owned.

Rav gave a thin-lipped smile and lifted his shoulders in a shrug that looked like it took far too much effort. Gunawan pulled off his glasses to rub his eyes and slumped in his chair.

Both men had aged five years since *Heartbreak* was announced a couple months ago. Of course they were done with Surya's bullshit. She'd only dealt with him for months. But them?

"Should we make a complaint then? I'll support anyone who wants to. I'll make my own too." Gunawan and Ravi glanced at each other but didn't answer. "Oh. You don't see the point in talking to HR," she guessed, and waited for confirmation.

Rav shook his head.

Shit.

Had *any* of the department heads protected the employees from Surya? Who were they compared to the board members—even a whole group of them? This wasn't Australia, where HR complaints against a senior would spark an internal investigation. How many complaints from lowly staff members would it take to oust a board member here? And not just any board member—one who was related to one of the directors, and with whom MERAHPUTIH had advantageous business dealings?

Naya said, "I'm so sorry."

"Why are you apologising?" Edhi said, appearing in the doorway with Tini. "It's not your fault. The really crappy thing is that we're so used to it, we stopped noticing how bad it was until you showed up and he took an instant dislike to you."

Tini muttered, "Talk about emotional abuse."

A hot and stifling dread expanded in Naya's belly at Tini's comment. Because, in a way, it *was* her fault. Her secret DEWI power had made it so much easier to see Surya as nothing more than an angry wasp buzzing about. Surya's venom hurt, but she could handle his stings, as unwelcome as they were. More importantly, she finally got it. The rest of the staff didn't have the luxury of a powerful alter ego—or a lover who was king of the castle—to hide behind. And the shittest part? The staff rallied around each other with no assistance from The Elders, who were probably just as terrified of Surya, if not on the prick's side. And... fuck—the staff had rallied around *her* too, but she was such a self-involved asshole that she'd prevented Endah and Owen from doing something that would help *everyone*, all because of her own fear of... *of what, really?*

Somewhere along the way, DEWI had commandeered all of Naya's backbone.

The Bevy went back to their own spaces, and Naya sat alone in her office, hugging herself as she stared out the window. From her side of the building, she saw the pristinely manicured grounds Pak Yanto and the rest of his landscaping crew kept. Some visitors sat on the park benches and steps of Hamdan. A tour full of primary school kids exited the exhibition.

She remembered visiting when she was a little girl too. Back then, the buildings were void of greenery and the hulking installations didn't adorn the gardens. MP was grey and unwelcoming until she stepped through the doors of Purnama. The foyer of the main gallery was vibrant and friendly—full of colour, and pretty images that filled young Naya with wonder and possibility. It could have been that visit that made her want to become an artist, and something about that memory made her feel a bone-deep resentment at how they'd been led to believe the board and—yes, even the directors—had more of a claim on the gallery, and art, than she did. As if the person with the money was more important than the artist. As if the labour—mental, emotional, and physical—of the workers who loved the gallery, who kept the place swept and pruned and filled with visitors, wasn't as important as the people at the top who made all the big financial decisions.

She took a deep breath. It was time for Naya to reclaim her back-bone. She needed to be more like DEWI, for fuck's sake. Maybe it was time for Srinaya Matthews to be *that person*. How many lowly staff members would it take to oust a board member? Maybe the answer was one, with an esteemed benefactor as a power-up.

She DMed Owen:

> Busy? I need a pep talk

He called straight away and her heart did that annoying flip-flop thing it always did whenever they reconnected. "Hello," she breathed.

"I love you. You're clever. You're charming. You're sexy. You're revered by your team. Your arse should be one of the natural wonders of the world. You're an incredible human who makes the most beautiful art and you suck and fuck like the dirtiest whore. You're a gem."

She let out an unattractive cackle as she rubbed that spot very close to her heart, and the tightness in her shoulders eased. "Thank you."

"Are you okay?"

"*Mm hmm*. Design meeting," Naya answered.

"With Surya?"

"*Mm hmm.*"

"Remember—DEWI wants to work with you."

"Yes yes, I'm amazing, but also, I'm about to throw myself under a bus."

"Hang on—what? Why? Naya, what are you doing?"

"You're kind of—*ugh*—you're about to get your way," Naya grumbled.

"Please explain."

"Surya's being a jumbo-sized cock—"

"Gross."

"*Shush*—so we're coming out into society. People are going to learn you're courting a woman of ill-repute. Hope you're ready for the attention, Owen. Because the gossip..." She rubbed her temples at the thought of the terrifying network of receptionists and assistants who exchanged rumours like precious gems, whispering the news far and wide: Owen Jameson—golden king of MP, built like the hero of every smutty fantasy book ever written—was dating the fat, foul-mouthed, and rough-around-the-edges Naya Matthews.

She baulked.

No. Backbone, Naya. She soldiered on, "But it's the quickest way to just—*ugh*. Whatever. Just be on standby, please? I'm going to need you to flirt with me in front of Surya."

"Srinaya Matthews, are you about to cause a fuss?"

thirty-three

The Bevy filed into the large boardroom and waited.

And waited, and waited, and waited.

Fifteen minutes later, Edhi hummed the *Jeopardy!* theme song. By the seventh round, all five members joined in, and then Surya moseyed in like the imperious piece of shit that he was. He tossed his notebook and pen on the table and collapsed onto the leather chair with a grumble. The high-backed chair dwarfed his rangy frame; Naya would've snickered at the sight if the look on his face didn't remind her of some tyrant-king ruling on a throne he didn't deserve.

"Well?" he said, hands raised impatiently.

"Good afternoon, *Pak*. Did you receive the files we emailed you?" Naya asked, voice calm but commanding.

"Yes."

"Do you have any questions about any of the designs? Anything that needs to be clarified?"

Surya glanced at his watch, refusing to look at her as he answered, "I haven't looked yet."

"Production has to start as soon as possible," she pressed.

"I'll look when I have time."

Gunawan offered, "If you're too busy, is there someone else from your company we can liaise with? We don't want to disturb you if you have more important things to work on."

Ah, Gunawan. Sweet, diplomatic Gunawan.

Surya's voice went sharp. "We still have a couple of months—"

"We have four weeks," Naya interjected icily, but Surya gave her a micro-shrug.

Okay then. Another tactic. "Alright. Well, in that case, while we wait for you to get back to us, Ravi will look at backup manufacturing houses."

Oooh, Surya didn't like that one bit. "What?" he challenged with a scowl.

She turned to Rav. "I actually have a friend who owns a studio in Bandung. Remind me after the meeting and I'll send you the details so we can get a quote."

Rav nodded and scribbled in his notebook.

Surya sputtered, "My factory has been making the soft goods for MP for over ten years."

"But if you can't get it done in time, we'll need to find somewhere else that can."

"My company and MERAHPUTIH have a deal."

Naya spoke more slowly, enunciating every syllable. "But. If. You. Can't. Get. It. Done. In—"

"Of course I can get it done in time!" Surya snapped.

Naya ignored the almost-shout. "Wonderful," she said sweetly, clapping her hands and interlacing her fingers. "Edhi, make sure you add that note. Pak Surya is guaranteeing we'll get the products delivered on time."

Edhi muttered as he scrawled, "Pak Surya...guaranteed... timely... delivery. What's the time? 3:26 PM on—what's the date? Ok, done."

"Thanks Edhi." Naya pasted a polite smile on her face that didn't reach her eyes. "Was there anything else?" she asked her team. They shook their heads. "Awesome. What about you Pak Surya? Anything to add before you pop off back to your office to look at the work we sent you?"

Surya blinked his beady eyes like a languid, sun-drunk gecko. "I'd like to have a word. Alone."

"Anything you say to me can be said in front of my team."

"The DEWI mural."

Naya beamed. "I know! Isn't it exciting?"

The man came forward with his elbows on the table, lean arms crossed. "Are you working with DEWI?"

"I'll liaise with the team when they arrive. I'm hoping to help them paint the mural but it all depends on how—"

Surya jabbed his finger in Naya's direction and she hated that she flinched. She really wanted to smack his hand away. "I got their email. You went over my head to push me out of the project," he accused.

"No—*you* did that to *me*," she spat back, her cheeks heating as her anger rose. She leaned forward too, mirroring his body language by crossing her arms. "You went over *my* head. And the directors'."

"I don't know what you're talking about."

She huffed a mirthless laugh, and turned to The Bevy. "I was hoping to spare you all the drama but Pak Surya emailed DEWI offering a mural, and DEWI forwarded it to me. He didn't get approval to make that kind of offer."

The Bevy glowered at him. This wasn't merely an affront to Naya and the directors; the Bevy had spent countless hours working on *Heartbreak*—early mornings, late nights, and weekends—and Surya thought he could swoop in and take DEWI as his own personal win?

Naya shook her head slowly at Surya. "Offering the Purnama, without consulting the bosses," she tutted at him.

Surya's bottom lip jutted out defensively. "Well, my aunt—"

"Yeah, yeah," she groaned as she rolled her eyes. "God forbid we forget your aunt, the legacy director. You didn't tell the other three directors though." Surya didn't respond. "Of course, the other three would be crazy not to approve it once they found out DEWI was interested because a DEWI mural's like a leap year—they don't come around very often." She winked. "What you didn't expect was DEWI asking me if they could do a mural *before* your offer to them." He huffed just as Naya crooned, "I mean, really, Pak Surya, we all get what we want, don't we? I get the offer from DEWI, DEWI accepts your offer of the Purnama, and the directors have a beautiful mural that is amazing PR for MERAHPUTIH. Your aunt must be so proud."

Surya leaned back in the leather chair, resting his left ankle on his right knee, fingers interlocked over his sternum. "You," he mused, "are a pebble in my shoe, Mbak Naya."

"And you—" Naya replied airily, feeling her backbone straighten and strengthen like it was forged out of steel—"are a thorn in our side."

Surya's blank facade cracked at her words. She was playing with fire now.

"The person with power punching down," Naya noted. She tapped her chin in thought and then gave him one of those sickly sweet smiles he liked to give Owen. "Perhaps you should start a creative project to work through your insecurity, Pak. Highly recommend painting. It's very therapeutic."

Tini raised her hand and exclaimed, "Oh! We have a painting workshop starting next weekend, Pak Surya. It's called Creative Healing: Self-Expression and Self-Care. It goes for six weeks. It would be perfect." Tini's pretty eyes were big as she feigned innocence.

Edhi pursed his lips to catch his giggle.

Naya sent a text on her watch and then looked up at Surya. "Can we call a truce or something? Because this is getting old."

Surya looked both amused and bemused. "You're trying to negotiate with me—a board member who has a decade-long manufacturing contract with MERAHPUTIH?"

"Don't forget your aunt, the legacy director. You certainly never let us forget."

Surya snorted, his eyes scanning every single one of them with a look that screamed, *You are nothing.*

"Fine," she sighed, feigning defeat. "There must be some other way to inspire you to change your mind though. *Hmm.*"

The boardroom door flew open; everyone except Naya flinched. Owen appeared, his broad shoulders and towering height making the doorway look tiny. His hands were in the pockets of his pants as he searched the room with a frown on his beautiful face. Surya scrambled to stand, but Owen spotted Naya and his whole face lit up, eyes aglow, ignoring Surya.

"*Sayang*—there you are. I've been looking for you," he gruffed affectionately in his deep Australian accent. He gave her the most devastating smile, wintry eyes sparkling.

Naya's cheeks warmed, although she put on a fake tone of derision. "I know. My watch has been blowing up with your texts." She held up her wrist. "Seven, Owen."

He jogged in like a cheeky child and sat in front of her on the table. He took her hand and kissed it. "What are you doing, love?" he asked, booping her nose. She playfully slapped his hand away.

The Bevy stared—mouths agape.

She gestured to everyone in the room. "Important meeting. Trying to be professional."

Owen looked around at her team members as if only then realising she wasn't alone. His brows shot up and his face lit up again for them. "Oh, hey, team. How are you all?" he said casually. "That is a very cool shirt, Edhi."

The team murmured dazed hellos, and Edhi fiddled with the collar of his hot pink shirt. And then Naya said, "You forgot someone," jerking her chin to the person behind him.

Owen looked over his shoulder, surprised and disappointed to see Surya. His voice went flat. "Oh. Surya. Didn't see you there." He turned back to Naya just as Surya started to say something. "Are you almost finished? I've been waiting for ages," Owen complained.

Naya chuckled as he tucked her hair behind her ear and flicked the strands over her shoulder—an innocent move, but no one would mistake it for anything but an intimate touch between lovers. She turned to Tini, who was trying to suppress a smile, and pointed her thumb at Owen. "Who knew a legacy director could be so clingy."

Owen did that adorable lazy shrug-cheeky grin combo thing and then pouted. "I haven't seen you at all today. I miss you. Let's leave early."

She pouted at him. "I can't. I have to wait until Pak Surya finishes looking over the email we sent him. We need to make sure there aren't any issues with the design notes so they can start production right away."

Owen twisted around to look at the man who had the *fucking audacity* to keep him waiting even longer and flashed him a grin that was all teeth, and Naya couldn't help but remember that comment Endah made a few days before about Owen and his terrifying toothy smiles. "I know you'll get it sorted, love, just like you got that whole DEWI debacle sorted," he crooned at her, while he stared flatly at the man shrinking back into the chair. The Golden God of MP paused for dramatic effect, and Surya's eyes darted up to his face and then away again. "I'm relieved, Surya, that your faux pas didn't scare DEWI away. That comment you made in the email to them, about the unknown artists—" He turned back to Naya—"how did it go?"

Naya recited, *"...Your contribution will distract from an otherwise humble event that has been curated with works by unknown artists, since it has been planned at the last minute."*

Ravi let out a scoff then, shaking his head, and Owen turned to him. "I know!" he laughed. "Joyce Setianingsih, and Ali Suleiman—*unknown artists.*" Owen stood to face Surya, leaning his divine body over the glossy boardroom table. "You sure MP's the right place for you? It's probably a good idea to actually *have an idea* about art to sit on the board of an art gallery. No matter who you're related to."

Surya's jaw ticked. He looked at his hands.

Owen's voice had gone as smooth as a newly sharpened knife. Naya couldn't wait to get the esteemed benefactor alone, let him use that lofty tone and sharp tongue on her. She reached for Owen's hand and gave it a squeeze.

"Approving the designs won't take longer than an hour." Owen's voice went up at the end as if it was a question but Surya nodded quickly at the command. Owen sighed sulkily and turned to Naya. "I'll be in my office being bored. Come hang out with me while you wait, yeah? Bye, team."

And then he put his hands back in his pockets and sauntered out, looking over his shoulder to wink at Naya and bite his lip before disappearing round the corner.

The minute of silence was *delicious.*

Naya flopped back in her leather chair, crossing her legs and interlocking her fingers over her belly. "How's *that* for inspiration?"

Surya looked defeated, and utterly offended by it. He stood up, mumbling something about going back to his office to check the design files and getting back to them in less than an hour, and then rushed out of the boardroom.

$$\downarrow$$

O leaned against his desk, waiting for Naya to show when Surya walked past, sulkily dragging his feet. The man didn't turn his head to acknowledge O as he continued along the wall of glass, but his eyes flashed O's way. Surya was side-eyeing *him*, looking all offended. Betrayed, even—as if they were aligned in the first place, as if it was ever some *us vs them* situation where board members and directors were on one team while the rest of the staff were on the other.

He rubbed his eyes, imagining the rot that had appeared at MERAHPUTIH right under his nose, oily and black, its roots spreading deep and wide. If Surya was the source of this rot, did it start ten years ago when the manufacturing deal had been signed and his family had been given the board seat?

Could they have been so blind to it all? For a fucking decade? How did they only find out only when Endah happened upon Surya berating Naya in front of a room full of people? Even the department heads hadn't done anything to defend her. Was it fear? Carelessness? Competition—every man for himself?

None of them had complained. That wasn't due to their complacency—he was sure of it. No—they didn't think anything would actually be done. They didn't believe they were supported, and rightly so, because they fucking *hadn't* been—so they just kept their heads down and hoped to stay out of Surya's way while doing whatever they could to protect each other.

What would his mother think? And his *grandmother*—who started the place he'd spent the last few years neglecting? God—and Ibu Tuti. How could *she* be okay with this?

Anxiety crept up his spine, the same black tendrils as MP's rot coiling around his insides, coaxing him into a shame spiral when Naya appeared at his door, all smooth curves and sharp strength, a wicked smile on her face. Without faltering her steps, she strode right up to him, her pretty lips turned up into a sly little smile as she said, "Thank you for playing along. You were perfect."

His mood lifted as soon as she spoke, and he felt less burdened at the sound of her husky voice. "*You're* perfect. You know I wasn't play-ing," he answered, moving to touch her but then snatching his hand back, glancing at the staff who were failing spectacularly at getting back to work.

Naya looked over her shoulder; Ravi and Edhi were standing by Ravi's office, and Tini was leaning against the side of her cubicle, wait-ing. She gestured at Naya and mouthed, *Come on*. The rest of the juniors frowned at Tini's flailing arms, and then turned in O and Naya's direction. Naya covered her face with one hand and grumbled as she turned back to O. God love Tini's audacity. He didn't know whether he should chastise her for being grossly unprofessional or give her a raise.

"You okay?" he asked, and he bowed his neck to see her face better.

Naya's eyes were downcast, her black lashes fluttering against her blushing cheeks as she stepped closer between O's feet. "I guess," she said—voice quiet, "we're not hiding anymore."

O swallowed. His body wanted to lean towards her, but he willed himself to stop. "Srinaya," he murmured, "we had a timeline; the exhibi-tion opening is still weeks away. This is all happening faster than you wanted."

The rot began climbing again, little by little.

Naya nodded. "I know. I'm surprised at how *movable* I've been since meeting you, Owen. Maybe I'm not as headstrong as I thought. Or maybe it's just you." She placed her hand on her chest as she said, "Immovable object," and then gestured to him, "Unstoppable force."

She stared at his mouth as if she was too shy to look into his eyes.

They stood in front of each other for about three breaths-worth of silence before they burst out in awkward giggles. "This is ridiculous," he complained. "I've seen you naked a thousand times, and we've said some shockingly dirty things to each other, but standing this close to you in front of our audience out there is the hardest fucking thing..."

She snickered and clasped her hands behind her back, looking adorably coy *and* like she was trying to behave, but her body leaned towards him too. It happened all the time whenever they tried to resist each other—their bodies just seemed to pull together like magnets and they couldn't do anything to stop it. But he didn't want this to be some performance for other people. Yes, it was a public statement that, through Naya's connection to him, *everyone* was off-limits to Surya.

But this couldn't be forced.

Back at Cinq-Huit, Naya mentioned something that had cemented itself in O's mind. "But... I don't want you to feel like you're *cheapening* what we have by doing this..."

She nodded, remembering her words. "Thing is, I've been protecting myself but doing a disservice to you and me. We're not doing anything wrong—I finally believe that. And... you were right: my connection to you, and *Oom* Bakti, and *Ibu* Endah means I can borrow your power to protect the staff." She tucked her hands into her pockets. "I'm not going to lie... I hate that I couldn't fix this on merit alone, and I really am going to hate all the intrusive comments and questions—" She grimaced at the thought—"but this is important."

She looked to the cubicles again, at the expectant faces of her fellow curators who congregated in the open office space, pretending not to stare.

O took a deep breath—heaviness creeping up his sternum like heartburn. "I've done a really shit job here," he muttered, squeezing his eyes shut.

"No, Owen. This isn't all on you. You haven't been here."

"Exactly."

"No. Stop. Look at me." Her soft fingers squeezed his forearm and he opened his lids to those big sad eyes so full of love and kindness. Far more kindness than he deserved. "You are not the only one responsible.

Hey—no. Owen. Listen to me. This *is not* all on you. There are others who are here all the time—who are aware of how toxic the culture is—*they* should have done something."

"I'm going to do something."

"I know," she soothed. "I wanted to do something too, and this was the quickest way, even if... even if it exposes me..." O watched as her mind ticked over. "I'm tired of being scared. I'm tired of keeping my head down and keeping quiet when, really, nothing about me is quiet."

She gestured at her body—at the way she looked.

Her fat body stood out wherever she went. It wasn't only her size, or her bold tattoos or piercings, or even the way she dressed. There were plenty of others who dressed the same, whose skin was inked more heavily than hers. There was just something about *Srinaya Matthews*. People turned her way. She was like the sun; people couldn't help but get pulled into her orbit, and they either basked or resented the heat.

"I don't really fit, and I don't know why I keep trying to *make* myself fit. I keep stopping myself from ruffling feathers, when it happens anyway. All I have to do is walk into a room and—" She raised her hands in surrender—"feathers are ruffled." She took a step closer, standing between his knees as her voice went soft and needy. "If I'm going to ruffle feathers without meaning to, I should probably just enjoy myself."

Her plump lips parted, curved upwards in a little nervous smile. O reached for her hand and brushed his lips over her palm, and Naya stroked his cheek with her fingers.

Tini jumped up and down.

O needed more. "Come here, love." He pulled her in, holding her close and Naya's arms wrapped around his neck. He buried his face in her hair and inhaled the scent of coconut and cinnamon. He glanced at the glass and huffed at the gawking curators. He murmured, "They're watching us like we're bloody pandas at the zoo."

Naya turned to look as well, and the whole floor—minus Surya— was milling about giving them thumbs ups, or punching the air in victory, or golf-clapping.

"Oh god," she groaned, and then buried her face in the crook of his neck again.

He purred, and since her hair hid his face from view, nipped at the soft skin on her shoulder. "Hey—it's still just you and me, okay?" he lied, because he couldn't ignore the bloated and ugly shame that sat squarely on his shoulders. It really *wasn't* just the two of them—it was Naya, and him, and his negligence in keeping the staff safe, and Naya sacrificing their privacy for the greater good, and his dead grandmother and mother hating the coward he'd become, and the big Chidori lie.

He held her tighter; he couldn't lose her.

From the main office, they heard a resounding *Aaaaaaaaaaw.*

Naya called out, "Get back to work!"

thirty-four

Naya was coaxed out of her late afternoon nap on Owen's daybed by a warm caress on her lower back. Not ready to open her eyes, she just murmured—stretched her toes. She heard the little pops of buttons, the sound of a zipper, and the rustle of fabric being tossed over furniture, and then she felt the dip of the mattress as a warm, almost-naked body settled behind her. A scratchy cheek caressed her neck. She inhaled deeply and tasted citrus in the back of her throat.

She turned to face Owen. Half his hair was tied up and his high forehead and furrowed brow made him look more broody than usual. The dark circles under his eyes were worse; she knew he'd been having trouble sleeping, but she had too much on her own plate to deal with it.

He stroked her hair and said, "I went back to pick you up but you weren't there. What happened?"

She buried her face in the crook of his neck and let out a petulant little *hmph*. "*Ibu* Desi gave me tips on how to butter you up so you'd propose. In the middle of a budget meeting. There were innuendos, Owen."

His jaw clenched.

Naya didn't mention how she hid in a bathroom cubicle on the second floor to silently seethe after *Ibu* Desi's unsolicited relationship advice when three staff members entered, giggling as they made obscene comments about Owen's body and disparaging remarks about hers, speculating on sexual logistics. *I mean, she's pretty for a fat woman but do you think it's because she's the only other* bule *here? Maybe he goes elsewhere for sex. How can she satisfy him? He's... god—he's* perfect *and she's... not. At all.*

"And two days ago," she continued, "Astrid from accounts congratulated me, and I thought it was for how well the plans for the show are going, and it felt so fucking good to be acknowledged for my work. But then she was all, *You caught a big fish—how did you do it?*" Naya made her voice extra high and squeaky to mock Astrid and then regretted being mean. She pressed the heels of her palms into her eyelids. "Everyone's staring at me again," she mumbled.

"They're staring at me too."

Naya rolled her eyes. "They always stare at you." How could they not? He was gorgeous and hard to miss.

He huffed. "They always stare at you too."

She frowned at him. "No, they don't."

Owen's brows shot up in insistence. "Yeah, they do. I notice. They watch you all the time, even before we went public."

"Well, that doesn't make me feel better."

"It should. They're intrigued, Naya. You fascinate them. No scowls or sneers." She couldn't be bothered correcting him. Owen ran his lips over her ear. "What do you need?"

A frustrated groan came out. "For them to stop pointing at me and making comments. I haven't *up-levelled* because I'm with you. It doesn't make my work for MP better, and it doesn't make my personal artwork better." He nodded but his lips thinned. He looked so sad; had she hurt his feelings? "You know I don't mean being with you isn't the best, Owen, because it is," she said softly. He gave her a weak smile and nodded again. "It's just that... I'm angry at myself for not being more prepared for all the gossip and interest in our private life. Surya hasn't been back at work since, and I know that was exactly why I did it, so my plan worked, but—fuck. I was a whole human being with a pretty interesting life before they labelled me *the future Mrs Esteemed Benefactor.*" Owen made a weird little sound—like a raspy intake of breath. She ignored it and barrelled on. "For thirty-five years, in fact, I was known as Srinaya Matthews. Now I've been stripped down to being *Mr Jameson's Girlfriend From The Fifth Floor*."

Naya rolled onto her back and looked up at the trees sheltering the outdoor deck. The daylight began to fade, and the leaves looked black in front of the light blue-grey of the sky.

Owen stroked her belly—his little *Naya line* deep between his brow. He looked out at the garden as if he couldn't meet her eyes. She tilted his chin down to kiss his lips gently. "I love being with you. So much. I hate that I've lost my sense of self at MP."

His eyes finally flicked to hers. "Both things can be true," he recited.

Naya smiled mirthlessly. "Yeah," she answered, and then with more solemnity she repeated herself to ease the vulnerability that wouldn't leave his beautiful face. "I love being with you. I love you. My personal life is so much better with you in it."

Owen rested his chin on her shoulder. "I love you too. It's early days. We'll be old news soon. The timing's shit—I know, what with *Heartbreak* only three weeks away—but you'll get it done because you're wonderful."

Naya melted against him, comforted by his trust and confidence in her, and then lifted her nose to the pulse point in his neck to inhale his lovely scent—oranges, grapefruit and brown sugar invading her senses. She sighed in pleasure. "You smell like summer, Owen. You make me miss Melbourne," she said.

He leaned away to search her face, eyes dark and cheerless, and then he pulled her so close her arms were trapped between them, his mouth covering hers in a heavy, bossy kiss. "What *else* do you need?" Owen breathed into her mouth.

"Distraction," she moaned.

He was hungry—his lips and tongue unrelenting as they explored her mouth, and then made his way down her neck and chest. He impatiently peeled away her tanktop and suckled on her nipples, the click of metal against teeth and the little growl at the back of Owen's throat sending jolts of pleasure to her clit. A big hand reached beneath her underwear, fingers stroking her pubic hair. She moaned, heat spreading from her belly outwards, her cheeks burning and her calves feeling tight. Ridding her of her briefs with a frustrated curse, Owen's clever fingers parted her pussy lips and then brushed against her clit, and Naya gasped at how uncomfortably sensitive she already was.

She needed to feel Owen inside her—stretching her open. "Fuck me with your fingers," she demanded with a whine, and the glint of approval in his stormy eyes inspired a fresh surge of slippery juices to well up within her.

He used two fingers, sliding them in and out, twisting, and then curling them upwards to that gorgeous spot deep inside that made her lose her breath. He watched her face carefully—studied her reactions to his strokes. She parted her legs wider, licking her own fingers to get them slick and circled her clit, her whole body on fire. "More, Owen," she whispered. "Another," and Owen looked practically masterful when he slid another finger inside her, making her whimper—making tears form and fall down into her hair.

That lovely sunshiney smell mixed with her wetness and the musky scent of his own arousal fogged her brain and coloured her vision until all she could see when she closed her eyes, submitting to overwhelming pleasure, were streaks of gold on warm chocolate brown, and amber with a flash of cold grey.

His erection grazed her inner thigh and she reached down to wrap her hand around him. God—his cock was incredible—everything about it. She loved his velvety foreskin, so warm and soft under her fingers. Naya looked down to watch his rosy cockhead appear as she stroked him, twisting her wrist just the way he liked. A little bead of pre-cum appeared on the tip, and she wiped it with her thumb and brought it to her mouth—hummed in delight at how right he tasted.

"The face you make when you taste me—it's like you've discovered chocolate or something," Owen said, blushing. "Your eyes roll back, and your cheeks go so pink. Such a compliment, Naya."

He pulled his fingers out of her and licked them clean. He moaned a curse. His lids closed, enraptured. It felt so fucking wrong to not be filled by him. She whimpered, and when his eyes reopened, two terrifyingly large pupils stared back—his nose wrinkling in a feral sneer as he swiftly manoeuvred himself to lay between her legs.

He kissed her pubic mound, nuzzling the hair there. And then he parted her pussy, spreading her lips open and dragging his tongue heavily against her. She sobbed when he suckled on the slippery skin that hooded over her clit.

Owen was almost fluent in the language of her body—understood her intricacies—her sounds, her breath, even the different ways she bit her lip or ran her tongue against her teeth. He gave her overwhelmed bundle of nerves a reprieve when she rasped his name. God—she loved the way his name felt in her mouth.

He pushed her legs further apart and drove his tongue into her pussy instead. She felt obscene, her naked body splayed under the milky-coloured Jakarta sky with Owen's face pressed firmly against her, eating her out. His lips and tongue were stubborn in their exploration, and the vibrations of his moans on her skin made her hips shake.

He looked up at her, resting his cheek against her thigh, mouth glistening.

He said, "Teach me how you come, Naya. I want to know where that secret little spot is." Naya smiled down at him, touched by his undeviating focus when it came to learning everything he could about her. He tilted his head in thought and then grinned mischievously. "Maybe we can tattoo a little *x* there."

Naya giggled and shoved his face away when he nipped at her soft belly, and then he dashed inside his bedroom to retrieve her vibrator.

He returned and settled between her legs again, thick muscular thighs pressed against hers, his eyes bright and alert for his lesson. She tilted her hips up, parted her pussy lips and then stroked the sensitive little place that made all the difference—to the right of her clitoris. "Right here," she sighed, and Owen leaned closer to see.

He turned her vibrator on, ran his talented pink tongue over the soft silicone to get it as wet and slippery as she was, and pressed it into the spot. *So close.* She guided his hand. "Almost. Just a little—*Yeeees.*"

She pressed her pelvis against the sextoy, slightly away from her clit and into the soft flesh of her inner labia, and her lids fluttered shut. Her clitoris had always been far too sensitive—wasn't built to take all the focus—but aiming the toy only a few inches away made the rumble of her vibrator thrum through her body.

"Here?" Owen asked, and Naya gasped.

He looked so pleased, so very very haughty, like he wanted to gloat. "*Hmm.* So, about two finger-widths to the left. What about on the other side?" he asked, and then he moved the toy over and Naya's spine bowed and she cried out a curse. He bared his terrifying teeth at her, laughing devilishly.

Oh shit. She was in so much fucking trouble.

He slid three fingers deep into her cunt again without warning while his other hand pressed her toy firmly to that secret spot. He curled his beautiful fingers upwards like he was beckoning her, coaxing her orgasm out. *Come, Srinaya. Come here.*

Naya's pelvis bucked upwards and she grunted. She curled her toes, panting. He watched her closely—paid attention to those little signs her body gave him, like he was memorising some kind of combination that unlocked a vault deep inside her, wrenched open the door to her treasure.

He didn't need to tattoo an *x*. Owen's voice was a growl when he uttered, "There it is."

He did something—she wasn't sure what, but she stopped breathing as an orgasm was plucked out of her. She squeezed her eyes shut when stars blurred her vision, and he leaned over her. "No, look at me," he commanded.

Naya forced her eyes open again, tears spilling from her eyes as juices spilled out of her pussy, all over Owen's hands. He murmured, "Beautiful, Naya," just as she begged, "Owen, please—"

Owen moved and Naya braced herself. His eyes were full of forbidding humour. She knew that look—loved how he could somehow tell when she needed more than pleasure. She needed to be pulled out of her head. No thinking—just feeling. She needed *too much* pleasure, so much that it stretched over to pain.

Owen pushed her legs open and up, her knees to her chest, pinning her with that gorgeous unyielding body, putting his weight on her to keep her still as he spat in his hand to wet his hard cock, and then pushed into her. Naya hummed, the burn of his dick stretching her pussy such a welcome sensation, all thoughts of MP forced out of her mind. She growled, digging her sharp nails into his biceps, and hips, and chest, scratching down his stomach, leaving pretty red lines along his skin. He hissed, freeing one of her legs to wrap his hand around her throat, and she did the same, reaching up to grip him under his jaw. He laughed like a villain, that toothy grin appearing again.

He was cruel; made it hurt. Naya cried and begged for more. She could tell she would feel the heavy ache for days after and that made it even better. For the first time since their very first encounter, he pinned her wrists above her head and she didn't protest. "Perfect, *yeees, perfect...*" she moaned, over and over.

She came again, gushing over Owen's cock as he held her toy firmly to her not-so-secret-anymore spot, her spine curving and hips trembling, with him murmuring dirty words in the most soothing tones in her ear. He fucked her so hard it knocked the breath out of her; every time she tried to say his name all that came out was the first syllable—*Oh, Oh, Oh.*

"Sweet Naya," he sighed as he got close, his breath rasping as he grunted. "Fuck, yes," he huffed, and his entire body—not just his hips—strained forward and back as he spilled into her, teeth clenched, eyes wide and pained.

As they lay together catching their breath, Naya luxuriated in the mingling of the cool air whispering over her sweaty skin, and Owen's hot and sticky body still tangled around her. She was happy and sated —well-taken care of. The burdens of the week dissipated and all that was left was comfort and safety and love.

She rolled over, propping her chin on his chest and said, "We must have been lovers in a past life. That day I met you on the steps? Somehow, I already knew you."

Owen's face changed; his bliss morphed into something dark again, but Naya didn't have it in her to question him about it.

thirty-five

Naya was sullen and distracted again—she seemed to retreat further into herself with every passing day.

Endah and Mar were right: gossip was a *thing*. O and Naya's relationship was a reality tv show—all for everyone else's entertainment. *You must go to fancy restaurants now. Oh my god, your kids will be so good-looking. They'll have light eyes! Does he buy you expensive things? Ask him to buy you a car so you don't have to take any more taxis! When are you moving in together? Does he have any single friends? Does he look even better naked? He does, doesn't he? I'm invited to your wedding, right?*

His misery was constant now; his anxiety grew like a cancer, spreading, making it harder to breathe. He hid in the bathroom during a panic attack, the door locked and the shower running as he pressed his back to the cold tiles, counting five things he could hear that weren't his own sobs muffled by a towel in his mouth.

He hadn't been to therapy in ages but couldn't bring himself to make an appointment, telling himself it was fine. It would be okay. He'd be okay; the attacks would stop soon enough. He had Naya now so life was good. He could get by with just her and his medication. Nothing else mattered.

Stefan invited them to the bar for dinner. O dreaded a rowdy Friday night at Le Roy but Naya was desperate to shake away the stress of another week and begged him to come with her. *You said you wanted to get wasted and dance with me at Le Roy. I need some fun, Owen. It's been a week. Help me forget again.*

So they ate dinner and then Stef offered them shots and MDMA, and they hid in the darkest corner of the bar, tucked away behind the DJ booth, making out like twenty-somethings on a sticky vinyl bench. Naya straddled O's lap, lazily flicking her tongue against his. One hand cupped her arse under the waistband of her jeans, the other stretched wide between her shoulder blades. Her skin was scorching. The pleasure was torturous.

They were alone in the little alcove; O gave anyone who tried to sit close a sharp, *No*, and they left in a hurry.

Naya giggled, apologising to them for the big mean *bule* she was wrapped around. "He has big scary teeth. He'll bite," she laughed, eyes crinkling.

He'd live with the anxiety if being at Le Roy made her laugh like that.

O's throat went warm and tingly and his lungs burned as if he'd run a kilometre at full speed. That was always the last sign his brain gave him as his body climbed its way to euphoria. Very soon, he'd reach the top, his whole body becoming light *and* heavy, and movements becoming fast *and* slow. He couldn't help the laugh that escaped him when the joy became so overwhelming, he wanted to cry. The music felt amazing against his skin.

Naya, so beautiful—so fucking devastating, smelling sweet and salty —moaned into his mouth. "*Ssssooo pretty,*" she slurred, running her fingertip down the bridge of his nose.

He stroked her hair, and his fingers had never touched anything so soft. It was like running his hands through water, the tingling in the webbing as the strands pulled through his fingers going straight to his rigid cock.

O gripped Naya's nape. Her eyes rolled back before her lids fluttered shut. The music was too loud for him to hear her purr, but he felt the vibration on her skin. When her eyes opened, her pupils were big and black and glazed, cheeks ruddy and sweaty. She took two of his fingers and sucked on them, pulling them out and then taking them back in, rubbing her tongue against them. Jesus fucking Christ. His dick got wetter.

And then it happened—he reached his own peak, like he had dived into the sea in the middle of a Melbourne winter, every nerve exposed. He hissed an inhale and then moaned his exhale.

He wrapped his hand around Naya's throat tightly, and like always, she lifted her chin, submitting, even with her movements extra slow and heavy. He pulled her closer, bringing the shell of her ear to his mouth and he growled, "I need to be inside you. Right now," and Naya shuddered in his arms, the crotch of her jeans pressed against his erection making him shudder too. "*Now*, Naya. Where?" he demanded, the panic rising.

Naya slinked off his lap without a word. She pulled him up; his body weighed a tonne. He rolled his neck and shoulders, the fabric of his tshirt feeling so fucking good as it moved and stretched against his back. Naya led him out of their little dark corner, past the bar where she called out to Stef and pointed down a corridor, and Stef threw her some keys and grinned knowingly at O, blowing him a kiss.

They ended up in Stefan's office—fucking on the man's desk. All their clothes off—thrown about the room, Naya bent over the cold wood, O's hand on the back of her neck, holding her head down as he pounded her from behind. She was soaked, her juices thick. His cock hit the deepest part of her but she loved it, never stopped begging for more, even when he could tell she felt pain—even when she flinched.

"Next week, Naya," he grunted, "I'll fuck you in my office." Naya moaned loud and low at his promise. "My *Presidential Suite*," he snarled, his hot wet breath in her ear. "You bent over like this. First thing in the morning. We'll hear people arriving at work. The blinds will be closed but they'll be there, just on the other side of the glass. I'll come inside your cunt, and then I'll lick you clean. You said you wanted to be spread open on my desk, yes? I'll make you come so fucking hard and you'll have to control yourself—not make a sound. Do you think you can be quiet? You're doing a fucking terrible job of being quiet right now, Srinaya."

He closed his eyes to picture the scene, but his brain flashed the blinds away, revealing him thrusting into her hard and fast for the entire fifth floor to see—their naked, sweaty bodies on display. The staff watched on with curiosity and arousal—their faces pressed up against the glass. *They're watching us like we're bloody pandas at the zoo.* His cock thickened even more at the fantasy and he hated himself for it.

And then his mind flashed back to that night in Melbourne, in that hotel room when she was just *xox N*, the feel of the soft, smooth skin of her spine under that red tshirt with the bleach stain like inverted blood spatter, a ghostly crime scene and, fuck—he was so guilty.

O shook the thoughts away. He looked down at the real Naya whimpering under him. "Fuck, yes yes yes, more, please. I need you, Owen, I love you. You're everything," she sighed, eyelids half shut as the euphoria clouded her mind.

Her sweet words subdued him. God, his nerves were stretched so tight. He felt overwhelmed—clingy and needy—as if he had to prove himself to her before she slipped from his grasp. "*Sayang*, I love you. Fuck. We should live together, Naya. Please? I'll build you the most beautiful house. You'll have a studio. A whole workshop. Anything. I'll make it just the way you want it. I'm so sorry. Please don't leave me. Please, please..."

Naya's voice was dreamy as she laughed, "Baby, you're babbling..." and O almost cried because it was the first time she'd ever called him any kind of pet name.

But O couldn't stop. The drugs and alcohol in his system wiped away any hint of a filter and it was time to lay himself bare. He turned her around and she wrapped her thick thighs around his hips. He nipped at her lips and jaw and tits as he fucked her slowly. Her tongue tasted like whisky and lemons. She smiled adoringly at him, beautiful chubby cheeks rosy and shiny. Naya murmured honey-sweet things to him and he hated them—he didn't deserve them: *You're lovely. You're mine.* Her pretty hands cupped his face and it was all too much. She could see too fucking much, all the way through his transparent skin to the lies within. O was a glass box with the blinds flashed away, revealing everything, and Naya saw him for the absolute *nothing* that he was—he was sure of it.

He took a breath.

"We slept together last year, Naya. Ten months ago… and I've loved you ever since. Please don't hate me."

Naya's eyes suddenly lost their glaze as she blinked. Her whole body stiffened and she leaned her head away to search his face. "What do you mean?" she asked, black brows furrowed. "Wait—what?"

She pushed him off.

thirty-six

"SAY THAT AGAIN," NAYA SAID, VOICE SHRILL. SHE SAT ON STEF'S DESK, horrified, arms crossed over to cover herself since the moment had been utterly ruined. The euphoria drained out of her, emptying her of everything but acute foreboding. "We slept together *ten months ago?*"

"Well—" Owen shoved his hands through his hair, and then he looked around the room for his jocks, stalling.

"Did we—or did we not—meet ten months ago?"

"I mean, you don't remember, so—"

"Don't be fucking coy, Owen," Naya snapped, pointing her finger at him.

"Look, it was the night of DEWI's show. You were getting high with friends at—"

"Chidori." Naya's eyes went wide, at first with recognition, and then confusion. "Oh my god," she whispered as she thought back to that night. "Denmark." She looked at Owen, imagining him coaxing her back to him in that hotel bed. His hair had been longer that night, and his full dark beard hid his face. "*You,*" she growled.

Naya arrived late to her alter-ego's afterparty. Her personal exhibition coincided with DEWI's, as always, and had been a success; she sold all but two pieces, *and* she'd made a killing at the DEWI show. And then she walked into the afterparty to be greeted by old friends she hadn't seen in ages. She'd been so happy to catch up with Meredith, Janet, and Liv, getting fucked up together like they did back at uni.

Liv brought some fancy molly and passed them around and they danced and laughed together, distracting poor Meredith from her shitty breakup.

The rest of the night was a haze of feelings: sadness for Mer, joy for her own success, anticipation for her move to Jakarta. But Naya remembered taking a beautiful man's hand, pulling him to DEWI's private room, his big body swaying precariously as he followed her in. "I called you pretty," Naya said to Owen, eyes shut as she replayed the night.

Owen huffed out a melancholy laugh. "Yeah. And you said I looked like a tree."

The Great Tingle Tree. Naya looked at the man standing in front of her—his stormy upturned eyes, his severe jawline. She had seen and touched every inch of him, and he'd done the same to her, but now she was in a tiny room with a stranger. Naked.

She slid off the desk, found her underwear and rushed to put them on. "I called you Denmark?" she asked, turning away to feel less exposed, trying to fill the six-foot-four-sized gap in her memory.

"Yeah. You climbed on top of me and invited me back to yours. And you mentioned Meredith's divorce, and said, *Heartbreak does—*"

"—*stupid things to people,*" she finished, and she turned around to glare at him.

She retrieved the rest of her clothes and hurriedly dressed in silence. Owen did the same.

Naya returned to Stef's office chair, his giant desk a barrier between them. Her mind reeled. She wrapped her arms around herself, skin cold and clammy.

She remembered the darkness of that hotel room on her last night in Melbourne; the soft sheets, the tickle of his beard against her neck, his sleep-soaked voice clear as a bell as he'd beckoned her back to him. *Hey. Stay.*

Her eyes prickled. When the tears blurred her sight, she met his gaze. "You used that line on me that day at *Pak* Mudi's."

Owen shook his head firmly as he sat on the chair on the other side of the desk. "No, that's not true. It wasn't a line," he argued, reaching for her.

She recoiled and Owen snatched his hand back as if he'd touched a flame. "I kissed you because something felt *very right* when you said that. What the fuck, Owen?"

"Look. Please let me explain."

"Yes," she hissed, "explain how the fuck I ended up half naked with you in my hotel room."

He gasped. "I-Naya-that's…No, I didn't take advantage. The last thing I remember is *you* asking to take advantage of *me*. You asked *me*. *Let me take advantage, Denmark*—that's what you said. And *I* said yes." His words rushed out, frantic.

She saw real fear and hurt, and she was fucking glad. She raised her voice. "How am I supposed to believe anything you say?" Her head spun. She took a deep breath but couldn't quite grab at that last little bit of oxygen her lungs needed.

"Because I'm telling you now," Owen said, voice strained. "You never would've found out if I didn't. But I've wanted to tell you for a while."

"Oh, ok then, *thank you?*" Naya spat out. "Thank you for finally telling the truth about lying to me since the very beginning."

Owen buried his face in his hands. "The part before I blacked out was… I don't know—fifteen minutes max. It didn't matter," he mumbled.

"Is that why you kept it from me—because it didn't matter?" Her heartbeat quickened and the stabbing tingle of rage rose up her spine. "Is that why you're here in Jakarta? Because it didn't matter?" Owen refused to look at her. "I woke up without any underwear on—*does that not fucking matter?*" Naya asked, raising her voice. His eyes narrowed in a wince. He'd never seen her angry before—had never experienced how loud she could go. *Just you fucking wait,* she seethed.

He looked down at his feet and took a deep breath in, trying to control the tremble in his voice. He spoke quietly, "No—you're right. It all matters. It meant the world. And I should've told you that day on the steps. I don't know why I lied. I was scared too—I'm always scared, Naya. But… you woke up before me. You left *me*." He tilted his head as his own words sunk in. He frowned at her. "You… you just ran out of there and didn't even care enough to say goodbye. To *see* me."

"Well, you found me anyway, didn't you?"

Owen's voice got hard. "Eight months later."

"Going for the long con?"

His jaw ticked but he didn't snap back. "I planned on telling you, but then you told me what happened to you, and I worried you'd think I'd gotten you the job and the exhibition, which *I didn't*—I promise you, I had no hand in that happening. You didn't… fuck your way to a win." He reached for her hand again. "I worried you'd think I stalked you, which I also didn't, Naya. I haven't lied about anything else."

A big fat tear fell as she avoided his touch, rolling her chair back until it hit the wall behind her to get as far away from him as possible. "How can I believe you?" she croaked.

He looked wounded, and Naya felt sick because all she wanted to do was go to him and comfort him, and ask him to comfort her in return. But he'd caused all of this. He'd made decisions for her without her knowledge and consent—just like Sal. He'd *managed* her—

Endah.

Endah said, *Remember how much you love him when you find out he's managed you, as you say, Naya. He really can't help it—*

"Endah knew, didn't she?"

Owen nodded, squeezed his eyes shut in shame, and then his eyes met hers. He shook his head in a silent plea, that deep V appearing between his brows.

"You know what the kicker is, Owen?" Naya said, voice cracking as she soothed the spot in her sternum that ached whenever she thought about how much she loved him. "This is about trust. You don't trust me to be sensible. You think you know better."

Owen sat forward, his grief morphing into offence. "How can you say that to me? I was heavy-handed at the beginning because I didn't understand what you'd gone through. But you've been leading this ever since. *That's* how much I trust you."

She wanted to be petulant—to lash out. She didn't fucking care anymore. "I've done so much for you. For us. I've given up so much."

His stupid, handsome face scrunched into a sneer. *"Given up? What have I asked you to give up?"*

Naya couldn't answer that, but she *felt* it. She'd changed—broken her own rules. She'd moulded herself into someone she hadn't been before he appeared. The second time. She lifted her chin defiantly. "And you waited to tell me until after we fucking *came out* to the company!"

"I didn't ask you to do that."

"And now I'm going to look like a fucking idiot when they find out we broke up."

"Is that what you really want—to break up?"

Yes. No. Fuck. Her brain was too full—swollen. "Did you get me the job at MP?"

"I literally just said—" Owen stared incredulously at her. He chewed on his lip as he tried to swallow his mounting annoyance. "No. I told you—I didn't get you the job. You did that all by yourself."

Her mind was having trouble grasping anything other than the screaming in her head: *Owen tricked you, Owen tricked you, Owen tricked you.*

"Then how did I come to work at a place that you practically own eight months later?"

The growl that came out of his throat was a sound she'd never heard before—the worst fucking sound. He raised his voice as he answered, "Oh my god, why can't you believe that you got the job because you're just that fucking good, Srinaya?"

She stared at him blankly.

Running both hands through his hair, he stood, moving away to lean against the door. "Look. I'd been at DEWI's show and then I went to Chidori. Total fluke that I went. Wasn't planning it. And then you walked in. And I noticed you straight away. I couldn't stop looking at you. You were fucking radiant, like a rainbow in a room full of beige. And then a friend of mine appeared, and they offered me a sip of their drink because… they know how I can get, and like a fucking asshole, I downed the whole thing not realising they'd spiked it. And I met you just as it started to kick in—just as I was leaving. And I was so fucking glad, Naya, because I'd been mustering up the courage to speak to you all night, and then there you were, in front of me, asking if I was okay. And I hadn't been. All night, I hadn't been okay, and then I was as soon as you spoke to me." His eyes scanned over her face. "And you were fucking *adorable.* So sweet, and sad, and curious. And you were *off your face,*" he laughed joylessly, and then his face darkened even more. "Why weren't your friends looking after you?

"And then… we were in that room, and you were straddling me on that couch, and I said it wasn't a good idea because you were fucked up, but you insisted, and I tried to behave. I fucking tried, but then—" He swallowed—"I peaked, and you said, *Let me take advantage, Denmark,* and of course I said yes. And the next thing I know, it's morning, and I'm alone in a hotel room." He rubbed his chest right above his heart— "I've experienced a lot of loss in my life but when I woke up in that bed alone, Naya, and I had no way of finding you, it *killed* me. I don't give a shit how dramatic that sounds. And I pined for this person I didn't even know for months—and felt like a fucking loser the entire time for feeling the way I did, until I accepted that you were just going to be out there, existing. Without me. I thought I'd never see you again but was so glad for all the people who were going to get to meet you."

Owen covered his face with his hands, rubbing his eyes. He pulled out his phone, swiping and tapping it as he continued his story, "And then, eight months later, I get an email from Endah telling me a new curator is having a hard time, and to come and show my support because she's amazing."

He paused to search for the email and held up the picture of her Endah had sent. Naya recognised the photo. "...and it's *you.* I was walking down Swanston St, and there you were. So, yes. I go to Jakarta. I meet you, and Endah was right—you *are* fucking amazing and I wasn't going to walk away." He swore under his breath. "I don't believe in God. Hard to believe in divinity when you've lost as much as I have and can feel so utterly *shit* like I can. But now that you know how we met and where we ended up, don't you think it feels a little bit cosmic? *Sacred?*"

Owen crouched in front of her. She flinched but didn't move away. He leaned in closer. "Look at me, Naya. Please," he asked gently, and she did. "You think I hold the power in this? You think all the money and influence I have, the fucking title no one will let me forget—*esteemed benefactor*—" He spat out—"makes *me* the one holding the cards here? Are you fucking kidding me?"

She didn't know what to say to him. She was so angry and sad and lost—bereft of love and laughter. Tears dripped off her chin; she hadn't noticed them before. "But… you lied," she slurred.

Owen tilted his head to study her, eyes red. "You want to fight me—not forgive me," he said in the saddest fucking voice, and as tears formed, and he wiped them away, a horrible wave of nausea and hopelessness washed over Naya—as if their terrible conversation had forced her comedown to the surface ahead of schedule.

A comedown, a hangover, and heartbreak rushing out all at once.

"I don't want to fight," he murmured and stepped away immediately, eyes downcast, "So, I'm going to go. Take Ibrahim. I'll call a taxi."

Before she could think, she opened her mouth. "I don't need any more fucking favours from you. I'll find my own way home."

He stared silently, for ages, and the longer he didn't say anything, the worse Naya felt for all of it—for saying mean things, for being lied to, for telling everyone about them.

And then Owen broke eye contact, rubbing his face with a trembling hand, and opened the door. Naya grimaced as the thumping music filled the little room and assaulted her senses.

Her stomach turned.

Owen looked back at her from the doorway. "I wish I could forget *this* night," he said, and then left.

thirty-seven

Naya cracked open her eyelids and immediately regretted the sliver of light that pierced her pupils. An ice pick must've been lodged in her brain—there could be no other reason for the sharp pain in the back of her skull. And then she remembered what happened at Le Roy: one moment Owen was giving her mind-blowing pleasure, asking her to move in with him in that extravagant-yet-vulnerable way of his, and the next, he confessed to being the mysterious Dane from her after-party, who'd clung to her like a limpet for most of the night, to her delight. She'd welcomed his clinginess; her body wanted him, even if the midnight blackness hid him from her.

The pounding headache felt like a mild bout of brain freeze compared to the ache that Owen had caused in her heart. She groaned and very slowly opened her lids again, breathing through the wave of nausea that crashed over her as her eyes attempted to focus. She slowly sat up, realising she was in Arum's guest room. Her best friend was sitting in the armchair next to the bed, hugging her knees, smiling at Naya. Naya groaned again.

"Hey, bud," Arum said far too brightly.

"Is he okay?" Naya asked.

"'Course not. Don't be stupid."

Naya's eyes burned as the tears slowly appeared. "Oh, bud," Arum said sympathetically.

"He tricked me."

"*Mm hmm,*" Arum answered in a familiar tone that set Naya's nerves on edge all over again.

"He *tricked* me, Arum."

Arum tilted her head to one side as she winced. "Naya, your serotonin levels are way too depleted to get into it," she said with a little less care.

Naya sat up straighter, scrunching her eyes shut, the pressure in her head throbbing with every shuffle. "You think *I'm* in the wrong?" Arum crossed her arms but didn't respond. "He met me ten months ago at my afterparty. We may have fucked, Arum! He fucking snuggled me all fucking night," Naya said angrily.

Arum gasped, eyes wide. "How *dare* he? What a cunt!" she exclaimed. "What other awful things did he do?"

Okay. Naya wasn't going to get anywhere trying to make their first *actual* encounter sound terrible. Arum looked at Naya as if she was still waiting to hear the bad part as Naya continued, "He didn't tell me."

Arum's lips thinned. She was clearly *not* moved by Naya's revelation. "Arum, he didn't just not tell me. He outright *lied*. He said we met at MP. More than once."

Arum shrugged her shoulders. "But what's so bad about that? You would've ended up together anyway."

If Naya's leaden body wasn't screaming at her for more rest, she would've thrown a pillow so hard at Arum, the little pixie-witch would've toppled out of the chair. Instead, Naya pointed to the door. "Go away."

Arum squawked, "No. This is my place, and I love you and I'm being a good friend."

Naya flopped sideways and buried her face in a pillow. The bed dipped just a tiny bit under Arum's slight frame as she sat next to her. "Sri, I understand you're hurting, and that fucking sucks. But I've never been the type to baby you, so I'm not going to start now. If you wanted coddling, Stef should've taken you back to his—not mine."

Naya turned to Arum, who looked down at her with those big, perfectly winged eyes. Arum said, "He shouldn't have lied. That was wrong."

Finally. Some validation, even if she knew the woman next to her well enough to brace herself for the next bit. Arum took a small intake of breath before saying, "You've outright lied too. Granted, different types of lies, *yadda yadda*—" Arum twinkled her fingers as if *shooing* the point away like it were a fly—"but you're withholding something pretty big from him."

Naya bristled. "DEWI's got nothing to do with this. DEWI came before."

"Oh, come off it, Sri. You can't really be this obtuse. You met Moose at a party for your alter ego in Australia. Sure—it's all a blur. That sucks. But I remember you telling me about the mysterious man you walked out on when I fucking picked you up at the airport. You said you wished you could've stayed there all weekend. You said there was something about him."

Telling Arum about the Danish man with no name and face had escaped Naya's memory. She cringed inwardly.

"And then," Arum continued, "two months later, you get a job working at the foundation his grandmother—and *my* grandmother— co-founded. In Indonesia. And then—*excuse me*, I haven't finished yet, so shut up—and then, the daughter of *another* co-founder comes to your rescue and gets Moose over here. And then *your* best friend falls for *his* best friend. And now your alter ego is going to paint a mural on the wall of the gallery that is his legacy. *My* legacy, Srinaya. Swear to Christ, it's like a Dickensian saga minus the tragic orphan subplot."

Naya muttered, "Owen's an orphan."

Arum threw her hands up in victory. "There you go then. One hundred percent Dickensian."

Naya rubbed her eyes, finding Arum's defence of Owen a hard pill to swallow. Her nose started to run as the tears very slowly welled up. Arum shuffled closer and stroked her hair. In that tough-love way of hers, Arum said, "When are you going to realise that you're the only person getting in your way? God damn, you're meddlesome."

†

O ended up in Endah's guest room, almost giving her an aneurysm as he stumbled through her door in the middle of the night. It had been almost twenty years since O had shown up at an ungodly hour, utterly fucked up, needing safe harbour—a place where he didn't have to be strong. The walls could come down at Endah and Agung's home.

Naya had been that—a safe and stable place he tethered himself to during dark moments. Now he was unanchored. Everything was dark grey, felt cold and hard, and weighed down by unanswered questions.

He drifted in and out of sleep all weekend. Sometimes he'd be alone, sometimes he'd open his eyes and Endah would be there, drinking tea or reading a book. One time, he opened his eyes and found her asleep on the couch. Shame stabbed at him. What a waste of fucking space he was.

He woke up on Sunday afternoon to find Mario watching tv—the volume low. O sat up slowly, his head pounding, feeling both hungry and absolutely disgusted at the thought of food. Mar looked up and smiled gently, his eyes kind. "Hey, mate."

"Is she okay?" O croaked, throat rusty. His mouth tasted disgusting.

"She will be," Mar answered.

"Where is she?"

"With Arum."

O didn't say anything, just rested his head against the bedhead and closed his eyes. The icy, foggy grey got stormier.

"What can I do?" Mar asked.

"I don't even know."

Mario moved to sit next to him on the bed, poured a drink of water and popped two of those fizzy electrolyte tablets into the glass before handing it over. "You'll be okay too, O."

He sipped the water and his stomach lurched. "I need to see her. Where's my phone? I'll call her."

Mar shook his head and said in a quiet voice, "Not right now, Owen."

"No—I really need to explain myself."

"Owen."

O's hackles rose and he sat up straight, ignoring the sharp spike of pain that shot through his head as he raised his voice, *"Don't* use that fucking tone with me, Mario. I hate it when people say my name in that patronising tone as if I'm an idiot."

To O's surprise, Mario raised his voice right back. "Then don't make me fucking use it on you, Owen. You're hungover, you're on your second day of coming down, and you're hurting. If you try to talk to her now, you'll fuck it up even more. *Listen to me*—no, shut your mouth and listen. When did you last take your meds?"

"Friday."

"Okay then." Mar tapped away on his phone. "My driver will go to your place to get some stuff for you. Clothes and meds. Is it on your bedside table?"

O nodded, wishing he could disappear. "I'm sorry."

"It's okay."

"I really did fuck it up," O commented.

Mario shrugged. "I'm proud of you for telling the truth though."

"Shouldn't've waited so long." O lay back against the bedhead and rubbed his eyes. "She said she'd given up a lot to be with me. I don't understand what she meant by that. I don't *think* I asked her to do that. Maybe I did. I don't know..."

Mar crossed his legs, hands resting on his knees. "Look," he said, "you were both off your fucking heads. Not the best time to be having a serious tête-à-tête about the state of your relationship. Don't know what you were thinking."

"I was off my fucking head. I wasn't thinking. I was *feeling."*

"Well that was a stupid thing to do, wasn't it?" Mario retorted.

O snorted out a pathetic little laugh, and Mario nudged his shoulder roughly, and then O's face went serious as he recalled more.

"She told me I don't trust her," he said as his brow furrowed, confused. He could hardly think straight—he was devoid of all good things. *"Do* I trust her?" O asked Mar, hoping he had the answer.

Mario hummed as he took in those words. "I think you don't trust *yourself,*" he said. "I think you think you don't deserve good things. You don't trust—"

"Not ending up alone," O cut in.

Mar nodded slowly. "Understandable, O. No one should ever lose everything at fifteen. That shit leaves a permanent mark."

O's eyes stung. The dark grey turned to oily black. "Fuck," he said in a trembling whisper. The darkness coated his lungs, creeping up his throat. It hurt to breathe.

Mar put his arms around O's shoulders. "Owen. You're okay."

"I don't know what to do," O said, collapsing in on himself—knees up, head down. He wished he could continue collapsing, compressing himself until he disappeared into nothing.

Mario sat closer and draped himself over O. "You're loved, mate. You're worthy. Hey—listen to me. I have excellent taste in friends, and you're my favourite. Endah and I will never leave you."

Hearing such kindness made O cry even harder, but once the worst of the sadness had been let out, the oily black receded to the foggy grey, and he felt relief.

thirty-eight

Two and a half weeks left until the opening of *Heartbreak*.

Naya let go of more duties, delegating work that required face-to-face meetings with other departments to Tini and Edhi.

"To challenge the two of you," Naya said with a fake smile plastered on her face when the real reason was that the thought of hearing one more fucking comment about her relationship with Owen would one *thousand* percent result in a very unprofessional outburst.

She hid in her office instead, responding to emails and finalising the plans for where each piece would go.

During lunch, when the floor was blissfully empty, she put the final touches to the mural design so Ru could work his magic and map out the image in order for it to be split into a grid and allocated to the volunteers on the day.

Everything was going well, workwise. Naya couldn't even bring herself to care. She hadn't heard from Owen and he hadn't appeared at work. Naya straddled the line between wishing he'd appear so they could be on the same floor while refusing to speak to him because *fuck him*, and wishing he would come bursting through her door and march right up to her and kiss her and then she'd push him away, and maybe even slap him. Because *fuck him*.

And then, her phone beeped and it was a message from Owen—*the asshole*—as if her *fuck him*-addled thoughts had sent out some beacon of desperation to him.

Her breath caught. She was so fucking relieved he'd reached out, yet still so angry at him. She snatched her phone.

Two voice DMs. She tapped the first one, and heard him inhale and then clear his throat, and at that moment, her longing for him outweighed her bitterness.

"Hey," he said quietly, awkwardly. Tears appeared. "I'm sorry if you aren't ready to hear from me. It's just—I'm not sure what you need right now. So, I just wanted you to know that, uh… I'm here, and I'm sorry." He exhaled, and she could picture his big shoulders slumping— imagine him raking his fingers through his hair. "If you don't reply in the next few days, then… I'll take that as a clear sign from you that you don't want this anymore, and I'll respect that decision." Another long pause. "I'm sorry. Truly."

She tapped on the second message, and his voice sounded frustrated—urgent. "Shit—I hope you don't think I'm trying to force you to talk before you're ready. I'm just… I'm not good with things being left unsaid, you know? Or silences. Mar told me to give you time, but I don't even know what the hell that means. Do I wait? Is there some unspoken number of days that everyone knows about but me?" His rambling was painfully adorable. Naya wanted to scratch his eyes out. "I kind of… prefer to talk it out. *Fight* it out, even." He sniffed a little laugh. "I don't know," he muttered. "Um, if you do need more time, maybe you could let me know? Jesus. Okay. Talk soon… I hope. Have a good day, Naya."

⊥

NAYA:

Hi

Thanks for giving me some space.

OWEN:

Hey. It's so good to hear from you. I'm sorry if I rushed you. I just don't know what to do in these situations... I didn't want you to think I was being distant

NAYA:

No I appreciate it

OWEN:

I'm here Naya. I'll wait until you tell me not to.

NAYA:

I'm sad

OWEN:

Me too.

NAYA:

And so angry.

OWEN:

I'm sorry I didn't lay all my cards out on the table

Fuck—and I'm sorry for how I finally told you. The timing was fucking awful.

Anyway, I'm here if you ever want to talk.

NAYA:

ok

You don't have to avoid MP. I know you hate working from home

OWEN:

Are you sure?

NAYA:

Yeah, I'm keeping my blinds down anyway

OWEN:

Oh.

Yeah ok.

Are people still being nosy about you and me?

NAYA:

Yes. I've delegated a bunch of meetings to Tini and Edhi so I don't have to deal with anyone but the team for now.

OWEN:

I'm sorry you were the one that had to deal with it. I don't think I properly acknowledged that.

NAYA:

Thank you. I really did feel like I copped it. But it isn't your fault that you didn't

Look, Owen, I'm not ready to feel ok

OWEN:

Ok...

NAYA:

I know we need to have a proper talk but I'm not ready to hear your side. I need time.

OWEN:

I understand.

NAYA:

But I wanted to say that I noticed you were struggling with something last week but I was too angry about all the shit happening at work to ask you about it, and I'm very sorry I didn't care. That was really selfish of me.

OWEN:

Thank you

NAYA:

I hope you're being kind to yourself and getting the support you need.

OWEN:

I'm trying to be.

NAYA:

Good

Ok I have to work

bye

OWEN:

Hey FYI, I may work in the office tomorrow or
Thursday if you're really ok with me being there... but I
won't bother you. Promise. Have a nice day.

NAYA:

you too

$$\dagger$$

That afternoon, Naya was on a roll with finalising the plans for artwork allocation when a knock on her office door interrupted her focus. "Come in," she groaned, "but seriously—this better be life or death, guys, or else I'll be the fucking death of you."

She almost spilt her tea all over her laptop when Endah stood in the doorway, hands clasped together and her feet pointing outwards looking so graceful. "Shit—sorry *Ibu*," Naya sputtered, "I thought you were one of my team members. "

Endah smiled pleasantly at her and said, "Srinaya. Have time for a chat?" Naya paused a little too long because Endah spoke again. "Please. I'll be quick."

Naya winced internally as she gestured to the couch. "No," Endah said, "let's go sit in the garden." She pointed to the blinds pulled down over Naya's window, darkening her office. "If you look outside, you'll see the sky is clear. It's a beautiful day, and I think you could do with a little bit of sunshine, yes?"

Naya gave her a weak smile and silently followed her out of the building. They slowly made their way past the copse of trees to the beautifully manicured garden. The hibiscus, jasmine and frangipani were in bloom and the sweet aroma that wafted on the breeze made Naya relax a little.

Endah broke the silence. "Owen stumbled into my house at three in the morning on Saturday."

Naya couldn't help the *ugh* that came out, and then she sighed. "*Ibu* Endah..." Her tone came out surprisingly insolent, but if they were going to talk about personal things, Endah would have to handle it.

"I'm not accusing you of anything," Endah said in a motherly voice. "I know he kept something from you, and he deserved the telling off you gave him." Naya scoffed. *Telling off.* As if what he did only warranted a slap on the wrist and a couple of sharp *tsks*. "You have every right to feel tricked, Srinaya. For what it's worth, I did give him a dressing down about it. We even had a little row that night at Cinq-Huit."

"Really?"

Endah nodded.

"I'm sorry."

"You have nothing to apologise for," Endah said.

She sat down on a park bench engraved with Owen's parents' names on it. A memorial, in the middle of the sweet-smelling garden. Endah said quietly, "Molly—Owen's mother—this garden was her idea. She never got to see it look like this."

Naya sat down and reached for Endah's hand. "I've heard a lot about how you showed up to support Owen, but I'm very sorry you had to do that while grieving your best friend. I can't even imagine how hard that must have been."

Endah squeezed Naya's hand in silent thanks, and then made her point. "Owen lost much more than I did, and it makes him cling tightly to the people he loves."

Naya slumped.

They didn't speak for a while, taking in the sweet floral scents of the garden and watching visitors walk along the pond to their left, admiring the giant koi.

"Listen, I know you hate being managed. But you *did* thank me for bringing you together, and you said you'd defer all decisions to me from now on. So, I think you should just break up with him."

Naya recoiled, a gasp escaping her. She felt instantly hot and angry and defensive, and telling Endah to fuck off was on the tip of her tongue. Endah's eyes crinkled knowingly at Naya's reaction, and her breathy laughter filled the air.

"Well, *that* was telling, wasn't it Naya? You're hurt, but it's definitely not over between you two." Naya flushed. Endah said, "That day you met him on the steps, I saw it—your mutual attraction. I told him not to play around with you. *Jangan main-main. Kalau kamu nggak serius, jangan deh. Cari yang lain.* I said he had to be sure, and then he told me he'd carried this torch for you for months but you didn't recognise him. And Naya, the look on his face when he talked about you…" Naya's brows furrowed. "I've never seen him light up that way. It was a very beautiful thing to see. He hurt your pride—I understand that. But it's not like he's the only one keeping secrets." Naya stiffened and Endah arched her brow, the smile of an evil genius growing on her face. "Oh, yes. Hiding in plain sight. Clever, Dewi Srinaya."

Naya's heart beat fast with fear. Endah waved her hand dismissively. "I'm not going to say anything. Although your anger is a little self-righteous and hypocritical isn't it, since he doesn't know your secret?"

Naya rubbed her temple in frustration. Were Endah and Arum scheming together? "But they're not the same. Mine is a ten-year-old secret that has *nothing* to do with him," she grumbled.

Endah rolled her eyes. "And Owen's secret is ten months old. Secrets are secrets, Srinaya. My goodness—the two of you are equally ridiculous."

Naya sighed, and closed her eyes, relenting. Endah said, "Be mad at him but forgive him. And soon. He's suffering, and I don't take you for a cruel and vengeful person. You won't find anyone as loyal, or kind, or passionate. He's just scared a lot of the time. He needs a lot of reassurance that he's worth it. And he *is* worth it." She patted Naya's hand and then stood. "There's only one Owen Jameson. Just like there's only one Srinaya Matthews."

Naya nodded blankly at Endah. "You haven't asked me anything about the show."

Endah shrugged. "*Untuk apa?* It will be amazing. Your professional life is thriving. It's not the part that concerns me," she said with a wink and then walked away.

thirty-nine

STEPPING ONTO THE FIFTH FLOOR JUST BEFORE LUNCH THE NEXT DAY, O's feet automatically veered to the left towards Naya's office. He course-corrected and made his way to the right, nodding at the juniors in their cubicles.

Tini whisper-shouted, "She's in there if you need her," with a flick of her chin to Naya, hidden behind the sturdy light grey polyester blinds. All her blinds were pulled down to the floor, even the one on her door. She had walled herself in—a protective barrier. From him, and from the speculatory whispers of the staff.

Did they know? Had she shared their... whatever this was... with any of them? Until O knew for sure, he'd happily play the part of Naya's loving partner. It wasn't a part, anyway. He would always, *always* love her. Whatever her decision, after her need for this distance.

O feigned a playful pout. "I've been banned from bothering her."

Rav stepped into his doorway, leaning against the frame with his arms crossed, eyeing O. His handsome face was stoic as always, but there was something challenging under all that calm. Perhaps she'd told Ravi. He greeted the man with a nod and turned back to Tini. "Check in on her every once in a while, yeah? Make sure she takes breaks."

"She doesn't want to be disturbed. At all. Everything is text or email only unless—and I quote—*it's life or death.*"

O let out an exaggerated sigh and shook his head. "Ah well," he said with another fake smile and roll of his eyes. "Naya can't be pushed." *Or rushed. Or managed.* And he'd done all three. "She's being a rockstar and I don't want to interrupt her."

The elevator *dinged* and Rav huffed sharply. Surya skulked their way. O clenched his jaw, turned to the curators and pointedly said, "I'm here. Just knock." He gave Rav and Tini *a look* and then marched into his office, ignoring Surya as they passed each other. He logged onto his laptop to make some long overdue calls.

Naya didn't leave her office once. Maybe she feared he'd go running after her but he was standing firm to his promise—she'd asked for space, so he'd give it. And while she worked through her own feelings, he would take the time to do the same.

He realised he hadn't been to therapy since she'd stood him up. He'd buried himself in all that pleasure and love, thinking it would sustain him, and ignored the growing anxiety—a clear sign of an impending break, but one he never saw coming until it was too late.

His mood slowly improved though; his mind was clearer. Bad mental health weeks would forever be a constant in his life but he'd gotten better at climbing out of the hole once he found himself there. Still... he hated how he dragged Naya into his black days with him instead of asking for help.

The ceiling lights switched off; the entire office was bathed in darkness save for the dim exit signs, his desk lamp, and the thin strips of light between the gaps of her blinds. Had she gone out at all for food or water? She could be so terrible at basic self-care when she fixated on work.

OWEN:

I'm sorry if I'm overstepping, but I've been here since before lunch and it's now 7:18 PM. I bet you've hardly eaten, if you've eaten at all...

NAYA:

Shit I didn't realise how late it was. I'll get some food soon

OWEN:

Ok. I'm leaving now. Look after yourself, please?

NAYA:

I will. Promise.

$$\perp$$

On Thursday, O arrived before any of the other staff. He dropped off a small package on Naya's desk with a note:

Please don't read too much into this.

—O.

The curators arrived in dribs and drabs while he was on a Zoom session with Sheridan, his therapist in Melbourne, and O's heart warmed at the sounds of the juniors' chittering filling the office. Tini and Nur skipped past arm in arm, waving at him and he waved back with a smile.

And then Naya arrived, wearing her *Fuck Off Headphones*—the bright red ones that were a clear sign to stay away. She gave the team some direction for the day ahead and then disappeared into her office. She didn't look over in O's direction, and he told himself it was nothing personal, although it definitely felt like it.

Sheridan said, "We could speculate on the whys all day, right? Like, yeah, there's a good chance she's avoiding you, which she's absolutely allowed to do. She's busy, and hurt, and dealing in her own way. Or maybe she went blind over the weekend and she couldn't see you but she's very spatially aware and doesn't bump into things which is how she made it safely to her office without help." O snorted, but Sheridan wasn't done. "Maybe she isn't an *ambi-turner* anymore. Maybe she's working on her *Blue Steel*."

O guffawed. It was so fucking good to laugh. He thanked Sheridan. Sheridan beamed. "You're welcome. You just deal with you, yeah?"

Not too long after his session ended, his phone beeped.

Aud Pitch

And then the blinds in Naya's office opened halfway, letting more light into the space between them, and the one on her door rolled all the way to the top, and when she appeared behind it, she gave him a small smile, and O held himself back from crying because it was one small step in the right direction.

forty

THE PURNAMA'S RENOVATIONS FINALLY FINISHED ON FRIDAY AND NAYA took the Bevy down to the empty gallery late in the afternoon to celebrate with bottles of grape Fanta. They roamed the empty halls arm in arm, giggling like school kids as they sipped their drinks. Naya hooked her arm in the crook of Rav's elbow and as they walked, Rav asked, "Are you okay?"

She gave him a weary smile. "Yeah, you?"

"You haven't been yourself. We've been worried."

She loved how he cut to the chase. No games. You always knew where you stood with Ravi. She steered him away from the rest of the team to quietly stroll through the east wing. "It's been a lot."

"*Heartbreak?*"

Naya blinked at him and a startled laugh came out. "*Heartbreak* and heartbreak."

"He didn't hurt you, did he?"

Her eyes went wide and her smile disappeared. "*No.* Well, yes. We hurt each other. Kept things from each other."

"I'm sorry."

Rav didn't say anything else as they walked all the way up the left wall admiring the fresh paint and brand new lighting and then at the very end of the wing, they looped back and walked along the other side.

Naya mused, "We've never had a personal conversation before."

Rav answered, "You're a closed book."

Naya squawked out a *Ha!* "Take's one to know one," she retorted, and Ravi laughed, and it was fucking glorious to witness the rare smile on her serious colleague's face.

The conversation with Ravi replayed in her mind all weekend. She'd let Rav think she and Owen were over, and the thought of that ever being true felt so awful—caused a bone-deep heaviness in her chest that made her feel worse than when she'd found out he'd lied in the first place. That was surely a sign.

Two weekends away from Owen. It was absolute torture made in no way better by the fact that it was what she needed—some distance to gather her thoughts. It wasn't about punishing him anymore. Not *really*.

She had more chats with Arum and Mario over the second weekend —Arum telling her (lovingly) to get over herself, and Mario encouraging her to take all the time she needed but to please be kind to Owen, because his dark days could get *really* dark, and he tried so hard to deal with them on his own.

"I'm not angry anymore," she confessed over dinner on Sunday night. "But... the hurt's still there."

"You know, he called me the morning after," Mario revealed, and Naya frowned. "Yeah, I knew," he said, shrugging. "I keep secrets for my friends. Especially for O."

Naya swallowed her disappointment. She would've done the same thing, and Arum was keeping a secret from Mario for her.

"You should've heard him," Mar continued. "All frantic—remembering his parents and how his dad had talked about falling in love with his mum the first time they met, and..." Mario shook his head ruefully, and Naya lost her breath. "Even our friend Alexis contacted me to say they were worried about him. It was their spiked drink that Owen stupidly—"

Naya shot forward in her chair. "Alexis Charles?" she and Arum asked in unison.

"Yeah… What—how do you know Al?"

Arum grinned. "We banged them."

"Not at the same time!" Naya rushed out.

Arum stuck out her bottom lip and glared. "Ouch. Unsure why you needed to clarify that with such gusto, bitch."

"Not now," Naya growled, dismissing her bestie. "How do *you* know Al?" she asked Mario.

"We banged them. At the same time." Mar mirrored Arum's grin. He waggled his brows conspiratorially at both Naya and Arum's gaping mouths, and then he snorted out a laugh. "I'm joking! We met them at some uni party."

"You turd," the pixie-bitch grumbled affectionately, punching him not so lightly on the upper arm.

For god's sake. They had all been in each other's orbit all this time, and Naya couldn't see it as romantic, or serendipitous. It just felt like so much wasted time. She could've been loving Owen years ago instead of being so hurt and worried about… Fuck—why was she still so fucking *scared*?

She wrung her hands together. "What did Alexis say?"

"That they bumped into O, who was spiralling about not being brave enough to speak to… you."

Naya's lip quivered involuntarily.

She held up her finger and apologised, and scrambled for her phone.

NAYA:

Ally 🩶 I'm here with Arum and Mario Murni

We're talking about a mutual friend… Owen Jameson?

And then Naya braced herself for the deluge of chaotic DMs that were about to dump on her like an avalanche.

Her phone *ping-ping-pinged* for over a minute.

ALEXIS:

Baaaaaaabez. 🤍🤍🤍🤍

So good to hear from you!

OMG HI MARIO!

Awww, I miss Mar so much.

How hot is he?

Wish he was into dick because I'd be all over that if he was.

But Owen Jameson.

Now HE is one heavenly specimen.

I saw him at DEWI's afterparty looking like some hot pirate. That beard!

Wanted to yo-ho-ho his bottle of rum 😈

But I drugged him instead 🙄

UNINTENTIONALLYYYY

No regrets tho.

That boy was wound so fucking tight!!!

Swear I bumped into him mid panic attack

Offered him a sip of my Special Floaty Funtime Cocktail and the fucking arsehole downed the whole thing!!!!

Rude.

Poor thing would've been fuuuucked from it.

I told him to go home asap.

NAYA:

Why was he freaking out?

ALEXIS:

Crowds. Noise

Was shocked to see him there. Especially alone

He's SO shy

It's adorable

Imagine looking like that and being too shy to walk up
to a person you've been desperate to talk to all night

NAYA:

Did that really happen??

ALEXIS:

Yah!!!

He'd gone all heart-eyes for some lucky bitch

Can't say I approve of his tastes tho

NAYA:

Um why not

ALEXIS:

Apparently she was wearing clothes covered in paint
or smth

TO A DEWI AFTERPARTY

Can you believe???

NAYA:

Alexis, when did you get so snobby?

ALEXIS:

MOHOHO that's what Owen said!!!

He got so defensive on her behalf.

It was tres adorbz

But seriously!

If you go to one of the most talked about art events of
the year dressed like a pre-makeover Laney Boggs,
you better be ready for my very mean opinions.

NAYA:

It was bleach.

ALEXIS:

Huh?

NAYA:

It wasn't paint. I had bleach on my tshirt. Well, I probably had paint on my jeans

ALEXIS:

SRINAYA

FUCKING

MATTHEWS

kcfbs ksnave shekel sl

Are you telling me YOU were the mysterious person who got Owen "Shiver Me Timbers" Jameson into a state?

NAYA:

Guilty

ALEXIS:

AAAAAAAAAAAAAAAAAHHHHHHHHH

What the fuck were you wearing???

NAYA:

My studio clothes!

What did Owen say when you bumped into him?

ALEXIS:

Oh Naya he looked so lost

He was searching for you

You lucky bitch.

I'd give my left arm to have one night with that boy.

I wanna climb his mast

Hoist his sails

Polish his deck

NAYA:

You're ridiculous

ALEXIS:

Woooow... it was you

WAIT

That means YOU were the evil bitch who left him high
and dry 😟

Srinaya 😳

you hurt him

Like really hurt him

That was mean. 😾

No one hurts Owen

He was so sad, Naya 😾 😾 😾

How could you do that??

I texted him a coupla days later and fuck, Naya

Lemme paste our chat

NAYA:

No! Don't violate his privacy.

ALEXIS:

Shut up. This is important.

☨

CHAT WITH OWEN JAMESON - 24/09/23

ALEXIS:

Hiiiiiiiii bbyyyyyyy

Hope the comedown wasn't toooooo awful???? 😬

OWEN:

It was fucked. You made me black out, Al.

ALEXIS:

EXCUSE ME.

You did that all on your own tyvm 😾

I offered you a sip to mellow you out

I mean yeah I probs shoulda told you what was in it

But you took the whole thing! 😤

OWEN:

True. Ok. That was shitty of me.

I'm sorry for being a dick and drinking it all.

ALEXIS:

It's ok 🩶 I'm sorry for drugging you

OWEN:

What the fuck was in that anyway???

ALEXIS:

All the things, babezzzzz

OWEN:

Jesus, Alexis. I hope you're not drinking those every weekend.

ALEXIS:

No, only special occasions.

And bumping into you at a DEWI afterparty was defs a special occasion!!!

OWEN:

I met her. The red tshirt person

ALEXIS:

OMGOMGOMG AND?

OWEN:

She was gorgeous. Sulky, playful, brazen. She came onto me... asked me to go back to her hotel room.
And yeah

ALEXIS:

YAYAYAYAYAYAYAYYAY!!!!

OWEN:

But I blacked out

Can't remember what happened after

There are flashes but I don't know how far we went. I
hate that I can't remember.

I hope she doesn't think I took advantage...

I don't think she did; she left me a thank you note... so
yay me?

ALEXIS:

Wait- she left you in her hotel room? All alone??

OWEN:

Yeah. She'd gone when I woke up

ALEXIS:

Oh Owen that sucks

I'm sorry

WHAT A BITCH

OWEN:

Don't say that

ALEXIS:

That's not ok!

It's so shitty!!!

OWEN:

Thank you for being angry for me

ALEXIS:

Are you ok????

OWEN:

Not really

ALEXIS:

Oh love

OWEN:

But I will be

ALEXIS:

Fuck yes you will!!

GOOD RIDDANCE.

Aud Pitch

OWEN:

No

I'm glad we met, even if I can't remember 90% of it.
The tiny moment we shared was great.

And it wasn't that we said anything all that profound to
each other... there was just... I don't know. Something
there.

For me, at least

She was fucking adorable

Dark eyes, but kind of bright too? And she wrinkled
her nose in this naughty way that fucking killed me.

I'm grateful

Taking comfort in knowing that she exists... walking
around making people turn her way. And for a night,
she turned my way

That makes me feel pretty special.

ALEXIS:

You're a lovely person, Owen.

OWEN:

Thanks Alexis.

ALEXIS:

Want me to come over wearing an ugly tshirt and you
can reenact all the filthy things you want to do to her?
Happy to be her stand-in 😏

OWEN:

Literally just spat out my coffee all over my jeans, Al.
You arsehole.

Tears flowed freely down Naya's cheeks, her eyeliner and mascara smudging as she wiped the saltwater away with her knuckles.

Mar reached across the dining table to stroke her hand.

"I'm a selfish, horrible person," Naya sniffled.

Arum answered in a tone reserved for cats, dogs and babies. "Aw, Sri. Selfish? Yes. Horrible? Debatable."

forty-one

Naya didn't sleep much over the week—mind sharp and ready before the sun crested. She spent the dark mornings in her studio, doing last-minute tweaks to the mural design and prepping for Ruben and his chaotic personality as he acted the part of entitled DEWI 2IC.

Something made her leave her house extra early that day, and she found herself at work before 7AM. The main doors to the admin building were still locked, so she meandered through the trees lining the thick fortress-like walls on the three sides of the campus. Then she lay back on the steps and waited, earbuds in, listening to a playlist she and Owen made together over their blossoming romance, each song the soundtrack to a beautiful memory.

She stared up at the hazy sky, the grey-white clouds stringy like fake Halloween spiderwebs. Too many thoughts crawled through her brain. Too many regrets. She tried to rationalise away the sadness when she felt a light tap on her leg.

Naya opened her eyes and found Owen sitting a few steps below her, a tentative smile on his face, just as he had during their first—no, second—meeting. She didn't bother to sit up this time, although she pulled out one earbud and handed it to him.

"I discovered a song the other night," Naya said as she searched for 'Circle the Drain' by Soccer Mommy.

She tapped on the lyrics of the song, pressed play and handed her phone to him. It was about how, even when everything seems okay—when life's good and beautiful, people still struggle to be happy. They put on a brave face for loved ones, pretending nothing is wrong, losing the tug of war that pulled them into the depths of despair. And they did it silently, trying very hard to not let others know, because they didn't want to drag loved ones down with them.

But I'm so tired of faking...

"Is this what it's like?" Naya asked.

Owen flicked her a quick look and then turned away, nodding. "Yeah."

He slumped, elbows resting on his knees. Naya reached over to touch his arm. "I'm sorry you went through that alone."

Owen brought his knees up and wrapped his arms around them. He didn't look like the esteemed benefactor. He looked *small*—just a man carrying far too much on his shoulders.

They sat silently, the tension still there, but neither of them shied away from it. It was a new shared memory—kind of like how slicing into the earth and seeing the different layers of rock could tell you the history of the land. This new layer would mark their first dark moment together.

Owen broke the silence. "Want breakfast?" He held up a bulging canvas shopping bag.

Naya rolled her eyes and tsked. "If you were anyone else I'd swear you were trying to weasel your way back into my good graces via my stomach."

"Is it working?"

Naya gave him a teasing wink. "Depends on what's in that bag."

Owen waggled his brows, and for the briefest moment, it felt normal between them, and Naya almost burst out crying.

He led her into the building. Owen Jameson of course had access to the building.

They sat in his office, on separate couches but at the ends closest to each other. She broke the silence. "Would you like to talk? I'm ready."

"Yes," Owen answered quickly. He gestured for her to start.

"You said you spotted me at Chidori and had to meet me." He nodded. "How can that be?"

"What do you mean?"

"Why me?"

"That's a ridiculous thing to ask me. I saw you and had to meet you," he said with a shrug, not feeling the need to question his instant attraction to her, or his impulse to seek her out.

She looked down at her coffee cup, running her fingertip around the rim. "It's not like you to be insecure," he commented. His brows were furrowed low, making him look cross.

She rubbed her eyes. "I'm tired. And anxious." *And lonely, and scared.* She'd never admit it but she was desperate for praise, to be told she was smart and hardworking and beautiful, especially from him.

"The other night, I recall saying you were like a rainbow. I stand by that very cheesy description," he said sheepishly.

Well, there you go.

"I was leaving to Jakarta that day. That's why I left so early." He absorbed her words and nodded slowly. "I... didn't want... to leave you," she said regretfully.

"It's okay."

"It's not. I should've woken you. Said goodbye."

They were both silent then, sipping their coffee. Naya studied his expression. He looked as tired as she was. She fought the urge to sit beside him, maybe even rest her head on his shoulder.

"May I ask you a question now?" he asked, interrupting her thoughts.

Naya nodded, bracing herself.

"You said you'd given up a lot for us and that I didn't trust you. What did you mean?"

Naya sighed, ashamed. "No, look. You were right—you stepped back after I told you not to push. From then on you were great—you let me lead and I really appreciate that. Thing is, I've done things with you that I wouldn't've done in other relationships. But I did them because I wanted to—not because you made me, or even asked me to. I moved so much faster than I ever have since... well, since a different time. I *have* changed, and I blamed you but you didn't cause it. I was lashing out when I said that. I'm sorry."

Owen's Naya lines were pronounced—his stormy eyes desperate. "Then, what is this?" he asked forlornly as he gestured between them. "What do you need for this to not feel so fucking horrible anymore?"

Naya leaned her head back onto the couch and breathed deep, recalling their meet-cute on the steps of MP, and all the days they'd shared after, and how Owen had the privilege of remembering an extra moment of intimacy that was fuzzy in her mind.

"I woke up that night." She closed her eyes to remember him in the darkness—a midnight deity made real, offering himself up to her.

"You did?"

She nodded. "It was dark; I couldn't see you. But you reached for me. Pulled me back. Held me so—" Her voice wavered—"greedily, like I was a prize. I was safe, and cared for. It was so fucking sweet." She opened her eyes to gaze at Owen. *Denmark.* Shorter hair, full beard replaced by chocolate stubble on that perfect, golden face, but she should've known. Should've trusted the way her body and heart responded to him, as if the memory of his words—*Hey, stay*—unlocked something; made her imprint on him.

Her nose prickled and her eyes stung. "You held me the same way our second night together. After Cinq Huit."

His eyes brightened a little, like he was relieved to know he'd left something-a crumb of a memory buried in her.

Naya swallowed. "I wondered who this mysterious man from Denmark was. I… missed him, wondered if he ever thought of me. And I feel robbed of a proper reunion with him. God—that sounds so fucking ridiculous when I say it out loud." She pinched the bridge of her nose.

"I don't know what I would've done if you appeared on the steps and said.. I dunno— *I spent a night with you and all I got was a lousy thank you note*, but I think I would've been over the moon." She bit her lip, imagining that alternate beginning for them. "I think I would've insisted on taking you out to lunch so you could tell me all about your-self, and I would've kissed you and—" She sighed—"maybe all that stupid fear about being accused of fucking my way to the top never would've been a thing if I knew our backstory."

"You think you would've chosen to be with me straight away?"

Naya smiled wistfully. "Probably."

Owen's mouth pinched into a harsh line. She took a sip of her coffee and then put her cup down with a little more force than she'd expected. "You managed me without my consent. By not telling me the truth, you took away my right to make up my own mind about us. And I hate that, Owen." She bared her teeth and shaped her fingers into claws in frustration. She looked him right in the eye as she kept going. "I also said horrible things the other night. I was in shock, and... wanted to cause maximum damage. But I do know you didn't get me the job at MP. I'm confident in my abilities, and I know you'd never do that, just like I know you're not some creepy stalker. But.. you thought *I* could think those things. You didn't trust me to understand and accept it—" Her voice cracked and tears appeared—"and that hurts so much." She rubbed the skin between her brows with her thumb.

Owen moved to sit on the coffee table directly in front of her. They were so close she could smell his sobering summer scent but he didn't touch her. It felt like they were back at that moment when he showed up at her house. They would go only as far as she wanted.

He bent forward and said, "It's not about not trusting you." He winced at his next sentence. "In some ways, it had nothing to do with you at all. You just got tangled up in it. It's about not trusting *myself*." He focused on his hands, fingers twisting together anxiously. His eyes went red and bleak. His voice went shaky. "I don't trust that I'm worthy of being forgiven, or that I'm worthy of love. I don't trust that I'm worth sticking around for. I expect people to disappear..."

His parents and sister flashed in her mind. You didn't lose the three most important people in your life in one go without coming out unscathed, developing deep issues around abandonment and distrusting that good things were there to stay. And then she had left him—*abandoned* him—after what sounded like a terrible mental spiral. She could only imagine his isolation and despair, especially now that she had a better understanding of his mental health.

"Well," she said, wiping her nose with the back of her hand, "you need to fucking work on that. Because I haven't disappeared. I'm tangled up in this—in you. Seems like I've been tangled for a lot longer than I realised."

Owen nodded sadly and held out his hand. Naya placed her hand in his, and the touch of his skin felt so fucking right. *Home, finally.* Of course. He had been home for ten months. She'd been missing him since Chidori, even if she hadn't realised it. He'd been right that night at Le Roy—this was bigger than them.

He closed his hand around hers and rubbed his thumb along her knuckles. "I'm so sorry I didn't tell you, Naya. I'm sorry my self-doubt was bigger than my trust in you. And I'm so very sorry I managed you —made decisions for you."

"Thank you," Naya said as she wiped her eyes, and then touched Owen's cheeks to wipe his tears away too. "You're forgiven. Of course I forgive you," she added, and the look of complete and utter relief on Owen's face, and how a whole new set of tears came streaming out of him, made the knot in her chest unpick itself and finally unravel. "That thing you said the other night—about this feeling cosmic and sacred? I feel that too. The universe managed us, and I should be mad about it, but I'm grateful."

Owen slid off the table and onto his knees in front of her, his strong arms enveloping her tightly. She wrapped her arms around his neck and stroked his hair. She closed her eyes, listening to his heartbeat and his breath. She sighed at the rightness of it all.

She pulled away to look at him. "Listen, I have more to tell you, but I really need a couple more days to get my head around some things. Will you give me just a few more days to focus on work?"

He ran his thumb over her lips. "Yeah, of course."

And then Owen took her hand in his again and shook it. "Hello. Srinaya Matthews, is it? I'm Denmark." He reached for his wallet on the coffee table and pulled out a small piece of paper tucked into a hidden pocket. He unfolded it with the utmost care, like it was so delicate it might turn to dust between his fingers. "I spent a night with you and all I got was this lousy thank you note."

He offered it to her and she took it, and read it, and yes—it was her silly note scribbled onto the hotel notepad paper:

Thanks for a night I wish I remembered. ;)

xox N

She gasped, holding the paper to her heart as he gave her one of his fucking disgustingly perfect smiles, his eyes crinkling with mischief, looking all cute with his red nose and freckles.

Naya's body wanted to explode with how right it felt. "Oh my god, don't," she gushed.

forty-two

MERAHPUTIH BUZZED. THEY HAD NINE DAYS BEFORE THE OPENING gala and a focused quiet settled over the whole company as the date loomed closer. The once empty flagpoles lining MP's driveway now flew colourful signage, and two vertical banners with angry splashes of colour from Joyce's beautiful painting graced the frontage of Purnama.

It was really, *really* happening.

Like teammates getting in the zone before a cup final, the light-hearted banter died down and the staff focused their attention on the crazy number of last minute details yet to be dealt with. Emotions weren't running high though; they were ready—knew their roles. They had a Plan B and a Plan C. Naya even had a secret Plan D.

One last installation piece hadn't arrived yet, and the intricate wooden frame Joyce had ordered for her painting—the fucking title piece of the show—had gotten badly damaged on the way to MP so she and her team were scrambling to figure out what to do. But the Bevy were unmoved. Whatever happened at that point was out of their control, so they wouldn't beat themselves up about it. *Que sera, sera.*

One thing needed following up on: the soft merchandising, which meant a meeting with Surya. He'd skulked through the office earlier that morning but Naya had yet to muster the energy to see him. She steeled herself and finally made her way to his office. Ravi appeared by her side with an encouraging wink, and Naya let out a sharp exhale, unaware she'd been holding her breath.

Rav said, "Buddy system, remember?"

Naya nudged him gratefully with her shoulder.

They knocked and heard a sharp, *Masuk.*

"*Permisi, Pak* Surya."

Surya turned his head to face her with a begrudging huff. He looked like one of those creepy ventriloquist dolls in his goofy black mock-turtleneck.

"We've requested updates from you and your factory but still haven't received anything."

Surya shrugged. "We have no updates to give then."

"Really? We're just over a week out and you have no updates for us? Was your company unable to deliver on your promise?"

"I didn't promise anything."

Naya sighed. She called out to Edhi in the main open space—*very* unprofessional, but what the hell. "Edhi, you wrote a little note about *Pak* Surya's guarantee, didn't you?"

Edhi popped his head through the door, "Yes, *Mbak* Naya. I have a note here that says, *Pak Surya guaranteed timely delivery.* I timed and dated it as well. Do you need that?"

"No, that's ok, Edhi. Thanks." She smiled acerbically at Surya. "Well there you go. Are you going back on your word?"

Surya didn't say anything. He just kept his reptilian eyes on her.

Naya walked right up to his desk and rubbed her forehead. Jesus Christ, she was exhausted. "*Pak* Surya, I'm talking to you on behalf of your *client*—MERAHPUTIH. You're not a board member right now. We contracted your company to do work for us and you guaranteed on-time delivery. I'd appreciate an ETA by the end of day. Thank you."

She turned to walk out with Ravi following a step behind when she heard Surya mutter under his breath, "*Dasar anjing bule.*"

Naya stopped dead in her tracks. Her heart pounded in her head. Did he really just—? She looked at Ravi, whose clenched jaw and sneer in Surya's direction made it absolutely clear she hadn't misheard what Surya said.

A wonderful, blazing rage rose up from deep within her.

"What *the fuck* did you just say?" Naya thundered.

The chatter in the open office died at the sound of her bark and Surya's eyes widened in shock. "You can't talk to me that way."

Naya let out a bitter laugh and stormed to his wall of glass, tugging a blind open. She went to the next one and opened that too, and then Ravi quickly stepped forward to help. She wanted everyone to witness what was about to take place. Surya sputtered in protest in his office chair. He stared out at all the startled fifth floor staff.

Naya growled, "What did you call me?" Surya puffed out his chest and stood his ground. "Ravi, did I hear correctly? Did *Pak* Surya just call me a *bule* dog?" she asked, speaking clearly and slowly so everyone on the other side of the glass wouldn't miss a single word.

Ravi gave her a tight nod and spoke up, "Yes, he did."

Angry gasps and rumbles floated in from the main office. Surya's eyes darted to the glass, where everyone was shooting daggers out of their eyes at him, and then back to Naya. She felt sweet relief to finally loosen her tongue, to unleash her honest feelings onto him.

"You are a piece of work, Surya," she said. "Honestly, I don't think I've met *anyone* as horrible as you, and boy—have I met some shitty people in my time. But you. You're the fucking king of shitty behaviour. Congrats." From the corner of her eye, she saw Lastri, Gunawan, and Chris move closer. Bolstered by their presence, she kept going. "You're toxic. You're sexist and fatphobic. And your discrimination against my heritage is gross. And the way—"

Surya cut in but Naya shouted over the top of him, using that booming voice that had been *dying* to come out for ages. "Shut your fucking mouth. I'm still talking," she roared.

Surya froze. He looked afraid and Naya wanted to wring even more fear out of him. She pointed her finger right at his face. "You've been throwing your weight around like you own the place since I got here, you pest. And you may have your sights set on bullying *me*, but it's pretty obvious I'm not your first victim here. Highly doubt I'm even your fiftieth. It sure as hell is going to fucking end with me, though. This is my official, *very public*, complaint against you."

"I'll support that complaint, *Mbak* Naya." She turned to see Gunawan close to the glass, arms crossed. She had never seen him look so determined. Lastri and Chris flanked him, nodding their heads.

Ravi piped up, "Me too."

From her cubicle in the open office space, Nur—sweet, shy Nur—lifted her hand and said, "I have my own complaint to make."

Edhi added, "Me too. *Pak* Surya has directed very homophobic comments at me."

Other staff members murmured their own complaints to add to the growing list of grievances. Surya jumped to his feet, trying to use his body and crumbling social standing to force them into silence. Their rumbling only got louder.

"What could you possibly do—run to Mr Jameson?" He said with a snort. "He broke up with you! I heard he won't even go near your office."

"Oh, fuck off," Naya said, rolling her eyes.

He spat out, "I'll have you fired. You are *nothing*. I'm a board member. I'm not going anywhere. My aunt—"

"Oh *shut up* about your aunt, you nepotistic asshole," she said, throwing her hands up in frustration.

"What about your aunt?" Snapped a raspy, elderly voice from just outside.

Someone gasped.

The whole floor went deathly silent with the sudden appearance of *Ibu* Tuti Lestari—OG director and last living co-founder of MERAHPUTIH, clutching Mr Jameson's elbow with glossy red talons. They stood in the doorway of Surya's office, Tuti's puffed-up lips drawn into a disdainful pucker. She let go of Owen's arm and stepped in, her patent leather stilettos sounding like a whip crack against the wooden floors. For a woman measuring less than five feet tall, she took up as much space as Owen.

"What… about… your *aunt?*" she repeated.

She removed her gigantic Versace sunglasses perched atop her head and tucked them into her gaudy crocodile skin handbag, stern eyes never leaving Surya's face.

Surya laughed placatingly. "*Tante* Tuti. So lovely—"

Tuti spoke over him as she turned back to Owen, who looked like a violent squall in all black. "Does he invoke my name often, Little Owen?" she asked.

"All the bloody time," Owen replied, his icy voice as sharp as ever. Hands pocketed in his trousers as he leaned against the doorframe, his gorgeous face was stony—predatory eyes focused on Surya. He looked almost bored—calmly cruel, as if Surya was an annoying bug that needed to be squashed.

Owen's head turned to Naya and his face softened, and Naya's lip quivered. His brows furrowed in question; she wasn't okay at all but gave him the smallest nod.

Surya chuckled awkwardly, trying to diffuse the tension. "*Tante* Tuti, Mr Jameson, this is all just a misunderstanding—honestly."

Ibu Tuti's lofty gaze whirled back to Surya. "Is it? Who misunderstood? Did *Mbak* Srinaya simply mishear? What rhymes with *anjing*, I wonder?"

Surya's lips moved, but nothing came out.

Ravi spoke up, "*Ibu* Tuti, we came here to request an update for the merchandise Pak Surya's factory is producing for the show, per the contract MERAHPUTIH has with your family."

Tuti sauntered further in and sat on Surya's couch, plonking her handbag on her lap. "Surya isn't family," she replied as she rifled through the giant bag and pulled out a jewel-encrusted cigarette case. "I am *not* his aunt. *Ugh*, where is my lighter?"

Naya blinked. "He's not related to you, *Bu?*"

Tuti made a triumphant little sound, holding up the shimmering lighter like a prize. And then she shook her head. "No. His brother— the *actual* CEO of the factory—is just married to my niece."

Naya's mouth dropped open. So did the mouths of every staff member witnessing this absolute shitshow.

"Please, *Ibu* Tuti." Naya came forward as Tuti placed a thin cigarette between her fire-engine red lips and lit up. "Please tell me the staff haven't put up with him for years because of a lie."

"*Ibu* Tuti is family *by marriage*," Surya insisted.

"Enough, Surya!" the one true God of MP snarled—smoker's voice rough—and Surya flinched, hunching his shoulders as he dropped his gaze to Tuti's feet.

The powerhouse of a woman took another drag of her cigarette, drawing out Surya's discomfort. "You are an embarrassment. To your family, to MERAHPUTIH, and to *my* name. I am disgusted, and ashamed—" she said *ashamed* with such solemnity—"to learn about your behaviour." Her kohl-lined eyes glared down her nose at him. "But to actually witness it..."

The terrifying octogenarian shook her head slowly at Surya, whose eyes were still downcast. No one spoke. No one moved, except for Tuti, who crossed her slim legs in her skin-tight trousers.

Another drag of her cigarette, extending the tension. Even Naya found it painful.

"You're done here," Tuti declared. Surya, rendered speechless, collapsed into his chair. "And you will inform your brother MERAHPUTIH expects a refund for the 50% deposit, because our entire order will be gratis." She put out her cigarette in a half-finished glass of water on the coffee table. "And I want the products delivered in two days."

Surya gave the slightest, stiffest nod.

The co-founder's voice softened when she turned Owen's way. "Anything else, Little Owen?"

Owen finally entered the room to stand close to Naya, and Surya blanched. Burning anger radiated from him despite his icy countenance. He swung his arm to the wall of glass, to the faces in the main office watching the scene unfold. "You owe them an apology." He took Naya's hand in his, intertwining their fingers. "You owe Ms Matthews —an *esteemed curator* of MERAHPUTIH, and my *partner*—a fucking apology," he bit out, the syllables punctuated through clenched teeth.

Surya's face slackened with humiliation. He swallowed, took in a shaky breath and opened his mouth. Naya cut him off before he could spout more lies. "No. He won't mean it, so I don't want it." She looked at Edhi and Nur standing on the other side of the glass, and they both shook their heads in agreement.

Owen bowed his head to gaze down at her with admiration. "You're more gracious than he deserves." He took her hand and squeezed it tight. Naya dug her fingertips into his knuckles to keep from falling apart.

"*Mbak* Naya—Ms Matthews," *Ibu* Tuti said gently. Naya forced her teary eyes to look at the old woman. "Please accept my deepest apologies. Now, go. You still have work to do. I am looking forward to your show. I've heard great things." She smiled at Naya, and then flicked her fingers towards the door. "Go be with Owen. I have more apologies to make."

Owen nudged Naya gently and she forced her feet to move.

When Naya passed the crowd—their faces struck with shock and hurt—Surya's words hit her like a hard shove. She quickened her steps as the tears burned her eyes—her breath shallowing. Owen squeezed her hand harder and steered her into his office.

Her body shook. She was cold. Owen sat her down on the couch, kneeling in front of her as she took in too much, but not enough, air. Naya clutched her chest as she tried to hold all her emotions in—push them all the way back down, but she was so tired of fighting. She hiccuped when Owen's voice cut through the shock. *I love you, Naya.* Owen cupped her face. He called out for help and Ravi, Edhi, and Tini raced in to pull the blinds down—shutting out the stares, making their world smaller, back down to their little bubble. *It's just you and me, Naya.*

In the safety of his darkened office, and the warmth of his arms, she wept, great big raspy breaths, tears streaming down her face and chin and neck, her knuckles ghost-white as she clutched Owen's shirt. He held her firmly to him so she could bury her face in his shoulder, and only when she was certain her cries would be muffled did she let go. She wailed, high-pitched and pained, feeling so fucking sad, and insulted, and overwhelmed, letting go of all that pent-up rage. Owen stroked her hair and back, murmuring into her ear. "Lovely one, I'm so sorry... *Shh shh shh.* I've got you. So brave. You were wonderful, Naya."

forty-three

Naya fell asleep on O's couch, pretty eyes red and puffy. It hurt to see her so wounded by Surya's fucking awful words. Standing in that office while Naya forced herself to keep it together, O wanted so badly to peel off the cold facade of the esteemed benefactor and show Surya how red-hot he really ran. The keening sound she made as she broke down made his hands clench into fists, itching like mad to connect with Surya's face.

By mid-afternoon, Naya still slept soundly, and he was so close to shaking her awake so they could talk, and touch, and kiss. He gently removed the cushions and climbed over the back of the couch to slide into the narrow space behind her, sandwiching himself between her body and the backrest. She stirred enough to move over a touch, reaching behind for his arm and draping it over herself. She made a little purr as she settled back against him, and O buried his face into her hair and drifted off too. He had the best sleep he'd had in weeks.

He faded back into consciousness to warm fingers raking through his hair, and the scent of jasmine, and cinnamon, and all those other pretty smells that made up Srinaya Matthews filled his senses. He opened his eyes and Naya was facing him, big brown eyes puffy and red still, but she didn't look sad anymore.

"Naya," he rasped sleepily, "I'm sorry I stepped in. I just couldn't stand there and listen to him treat you that way. Are you angry with me?"

Naya pressed her forehead against his and hummed quietly. "How could I be angry? You defended *all* of us. That's all I wanted. You brought *Ibu* Tuti in. She is fucking terrifying, by the way. Wow."

She kissed his cheek, and O exhaled the last of the tension that had been stuck inside him since that night at Le Roy. He lifted his chin to invite another kiss, and Naya obliged, running her lips over the bridge of his nose to his other cheek.

"I love you," she whispered as she leaned her face closer. He felt her warm breath on his skin. "I think I've loved you for as long as you've loved me. I just didn't know it was *you*. Denmark. You shit. Please… no more big revelations from you." She smiled.

O pulled her in and chuckled into her mouth, and she let out a breathy, languid sigh that was *perfect*. All of it was perfect. And then, before their kiss got too hot and heavy, O pulled away from her sinful lips and nuzzled her hair. "Um, I actually do have another surprise. A present."

Naya looked at him quizzically. "Is it chocolate? Because I really want chocolate right now."

O sniffed a little laugh and shook his head. "I'll buy you a chocolate factory tomorrow. My surprise isn't edible. Sorry. But I do think you'll love it. It's in the archives."

Naya's eyes went wide as she sat up quickly. "You're taking me to the archives? Really?" she asked, her voice high. She was almost fizzing —vibrating at the thought of going deep into the vault where MP's art collection was catalogued and stored.

He nodded as he said, "Something very special arrived last week."

Her eyes crinkled into those pretty little crescent moons as she bit her lip. And then she threw her arms around his shoulders again.

⸸

They entered the deserted archives building and approached two heavy doors with a card reader and keypad on the wall next to them. Owen swiped his fancy keycard and then punched in a code, and the thick metal doors swung open. They entered a cold white corridor, and then turned down another, and then another.

Naya had never walked through the double doors that kept MP's vast collection; obviously, she didn't have the clearance. They passed locked door after locked door and she wondered what masterpieces were kept safely behind each one. She knew MP owned a Frida Kahlo, a Kandinsky, a Duchamp, and four pieces by Iabadiou Piko among so many other beautiful works. She should've been crawling along the hallways on her knees in veneration.

"What are you showing me?" Naya tittered impatiently as they turned one last corner. Owen stopped in front of a door. He swiped his keycard and his eyes glinted with anticipation. He pushed the door open, and she came face to face with a painting.

It was one of hers. *DEWI's.* It was two metres wide and one metre tall, bordered by an ornate white frame. The image was from an older series which would later inspire the Drewery Alley piece that Owen loved so much. It was a stylised nude femme with olive-brown skin; her back was arched as she used two fingers to hold her vulva open, but instead of the cosmos, plants and fruit of all shapes and sizes flowed out of her vagina. Duku, the rice plant, mangosteen, pink jambu, boni, orchids, jasmine, *sedap malam*, frangipani, and an array of tropical leaves all crammed together, bursting from her. The piece was called *Abundance*—an homage to the goddess, Dewi Sri.

Naya stood silent—mouth open wide. She gawked at the piece, and then looked at Owen. "A DEWI piece?" was all she could manage.

Owen nodded excitedly, expectant. "I bought it at their last show. It's been in storage in Melbourne but—" He looked a little sheepish—"I got it sent here because it's for you. I want you to have it. It reminds me of you."

Naya blinked at him and then looked at the piece again. And then a weird gurgle escaped as she started to laugh so hard no sound but wheezing and squeaks came out. After a good minute, she stood straight again, catching her breath, and faced Owen. He looked taken aback. "Do you not like it?" he asked, frowning.

"Oh, Owen, I'm sorry," she said, wiping away her tears. She took his hand and gave it a squeeze. "Sorry—that was a weird reaction. I'm not laughing at you. It's just such an unexpected gift."

Naya ran her hands through her hair. Like everything in her life pertaining to Owen Jameson, this was yet *another* instance where the universe was forcing her hand. Time insisted on moving faster when it came to their relationship. It followed its own rules, its own cosmic cadence. She relented.

She steeled herself and exhaled. "Owen. Thank you so much, but I can't take this."

His mouth turned into a tight straight line. He looked at his feet—shoulders curling inwards as he shoved his hands into his pockets. He nodded tightly. His body tried to lean away from her and her rejection, but Naya closed the gap instantly, reaching up to run her fingertips over his cheek. "I can't take it because I've already been paid for it. *Abundance* was twenty-two thousand dollars, if I'm not mistaken, minus Norton Gallery's cut. Still—feels a bit wrong to take your money and then take back my painting. Or are you asking for a refund?" She stifled her laugh by pursing her lips.

Owen blinked as he absorbed what she was saying. And then his stormy eyes went wide as he took a half-step back. He looked her up and down as if he'd never seen her before in his life.

"What?" he squawked.

Naya pointed at the painting, and then at herself.

"Y-You made this?" he asked.

"Yes."

"You're—"

Naya nodded.

"You're *DEWI?*"

forty-four

Naya put her hands up awkwardly. "*Surpriiiise*," she sing-songed with a grimace.

O just… blinked at her. A weird *Uuuh-uuuh-uh* escaped his lips. He couldn't form words. Too stunned—starstruck.

Naya stood in front of him and put her hands in the back pockets of her jeans, looking sheepish. He pulled at his collar and undid a button. Tried to swallow. His mouth was dry. He tilted his head and studied her. It was like he was relearning her—*DEWI has a little crooked tooth, DEWI has big tits, DEWI has a pretty laugh, DEWI tastes sweet and salty…*

"Are you upset?" she asked cautiously as she took his hand, but O was too busy taking her in to answer. Her face seemed to have changed but was also exactly the same. Naya was DEWI. His Naya. And then he looked down at her hand touching his and thought, *DEWI is touching me*, and his hand went all hot and clammy.

"Okay, Owen," she said in a soothing voice like she was trying not to spook a cornered stray dog, "there's another piece of mine in the building—the one for the show. It should be in the prepping warehouse. Can you take me to it?"

O nodded without saying a word. She gave him a big reassuring smile and laughed at his shocked face, and he led her back through the hallways to the large holding space used to house the work being prepped for *Heartbreak.*

Naya walked through the maze of works and stopped in front of the case that held the DEWI piece. *Her* piece. The lid was removed, and the piece sat snugly in moulded foam. She smiled wide when she saw it—a nostalgic smile—and then she studied it closely, brows furrowing, making sure it was as she left it.

It was a human heart—about five times larger than lifesize— sculpted out of porcelain. It had been smashed into pieces and then painstakingly glued back together using *kintsugi,* a Japanese technique where special glue is dusted with gold, creating bright shimmery veins that hold the broken pieces together, creating something even more beautiful in its imperfection.

At the front, in one of the ventricles, a piece was missing, leaving a jagged hole about the size of a golf ball. She named the piece *In Repair.*

"I used a hammer to break this," she said, voice distant. "It took me months to put back together. If only real heartbreak was that easy to fix," she mused. She walked around it, hands behind her back, and leaned in again. "I won an award about ten years ago. The Reginald Muse." Her eyes flew to him.

O's brows shot upwards. The Reginald Muse was a Victorian prize. The finalists went on to have international solo shows and plenty of press, and the first-place winner received a pretty sizable cash prize.

"What I didn't realise was that my ex was on the judging panel." Naya looked at the floor. She swallowed, and it looked painful. He stepped nearer. "Sal and I hadn't been in a relationship for a couple of years at that point, but we'd broken up on really good terms. I'd gradu- ated and wanted to travel and applied for artist-in-residence postings in different countries, but he couldn't come with me because he'd gotten a graduate tutor role at uni." She smiled wistfully and took a deep breath in. "I always thought we'd find our way back to each other though. But the timing was always off. I'd be single while he was in a relationship... then he'd be single and I'd be in a relationship...

"Anyway, when he and the other judges were choosing the two finalists, he was honest about our history. He told them we hadn't been together for years but he was voting for me because I deserved it—not because of our past relationship. The other judges appreciated his transparency, and they didn't disqualify me."

Naya closed her eyes, and O knew she was picturing her ex—this Sal. Her brows drew together, and the corners of her mouth curled downwards. She stayed quiet for a while, and when her eyes reopened, they were bright with unshed tears. "I didn't know he was a judge. I only found out at the awards ceremony. I was sitting at a table in the Hilton ballroom, and he appeared on stage when they introduced the panel. As soon as I saw him, I thought I was out of the running and was happy about it. He'd called me a couple of days before, and he'd told me he was single again, and I was finally single too. I didn't care about the award because I was so fucking happy that I was going to get *him*. There were plenty more art prizes for me to enter.

"But then they called my name, and I had to go up there and shake his fucking hand as he handed me that stupid fucking cheque. And he congratulated me and told me he hadn't lied to the people who ran Reginald Muse—that they knew we'd been together. And I realised then, as he gave me this friendly but detached smile that he'd—" She shrugged and shook her head in bitterness—"he'd sacrificed our relationship to let me win. Because Sal was all about doing the right thing —of following the rules, always. He knew it would look bad if we got together after he handed me a fifty thousand dollar cheque. He chose to let me win *money* instead of letting me win *him*. He made the choice for me. He *managed* me. Do you see?"

O's blood went cold. He reached for her hand, and she took it, her eyes darting up to him and then back at the almost-repaired heart.

"And then..." She paused, breathing deeply as she tried to keep it together. "Another artist who'd entered the prize—who knew us both at university—made an official complaint, accusing us of cheating. Accused me of *fucking my way to a win*. That's what she wrote on her socials when she smeared our names. Even though the people at Reginald Muse knew our history and accepted it, she wouldn't let it go. She flooded articles about me with cruel comments... Started a petition to pressure a gallery to cancel my show. It got so bad that someone even doxxed us, and I got weird mail, prank calls, people knocking on my door in the middle of the night..."

She wrapped her arms around herself as she remembered. "Winning that award should've kickstarted my career but no one wanted to go near me. It took years, Owen, and I had to start from scratch again. As soon as people saw my name on awards, or applications for shows..." She wiped her eyes and sniffed. "And I lost Sal."

Of all the scenarios O imagined, the truth was so much worse. "Srinaya, I'm so sorry," was all he could say as he pulled her to him. She buried her face in his chest, holding him tightly. "I'm so sorry that happened."

She sniffled some more and then exhaled as she let go of her bad memories, composing herself. "DEWI started because I was impatient. And desperate." She pointed at *In Repair*. "This was my very first piece. I won a smaller award with it. No cash prize. Just recognition. Ru—he's my assistant—went up to accept the award on my behalf since I had no interest in any of that." She smiled sadly. "People think he's DEWI, and I help them think that."

"Sneaky little devil," O teased.

She sighed, her whole body relaxing into his as he wrapped his hand around her nape. She pointed her thumb to the porcelain heart. "I'm donating *In Repair* to MERAHPUTIH."

He stumbled back, and Naya had to catch him before he bumped into a painting propped up against the wall. "Whoa," she said.

"Really? DEWI's—your—*DEWI's* first piece?"

She shrugged again. *Shrugged.*

Naya tilted her chin up to look into his eyes. Her black pupils flared when she blinked. He cradled her face and stared down at her— followed the shape of her brows, down her slightly aquiline nose, to the little dark beauty spots under her right eye. Her pouty little mouth. Her round pink cheeks. He had looked at that lovely face so many fucking times and had no idea, yet it was so obvious.

"Fuck—you're *DEWI*," he said, astounded. And then a lightbulb went off in his head. *"Sri.* Dewi Sri. Goddess. *Stefan.* Oh, that fucker—he was teasing me."

Naya burst out laughing. "I think he was teasing *me* and throwing hints at *you.*"

"Very angry fucking too, actually," O mimicked Stef's British accent, scowling.

Naya squealed and almost collapsed on the floor in a fit of giggles.

Of *course* she was DEWI. O was fucking blind.

He ran his thumb along her jaw and over her lips as he murmured, "Naya, DEWI, immovable object."

She tugged at his shirt as she gazed up at him. "Owen, Denmark, unstoppable force."

He smiled and stroked her cheek with his knuckles and she purred.

"Cosmic," O said.

Naya nodded. "Yes. Sacred."

outro

O MEANDERED THROUGH THE EAST WING OF PURNAMA, GREETING donors and visitors to the opening gala for *Heartbreak*.

The board members mingled with VIPs; Endah stood next to *In Repair* by DEWI as she discussed donations with a couple who were interested in becoming patrons of MERAHPUTIH after meeting Srinaya Matthews, the bright young star of the gallery.

Naya slipped away earlier in the evening after the speeches to make sure the Bevy were enjoying themselves, and he hadn't been able to find her since—the slippery little goddess. He shouldn't have been surprised; Naya had lofty career goals but shied away from the limelight.

He held onto his empty glass as he moved through the groups of guests dressed in their finest art gallery attire, using it as an excuse whenever he was about to get ensnared in a conversation. *On my way to the bar for a refill. Will try to find you later. Good seeing you though,* he'd say with a smile.

He made his way to the darkened room that housed *'I Am Just Waiting To Join You,'* pausing to watch the expressions of the folks silently taking in the entire sequence of images projected onto the haunting white tree. Some visitors clutched their chests in communion with the artist, just like that night when Naya talked about her vision for the show. *I love evoking that kind of emotion. I want people to hurt as they see the work.*

She had succeeded. Couples exited the room holding hands or wrapping their arms around waists and shoulders as they continued through the exhibition.

"That was so beautiful. So very sad," the gruff *Ibu* Tuti said as she held onto her son's arm. "It makes me miss your father."

O's heart hurt to hear those words from the last living co-founder of MERAHPUTIH.

He searched through the rooms, nodding and waving to people he recognised, then pointing at his empty glass to excuse himself as he walked on.

Where are you, Srinaya?

He continued past Joyce's moody painting mounted at the entrance to the exhibition. The bulky hand carved frame had gotten cracked on its way to the gallery and couldn't be replaced in time, much to Joyce's dismay, but Naya had the grand idea of working with the damage, creating more cracks and dents in the wood. By the time she and Joyce had finished hacking away at it, the frame looked like it had been unable to contain the rage on the canvas. An entire corner separated from the painting, and the larger chunks of loose wood had been mounted as if the frame had exploded outwards. The murmurs of awe as people took in the piece—so violent and haunting—made O's whole being flare with pride.

He stepped outside into the balmy night air, the quiet a reprieve from all the mingling. He spotted Ravi, Tini and Gunawan sitting on the steps of the admin building.

"Hello, Heartbreak Bevy," he said as he neared them.

They nodded their heads in greeting, and Gunawan spoke up. "Congratulations on the successful reopening of Purnama, Mr Jameson," he said, gentle eyes crinkling with pride.

The Bevy looked utterly exhausted after four gruelling months of planning a major exhibition from scratch, yet they still had that spark in their eyes—determination and focus. They were all on standby, ready to jump into action should an emergency arise.

O shook his head. "You deserve all the praise. Thank you so much for your hard work. And for supporting Naya. Her face lights up when she talks about you."

They all beamed—even Ravi. But then O went solemn as he added, "I also want to apologise for Surya's actions, and for my complacency. I should've spent more time here." His eyes met Gunawan's. "You've been here the longest, Gunawan. I can't imagine putting up with his behaviour for as long as you did. I'm very sorry."

Gunawan nodded—a little taken aback.

"Anyway, I saw Edhi flirting with the DJ so I didn't want to bother him, but I'd really appreciate it if you'd extend my congratulations to him too, and the directors will be sending out a company-wide email with an official apology on Monday."

Tini spoke up with a gleam in her eye. "We're just thrilled he's gone."

Rav muttered, "Dude was the worst."

And then Gunawan surprised them all by commenting, "I will not miss his black mock-turtlenecks. He looked like a Bond villain."

O sputtered out a laugh and Tini cackled in agreement.

"Have you seen Naya?" he asked them, wondering where on earth she would have disappeared to.

"She's staring at the mural," Ravi answered, flicking his chin in the direction of Purnama's south wall. "She's been staring at it for, like, an hour. She seems very nervous about having to work with that Ruben guy. I can see why *Mbak* Naya thinks he's DEWI. He's… a lot."

O smirked.

He met Ruben a few days before—once at Le Roy, where Ru listened intently to the instructions Naya gave him while giving Stef some very indecent looks, and then again just that morning when he'd barged into MP, acting the part of the dickish 2IC to DEWI, a crew of volunteers following behind as they set up, all of them studying each other carefully, wondering if DEWI was hidden among them.

Watching Naya get fake-bossed around had kept O entertained, especially seeing Ru insist on Naya's help in front of the Bevy when he barged in on a *Heartbreak* meeting. "Listen. The big boss told me to tell you that you've got to be available to them."

Naya frowned. "Yeah, but I'm also running a show. Like, MP's honoured, and *I'm* honoured, but—" She put her hands up and gestured to the other people in the room and the whiteboard behind her completely covered in notes—"massive exhibition opening tonight. Lots of last-minute things to do."

Ruben shrugged—unmoved. "DEWI wants your help. We'll start mapping the grid and setting up the equipment without you but we'll see you this afternoon to plan for tomorrow," he drawled, and then breezed right back out with his minions in tow.

Naya rolled her eyes and pretended to seethe. Such a good little performer.

He parted with the Bevy, and as he rounded the corner to the south wall, the spotlights that illuminated the front of the Purnama faded, only casting a dim glow on the wall Srinaya was staring up at.

She stood in a silk gun-metal grey jumpsuit with thin straps and a low neckline, her bold batik tattoo on her shoulder and chest unapologetically on display. Her hair was twisted and fastened using sparkly silver chopsticky things that must have been powered by magic because he didn't understand how her thick locks stayed up with only two of them stabbed in there.

All around her was equipment for the mural—crates filled with outdoor paint buckets and spray cans, a box full of brushes, tarps, and cleaning products. Two platform ladders had been brought in and a marquis assembled for the crew to rest under during breaks.

Srinaya looked so beautifully out of place among the mess—barefoot—holding her strappy heels in her hand.

She touched her lips absentmindedly, focused intently on the wall already mapped out into a grid by her, Ru and the assistants.

O moved out of the shadows, and she gasped when she noticed him —startled. "Owen," she breathed, clutching her chest, and then her eyes crinkled, and her pretty lips curved into a devastating smile. "Jesus—I really do need to put a bell on you."

She opened her arms as he came close, and he reached out to pull her against him, stroking her shoulders. "Pretty Sri," he murmured, "you're missing your show."

She made a dismissive sound and waved her hand. "It was mine during the planning. Now it belongs to the Bevy, and to the artists." She turned her head to look up at the mural again, brows furrowed.

"Onto the next project already, huh?" he asked as he nipped her ear. She leaned into him but kept staring at the wall. "What is it, Naya?"

"I'm nervous about the *kintsugi*. I just… it has to be perfect."

He held her tighter. "It will be. I know it's a new technique for you but you've tested the gold. It set perfectly. You've got this. You've done so many murals now and they've all been incredible."

She gripped his shirt—looked up at him with those dark eyes adorned with shimmery purple eyeshadow that brought out the copper flecks in her irises. "This one *means* the most," she said with a frown.

O ran his knuckles along her jaw and leaned in to nuzzle her temple —taking in her intoxicating scent. "Do you need another pep talk, love? Happy to tell you all about how I've planned to start a petition to get your arse on that UNESCO Wonders of the World list." He ran his hand down her body and squeezed her massive backside.

She tipped her head back to laugh, and O bent to kiss her gorgeous neck. "Or do you need more than talk, Srinaya? Do you need me to *show* you how wonderful I think you are?" He gripped her nape firmly with one hand and splayed the other on her waist as he led her back to press her against the wall. She dropped her shoes and made a breathy moan when her shoulders touched the cool concrete. She whispered his name, and her hand moved between them, brushing her magical little fingers over his hardening cock in his trousers.

He stroked his fingertips down her cleavage and slid his hand under the silk fabric of her bodice, brushing over her nipple. She sighed as she arched her spine.

"It's a beautiful mural. It's your best one yet," he said.

She'd shown him the night he found out the truth—that she was DEWI. The piece featured the white silhouette of a nude femme—not in the throes of orgasm like *Abundance* or the Drewery Alley piece, but reclining lazily on her side, ankles crossed together. Gold cracks crept over her body like the *kintsugi* in her *In Repair* sculpture. The femme was healed—scarred, yes, but those permanent marks made her stronger and all the more beautiful.

"It's about you, and it's about me, and it's about you *and* me," she'd said quietly. "It's for us."

track list

intro

Felix Da Housecat - Silver Screen (Shower Scene)

Hudson Mohawke - Behold

Rachel Chinouriri - Darker Place (Joe Goddard Remix)

Miguel - Adorn

1

The Cinematic Orchestra - Ode To The Big Sea

Rihanna - Sex With Me (Salva Remix)

Rachel Chinouriri - I'm Not Perfect (But I'm Trying)

Gigi - Terbang

2

Robotaki - The Possibility of a Dream Coming True

JPL - Close (Tutara Peak Remix)

Robotaki - Moonside

John Mayer - Last Train Home

Track list

3

Ramengvrl - I AM ME
ASL - My Whole Life
Alex Mali - Good Good
Mont Duamel - Eyes On You

4

Bay Ledges - Float
Jim-E Stack - Next To Me (feat. Lucky Daye)
Lenny Kravitz - Again

5

Eliza & The Delusionals - Nothing Yet
Middle Kids - Cellophane (Brain)
Jordan Rakei - Friend or Foe

6

Does It Offend You, Yeah? - Guess Who Just Rolled Back into Town
Gareth Donkin - GEEK OUT! (feat. quickly, quickly, The Breathing Effect)
Kris Bowers - Cultural Imports
Thandii - Not Just One

7

Cashmere Cat - Trust Nobody (feat. Selena Gomez & Tory Lanez)
She Wants Revenge - Tear You Apart
Lennon Stella - Kissing Other People

8

SIX60 - Closer
The Cinematic Orchestra - Child Song
Robotaki - Trial (Intro)

9

Big Wild - 6's to 9's (feat. Rationale)
Two Another - Jump
Remi Wolf - Woo!

10

USHER - Good Kisser
KOMMUNION - Lose My Cool (feat. Antony & Cleopatra)
Cashmere Cat - Secrets + Lies
Tyler, The Creator - I Ain't Got Time!

11

Blood Orange - You're Not Good Enough
Julius Black - Summer
Busty and the Bass - All The Things I Couldn't Say To You

12

Pink Skies - Spectra
The Cure - Close To Me
Blur - Girls & Boys
Arctic Monkeys - I Bet You Look Good On The Dancefloor
Pulp - Common People

13

GOON - Pink and Orange
Tom Misch - Smells Like Teen Spirit (Quarantine Sessions)
Robotaki - Limbo (eat. SHOR)

14

Domenique Dumont - La bataille de neige
Flying Lotus - This Cursed Life
Lauv - Steal The Show
ilo ilo - current
RÜFÜS DU SOL - Tell Me

Track list

15
Thilo - FLIGHT RISK
DanDlion - All the Way Up
ODESZA - Better Now (feat. MARO)
Dagny - Come Over

16
Snowmine - Let Me In
Sean Angus Watson - Let Me in
Blessid Union Of Souls - Let Me Be The One

17
Rihanna - Kiss It Better (Four Tet Remix)
Rationale - Reciprocate
Death Cab for Cutie - Marching Bands of Manhattan
Cashmere Cat - Night Night (feat. Kehlani)

18
The Cinematic Orchestra - Channel 1 Suite
Flying Lotus - Zodiac Shit
Prefuse 73 - Perverted Undertone

19
Air - Sexy Boy
Miguel - Funeral
Common Saints - Idol Eyes

20
Jacob Collier - Never Gonna Be Alone (feat. Lizzy McAlpine & John Mayer)
Harry Styles - Daylight
Victoria Monét - Jaguar
Four Tet - Locked

21

Laura Mvula - Let Me Fall

Mel Blue - Everything About You

Amber Mark - Lose My Cool - Franc Moody Remix

22

Billen Ted - People Ain't Dancing (feat. Kah-Lo)

Jungle - GOOD TIMES

Noga Erez - Quiet

Antwaun Stanley - Speed of Night (feat. Tyler Duncan)

23

Sara Diamond - Glass of Whisky

NASAYA - PATTERNS (feat. Sara Diamond)

Novo Amor - Same Day, Same Face

24

The Cinematic Orchestra - To Build A Home (feat. Patrick Watson)

Robotaki - Harbinger (feat. Jamie Fine)

Novo Amor - Anchor

25

Jordan Rakei - You & Me

Maxwell - Drowndeep: Hula

Holly Humberstone - I Would Die 4 U

26

Jacob Collier - All I Need (feat. Mahalia & Ty Dolla $ign)

BAYNK - Mine (feat. Cub Sport)

Brittany Howard - Stay High (Childish Gambino Version)

27

Client Liaison - The Real Thing

Fred again... - Baxter (these are my friends)

Jordan Rakei - Say Something

Track list

28
Spank Rock - Backyard Betty
M.I.A. - Come Around (feat. Timbaland)
Robotaki - Automaton

29
Tkay Maidza - 24k
Sampha - Treasure
Jordan Rakei - Eye To Eye

30
Nicholas Britell - Agape
Mitchell Yard - Room Full Of Love (feat. Lizzy)
Tyla - Water
DanDlion - All the Way Up (Choir Version)

31
Jordan Rakei - Freedom
Elbow - Mirrorball
Emotional Oranges - Be Somebody (feat. Tkay Maidza)

32
Does It Offend You, Yeah? - Battle Royale
MSTRKRFT - The Looks
Noga Erez - YOU SO DONE
Brigitte Bardot - Bonnie And Clyde (feat. Serge Gainsbourg)

33
Tom Misch - Chain Reaction (Quarantine Sessions)
John Wasson - Caravan
Frightened Rabbit - Get Out
Julius Black - A Form Of Self Defence

34

Julius Black - Together We Go Down In The Dark

Death Cab for Cutie - Summer Skin

The Cinematic Orchestra - Zero One/This Fantasy (feat. Grey Reverend)

35

The Rapture - House Of Jealous Lovers

Massive Attack - Angel (feat. Horace Andy)

Sia - Breathe Me

36

Jungle - Holding On

Flume - Say Nothing (feat. MAY-A)

SG Lewis - Heartbreak On The Dancefloor (feat. Frances)

Kavinsky - Nightcall

37

Artist(s): Tove Lo - True Romance

James Blake - Coming Back (feat. SZA)

John Mayer - Heartbreak Warfare

Julius Black - Dopamine

38

Yeah Yeah Yeahs - Spitting Off the Edge of the World (feat. Perfume Genius)

ford. - The Feeling (feat. Sonn, Hanz, Ralph Castelli)

Massive Attack - Paradise Circus

Gotye - Giving Me A Chance

Maroon 5 - Closure

39

Elbow - Lucky With Disease

Ben Abraham - In Your Eyes

Jordan Rakei - Lucid

John Mayer - In Your Atmosphere (Live at the Nokia Theatre, Los Angeles, CA - December 2007)

Track list

40
Eloise - Giant Feelings
Hermanos Gutiérrez - Cerca De Ti
Leon Bridges - River
H.E.R. - Hard Place

41
Soccer Mommy - circle the drain
Alanis Morissette - Tapes
Kennebec - Leaving The Canyons (feat. Samuel T. Herring)
Beyoncé - All Night

42
Mutemath - Blood Pressure
Does It Offend You, Yeah? - With A Heavy Heart (I Regret To Inform You)
Beyoncé - Don't Hurt Yourself (feat. Jack White)

43
xander. - Everlasting (feat. brillion.)
Trent Reznor and Atticus Ross - 8 AM, Christmas Eve
Andra & The Backbone - Sempurna

44
Sampha - Spirit 2.0
xander. - The Memories We Shared (feat. Rufus Dipper)
Trent Reznor and Atticus Ross - Epiphany

outro
Grey Reverend - Watch Me
Alexi Murdoch - Orange Sky
Brasstracks - My Boo

acknowledgments

I've just googled, *'writing book acknowledgments, tips and tricks'* and the big takeaway? Make sure it's good because everyone will read it and remember it.
So, no pressure.

Quinton Li, my editor. You took this mess of a manuscript and turned it into something pretty. It was a joy lurking in Google Docs as you edited and live-commented on my story. I'm sorry for being such a fucking creep.

Inez Joakim, thank you for creating the most beautiful cover. Thank you for seeing *me*. I am so deeply honoured that this book is adorned by something you lovingly created. When I grow up, I want to be you.

Zanni Louise, your generosity to aspiring writers everywhere is mind-blowing.

Bad Writers Club, you've given me a safe space to write utter shit. Being able to sit in a room full of curious people who want to talk about books and writing is a fucking dream come true. Donita and Amanda, I am so honoured to call you my friends.

The Chestnut Tree Bookshop, thanks for making the perfect matcha lattes and being a sweet escape when the walls of my house feel like a prison.

Jordan Krumbine, your creative fire keeps me going. I want to make you proud. I love you, friend.

Div Kelley (for reading this book 3 times you fucking champion), Amberlee Hong, Sandy Lin, Katharina Wynne (for coming up with MERAHPUTIH), Dunielle Vujasin, San May Tan, Les Burnham, Mark Nelson, Milton James Nelson, Emma Danks-Adam, and Kiel Adam.

The Weirdos (Liesl, Bec, Izzy, Heather, Jess, Dora, Jane, Felicity, Jenna, Chloe, and George) and the Expansion folks (Sammie, Carly, Kim, Tara, Sas, Emily, and Sarah). These two groups have been integral to my self-actualisation and healing journey. The beautiful balance of holding you, and being held by you is one of the biggest blessings of my life.

Sammie Fleming. Shining star. Wolf Mother. Teacher. Guide. So many roads lead to—or are paved by—you.

My father, Christopher. I inherited your nose and your love of books. Your copy of Delta of Venus by Anaïs Nin awakened something in me. You still insist it wasn't yours. Sure, Jan.

The rest of my family. I don't really know how you'd feel about being named in the acknowledgments section of a book as filthy as this one is, so I won't. But this is your official mention. You've made me who I am today.

Deities+Ancestors: BTD, Hades, Tante Merah, Lilith, Lucifer, and Yeshua (I burnt that Delta of Venus book in your name. So many horrible things are done in your name. I'm so sorry for that). Nenek (no—I'm not ready), Gran, Opa, The Ancient One.

My partner, Scott Pitch-Arthur. That time you woke me up at 1am because you'd finished my manuscript? You said you loved it. You said

about the author

Aud Pitch (they/them) is a Scottish-Indonesian geriatric millenial living in Naarm on the lands of the Wurundjeri People.

They dream up angsty romances and sling tarot cards—using the latter to plot the former.

They have always been a storyteller and have finally succumbed to the pull—and let go of their fear—of writing novels.

Diversity—especially body diversity—will always be an important part of their stories.

Aud is a Scorpio Sun, Sagittarius Moon, and Taurus Rising with Libra and Sagittarius stelliums.

It's a lot.

They can be a lot.

As you can see from this bio, Aud is a shameless lover of em-dashes.

instagram.com/thelittledeathxx

writing.exchange/@thelittledeath

threads.net/thelittledeathxx